Lincoln Peirce

BiG NATE

HERE GOES NOTHING

HARPER
An Imprint of HarperCollinsPublishers

BIG NATE is a registered trademark of United Feature Syndicate, Inc.

These comic strips first appeared in newspapers from June 9, 2008, through January 10, 2009.

Big Nate: Here Goes Nothing

Go to www.bignate.com to read the *Big Nate* comic strip.

Library of Congress catalog card number: 2012934240
ISBN 978-0-06-208696-9 (pbk.)

Typography by Andrea Vandergrift
18 19 20 PC/LSCH 11
❖
First Edition

More

BiG
NATE

adventures from

Lincoln Peirce

Novels:

BIG NATE: IN A CLASS BY HIMSELF
BIG NATE STRIKES AGAIN
BIG NATE ON A ROLL
BIG NATE GOES FOR BROKE

Activity Books:

BIG NATE BOREDOM BUSTER
BIG NATE FUN BLASTER

Comic Compilations:

BIG NATE: WHAT COULD POSSIBLY GO WRONG?
BIG NATE FROM THE TOP
BIG NATE OUT LOUD
BIG NATE AND FRIENDS

THE SHOW MUST GO ON

GUYS! GREAT NEWS! PRINCIPAL NICHOLS IS GONNA LET "ENSLAVE THE MOLLUSK" PERFORM AT THE ASSEMBLY!
WE **CAN'T**, NATE! WE'VE GOT NO LEAD SINGER!
YEAH, ARTUR'S OUT WITH CHICKEN POX!
SO WHAT? WE DON'T **NEED** ARTUR! HAVE YOU GUYS FORGOTTEN THAT **I** WAS OUR LEAD SINGER BEFORE **HE** JOINED THE BAND?
FOR-GOTTEN? NO.
TRIED TO FOR-GET, YES.
THAT'S THE SPIRIT, LADS! THE SHOW MUST GO ON!
PEIRCE

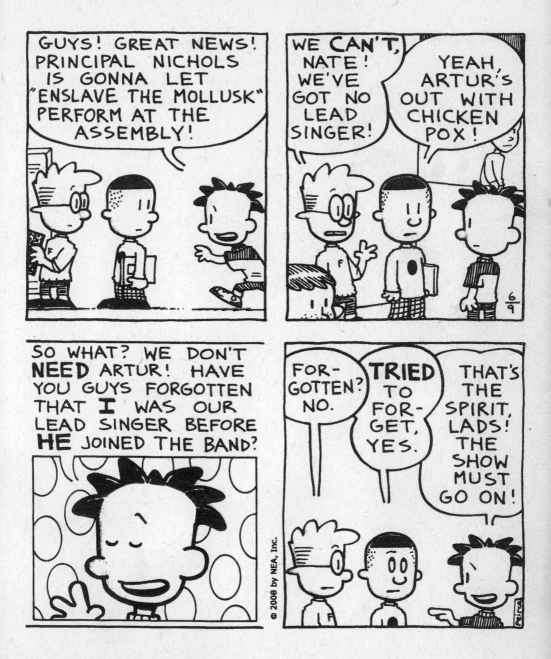

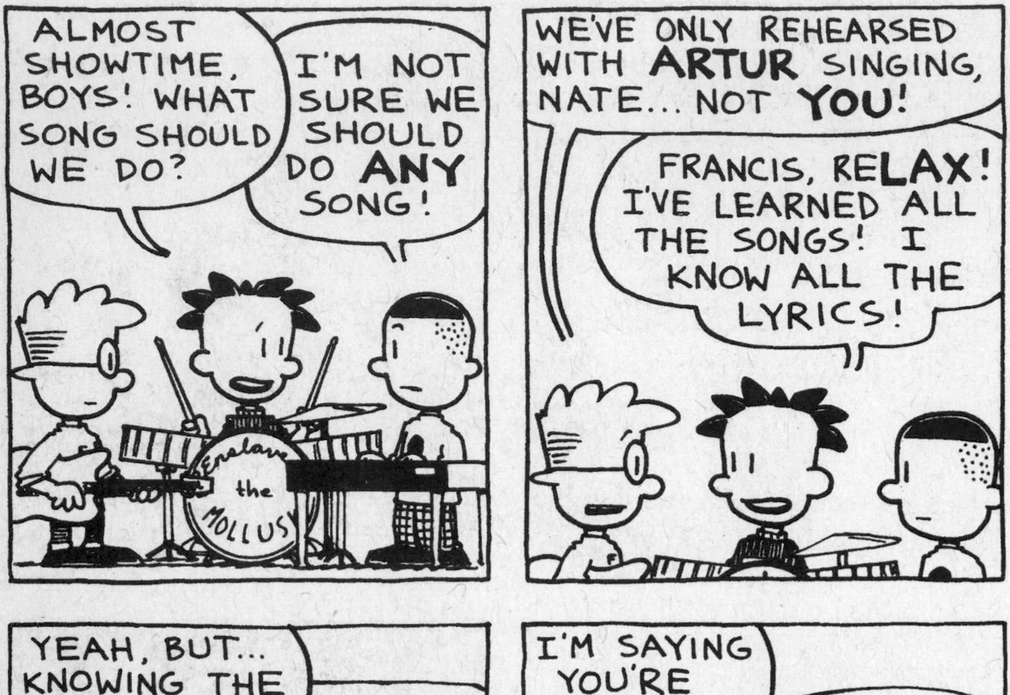
ALMOST SHOWTIME, BOYS! WHAT SONG SHOULD WE DO?
I'M NOT SURE WE SHOULD DO ANY SONG!
Enslave the MOLLUSK
WE'VE ONLY REHEARSED WITH ARTUR SINGING, NATE... NOT YOU!
FRANCIS, RELAX! I'VE LEARNED ALL THE SONGS! I KNOW ALL THE LYRICS!
YEAH, BUT... KNOWING THE LYRICS ISN'T... THAT DOESN'T...
DOESN'T WHAT? WHAT ARE YOU SAYING?
Enslave the MOLLUSK
I'M SAYING YOU'RE THE RINGO OF "ENSLAVE THE MOLLUSK."
KNOW YOUR LIMITATIONS, DUDE.
© 2008 by NEA, Inc.
6/10
Peirce

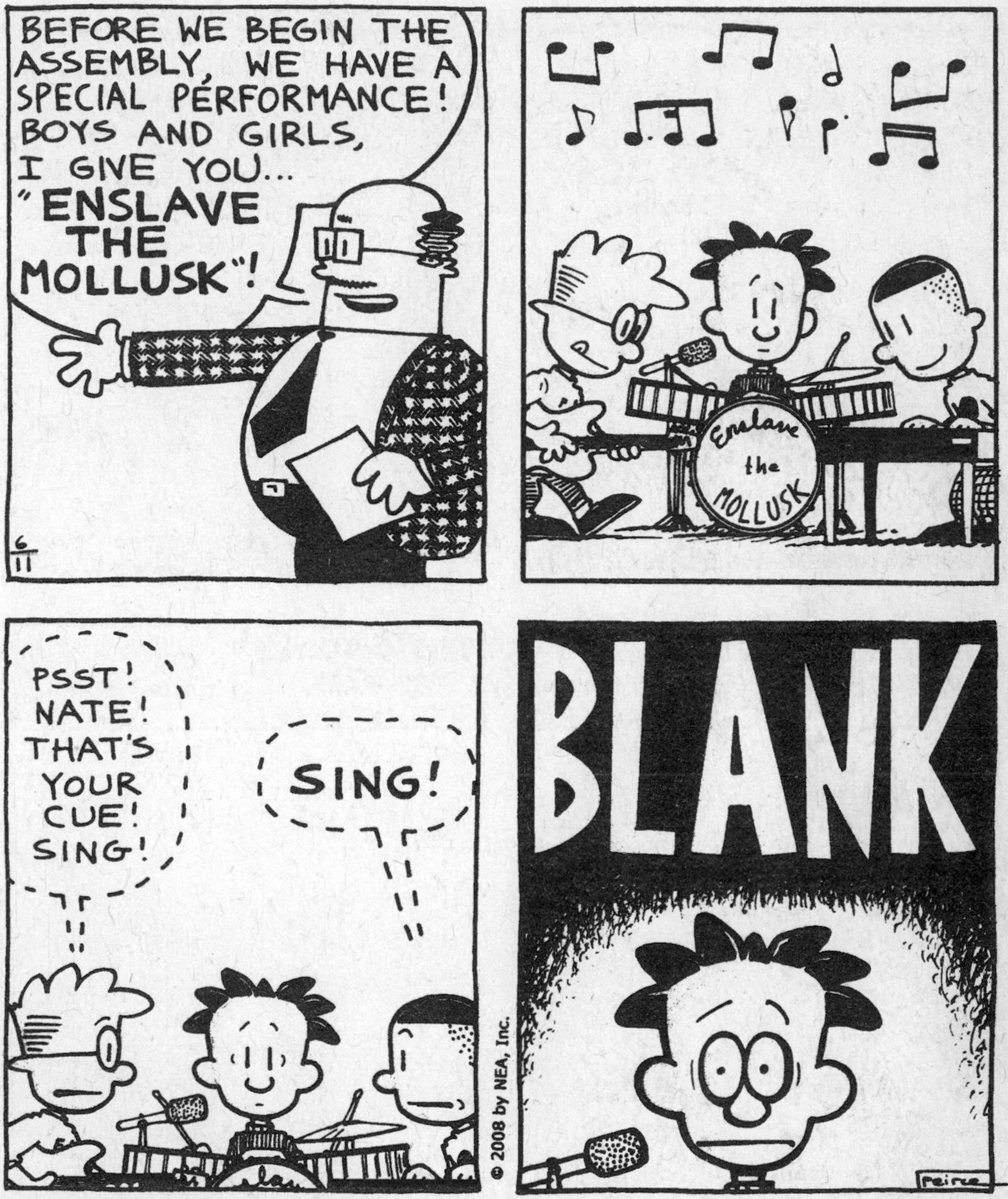
BEFORE WE BEGIN THE ASSEMBLY, WE HAVE A SPECIAL PERFORMANCE! BOYS AND GIRLS, I GIVE YOU... "ENSLAVE THE MOLLUSK"!
Enslave the MOLLUSK
PSST! NATE! THAT'S YOUR CUE! SING!
SING!
BLANK

GO AHEAD, NATE! SING!
SING!
WHAT IS YOUR PROBLEM?
NATE, THE WHOLE SCHOOL IS WATCHING!
WE'VE FINALLY FIGURED OUT HOW TO SHUT HIM UP.
LOOKS LIKE "HEART OF GOLD" IS NOW AN INSTRUMENTAL.
Enslave the MOLLUSK
6/12

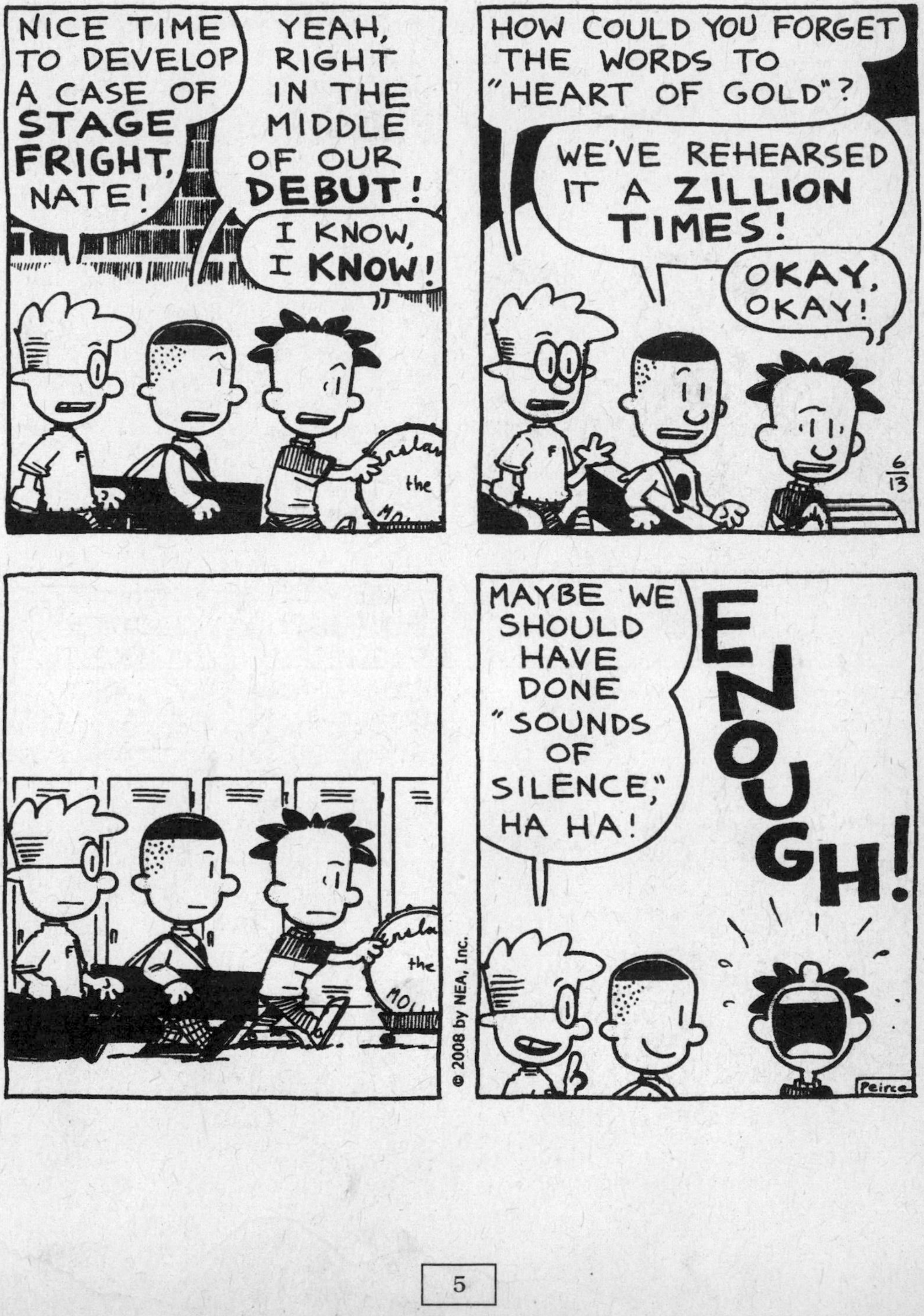
NICE TIME TO DEVELOP A CASE OF STAGE FRIGHT, NATE!
YEAH, RIGHT IN THE MIDDLE OF OUR DEBUT!
I KNOW, I KNOW!
HOW COULD YOU FORGET THE WORDS TO "HEART OF GOLD"?
WE'VE REHEARSED IT A ZILLION TIMES!
OKAY, OKAY!
6/13
© 2008 by NEA, Inc.
MAYBE WE SHOULD HAVE DONE "SOUNDS OF SILENCE," HA HA!
ENOUGH!
Peirce

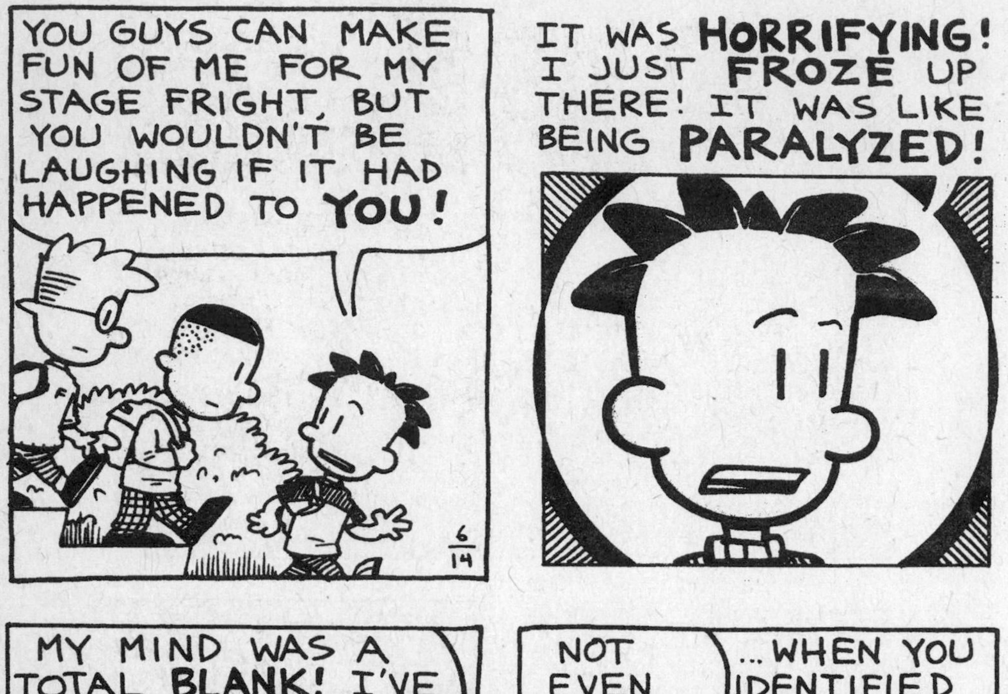
YOU GUYS CAN MAKE FUN OF ME FOR MY STAGE FRIGHT, BUT YOU WOULDN'T BE LAUGHING IF IT HAD HAPPENED TO YOU!
6/14
IT WAS HORRIFYING! I JUST FROZE UP THERE! IT WAS LIKE BEING PARALYZED!
MY MIND WAS A TOTAL BLANK! I'VE NEVER EXPERIENCED THAT BEFORE!
© 2008 by NEA, Inc.
NOT EVEN ON LAST WEEK'S SOCIAL STUDIES TEST?
...WHEN YOU IDENTIFIED APPOMATTOX AS THE GREEK GOD OF CREME-FILLED PASTRIES?

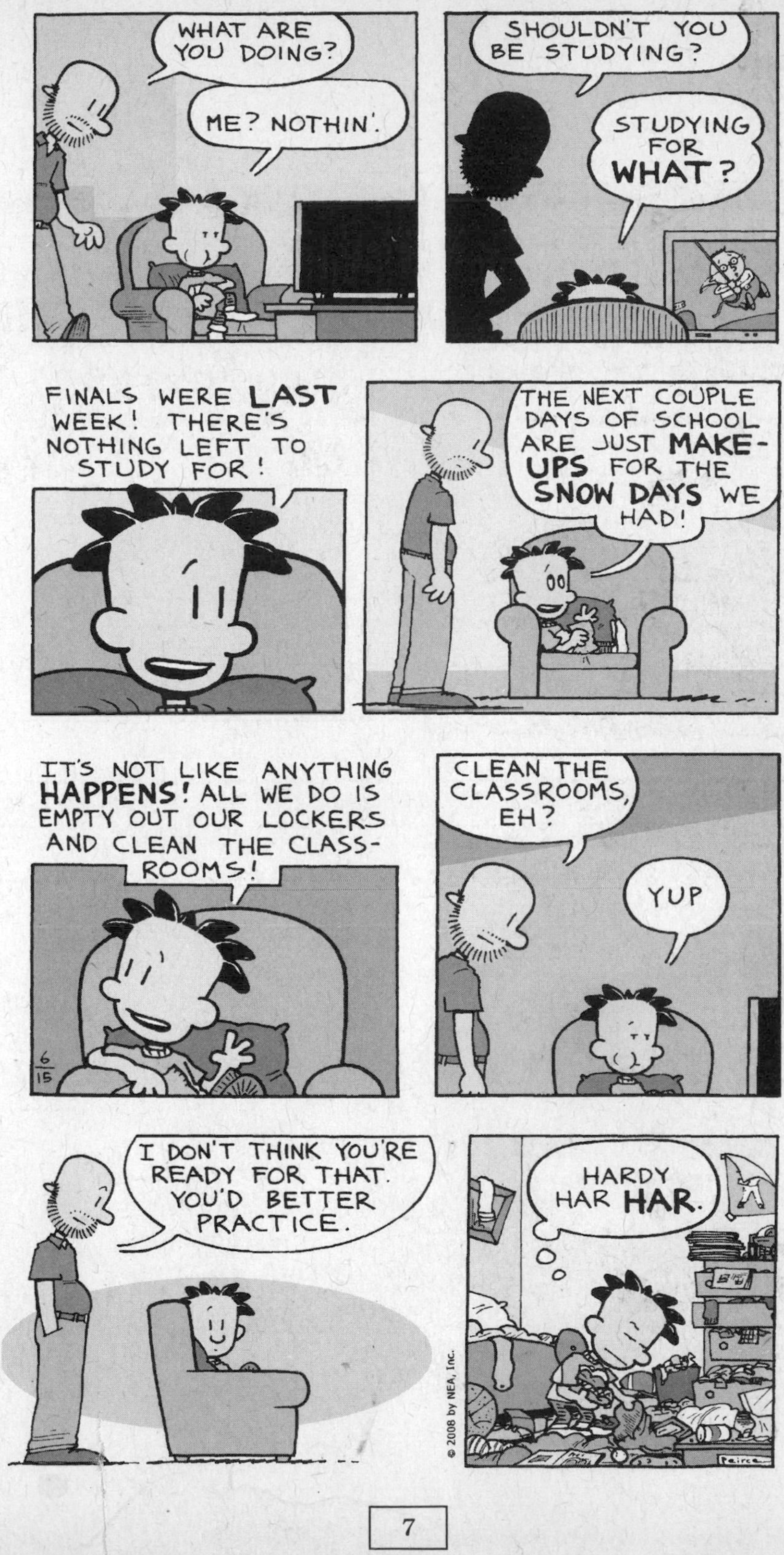
WHAT ARE YOU DOING?
ME? NOTHIN'.
SHOULDN'T YOU BE STUDYING?
STUDYING FOR **WHAT**?
FINALS WERE **LAST** WEEK! THERE'S NOTHING LEFT TO STUDY FOR!
THE NEXT COUPLE DAYS OF SCHOOL ARE JUST **MAKE-UPS** FOR THE **SNOW DAYS** WE HAD!
IT'S NOT LIKE ANYTHING **HAPPENS**! ALL WE DO IS EMPTY OUT OUR LOCKERS AND CLEAN THE CLASS-ROOMS!
6/15
CLEAN THE CLASSROOMS, EH?
YUP
I DON'T THINK YOU'RE READY FOR THAT. YOU'D BETTER PRACTICE.
© 2008 by NEA, Inc.
HARDY HAR **HAR**.
Peirce

PRANKED!

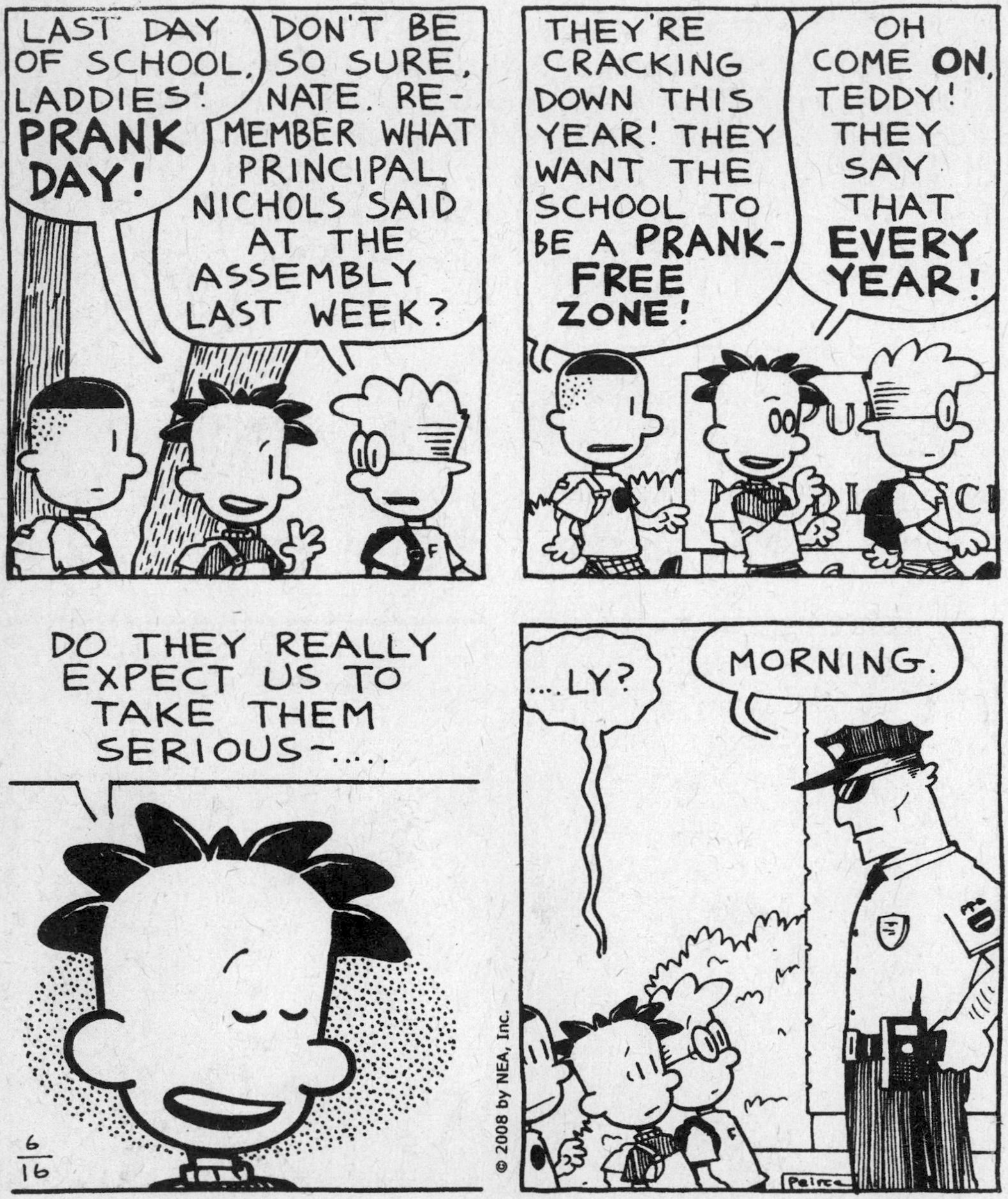
LAST DAY OF SCHOOL, LADDIES! PRANK DAY!
DON'T BE SO SURE, NATE. REMEMBER WHAT PRINCIPAL NICHOLS SAID AT THE ASSEMBLY LAST WEEK?
THEY'RE CRACKING DOWN THIS YEAR! THEY WANT THE SCHOOL TO BE A PRANK-FREE ZONE!
OH COME ON, TEDDY! THEY SAY THAT EVERY YEAR!
DO THEY REALLY EXPECT US TO TAKE THEM SERIOUS-.....
6/16
...LY?
MORNING.
© 2008 by NEA, Inc.
PEIRCE

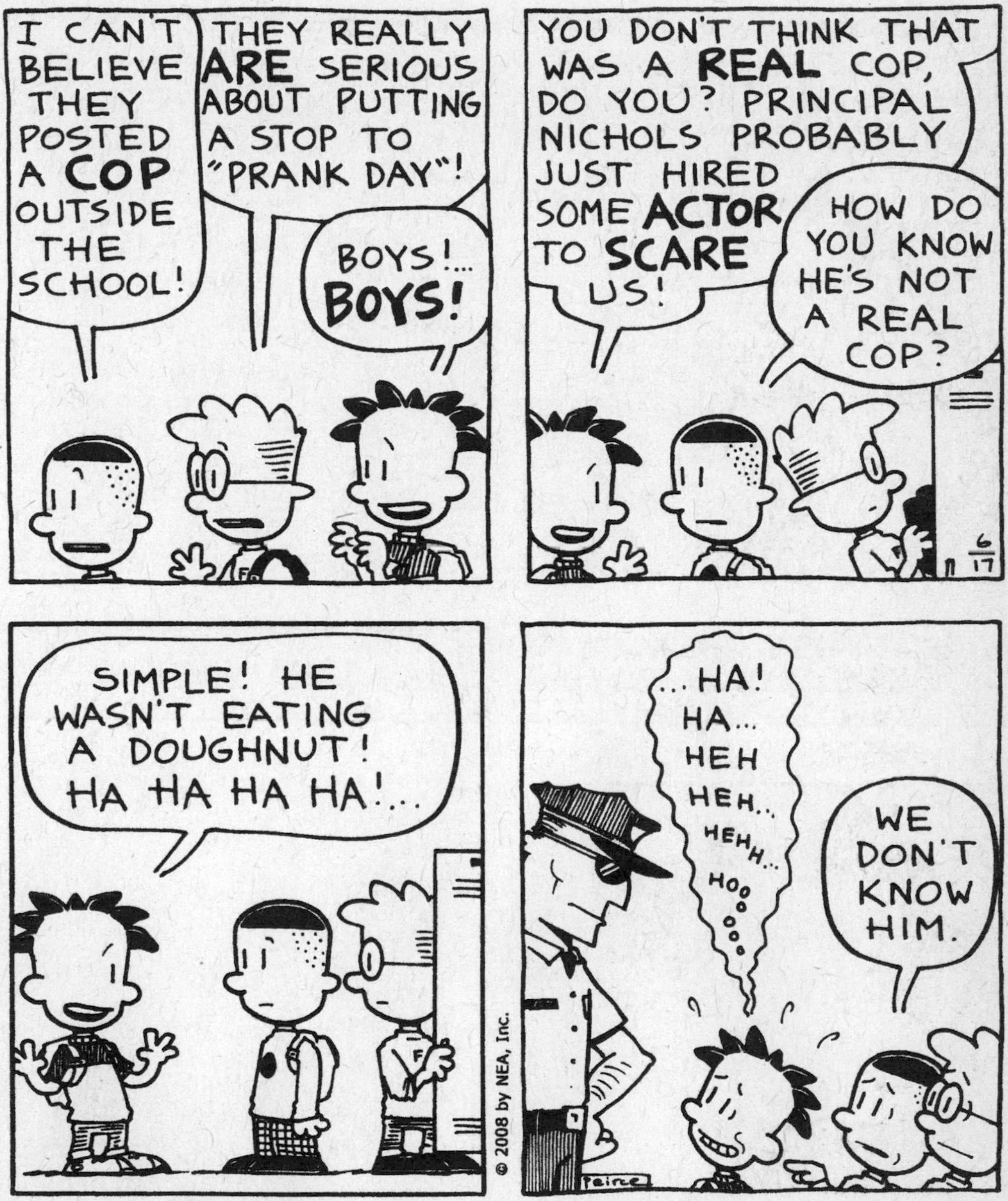
I CAN'T BELIEVE THEY POSTED A COP OUTSIDE THE SCHOOL!
THEY REALLY ARE SERIOUS ABOUT PUTTING A STOP TO "PRANK DAY"!
BOYS!... BOYS!
YOU DON'T THINK THAT WAS A REAL COP, DO YOU? PRINCIPAL NICHOLS PROBABLY JUST HIRED SOME ACTOR TO SCARE US!
HOW DO YOU KNOW HE'S NOT A REAL COP?
6/17
SIMPLE! HE WASN'T EATING A DOUGHNUT! HA HA HA HA!...
...HA! HA... HEH HEH... HEHH... HOOOOOO
WE DON'T KNOW HIM.
© 2008 by NEA, Inc.

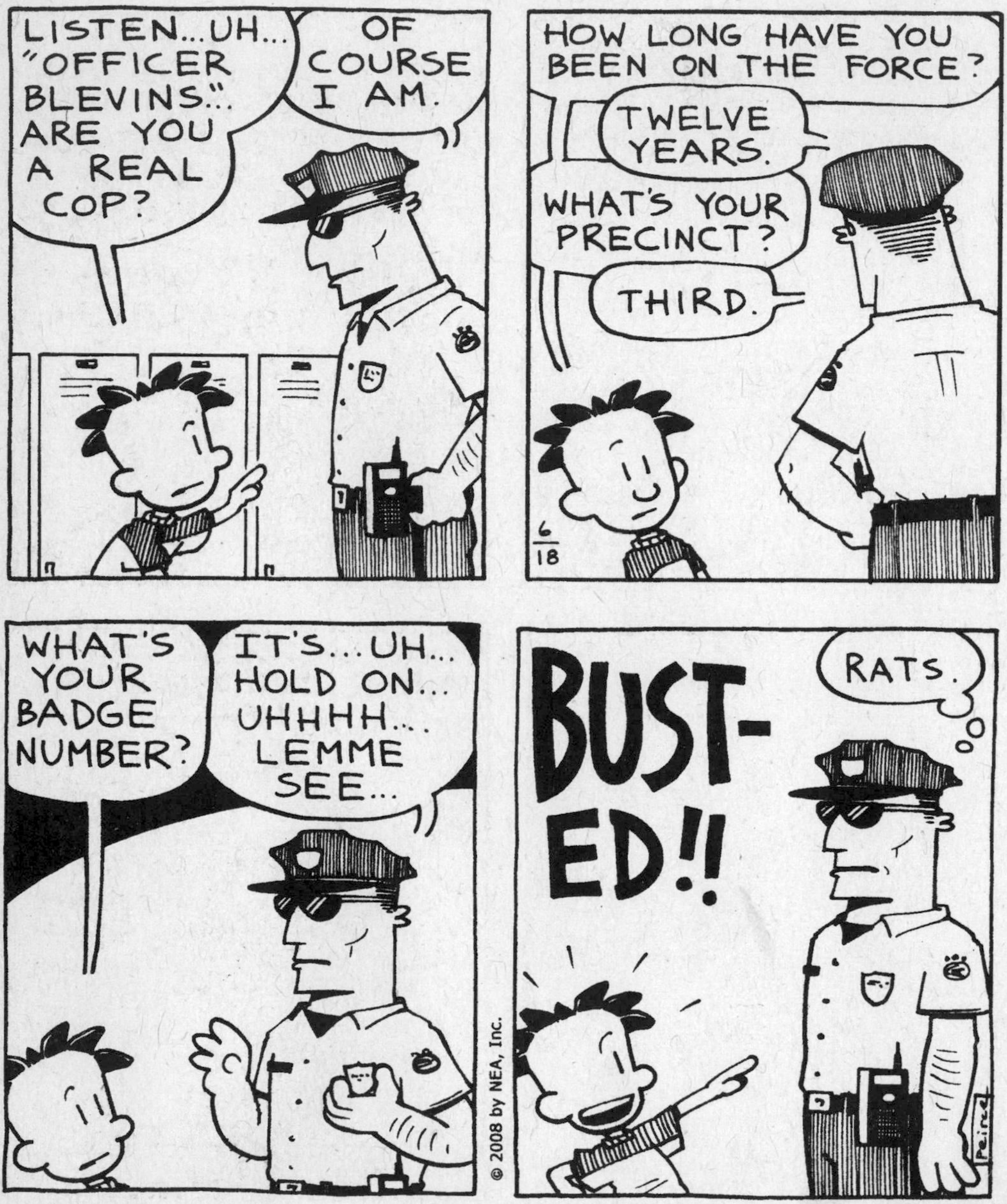

LISTEN...UH... "OFFICER BLEVINS"... ARE YOU A REAL COP?
OF COURSE I AM.
6/18
HOW LONG HAVE YOU BEEN ON THE FORCE?
TWELVE YEARS.
WHAT'S YOUR PRECINCT?
THIRD.
WHAT'S YOUR BADGE NUMBER?
IT'S...UH... HOLD ON... UHHHH.... LEMME SEE...
© 2008 by NEA, Inc.
BUST-ED!!
RATS.
Peirce

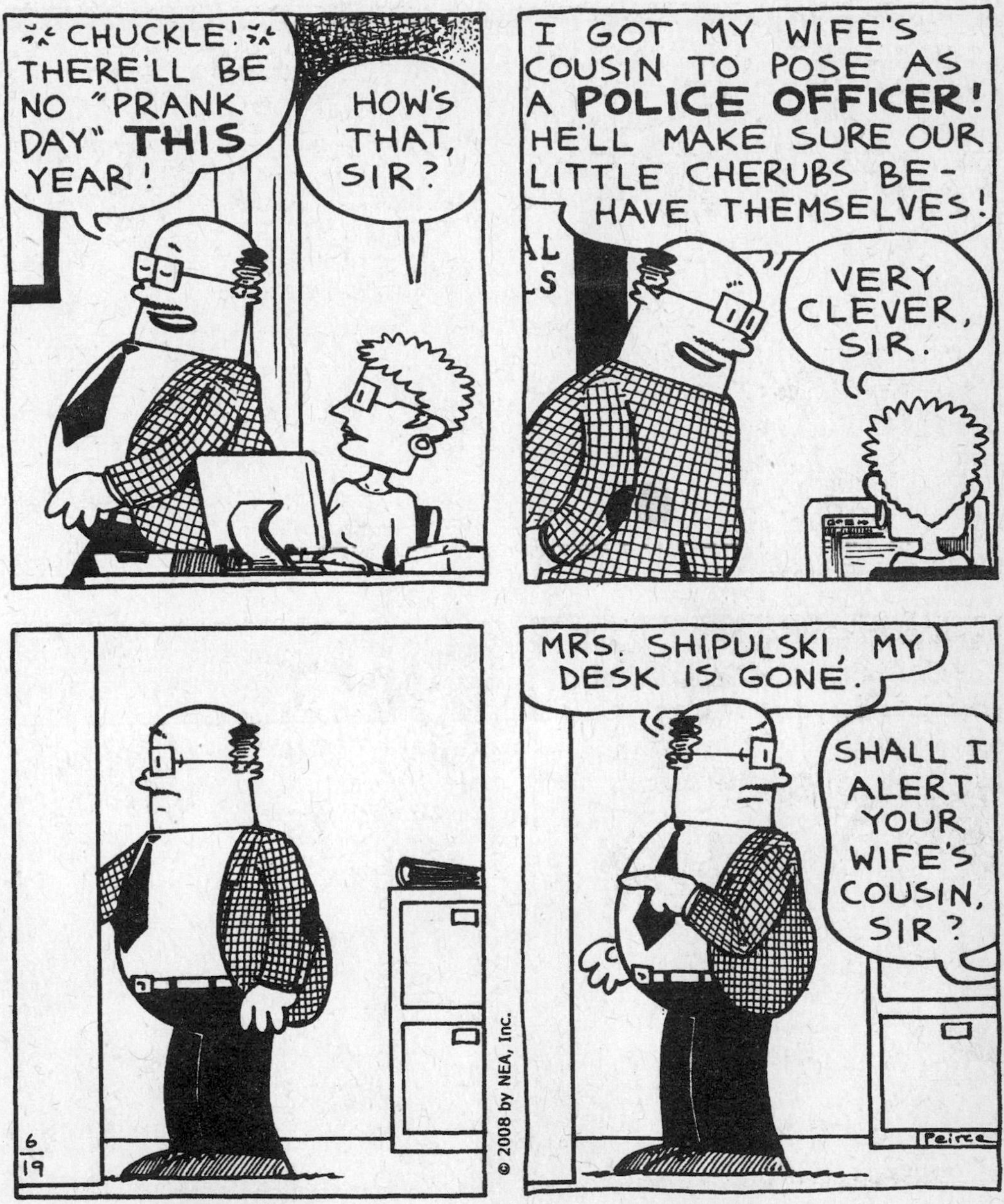
⁂ CHUCKLE! ⁂ THERE'LL BE NO "PRANK DAY" **THIS** YEAR!
HOW'S THAT, SIR?
I GOT MY WIFE'S COUSIN TO POSE AS A **POLICE OFFICER!** HE'LL MAKE SURE OUR LITTLE CHERUBS BE-HAVE THEMSELVES!
VERY CLEVER, SIR.
6/19
MRS. SHIPULSKI, MY DESK IS GONE.
SHALL I ALERT YOUR WIFE'S COUSIN, SIR?
Peirce

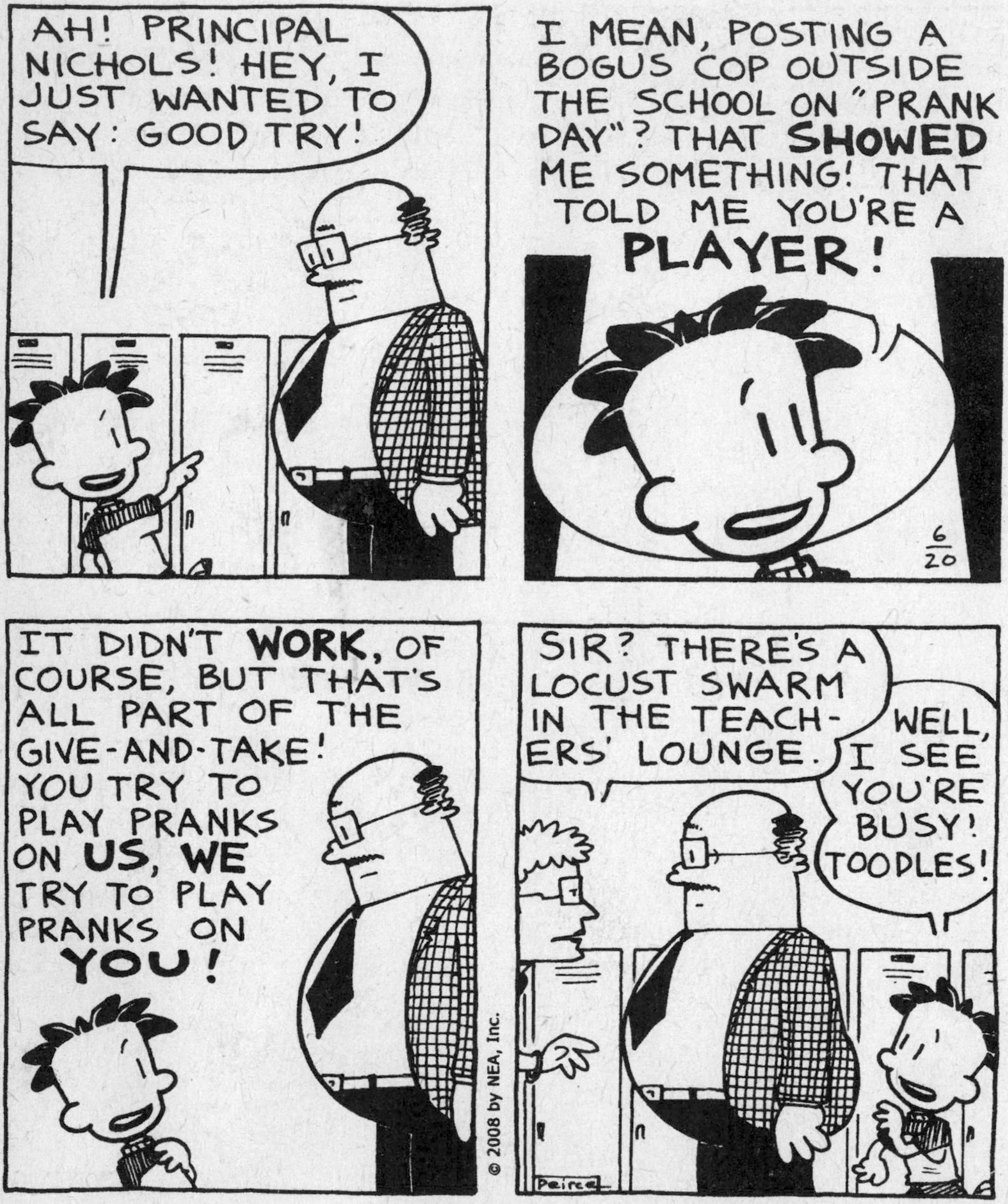
AH! PRINCIPAL NICHOLS! HEY, I JUST WANTED TO SAY: GOOD TRY!
I MEAN, POSTING A BOGUS COP OUTSIDE THE SCHOOL ON "PRANK DAY"? THAT SHOWED ME SOMETHING! THAT TOLD ME YOU'RE A PLAYER!
6/20
IT DIDN'T WORK, OF COURSE, BUT THAT'S ALL PART OF THE GIVE-AND-TAKE! YOU TRY TO PLAY PRANKS ON US, WE TRY TO PLAY PRANKS ON YOU!
© 2008 by NEA, Inc.
SIR? THERE'S A LOCUST SWARM IN THE TEACHERS' LOUNGE.
WELL, I SEE YOU'RE BUSY! TOODLES!
Peirce

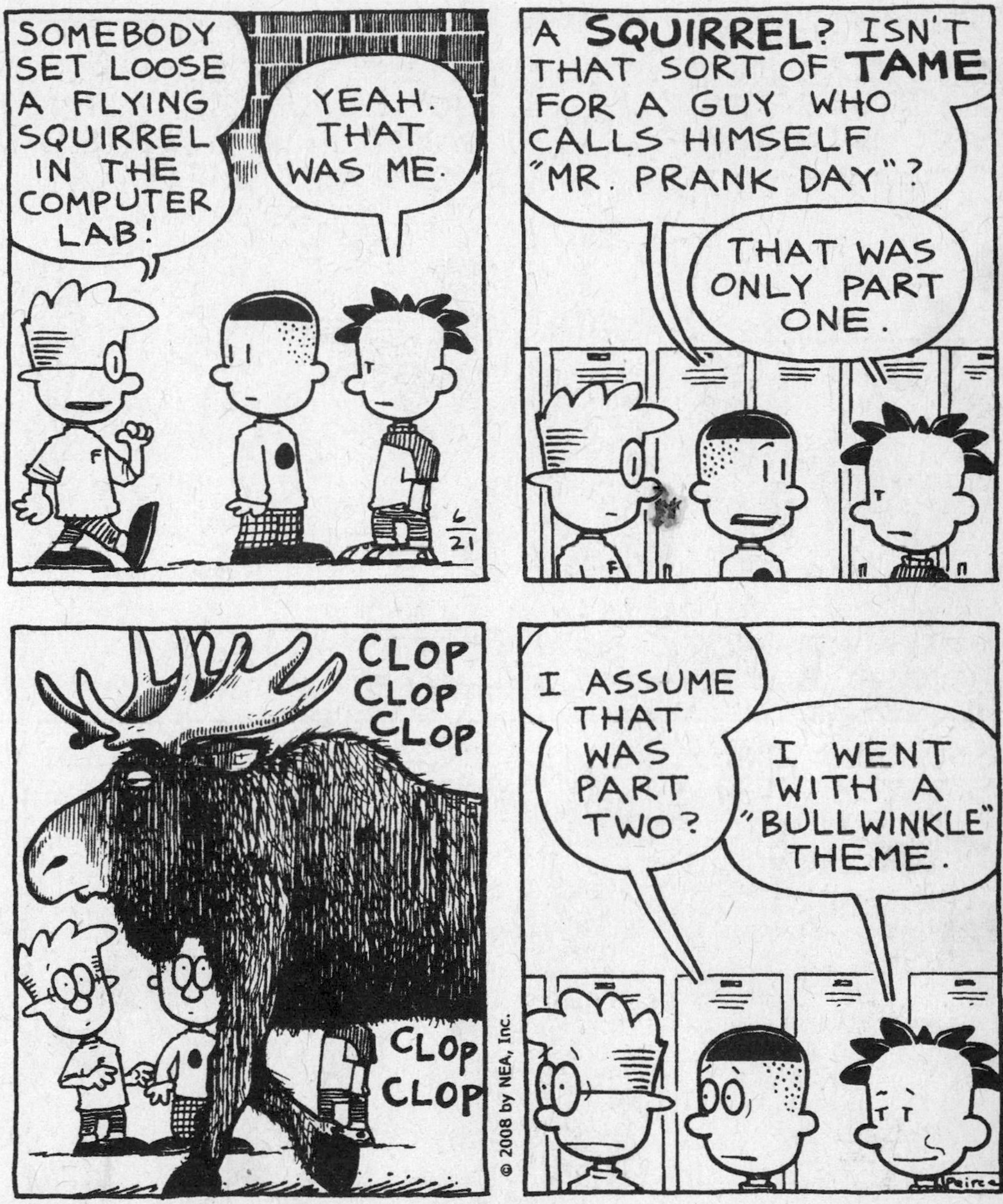
SOMEBODY SET LOOSE A FLYING SQUIRREL IN THE COMPUTER LAB!
YEAH. THAT WAS ME.
6/21
A **SQUIRREL**? ISN'T THAT SORT OF **TAME** FOR A GUY WHO CALLS HIMSELF "MR. PRANK DAY"?
THAT WAS ONLY PART ONE.
CLOP CLOP CLOP
CLOP CLOP
© 2008 by NEA, Inc.
I ASSUME THAT WAS PART TWO?
I WENT WITH A "BULLWINKLE" THEME.
Peirce

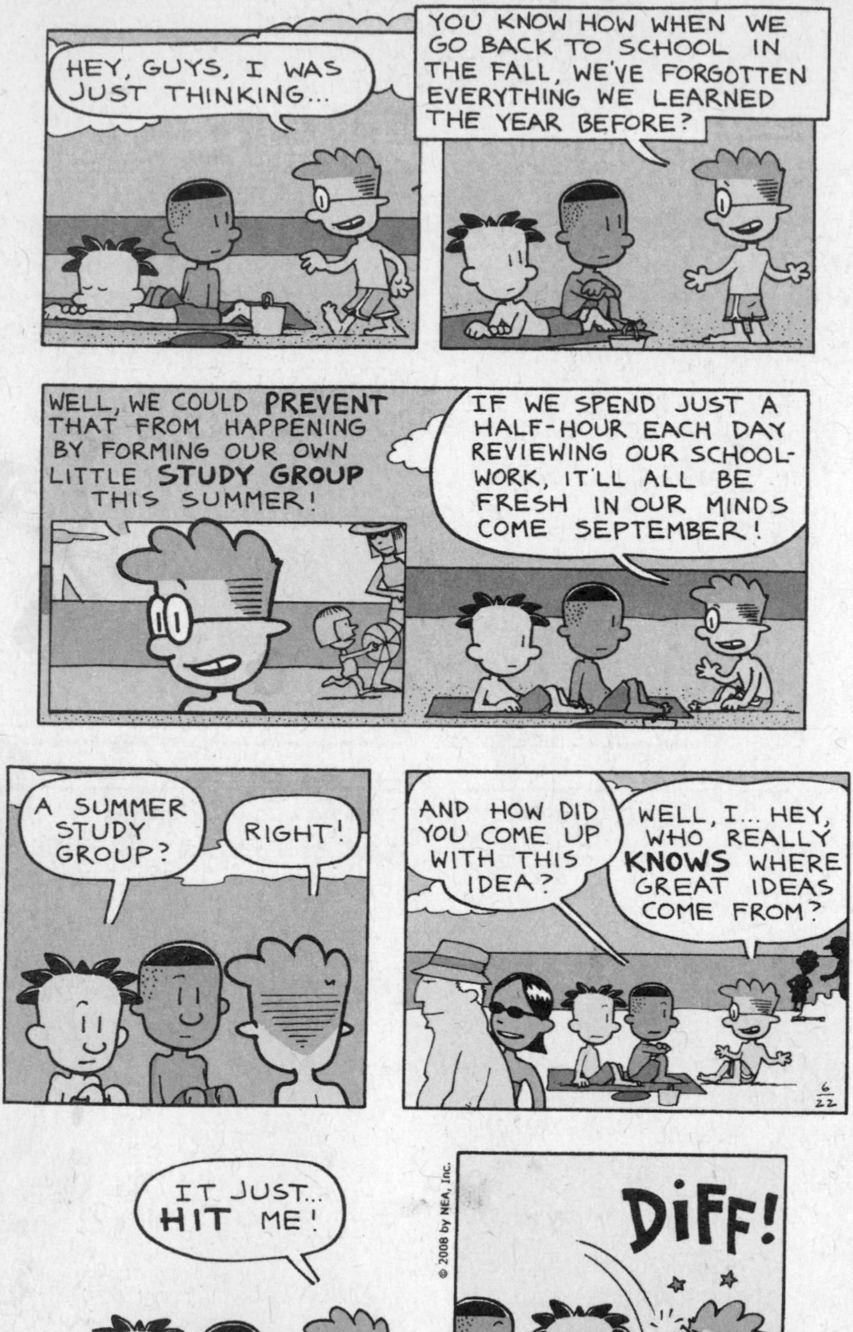
HEY, GUYS, I WAS JUST THINKING...
YOU KNOW HOW WHEN WE GO BACK TO SCHOOL IN THE FALL, WE'VE FORGOTTEN EVERYTHING WE LEARNED THE YEAR BEFORE?
WELL, WE COULD PREVENT THAT FROM HAPPENING BY FORMING OUR OWN LITTLE STUDY GROUP THIS SUMMER!
IF WE SPEND JUST A HALF-HOUR EACH DAY REVIEWING OUR SCHOOL-WORK, IT'LL ALL BE FRESH IN OUR MINDS COME SEPTEMBER!
A SUMMER STUDY GROUP?
RIGHT!
AND HOW DID YOU COME UP WITH THIS IDEA?
WELL, I... HEY, WHO REALLY KNOWS WHERE GREAT IDEAS COME FROM?
6/22

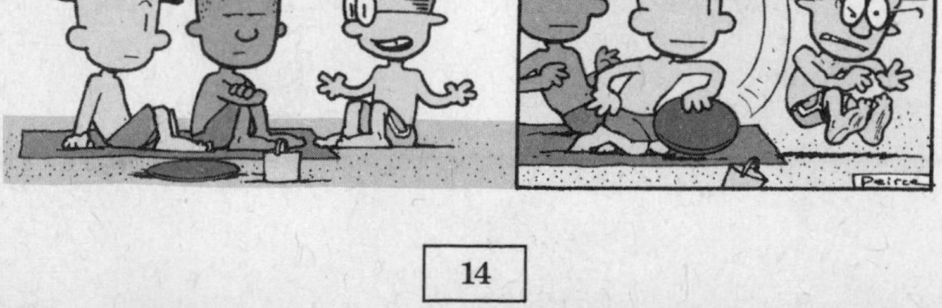
IT JUST... HIT ME!
DiFF!
Peirce

THE SUMMER OF NATE

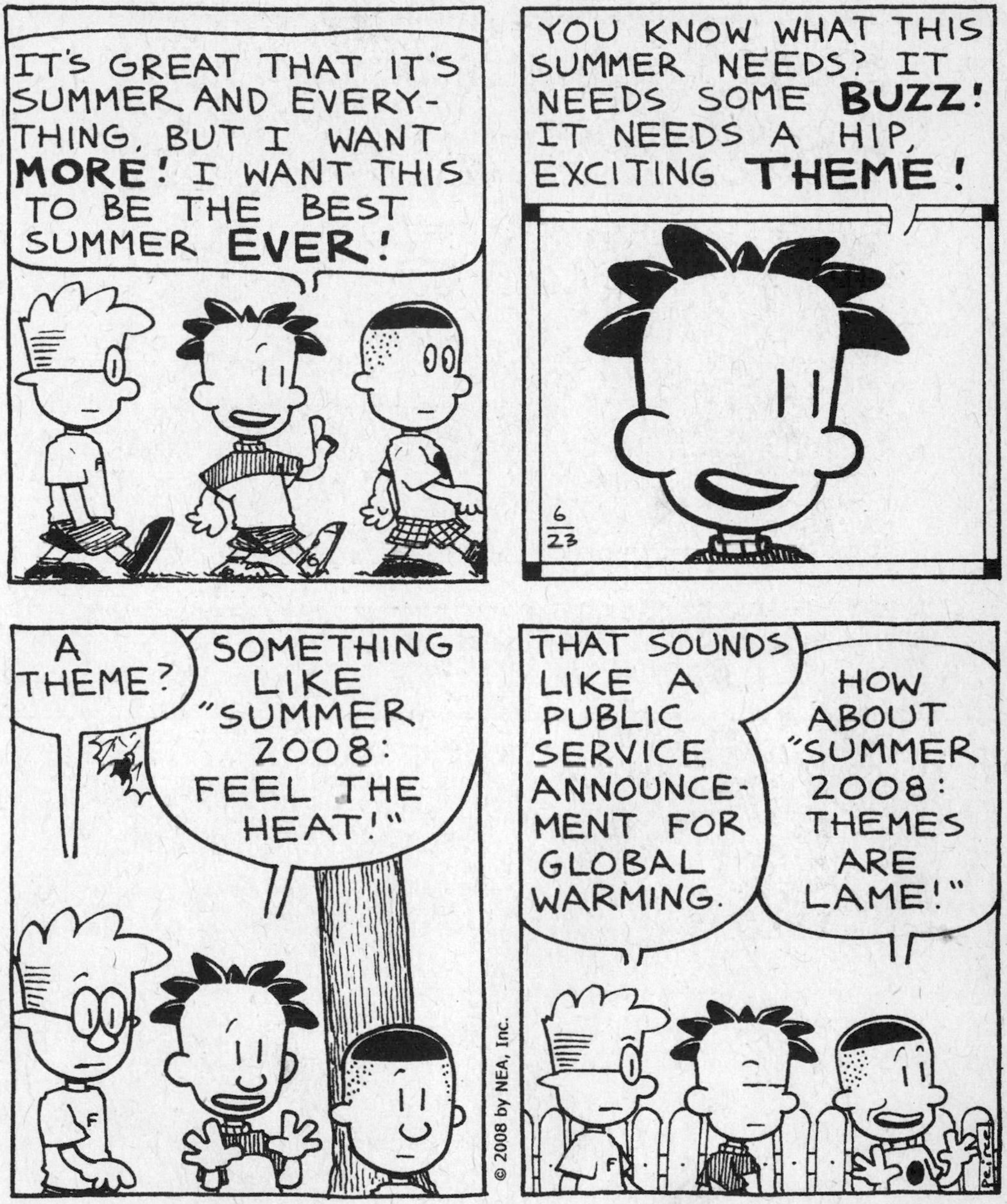
IT'S GREAT THAT IT'S SUMMER AND EVERYTHING, BUT I WANT MORE! I WANT THIS TO BE THE BEST SUMMER EVER!
YOU KNOW WHAT THIS SUMMER NEEDS? IT NEEDS SOME BUZZ! IT NEEDS A HIP, EXCITING THEME!
6/23
A THEME?
SOMETHING LIKE "SUMMER 2008: FEEL THE HEAT!"
THAT SOUNDS LIKE A PUBLIC SERVICE ANNOUNCEMENT FOR GLOBAL WARMING.
HOW ABOUT "SUMMER 2008: THEMES ARE LAME!"
© 2008 by NEA, Inc.

HERE'S A GOOD THEME: "2008: THE SUMMER OF NATE!"
...OR "SUMMER '08: GET READY FOR TEDDY!"
6/24
NOTHING RHYMES WITH FRANCIS.
Peirce

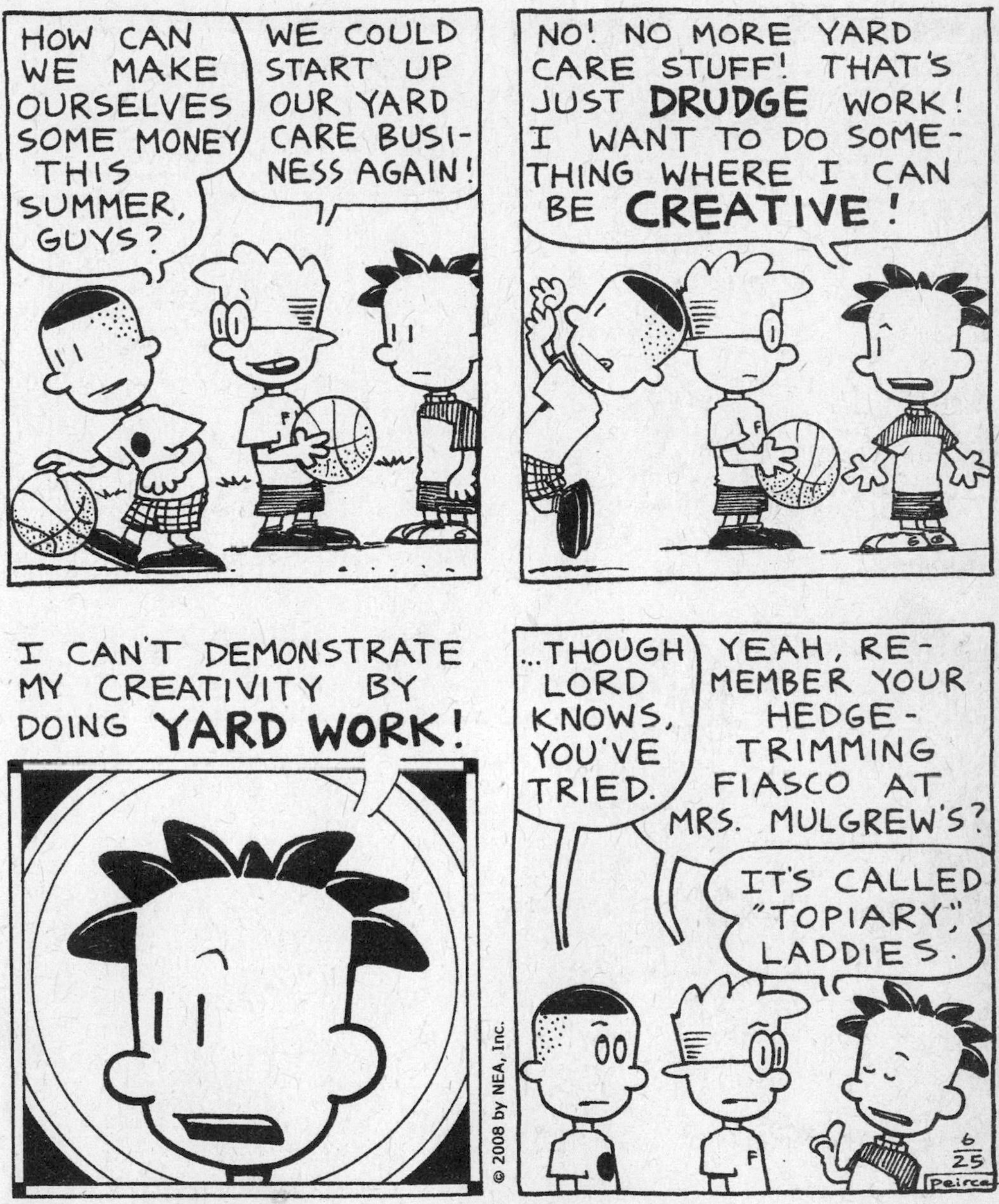

HOW CAN WE MAKE OURSELVES SOME MONEY THIS SUMMER, GUYS?
WE COULD START UP OUR YARD CARE BUSINESS AGAIN!
NO! NO MORE YARD CARE STUFF! THAT'S JUST DRUDGE WORK! I WANT TO DO SOMETHING WHERE I CAN BE CREATIVE!
I CAN'T DEMONSTRATE MY CREATIVITY BY DOING YARD WORK!
...THOUGH LORD KNOWS, YOU'VE TRIED.
YEAH, REMEMBER YOUR HEDGE-TRIMMING FIASCO AT MRS. MULGREW'S?
IT'S CALLED "TOPIARY," LADDIES.
© 2008 by NEA, Inc.
6/25
Peirce

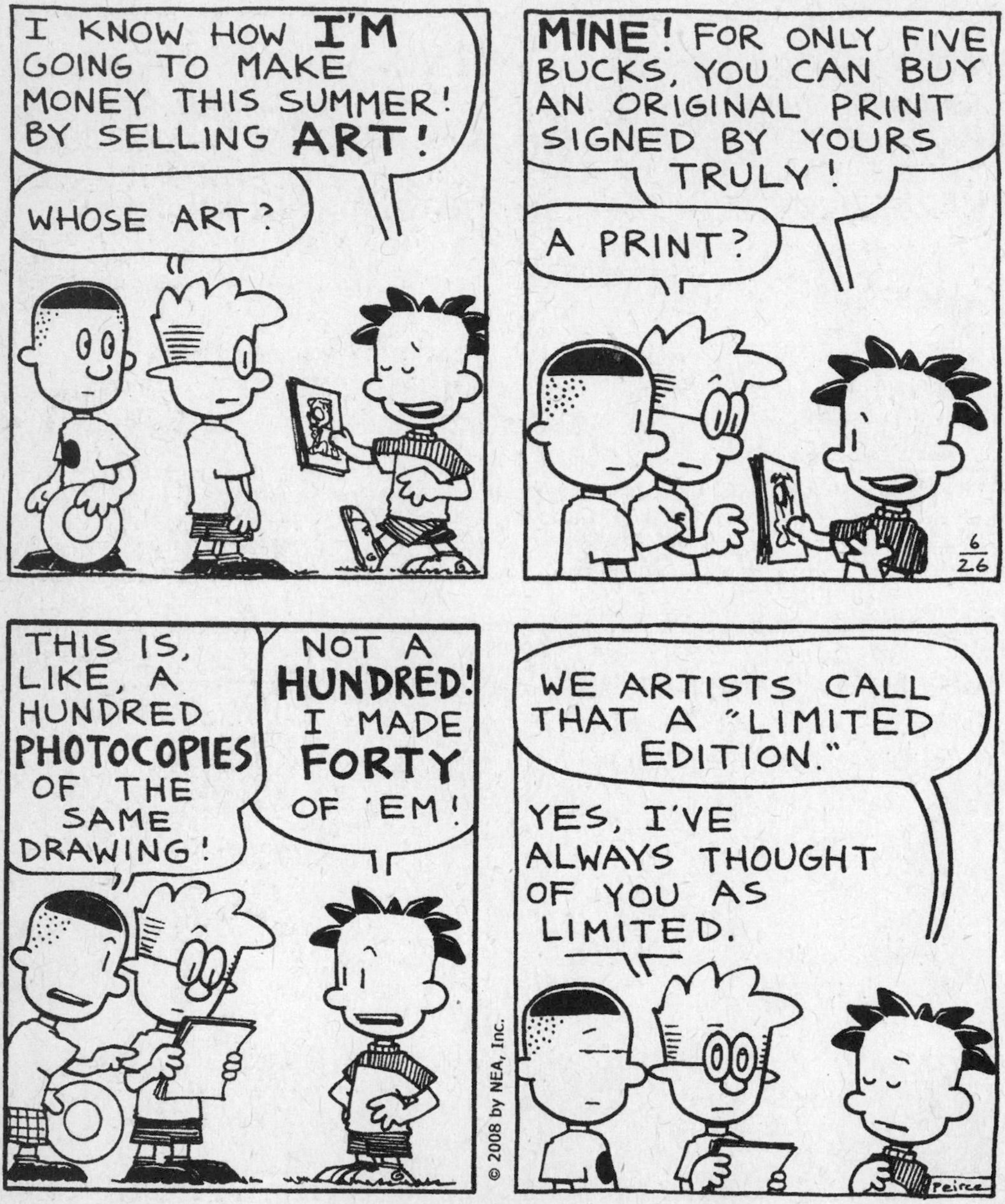
I KNOW HOW I'M GOING TO MAKE MONEY THIS SUMMER! BY SELLING ART!
WHOSE ART?
MINE! FOR ONLY FIVE BUCKS, YOU CAN BUY AN ORIGINAL PRINT SIGNED BY YOURS TRULY!
A PRINT?
6/26
THIS IS, LIKE, A HUNDRED PHOTOCOPIES OF THE SAME DRAWING!
NOT A HUNDRED! I MADE FORTY OF 'EM!
© 2008 by NEA, Inc.
WE ARTISTS CALL THAT A "LIMITED EDITION."
YES, I'VE ALWAYS THOUGHT OF YOU AS LIMITED.
Peirce

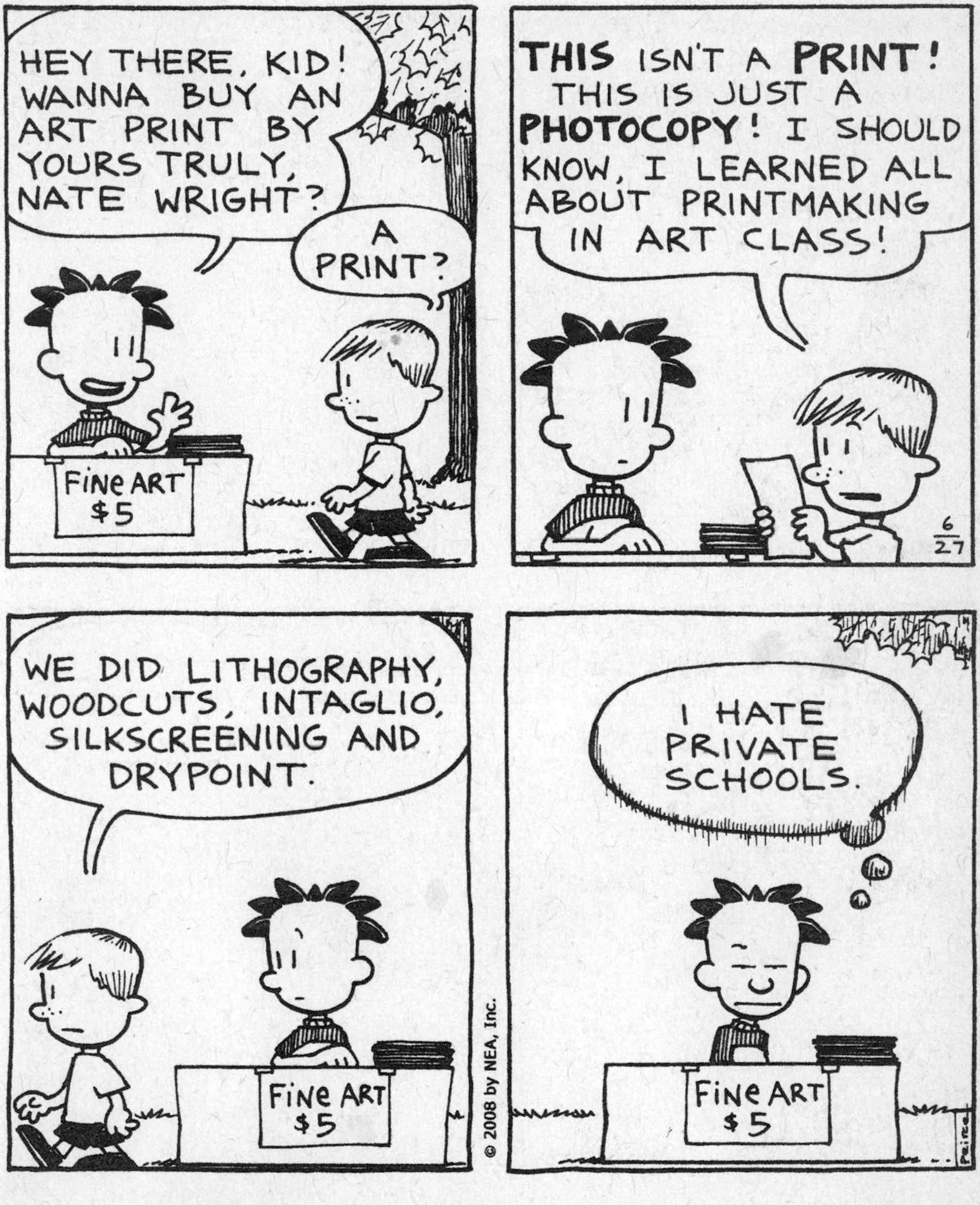
HEY THERE, KID! WANNA BUY AN ART PRINT BY YOURS TRULY, NATE WRIGHT?
A PRINT?
FINE ART $5
THIS ISN'T A PRINT! THIS IS JUST A PHOTOCOPY! I SHOULD KNOW, I LEARNED ALL ABOUT PRINTMAKING IN ART CLASS!
6/27
WE DID LITHOGRAPHY, WOODCUTS, INTAGLIO, SILKSCREENING AND DRYPOINT.
FINE ART $5
© 2008 by NEA, Inc.
I HATE PRIVATE SCHOOLS.
FINE ART $5
Peirce

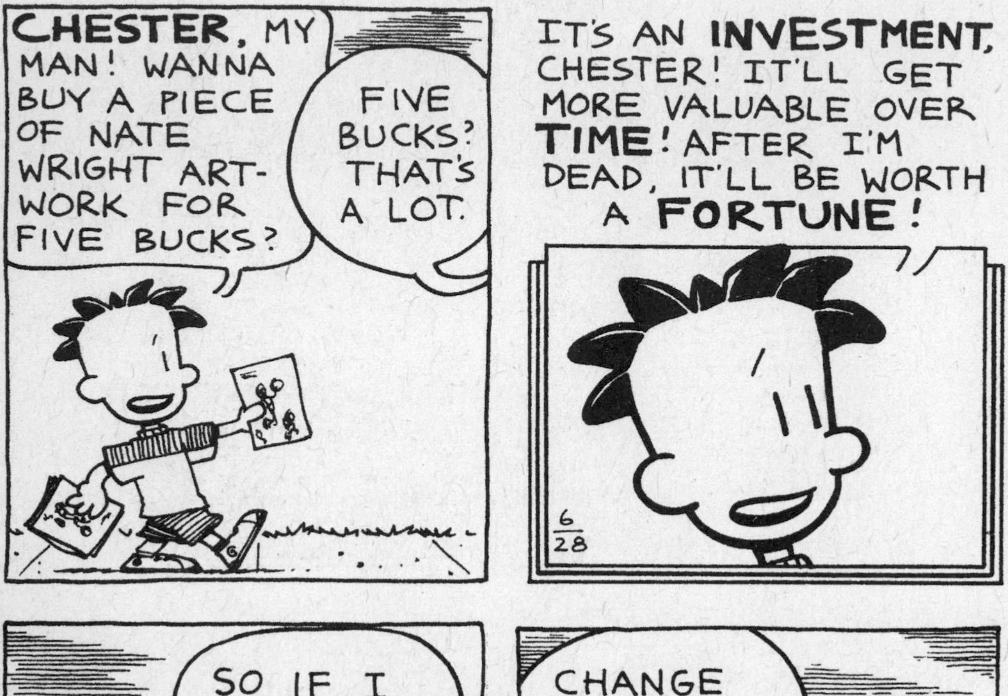
CHESTER, MY MAN! WANNA BUY A PIECE OF NATE WRIGHT ART-WORK FOR FIVE BUCKS?
FIVE BUCKS? THAT'S A LOT.
IT'S AN INVESTMENT, CHESTER! IT'LL GET MORE VALUABLE OVER TIME! AFTER I'M DEAD, IT'LL BE WORTH A FORTUNE!
6/28
SO IF I KILL YOU, I'LL MAKE MONEY?
CHANGE OF PLANS. I'M OPENING A LEMONADE STAND.
COME HERE.
© 2008 by NEA, Inc.
Peirce

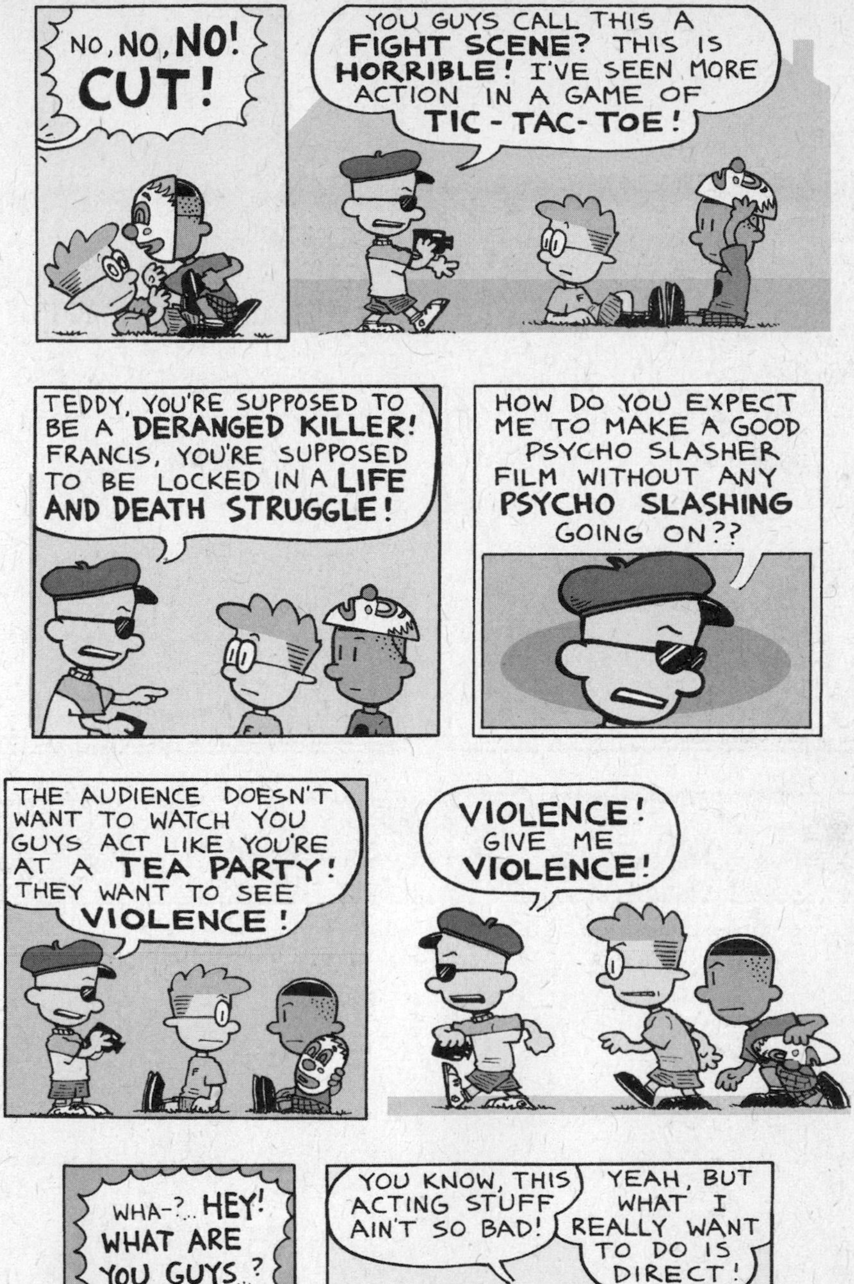
NO, NO, NO! CUT!
YOU GUYS CALL THIS A FIGHT SCENE? THIS IS HORRIBLE! I'VE SEEN MORE ACTION IN A GAME OF TIC-TAC-TOE!
TEDDY, YOU'RE SUPPOSED TO BE A DERANGED KILLER! FRANCIS, YOU'RE SUPPOSED TO BE LOCKED IN A LIFE AND DEATH STRUGGLE!
HOW DO YOU EXPECT ME TO MAKE A GOOD PSYCHO SLASHER FILM WITHOUT ANY PSYCHO SLASHING GOING ON??
THE AUDIENCE DOESN'T WANT TO WATCH YOU GUYS ACT LIKE YOU'RE AT A TEA PARTY! THEY WANT TO SEE VIOLENCE!
VIOLENCE! GIVE ME VIOLENCE!
WHA-?... HEY! WHAT ARE YOU GUYS...? NO!! OW!!
YOU KNOW, THIS ACTING STUFF AIN'T SO BAD!
YEAH, BUT WHAT I REALLY WANT TO DO IS DIRECT!
6/29
Peirce

WILD RIDE

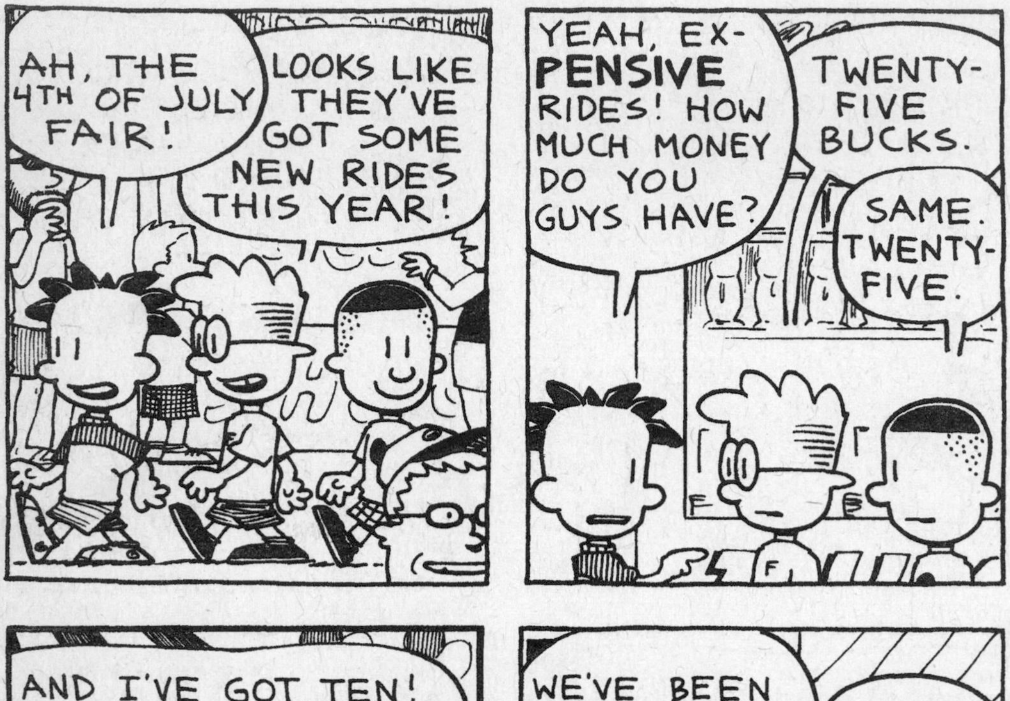
AH, THE 4TH OF JULY FAIR!
LOOKS LIKE THEY'VE GOT SOME NEW RIDES THIS YEAR!
YEAH, EX-**PENSIVE** RIDES! HOW MUCH MONEY DO YOU GUYS HAVE?
TWENTY-FIVE BUCKS.
SAME. TWENTY-FIVE.
AND I'VE GOT TEN! THAT'S SIXTY BUCKS ALL TOGETHER! TWENTY FOR EACH OF US!
6/30
© 2008 by NEA, Inc.
WE'VE BEEN HERE FOR TWO MINUTES, AND I'VE ALREADY LOST FIVE DOLLARS.
FAIRS ARE SUCH RIP-OFFS.
Peirce

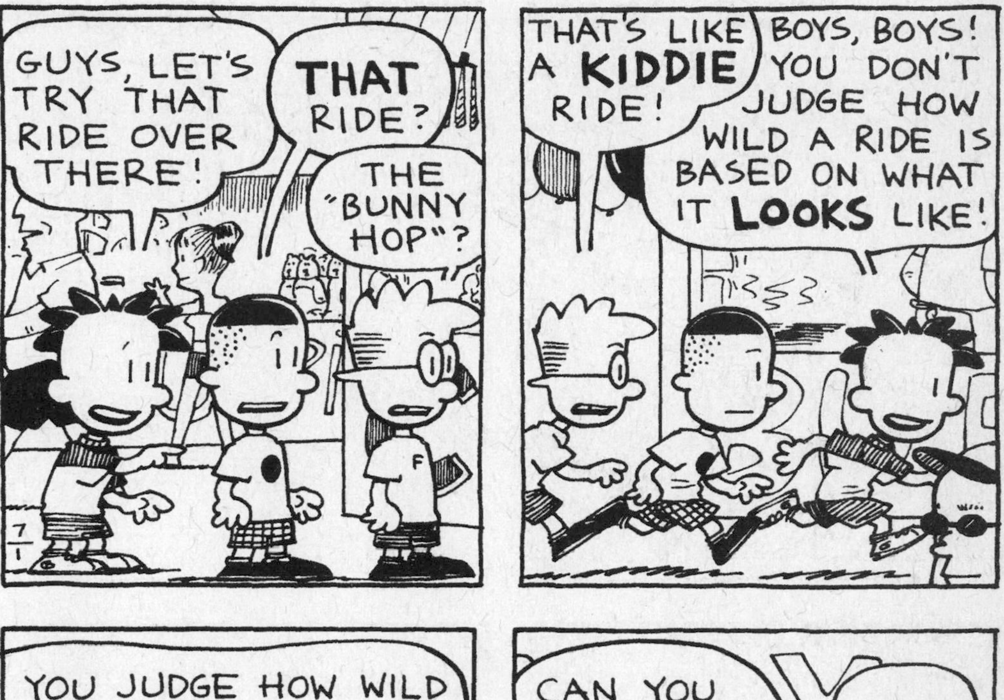
GUYS, LET'S TRY THAT RIDE OVER THERE!
THAT RIDE?
THE "BUNNY HOP"?
THAT'S LIKE A KIDDIE RIDE!
BOYS, BOYS! YOU DON'T JUDGE HOW WILD A RIDE IS BASED ON WHAT IT LOOKS LIKE!
YOU JUDGE HOW WILD A RIDE IS BASED ON WHAT THE GUY IN CHARGE OF IT LOOKS LIKE!
CAN YOU CRANK THIS BABY UP TO MACH 3?
'KAY.
Peirce

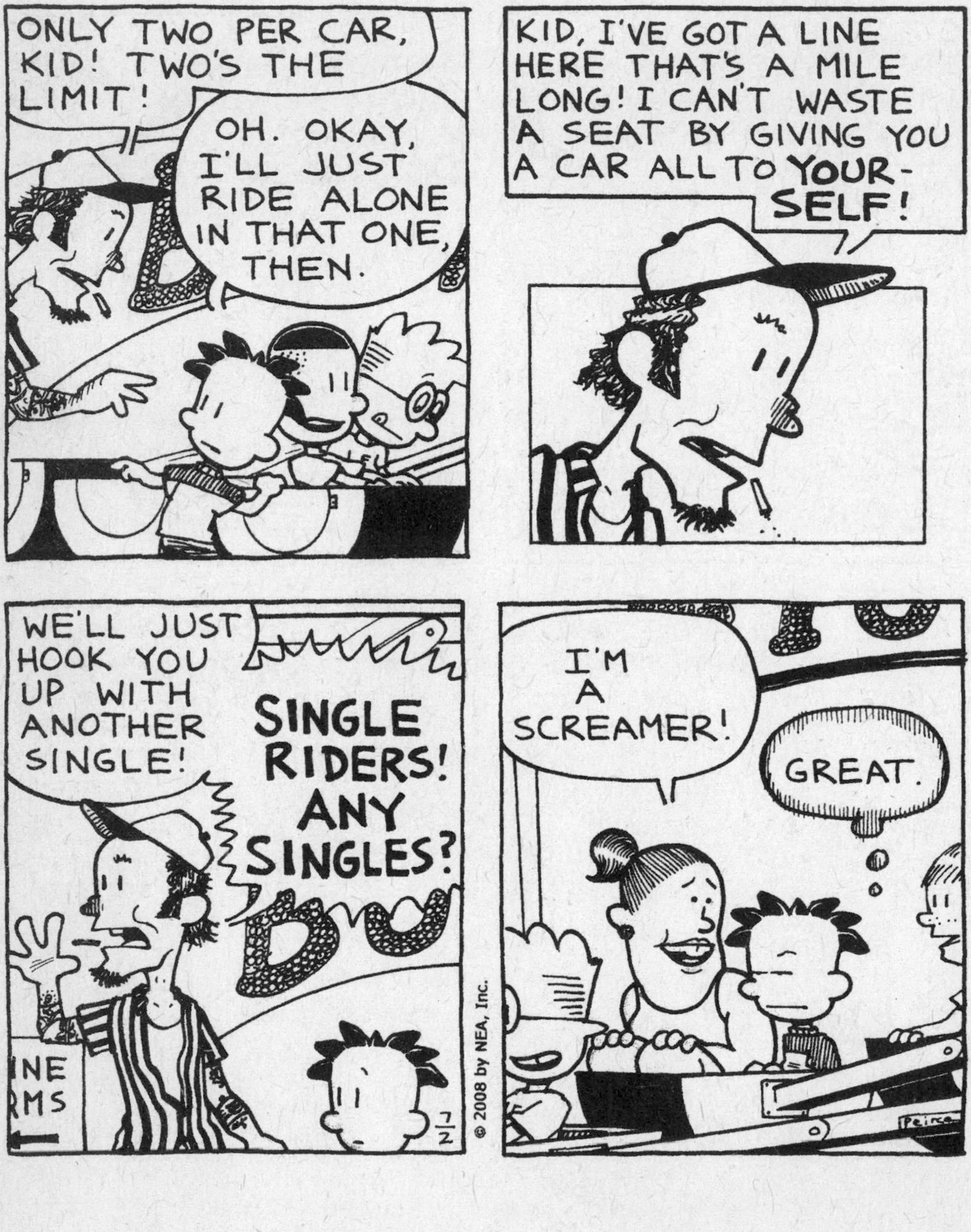
ONLY TWO PER CAR, KID! TWO'S THE LIMIT!
OH. OKAY, I'LL JUST RIDE ALONE IN THAT ONE, THEN.
KID, I'VE GOT A LINE HERE THAT'S A MILE LONG! I CAN'T WASTE A SEAT BY GIVING YOU A CAR ALL TO YOURSELF!
WE'LL JUST HOOK YOU UP WITH ANOTHER SINGLE!
SINGLE RIDERS! ANY SINGLES?
NE
RMS
7/2
© 2008 by NEA, Inc.
I'M A SCREAMER!
GREAT.
Peirce

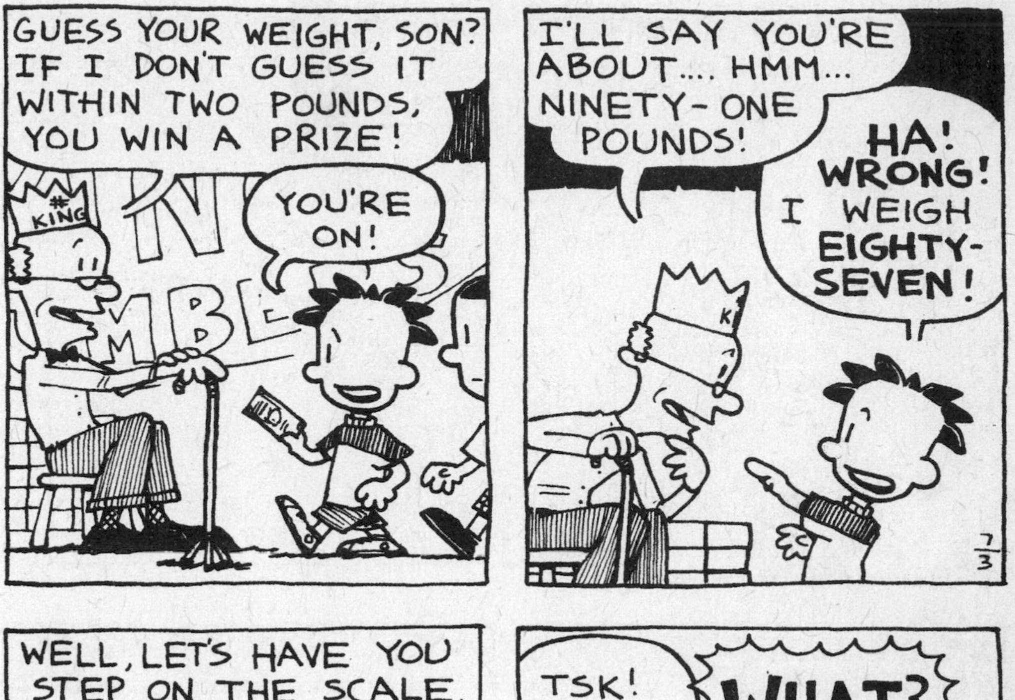
GUESS YOUR WEIGHT, SON? IF I DON'T GUESS IT WITHIN TWO POUNDS, YOU WIN A PRIZE!
YOU'RE ON!
KING
I'LL SAY YOU'RE ABOUT.... HMM... NINETY-ONE POUNDS!
HA! WRONG! I WEIGH EIGHTY-SEVEN!
7/3
WELL, LET'S HAVE YOU STEP ON THE SCALE, SHALL WE?
SURE!
© 2008 by NEA, Inc.
TSK! NINETY-TWO!
WHAT?
HE FORGOT ABOUT THE FIVE POUNDS OF FRIED DOUGH HE'S EATEN TODAY.
Peirce

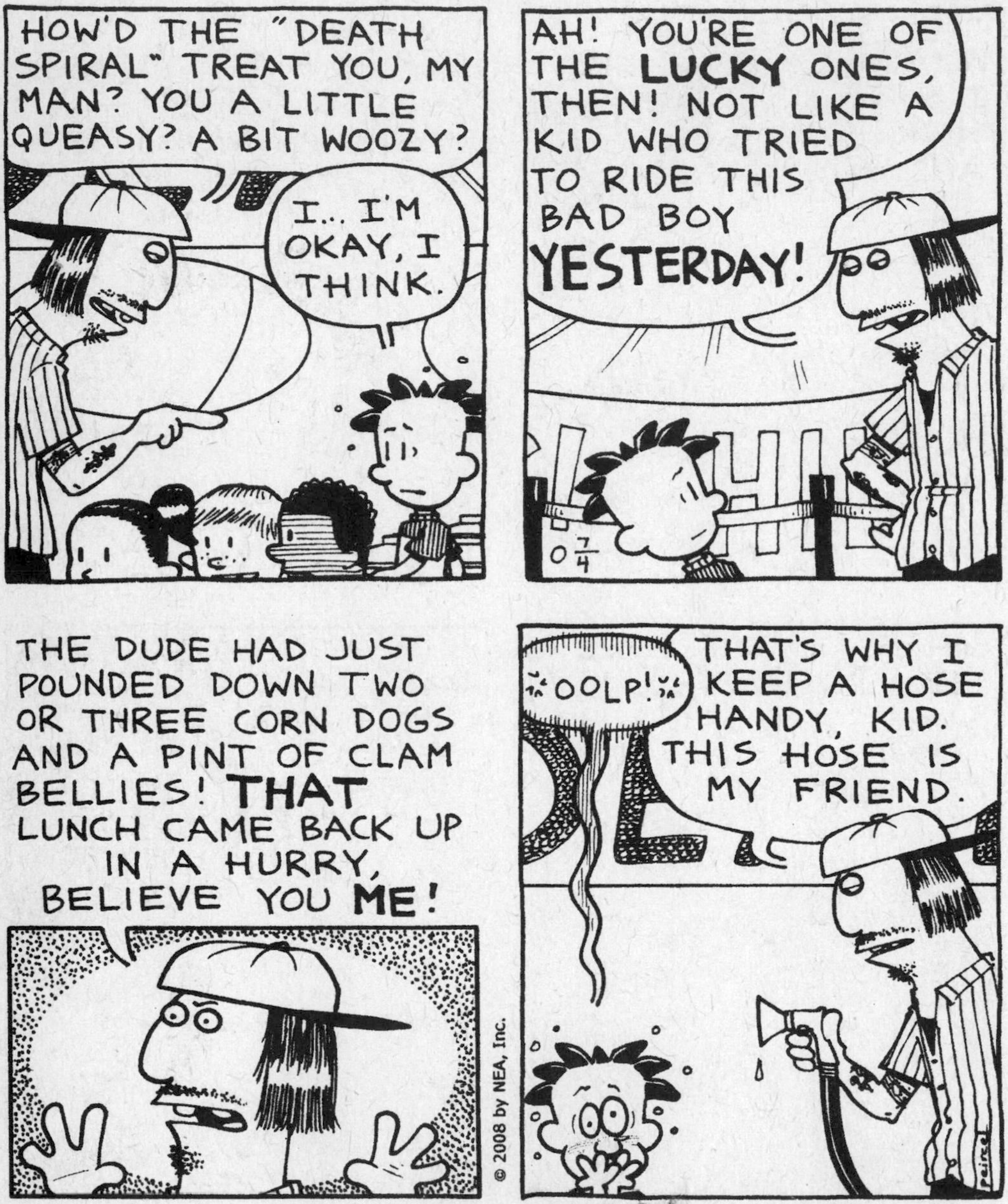
HOW'D THE "DEATH SPIRAL" TREAT YOU, MY MAN? YOU A LITTLE QUEASY? A BIT WOOZY?
I... I'M OKAY, I THINK.
AH! YOU'RE ONE OF THE **LUCKY** ONES, THEN! NOT LIKE A KID WHO TRIED TO RIDE THIS BAD BOY **YESTERDAY!**
THE DUDE HAD JUST POUNDED DOWN TWO OR THREE CORN DOGS AND A PINT OF CLAM BELLIES! **THAT** LUNCH CAME BACK UP IN A HURRY, BELIEVE YOU **ME!**
OOLP!
THAT'S WHY I KEEP A HOSE HANDY, KID. THIS HOSE IS MY FRIEND.

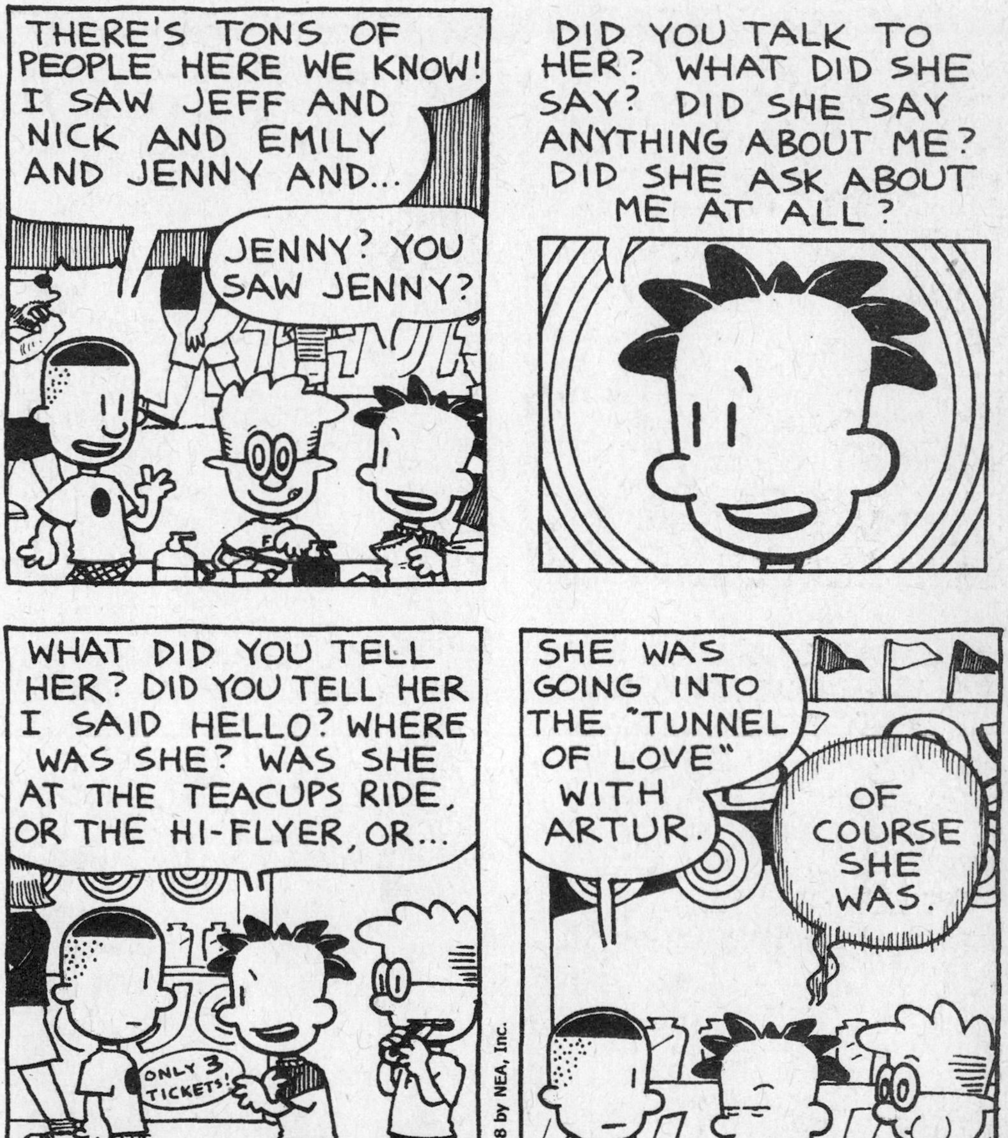
THERE'S TONS OF PEOPLE HERE WE KNOW! I SAW JEFF AND NICK AND EMILY AND JENNY AND...
JENNY? YOU SAW JENNY?
DID YOU TALK TO HER? WHAT DID SHE SAY? DID SHE SAY ANYTHING ABOUT ME? DID SHE ASK ABOUT ME AT ALL?
WHAT DID YOU TELL HER? DID YOU TELL HER I SAID HELLO? WHERE WAS SHE? WAS SHE AT THE TEACUPS RIDE, OR THE HI-FLYER, OR...
ONLY 3 TICKETS!
© 2008 by NEA, Inc.
7/5
SHE WAS GOING INTO THE "TUNNEL OF LOVE" WITH ARTUR.
OF COURSE SHE WAS.
PEIRCE

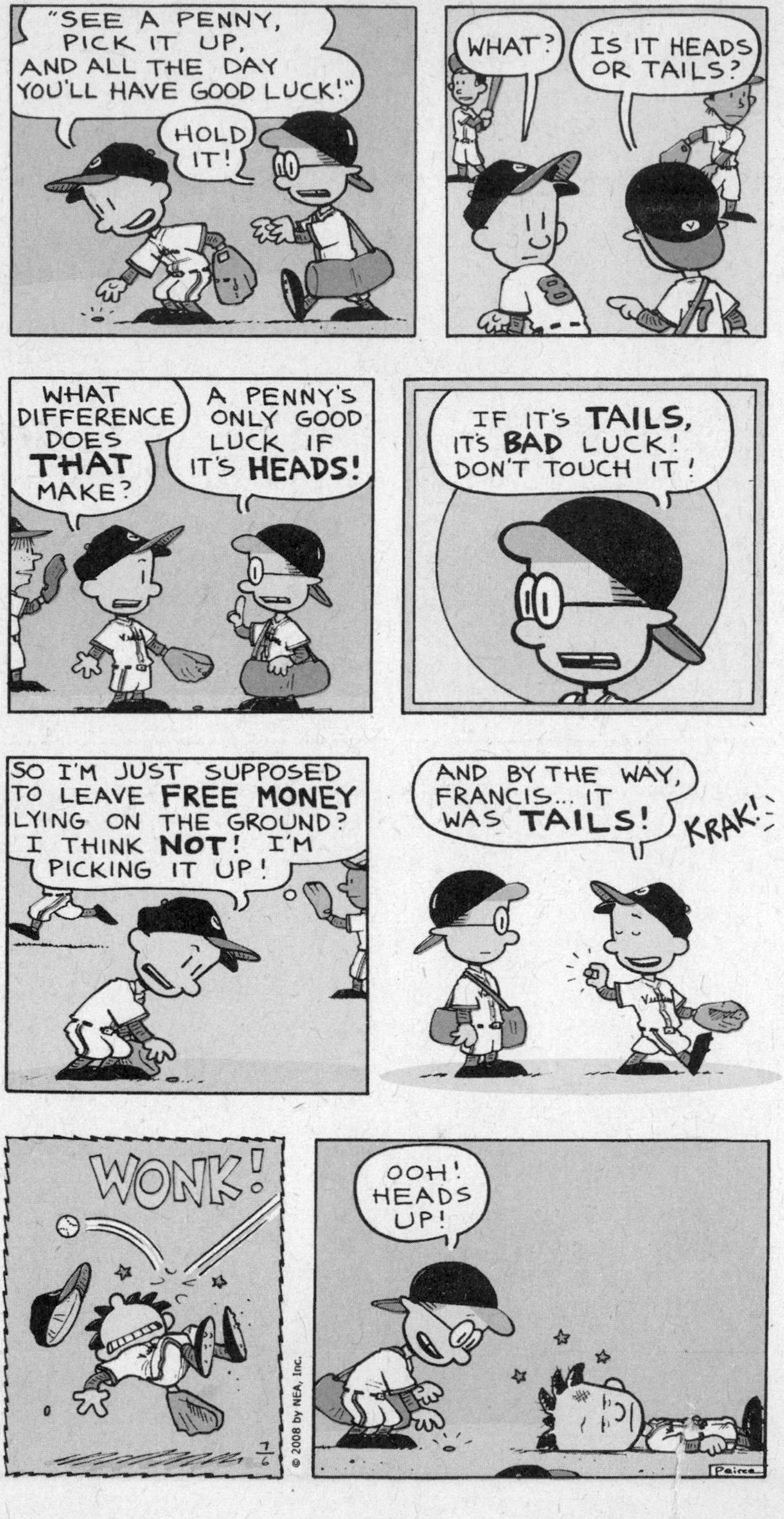
"SEE A PENNY, PICK IT UP, AND ALL THE DAY YOU'LL HAVE GOOD LUCK!"
HOLD IT!
WHAT?
IS IT HEADS OR TAILS?
WHAT DIFFERENCE DOES THAT MAKE?
A PENNY'S ONLY GOOD LUCK IF IT'S HEADS!
IF IT'S TAILS, IT'S BAD LUCK! DON'T TOUCH IT!
SO I'M JUST SUPPOSED TO LEAVE FREE MONEY LYING ON THE GROUND? I THINK NOT! I'M PICKING IT UP!
AND BY THE WAY, FRANCIS... IT WAS TAILS!
KRAK!
WONK!
7/6
© 2008 by NEA, Inc.
OOH! HEADS UP!
Peirce

WHAT BAD LUCK?

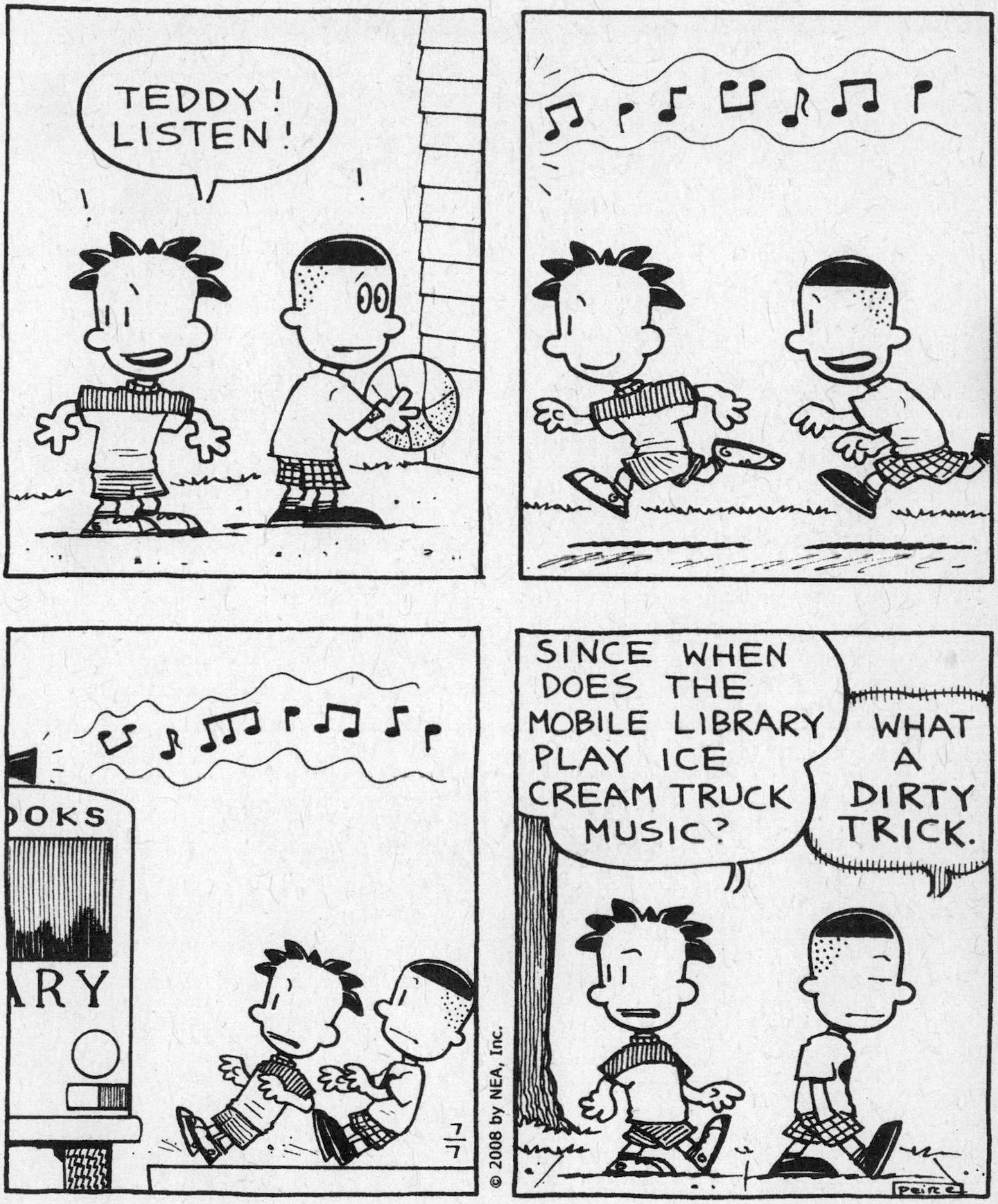
TEDDY! LISTEN!
OOKS
ARY
7/7
© 2008 by NEA, Inc.
SINCE WHEN DOES THE MOBILE LIBRARY PLAY ICE CREAM TRUCK MUSIC?
WHAT A DIRTY TRICK.
PEIRCE

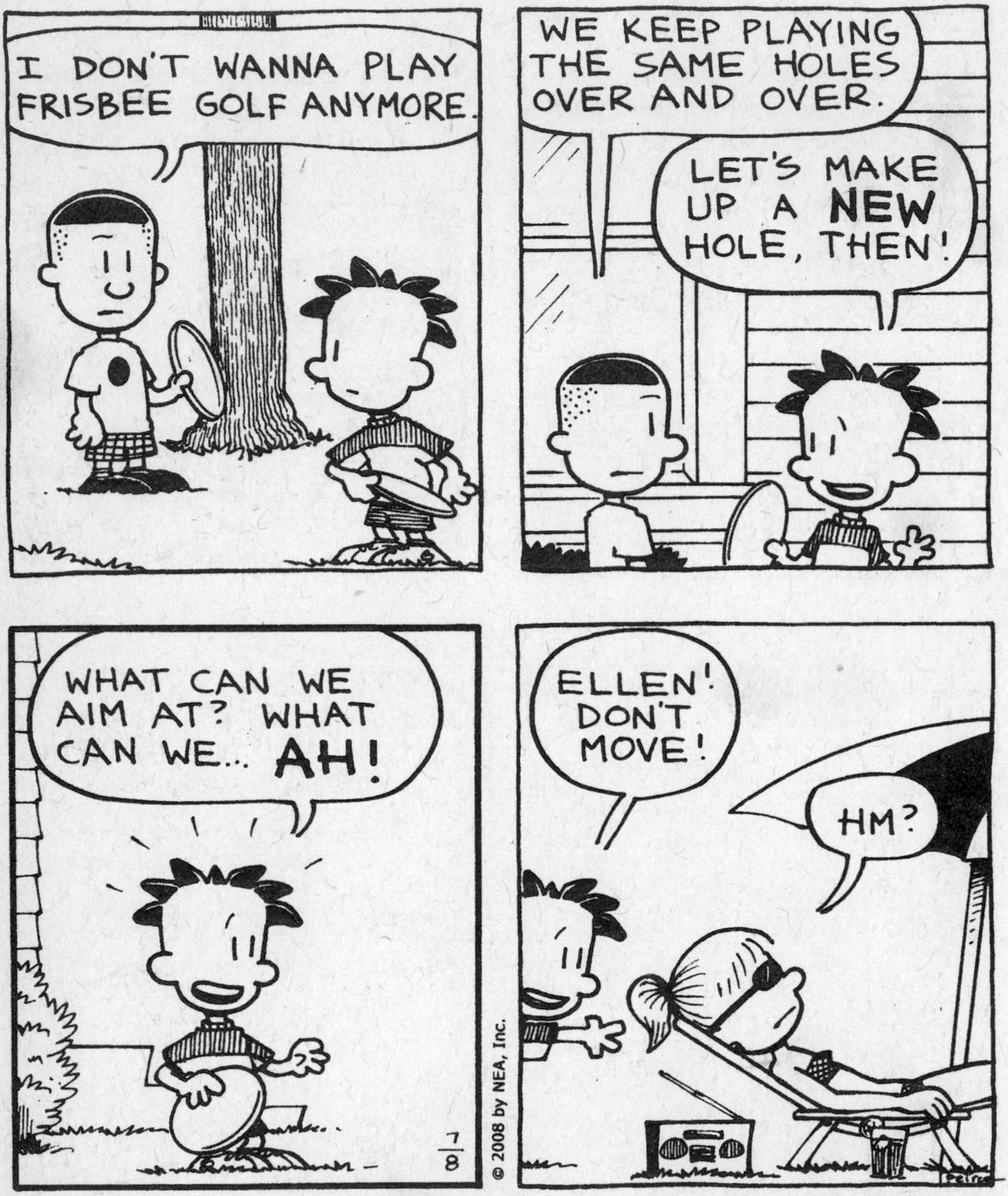
I DON'T WANNA PLAY FRISBEE GOLF ANYMORE.
WE KEEP PLAYING THE SAME HOLES OVER AND OVER.
LET'S MAKE UP A **NEW** HOLE, THEN!
WHAT CAN WE AIM AT? WHAT CAN WE... **AH!**
7/8
ELLEN! DON'T MOVE!
HM?

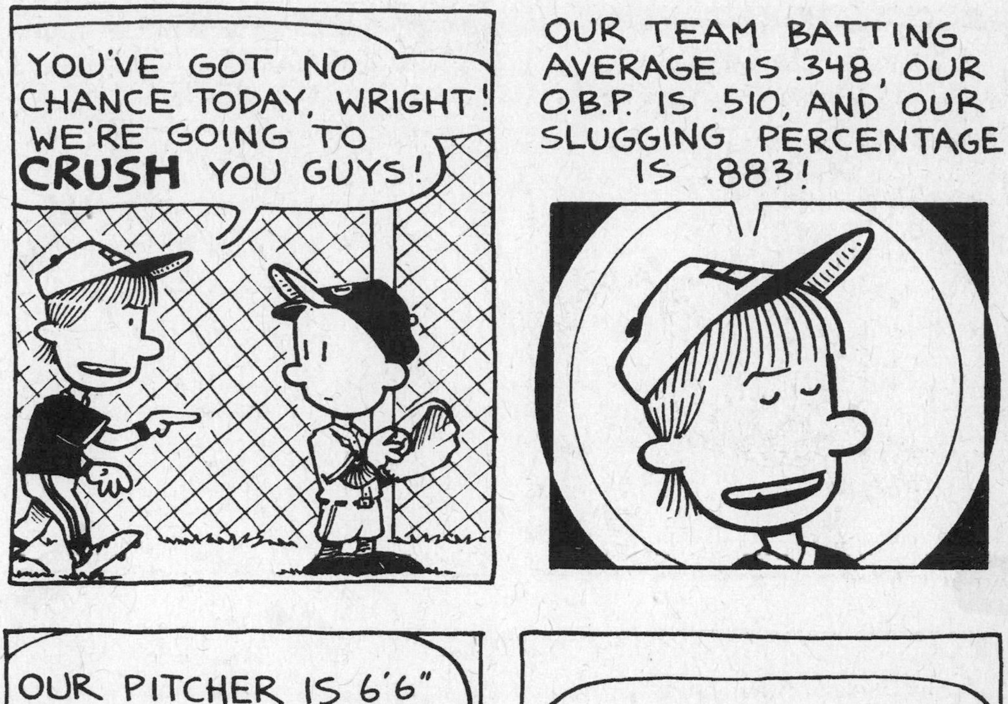
YOU'VE GOT NO CHANCE TODAY, WRIGHT! WE'RE GOING TO **CRUSH** YOU GUYS!
OUR TEAM BATTING AVERAGE IS .348, OUR O.B.P. IS .510, AND OUR SLUGGING PERCENTAGE IS .883!
OUR PITCHER IS 6'6" AND WEIGHS THREE HUNDRED POUNDS.
THERE ARE STATS, AND THEN THERE ARE VITAL STATS.
7/9
© 2008 by NEA, Inc.
Peirce

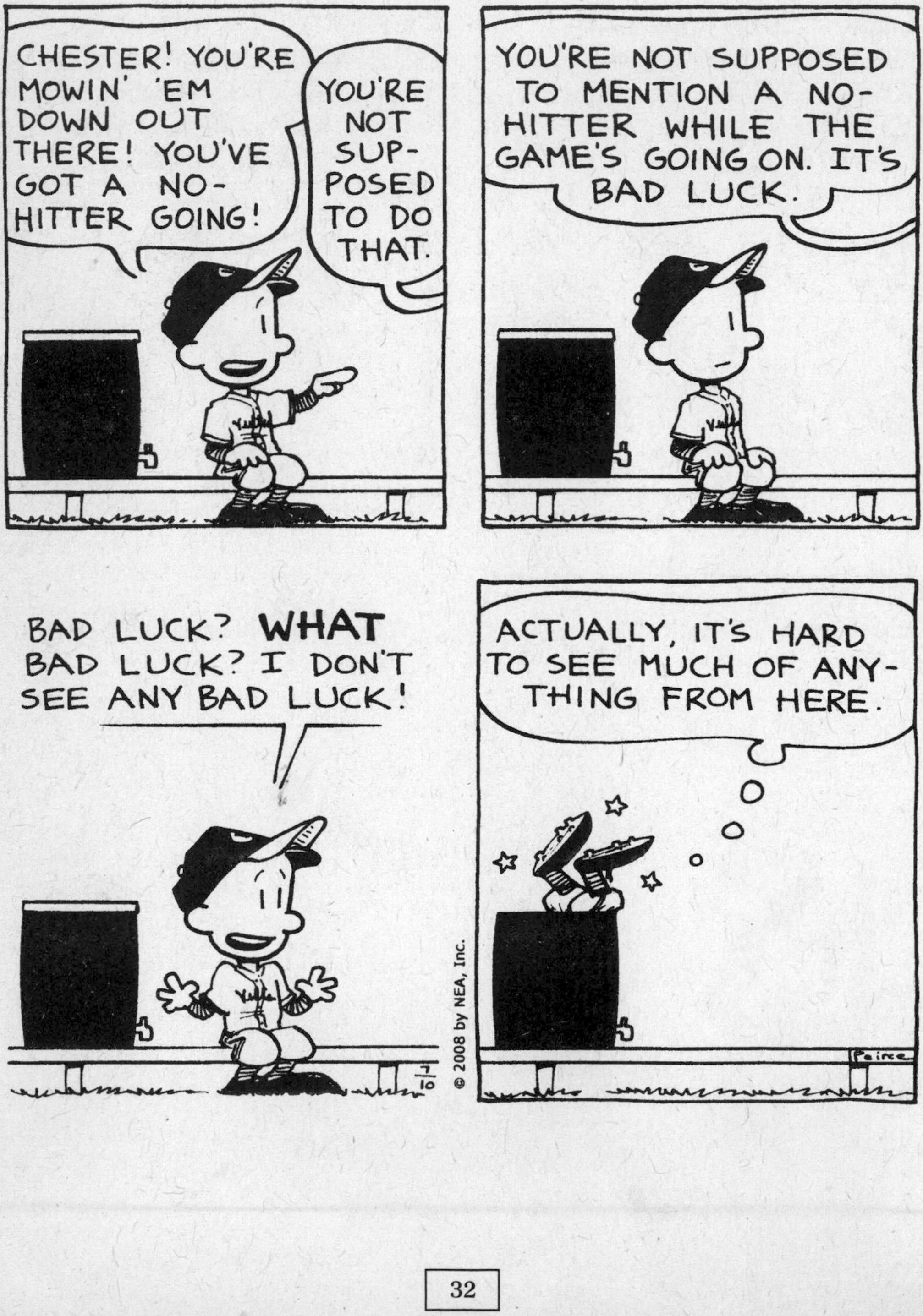
CHESTER! YOU'RE MOWIN' 'EM DOWN OUT THERE! YOU'VE GOT A NO-HITTER GOING!
YOU'RE NOT SUPPOSED TO DO THAT.
YOU'RE NOT SUPPOSED TO MENTION A NO-HITTER WHILE THE GAME'S GOING ON. IT'S BAD LUCK.
BAD LUCK? **WHAT** BAD LUCK? I DON'T SEE ANY BAD LUCK!
ACTUALLY, IT'S HARD TO SEE MUCH OF ANYTHING FROM HERE.
© 2008 by NEA, Inc.

DOGS=AWESOME

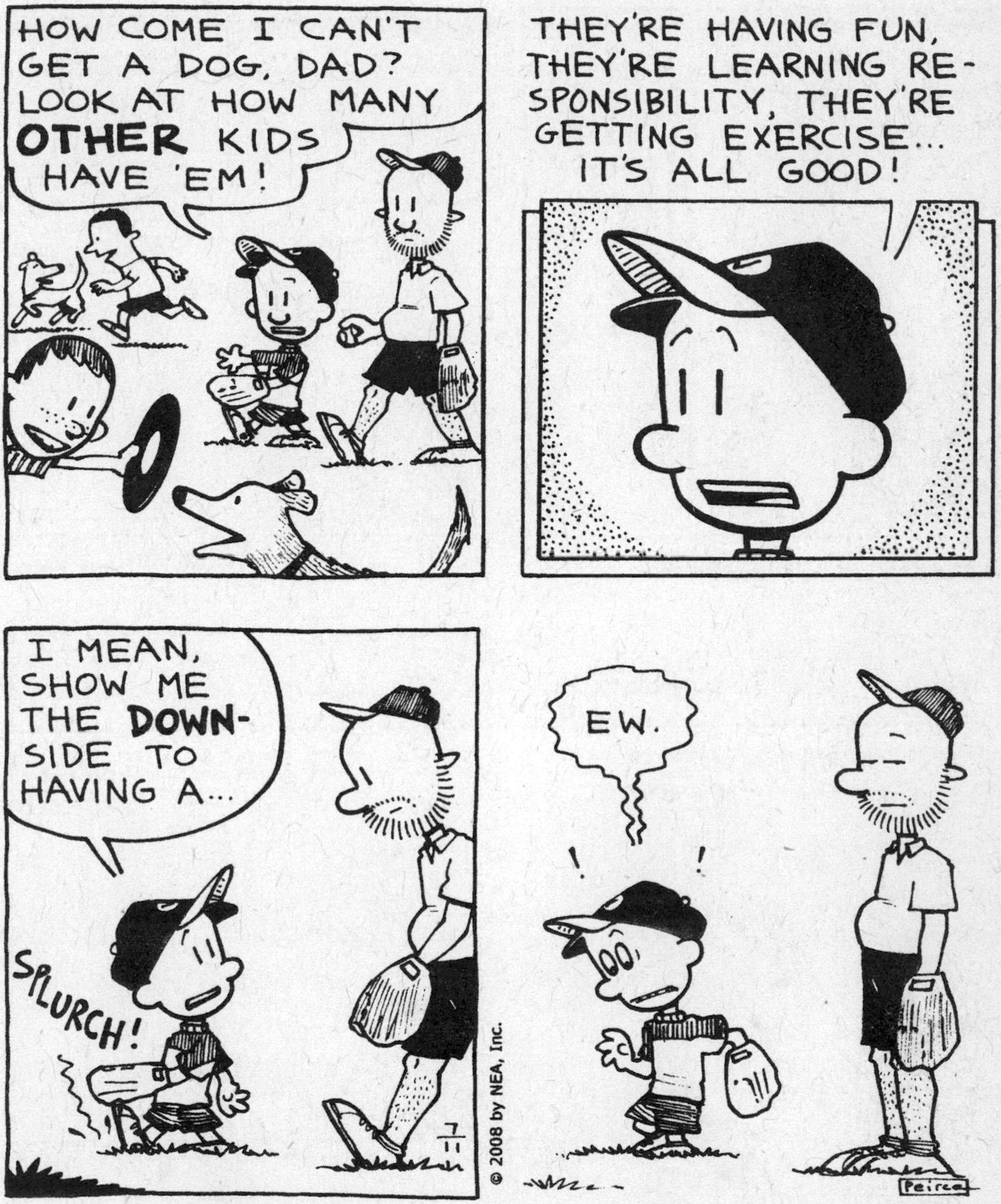
HOW COME I CAN'T GET A DOG, DAD? LOOK AT HOW MANY **OTHER** KIDS HAVE 'EM!
THEY'RE HAVING FUN, THEY'RE LEARNING RE-SPONSIBILITY, THEY'RE GETTING EXERCISE... IT'S ALL GOOD!
I MEAN, SHOW ME THE **DOWN**-SIDE TO HAVING A...
SPLURCH!
7/11
© 2008 by NEA, Inc.
EW.
! !
Peirce

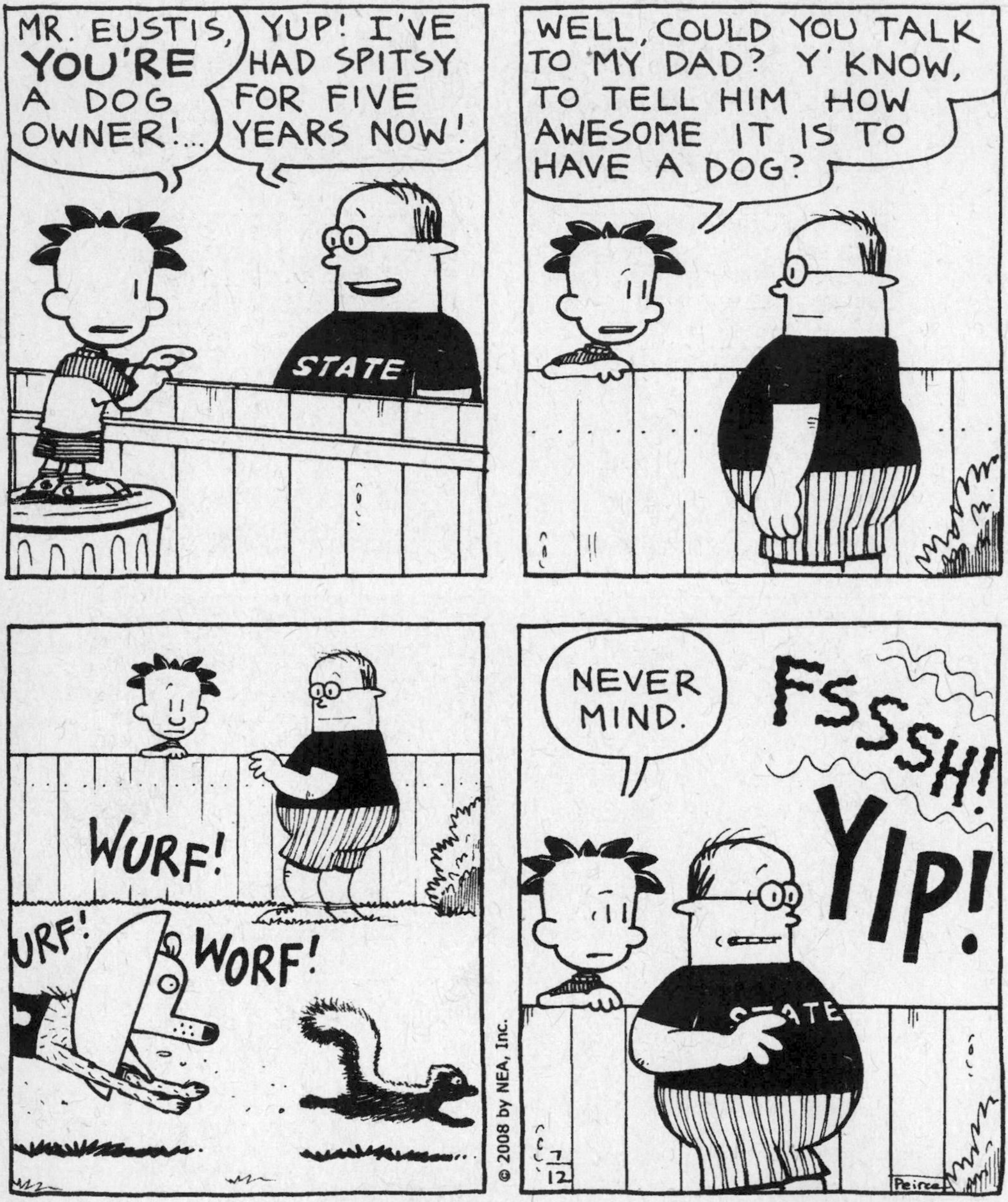
MR. EUSTIS, YOU'RE A DOG OWNER!...
YUP! I'VE HAD SPITSY FOR FIVE YEARS NOW!
STATE
WELL, COULD YOU TALK TO MY DAD? Y'KNOW, TO TELL HIM HOW AWESOME IT IS TO HAVE A DOG?
WURF!
URF!
WORF!
NEVER MIND.
FSSSH!
YIP!
STATE
Peirce
7
12

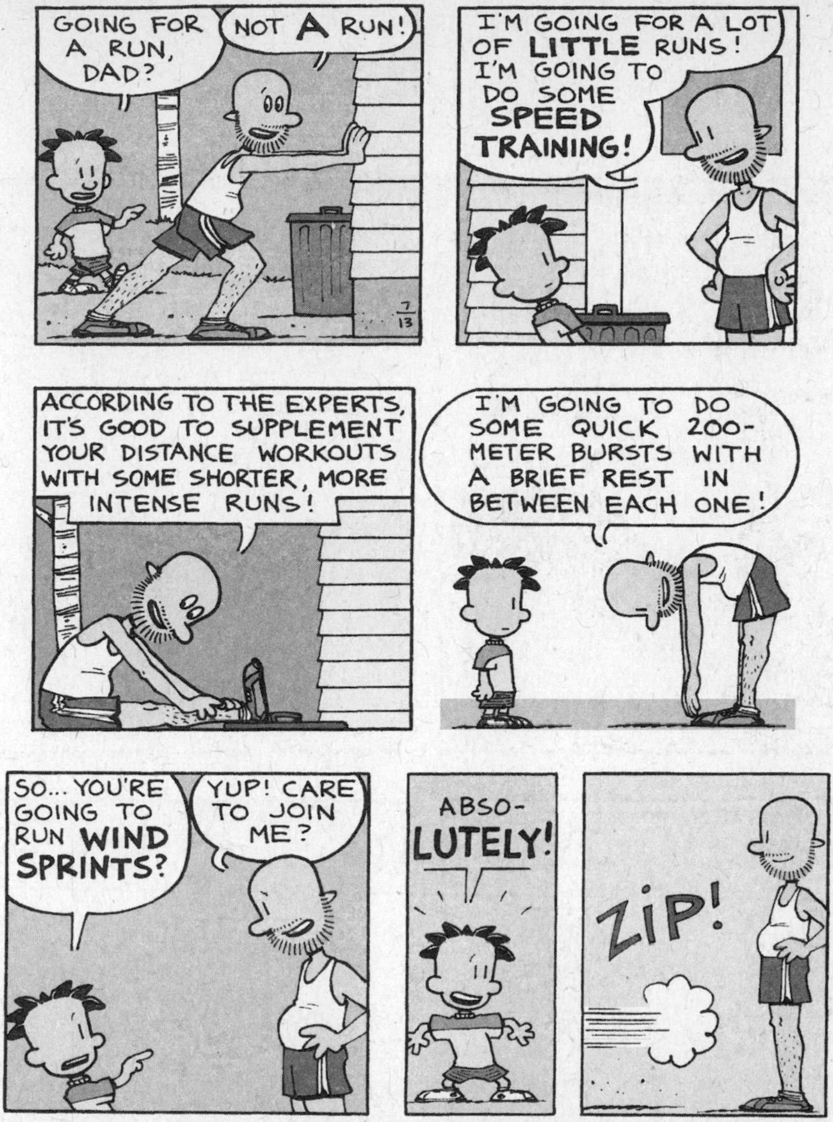
GOING FOR A RUN, DAD?
NOT A RUN!
7/13
I'M GOING FOR A LOT OF LITTLE RUNS! I'M GOING TO DO SOME SPEED TRAINING!
ACCORDING TO THE EXPERTS, IT'S GOOD TO SUPPLEMENT YOUR DISTANCE WORKOUTS WITH SOME SHORTER, MORE INTENSE RUNS!
I'M GOING TO DO SOME QUICK 200-METER BURSTS WITH A BRIEF REST IN BETWEEN EACH ONE!
SO... YOU'RE GOING TO RUN WIND SPRINTS?
YUP! CARE TO JOIN ME?
ABSO-LUTELY!
ZIP!
THIS SHOULD BE HILAR-IOUS!
© 2008 by NEA, Inc.
I'M TAKING BACK MY INVITATION.
OOP, HOLD IT. I'M GETTING TOO MUCH GLARE OFF YOUR HEAD.
Peirce

HUNGRY FOR VICTORY

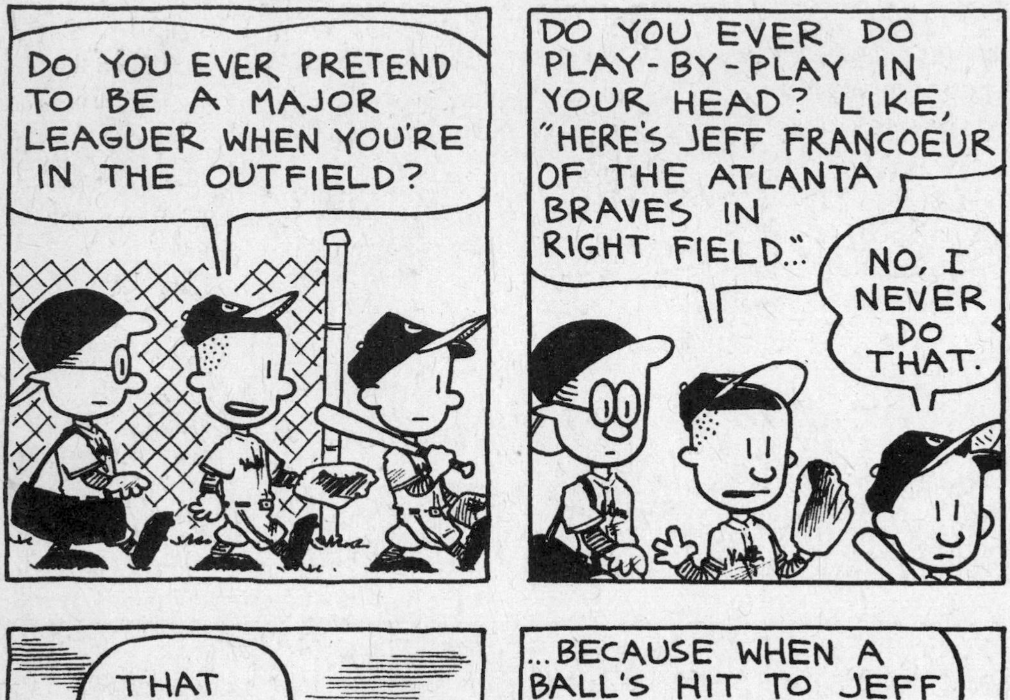
DO YOU EVER PRETEND TO BE A MAJOR LEAGUER WHEN YOU'RE IN THE OUTFIELD?
DO YOU EVER DO PLAY-BY-PLAY IN YOUR HEAD? LIKE, "HERE'S JEFF FRANCOEUR OF THE ATLANTA BRAVES IN RIGHT FIELD..."
NO, I NEVER DO THAT.
THAT MAKES SENSE.
...BECAUSE WHEN A BALL'S HIT TO JEFF FRANCOEUR, HE'S GENERALLY NOT BUSY BUYING A CHILI DOG AT THE SNACK BAR.
I WAS HUNGRY. SO SUE ME.
7/14
Peirce

DOUBLE DATE

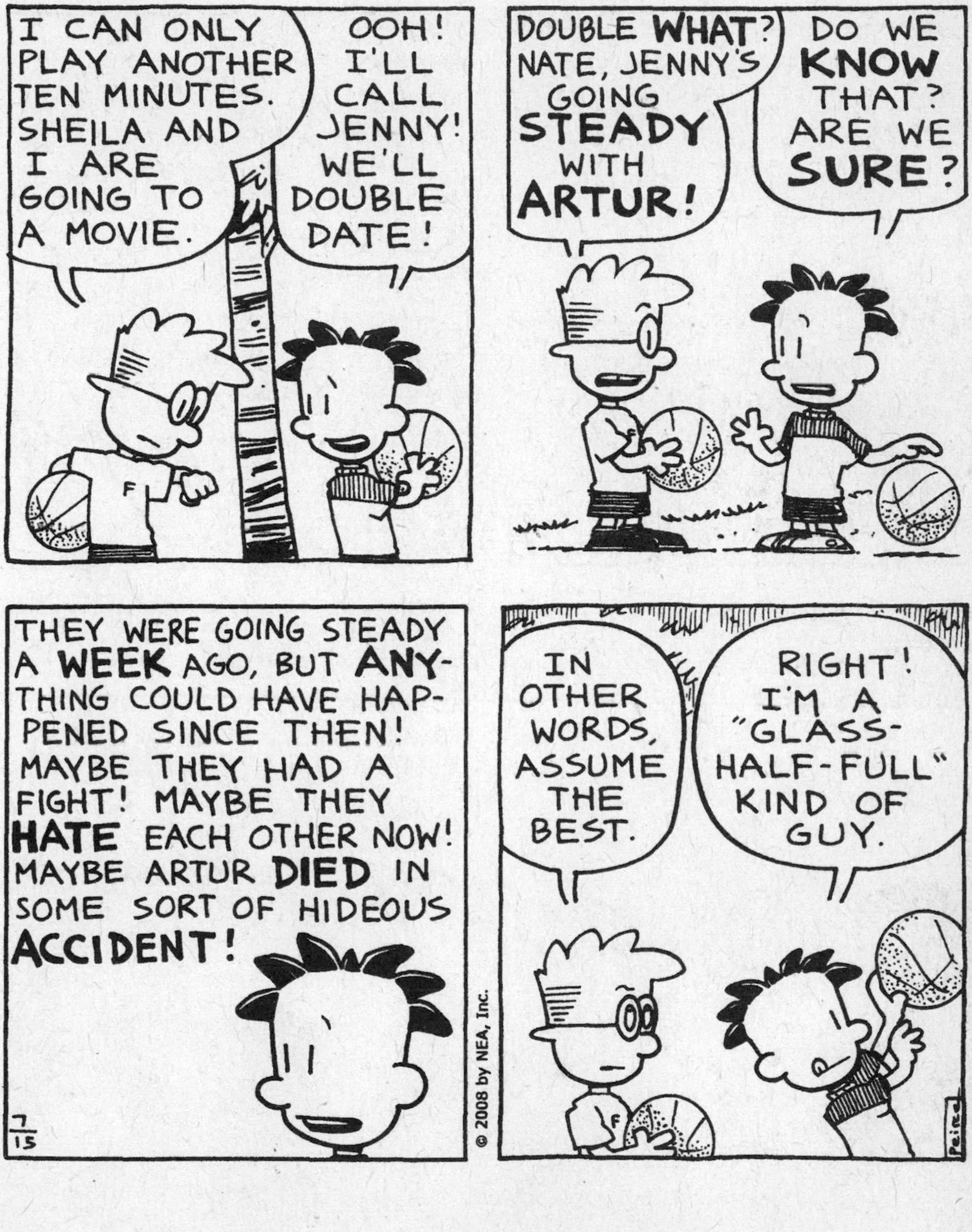
I CAN ONLY PLAY ANOTHER TEN MINUTES. SHEILA AND I ARE GOING TO A MOVIE.
OOH! I'LL CALL JENNY! WE'LL DOUBLE DATE!
DOUBLE **WHAT**? NATE, JENNY'S GOING **STEADY** WITH **ARTUR**!
DO WE **KNOW** THAT? ARE WE **SURE**?
THEY WERE GOING STEADY A **WEEK** AGO, BUT **ANY**-THING COULD HAVE HAP-PENED SINCE THEN! MAYBE THEY HAD A FIGHT! MAYBE THEY **HATE** EACH OTHER NOW! MAYBE ARTUR **DIED** IN SOME SORT OF HIDEOUS **ACCIDENT**!
7/15
© 2008 by NEA, Inc.
IN OTHER WORDS, ASSUME THE BEST.
RIGHT! I'M A "GLASS-HALF-FULL" KIND OF GUY.
Peirce

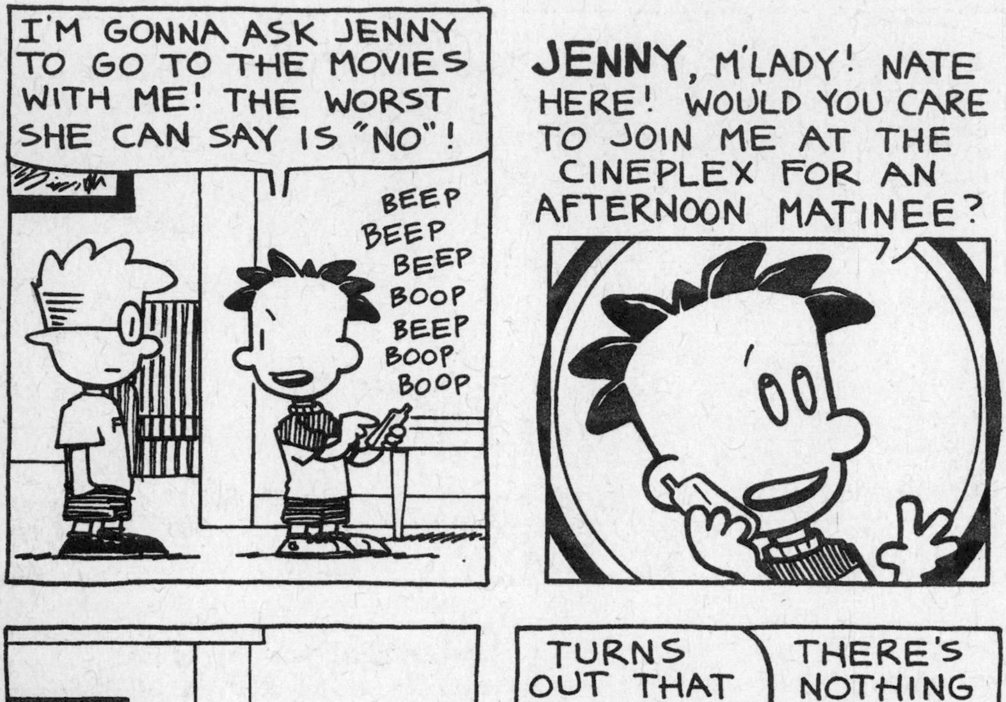

I'M GONNA ASK JENNY TO GO TO THE MOVIES WITH ME! THE WORST SHE CAN SAY IS "NO"!
BEEP BEEP BEEP BOOP BEEP BOOP BOOP
JENNY, M'LADY! NATE HERE! WOULD YOU CARE TO JOIN ME AT THE CINEPLEX FOR AN AFTERNOON MATINEE?
TURNS OUT THAT "NO" ISN'T THE WORST SHE CAN SAY.
THERE'S NOTHING LIKE A PHONE CALL FROM YOU TO EXPAND A GAL'S VOCABULARY!

SPECIAL DELIVERY

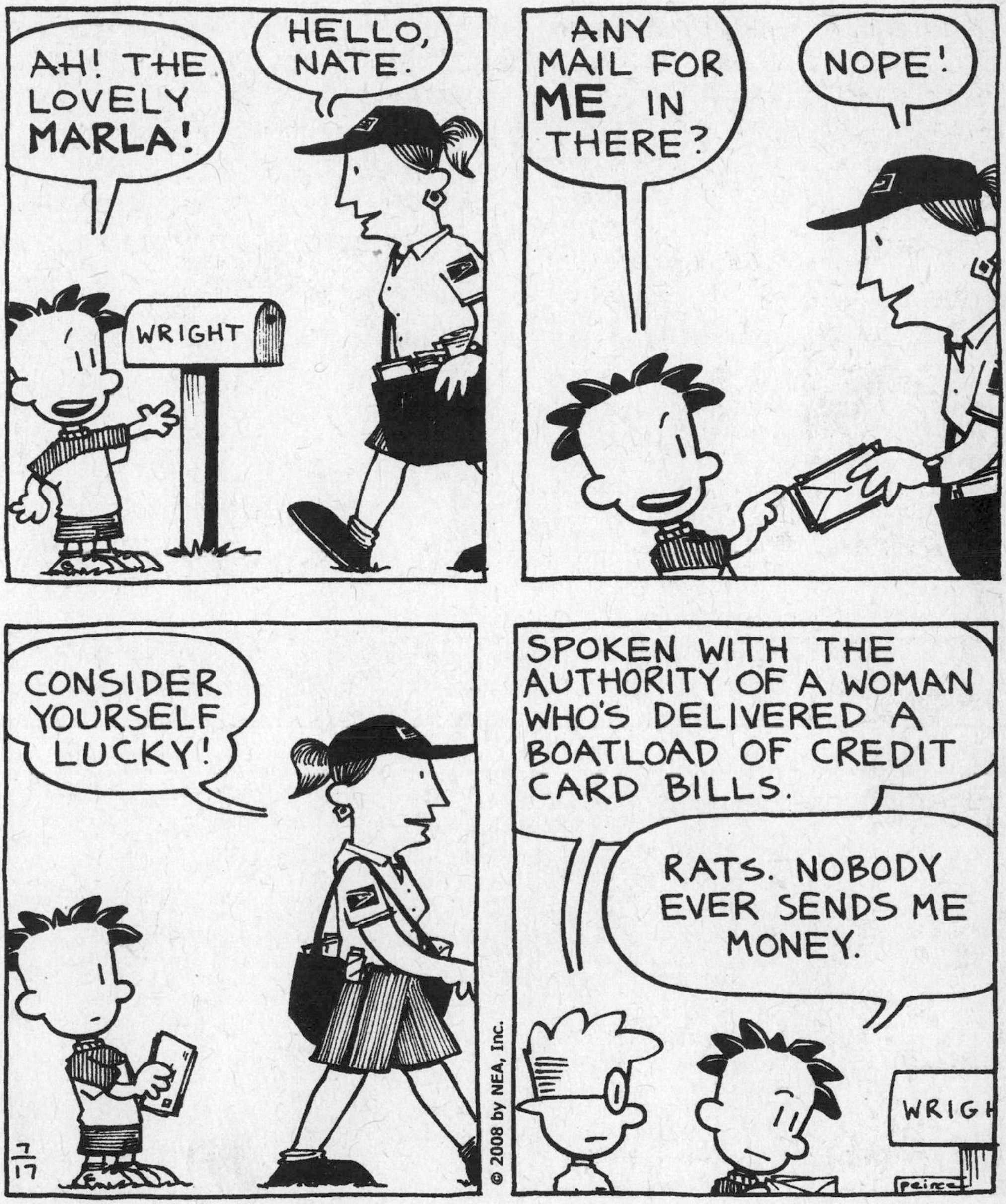
AH! THE LOVELY **MARLA**!
HELLO, NATE.
WRIGHT
ANY MAIL FOR **ME** IN THERE?
NOPE!
CONSIDER YOURSELF LUCKY!
7/17
SPOKEN WITH THE AUTHORITY OF A WOMAN WHO'S DELIVERED A BOATLOAD OF CREDIT CARD BILLS.
RATS. NOBODY EVER SENDS ME MONEY.
WRIGH

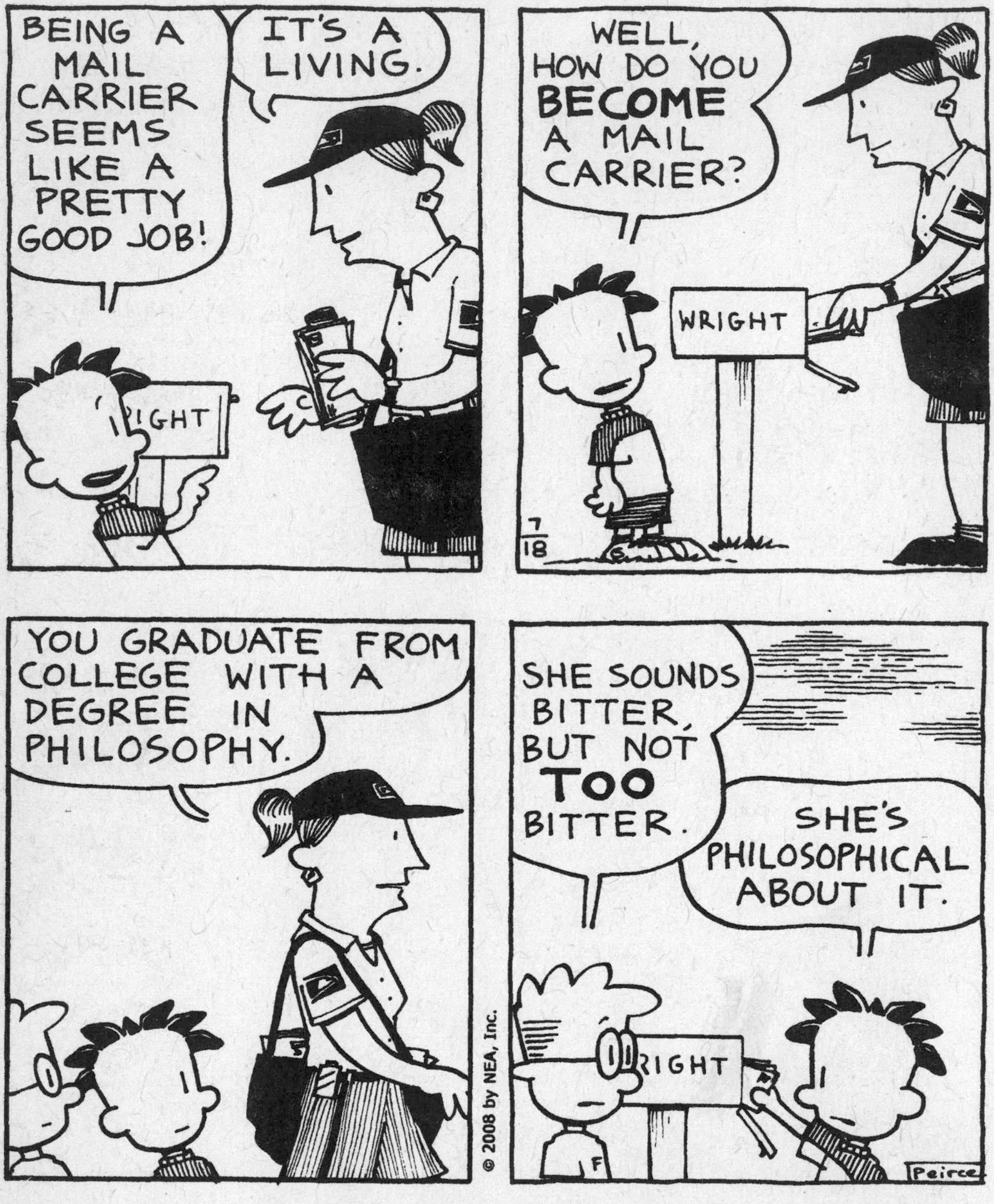
BEING A MAIL CARRIER SEEMS LIKE A PRETTY GOOD JOB!
IT'S A LIVING.
RIGHT
WELL, HOW DO YOU **BECOME** A MAIL CARRIER?
WRIGHT
7/18
YOU GRADUATE FROM COLLEGE WITH A DEGREE IN PHILOSOPHY.
© 2008 by NEA, Inc.
SHE SOUNDS BITTER, BUT NOT **TOO** BITTER.
SHE'S PHILOSOPHICAL ABOUT IT.
RIGHT
Peirce

DESTINATION VACATION

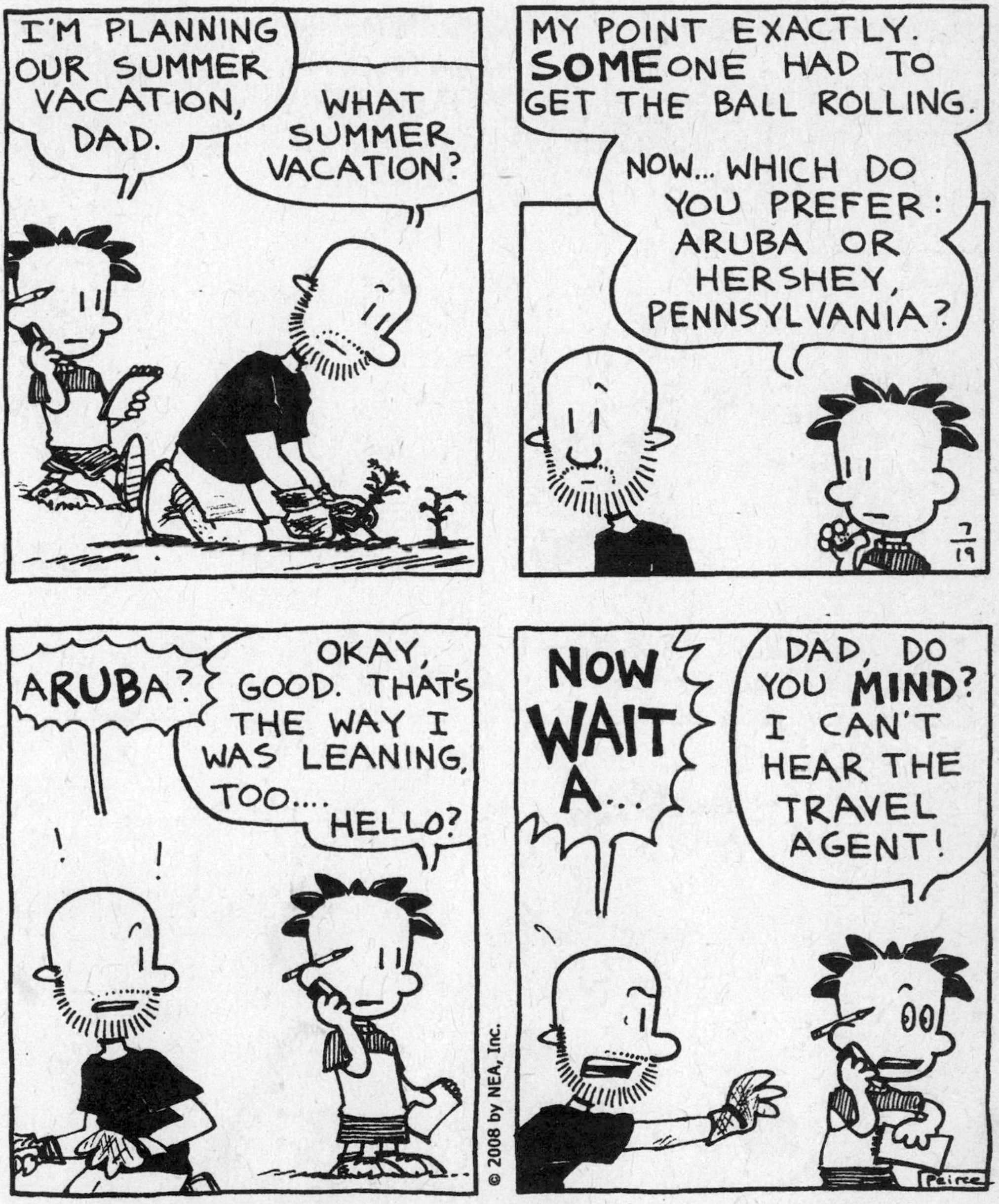

I'M PLANNING OUR SUMMER VACATION, DAD.
WHAT SUMMER VACATION?
MY POINT EXACTLY. SOMEONE HAD TO GET THE BALL ROLLING.
NOW... WHICH DO YOU PREFER: ARUBA OR HERSHEY, PENNSYLVANIA?
7/19
ARUBA?
OKAY, GOOD. THAT'S THE WAY I WAS LEANING, TOO.... HELLO?
! !
© 2008 by NEA, Inc.
NOW WAIT A...
DAD, DO YOU MIND? I CAN'T HEAR THE TRAVEL AGENT!
Peirce

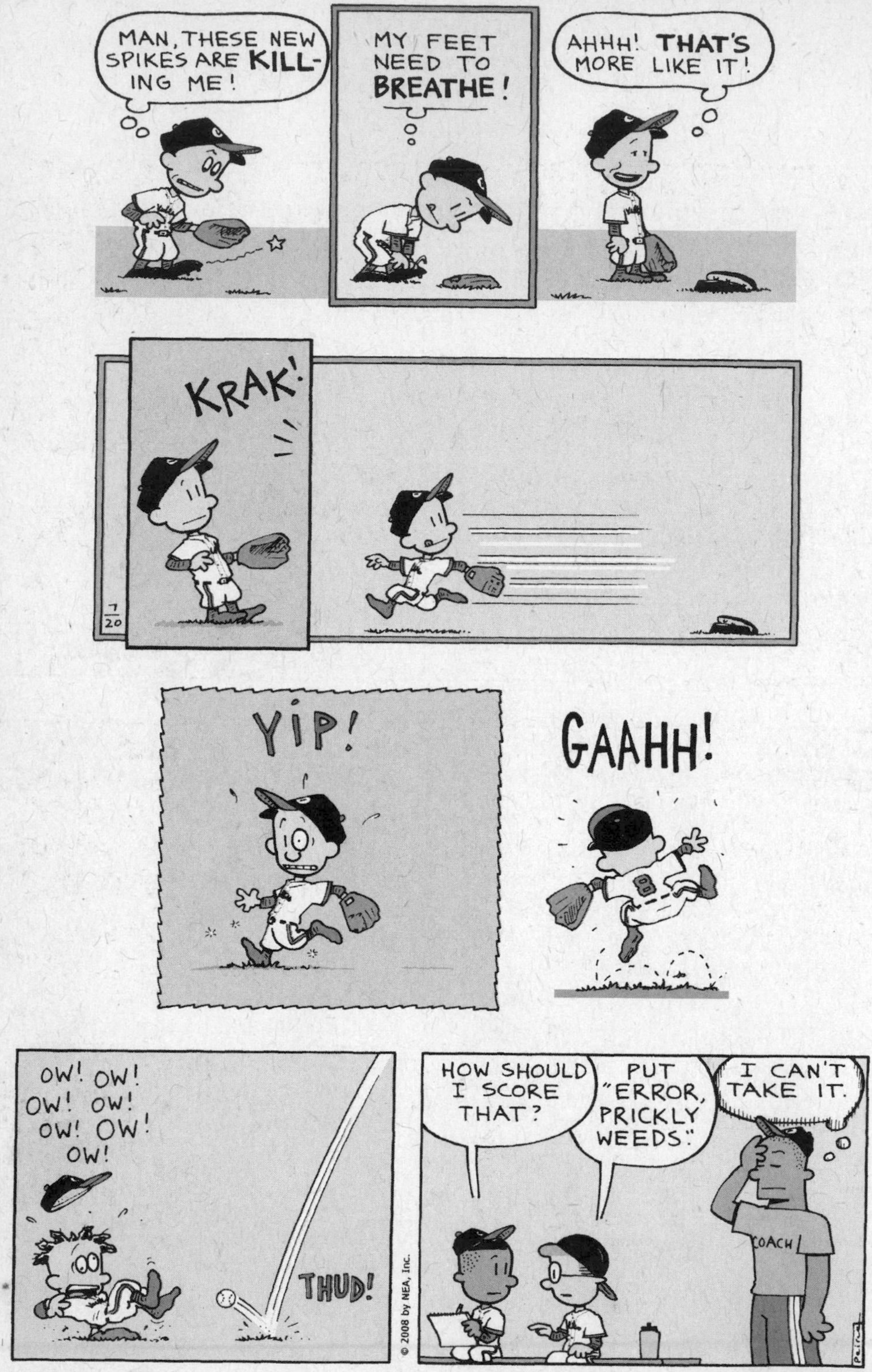
MAN, THESE NEW SPIKES ARE KILL-ING ME!
MY FEET NEED TO BREATHE!
AHHH! THAT'S MORE LIKE IT!
KRAK!
7/20
YIP!
GAAHH!
OW! OW! OW! OW! OW! OW! OW!
THUD!
© 2008 by NEA, Inc.
HOW SHOULD I SCORE THAT?
PUT "ERROR, PRICKLY WEEDS."
I CAN'T TAKE IT.
COACH

FAMILY (DYS)FUNCTION

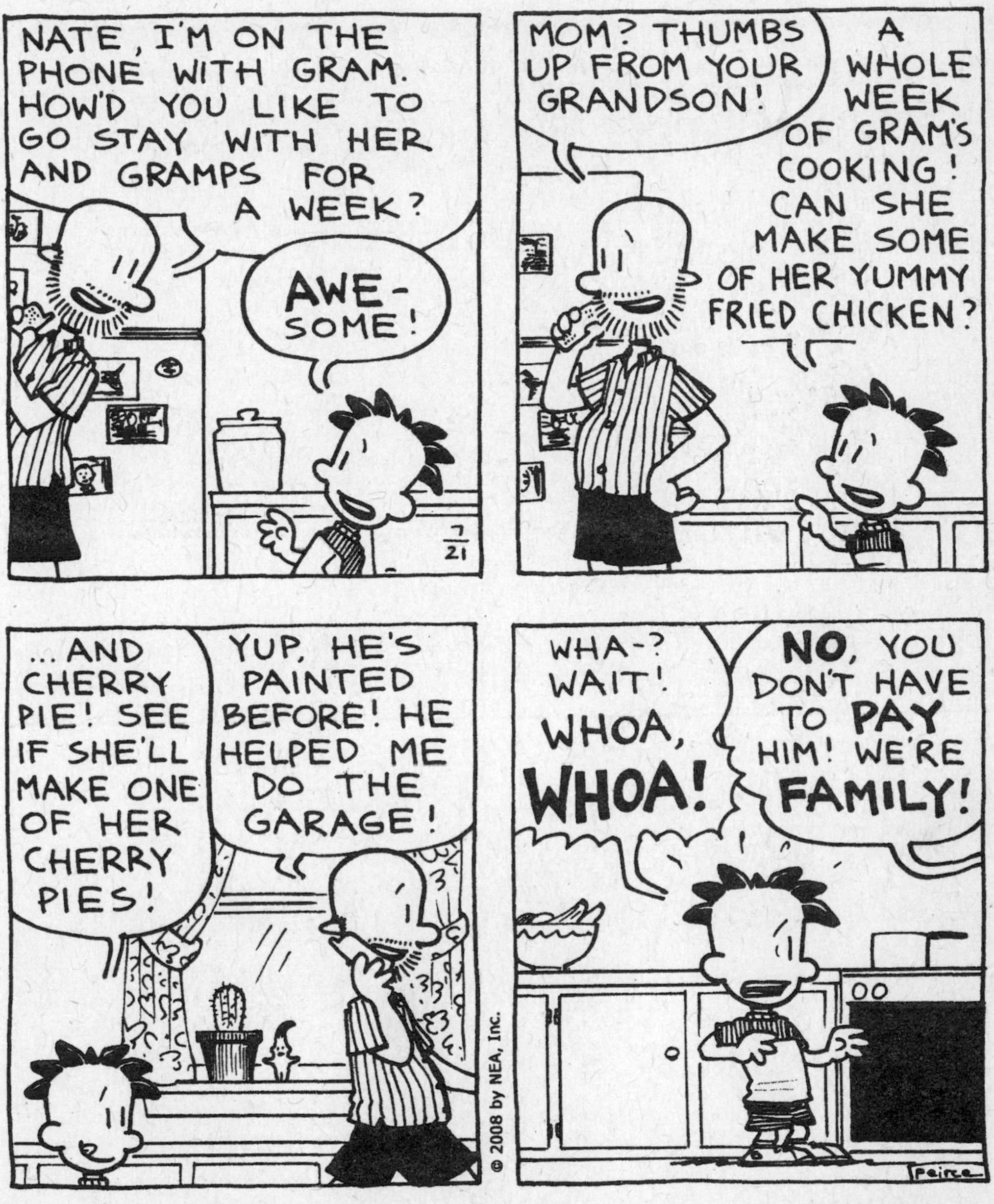
NATE, I'M ON THE PHONE WITH GRAM. HOW'D YOU LIKE TO GO STAY WITH HER AND GRAMPS FOR A WEEK?
AWE-SOME!
7/21
MOM? THUMBS UP FROM YOUR GRANDSON!
A WHOLE WEEK OF GRAM'S COOKING! CAN SHE MAKE SOME OF HER YUMMY FRIED CHICKEN?
...AND CHERRY PIE! SEE IF SHE'LL MAKE ONE OF HER CHERRY PIES!
YUP, HE'S PAINTED BEFORE! HE HELPED ME DO THE GARAGE!
© 2008 by NEA, Inc.
WHA-? WAIT! WHOA, WHOA!
NO, YOU DON'T HAVE TO PAY HIM! WE'RE FAMILY!
peirce

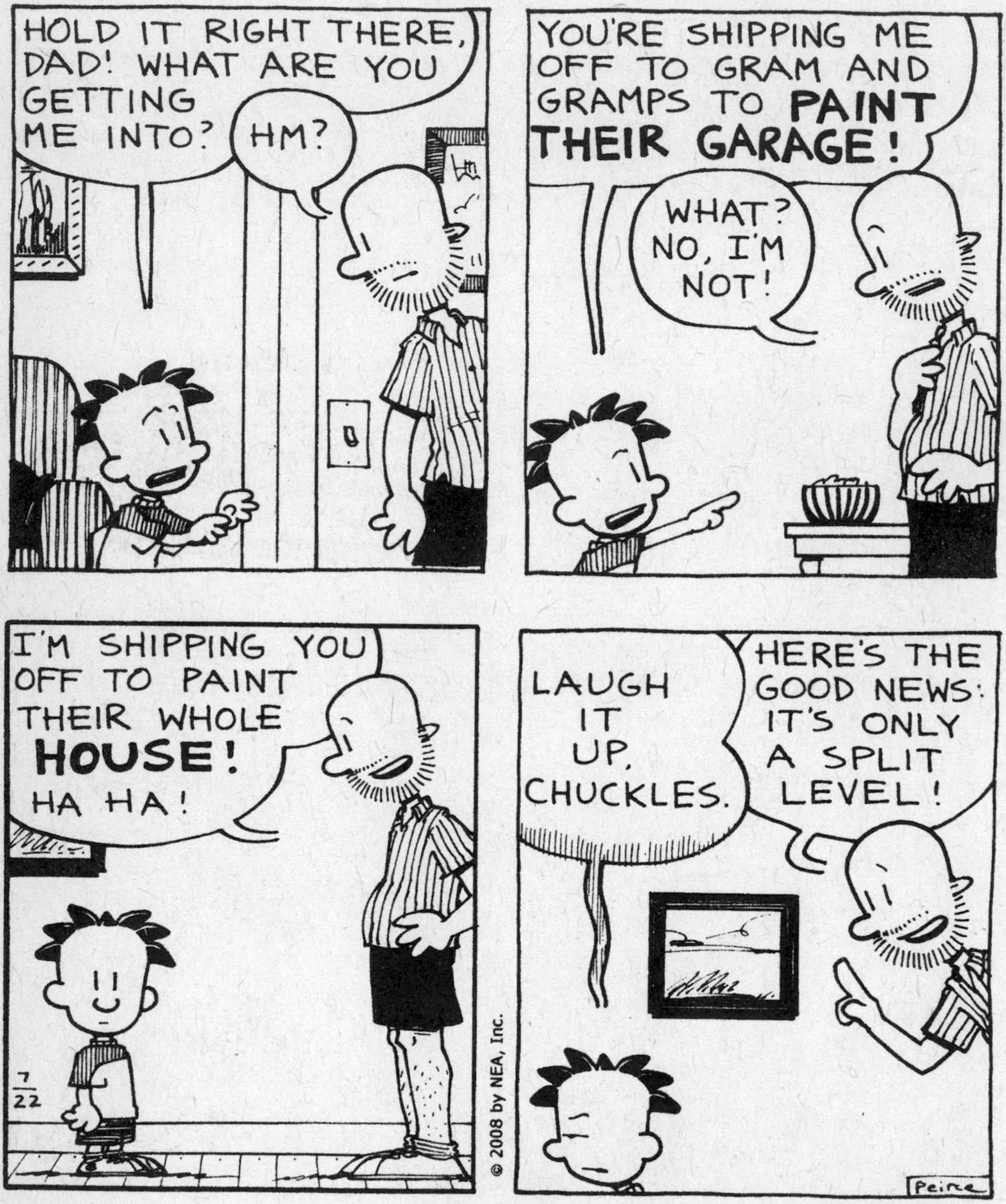
HOLD IT RIGHT THERE, DAD! WHAT ARE YOU GETTING ME INTO?
HM?
YOU'RE SHIPPING ME OFF TO GRAM AND GRAMPS TO **PAINT THEIR GARAGE!**
WHAT? NO, I'M NOT!
I'M SHIPPING YOU OFF TO PAINT THEIR WHOLE **HOUSE!** HA HA!
7/22
HERE'S THE GOOD NEWS: IT'S ONLY A SPLIT LEVEL!
LAUGH IT UP, CHUCKLES.
Peirce

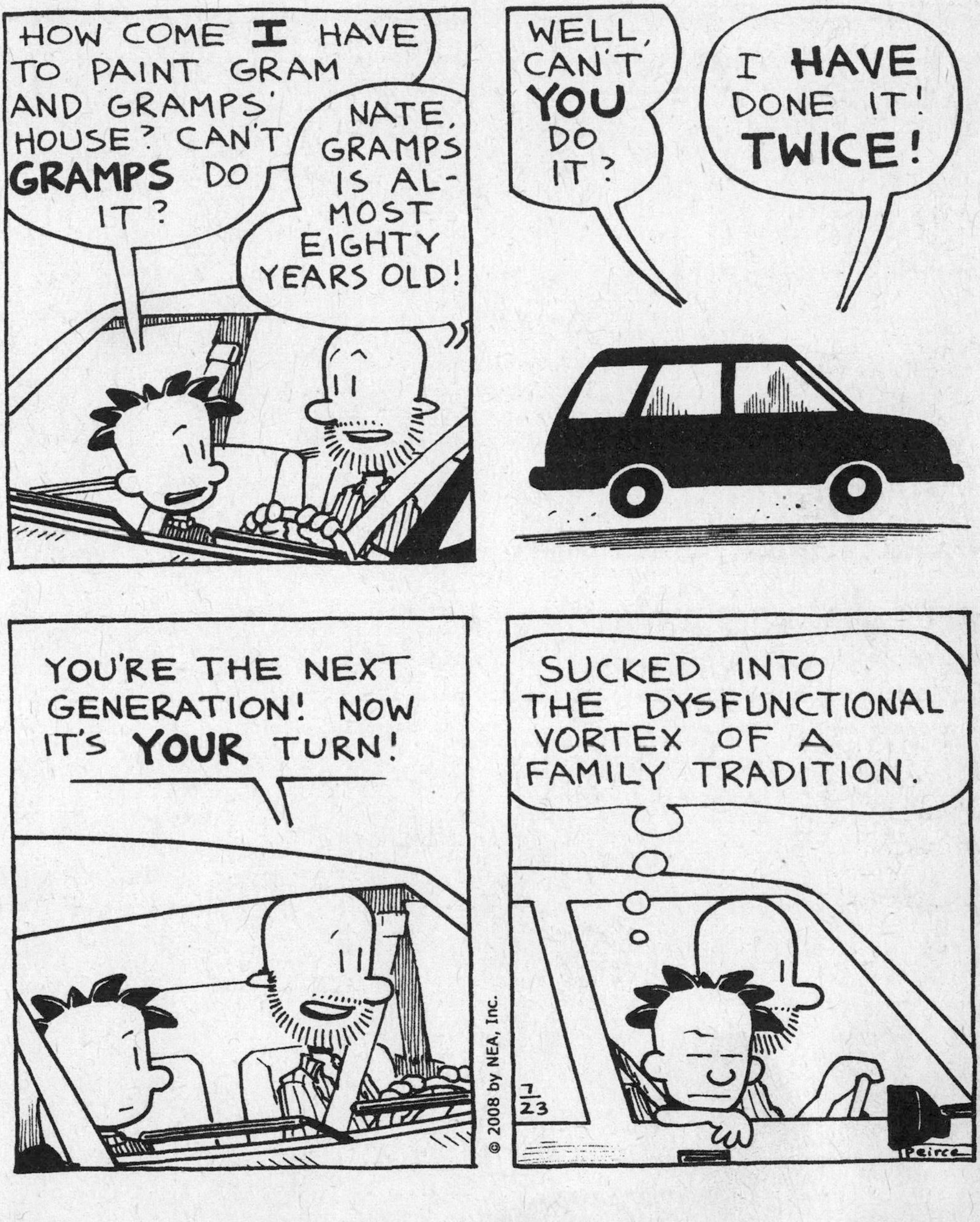
HOW COME **I** HAVE TO PAINT GRAM AND GRAMPS' HOUSE? CAN'T **GRAMPS** DO IT?
NATE, GRAMPS IS ALMOST EIGHTY YEARS OLD!
WELL, CAN'T **YOU** DO IT?
I **HAVE** DONE IT! **TWICE!**
YOU'RE THE NEXT GENERATION! NOW IT'S **YOUR** TURN!
SUCKED INTO THE DYSFUNCTIONAL VORTEX OF A FAMILY TRADITION.
© 2008 by NEA, Inc.
7/23
Peirce

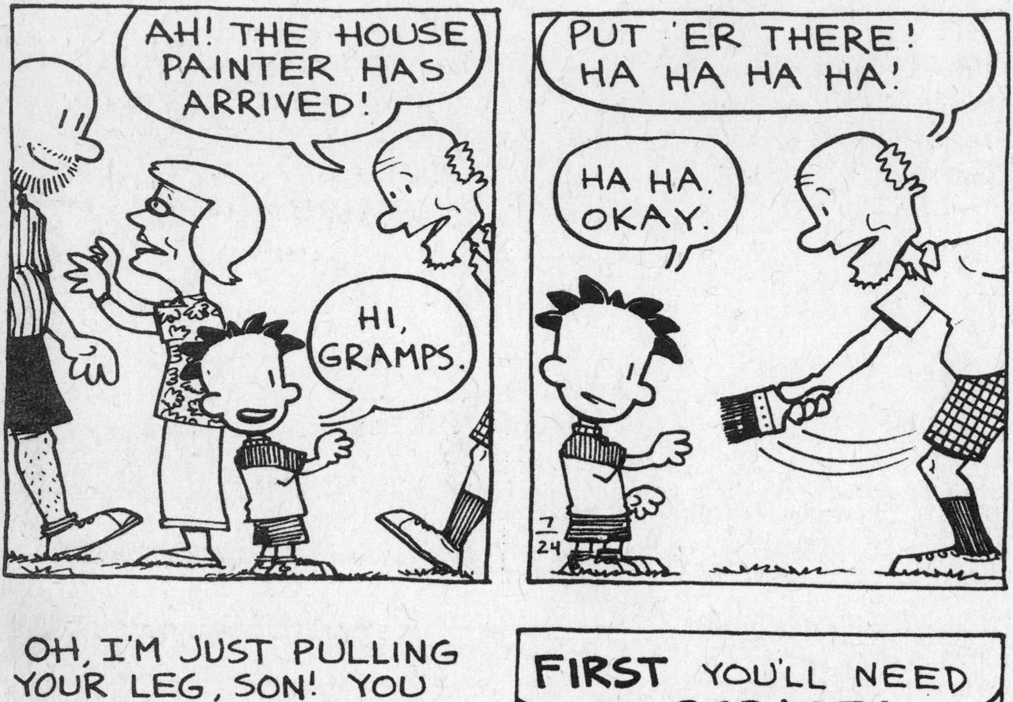
AH! THE HOUSE PAINTER HAS ARRIVED!
HI, GRAMPS.
PUT 'ER THERE! HA HA HA HA!
HA HA. OKAY.
7
24
OH, I'M JUST PULLING YOUR LEG, SON! YOU WON'T BE NEEDING THIS BRUSH RIGHT AWAY!
© 2008 by NEA, Inc.
Peirce
FIRST YOU'LL NEED TO SCRAPE!
GREAT.

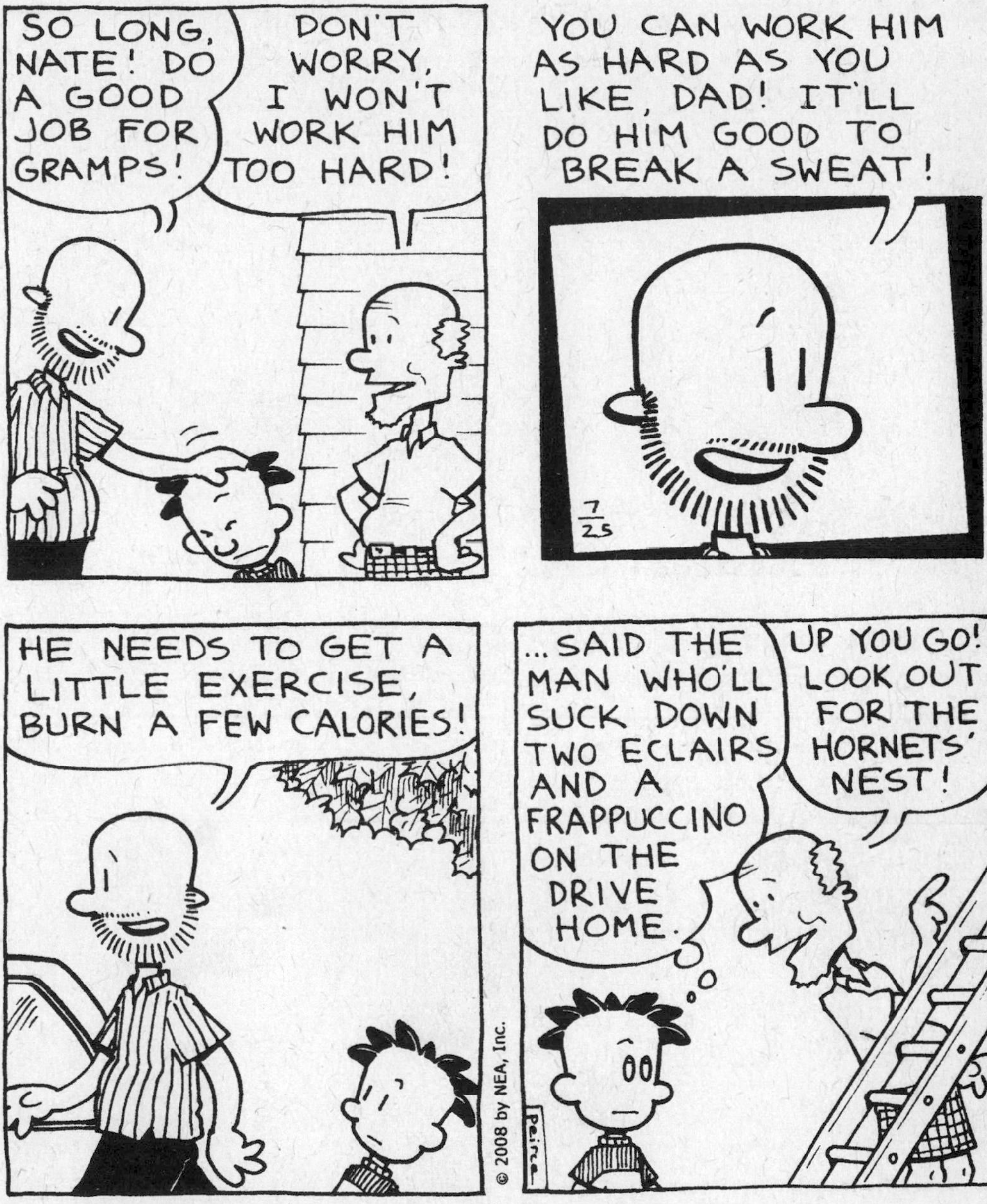
SO LONG, NATE! DO A GOOD JOB FOR GRAMPS!
DON'T WORRY, I WON'T WORK HIM TOO HARD!
YOU CAN WORK HIM AS HARD AS YOU LIKE, DAD! IT'LL DO HIM GOOD TO BREAK A SWEAT!
7/25
HE NEEDS TO GET A LITTLE EXERCISE, BURN A FEW CALORIES!
© 2008 by NEA, Inc.
Peirce
...SAID THE MAN WHO'LL SUCK DOWN TWO ECLAIRS AND A FRAPPUCCINO ON THE DRIVE HOME.
UP YOU GO! LOOK OUT FOR THE HORNETS' NEST!

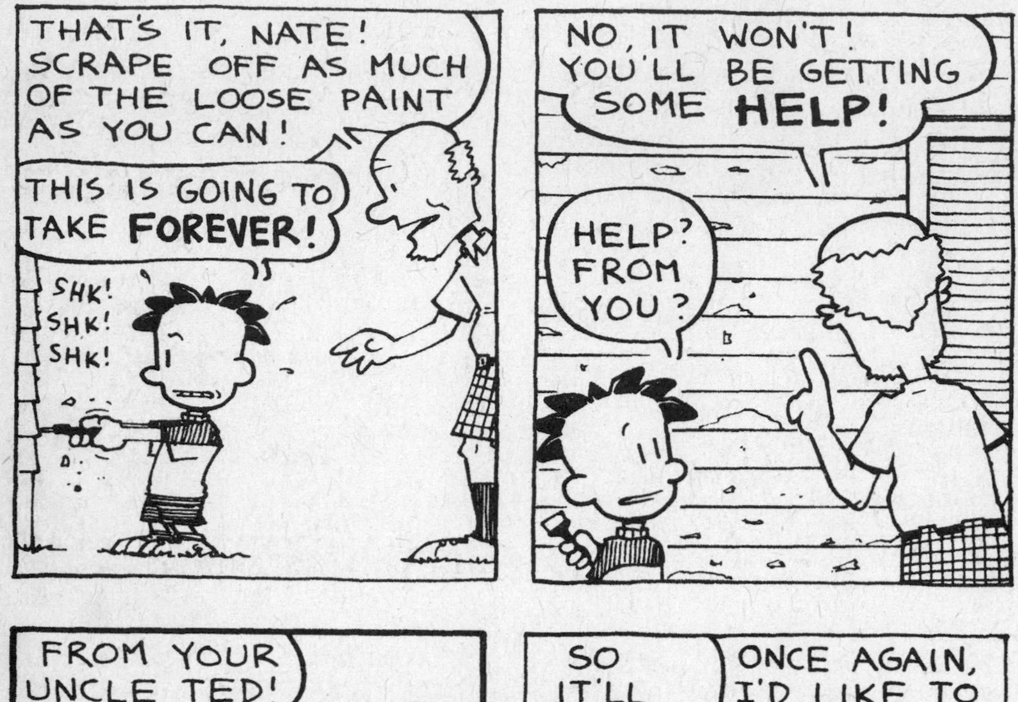
THAT'S IT, NATE! SCRAPE OFF AS MUCH OF THE LOOSE PAINT AS YOU CAN!
THIS IS GOING TO TAKE **FOREVER**!
SHK! SHK! SHK!
NO, IT WON'T! YOU'LL BE GETTING SOME **HELP**!
HELP? FROM YOU?
FROM YOUR UNCLE TED!
!
7/26
© 2008 by NEA, Inc.
SO IT'LL ONLY **SEEM** LIKE FOREVER.
ONCE AGAIN, I'D LIKE TO CAST A VOTE IN FAVOR OF VINYL SIDING.
Peirce

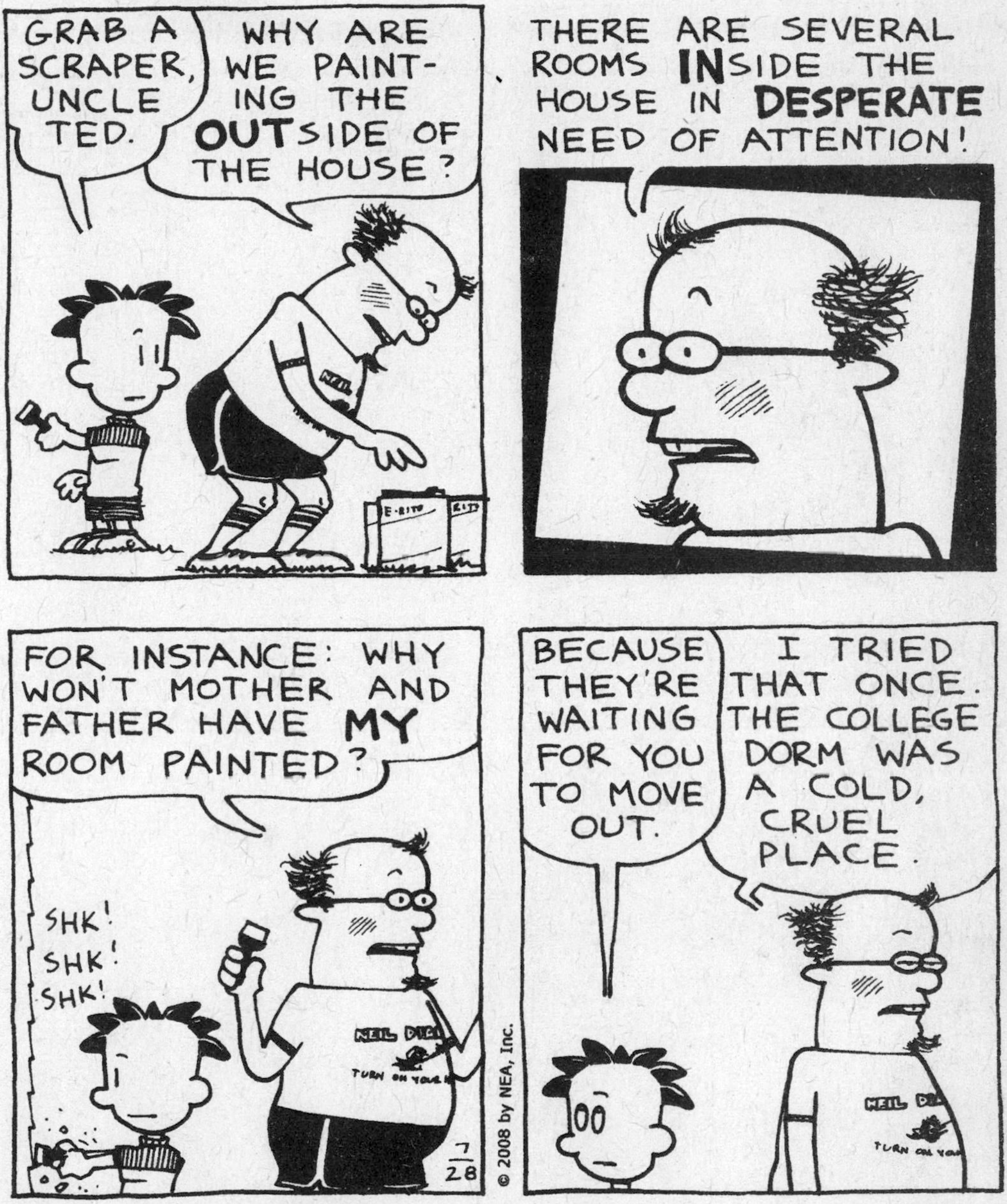
GRAB A SCRAPER, UNCLE TED.
WHY ARE WE PAINTING THE OUTSIDE OF THE HOUSE?
THERE ARE SEVERAL ROOMS INSIDE THE HOUSE IN DESPERATE NEED OF ATTENTION!
FOR INSTANCE: WHY WON'T MOTHER AND FATHER HAVE MY ROOM PAINTED?
SHK! SHK! SHK!
7/28
BECAUSE THEY'RE WAITING FOR YOU TO MOVE OUT.
I TRIED THAT ONCE. THE COLLEGE DORM WAS A COLD, CRUEL PLACE.

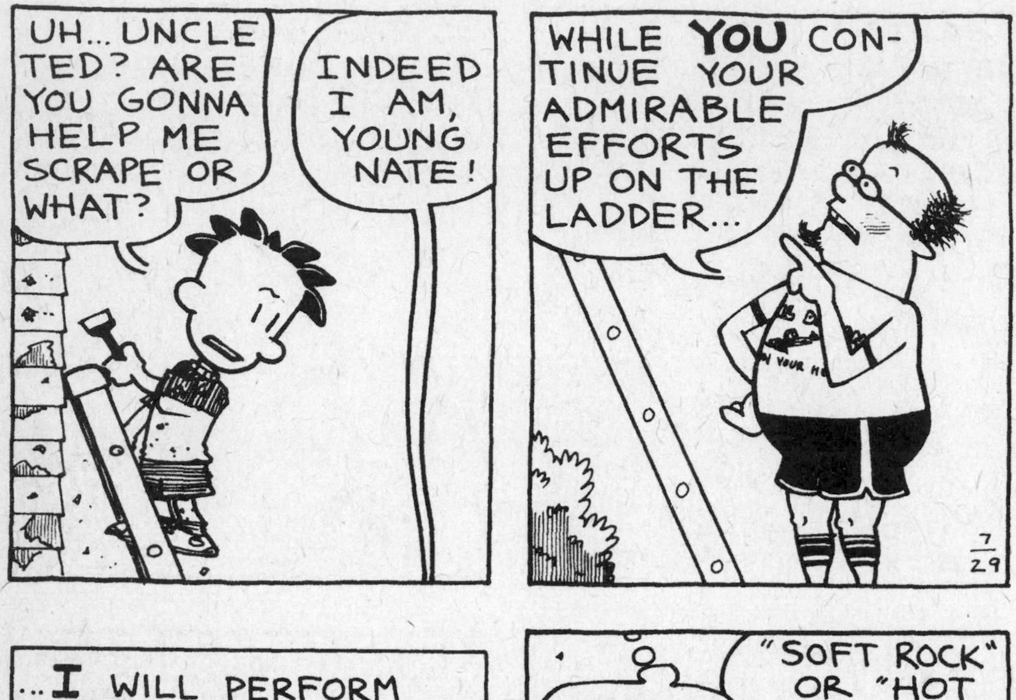
UH... UNCLE TED? ARE YOU GONNA HELP ME SCRAPE OR WHAT?
INDEED I AM, YOUNG NATE!
WHILE YOU CON-TINUE YOUR ADMIRABLE EFFORTS UP ON THE LADDER...
7/29
...I WILL PERFORM THE VITALLY IMPORTANT TASK OF PROVIDING ATMOSPHERE!
© 2008 by NEA, Inc.
GREAT.
"SOFT ROCK" OR "HOT COUNTRY"?

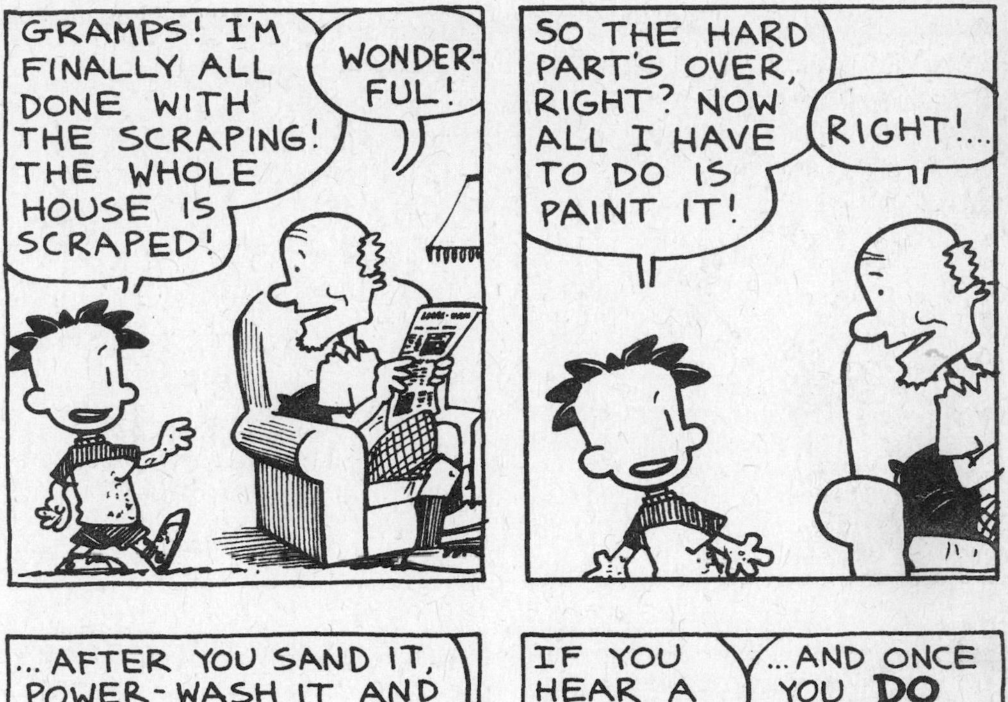
GRAMPS! I'M FINALLY ALL DONE WITH THE SCRAPING! THE WHOLE HOUSE IS SCRAPED!
WONDER-FUL!
SO THE HARD PART'S OVER, RIGHT? NOW ALL I HAVE TO DO IS PAINT IT!
RIGHT!...
...AFTER YOU SAND IT, POWER-WASH IT AND PRIME IT.
7/31
© 2008 by NEA, Inc.
IF YOU HEAR A THUD, IT'S JUST ME THROWING MYSELF OFF THE LADDER.
...AND ONCE YOU DO START PAINTING, REMEMBER IT TAKES TWO COATS!

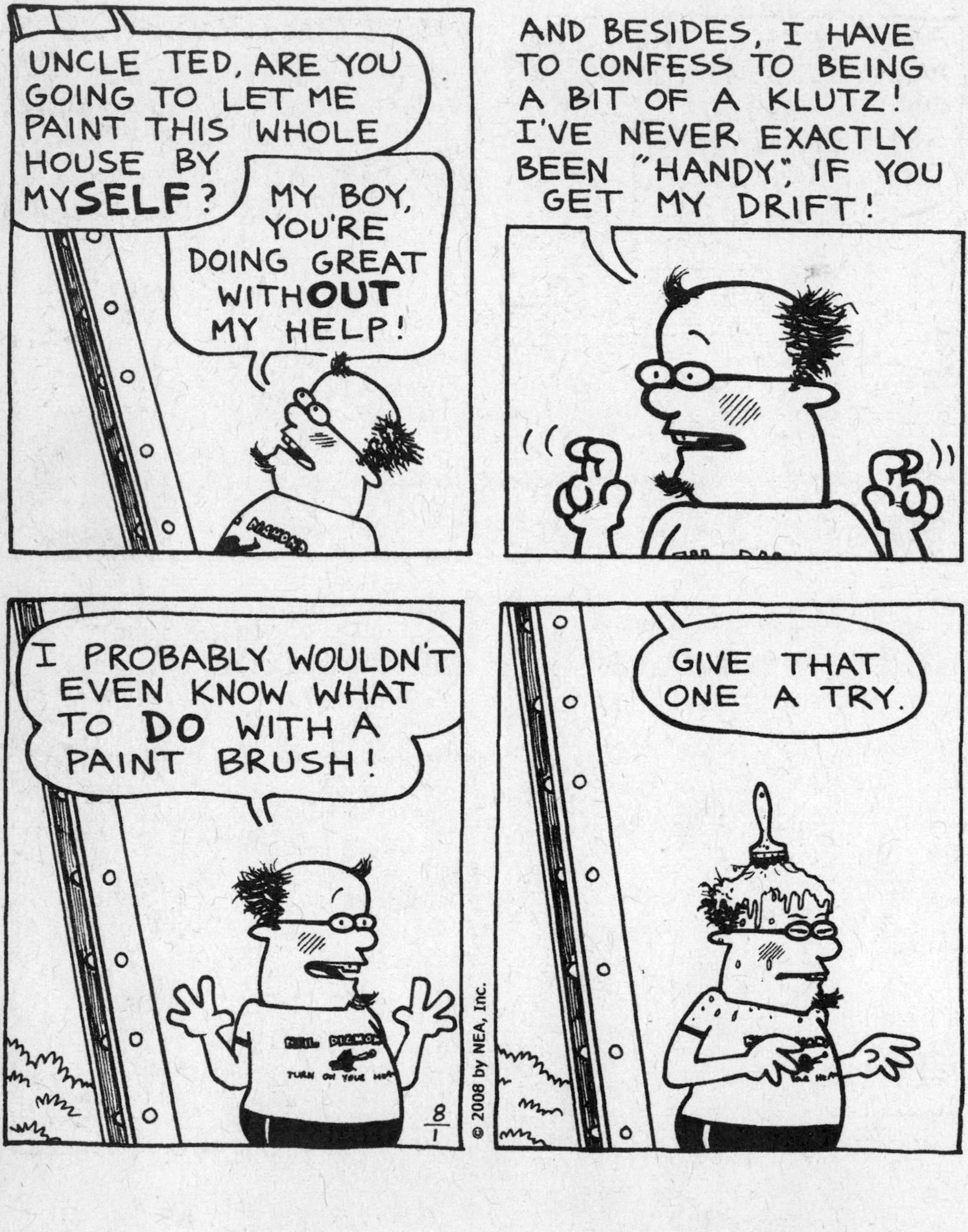
UNCLE TED, ARE YOU GOING TO LET ME PAINT THIS WHOLE HOUSE BY MYSELF?
MY BOY, YOU'RE DOING GREAT WITHOUT MY HELP!
AND BESIDES, I HAVE TO CONFESS TO BEING A BIT OF A KLUTZ! I'VE NEVER EXACTLY BEEN "HANDY," IF YOU GET MY DRIFT!
I PROBABLY WOULDN'T EVEN KNOW WHAT TO DO WITH A PAINT BRUSH!
8/1
© 2008 by NEA, Inc.
GIVE THAT ONE A TRY.

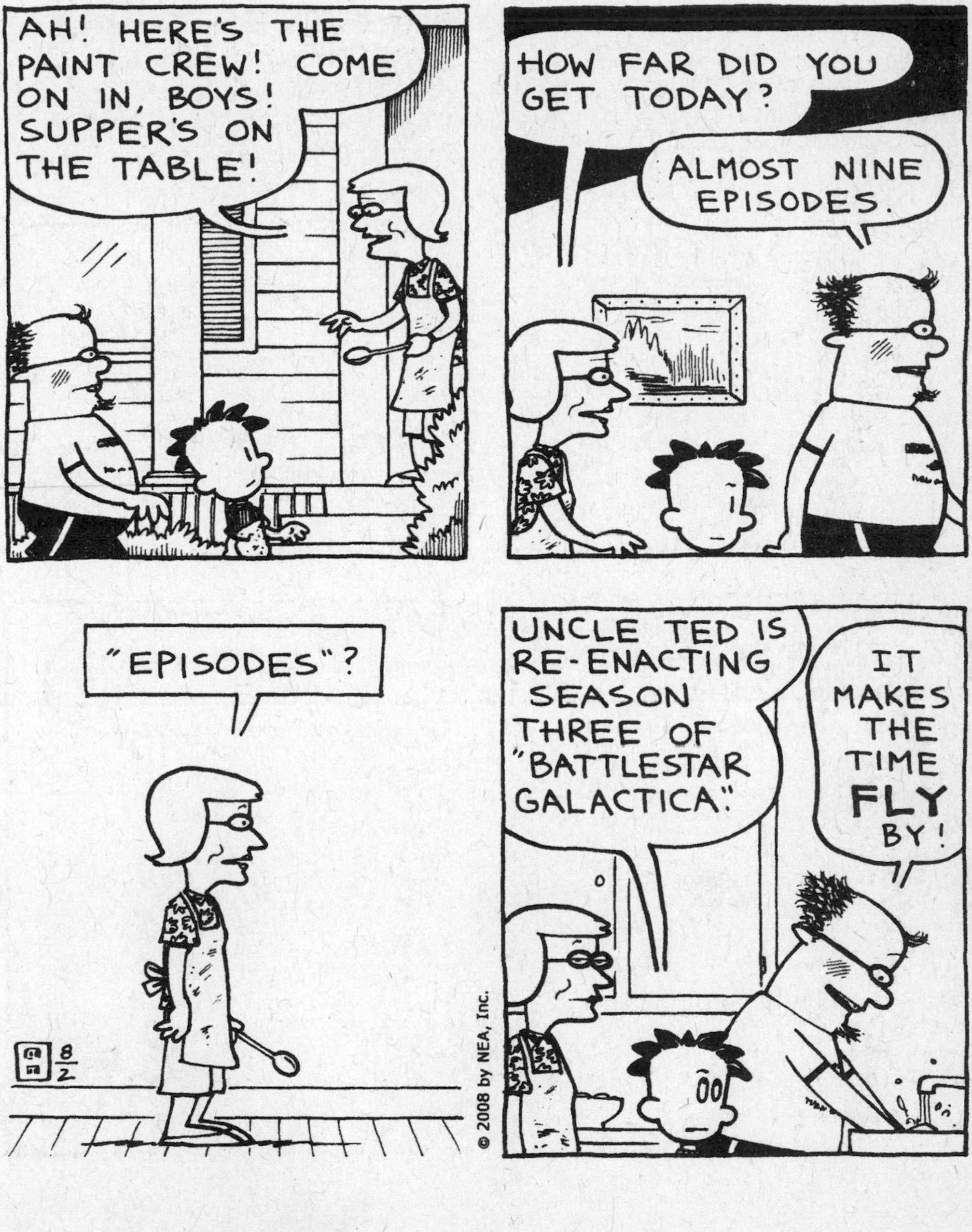
AH! HERE'S THE PAINT CREW! COME ON IN, BOYS! SUPPER'S ON THE TABLE!
HOW FAR DID YOU GET TODAY?
ALMOST NINE EPISODES.
"EPISODES"?
UNCLE TED IS RE-ENACTING SEASON THREE OF "BATTLESTAR GALACTICA."
IT MAKES THE TIME **FLY** BY!

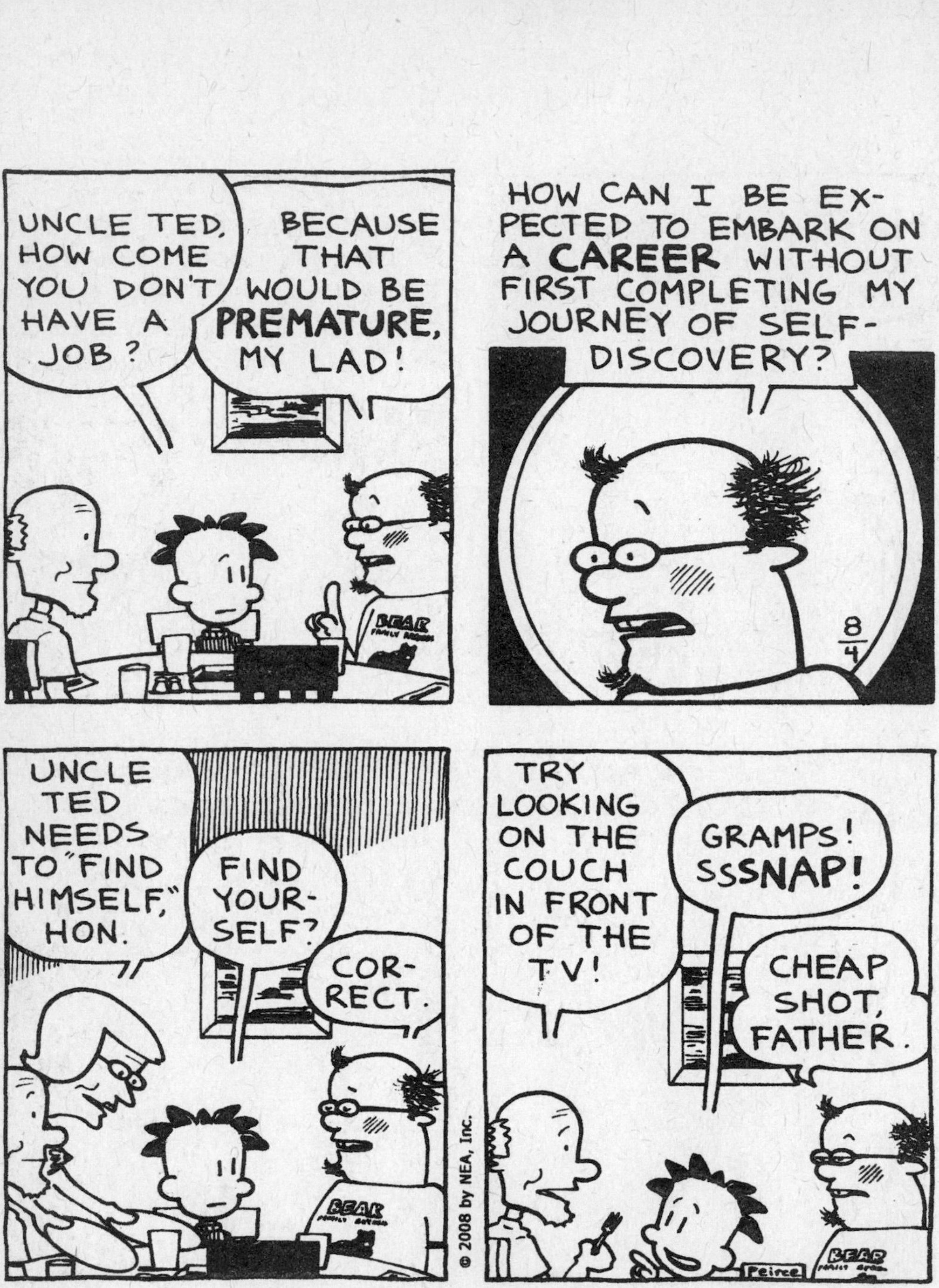
UNCLE TED, HOW COME YOU DON'T HAVE A JOB?
BECAUSE THAT WOULD BE **PREMATURE**, MY LAD!
HOW CAN I BE EXPECTED TO EMBARK ON A **CAREER** WITHOUT FIRST COMPLETING MY JOURNEY OF SELF-DISCOVERY?
8/4
UNCLE TED NEEDS TO "FIND HIMSELF," HON.
FIND YOURSELF?
CORRECT.
TRY LOOKING ON THE COUCH IN FRONT OF THE TV!
GRAMPS! SS**SNAP**!
CHEAP SHOT, FATHER.
Peirce

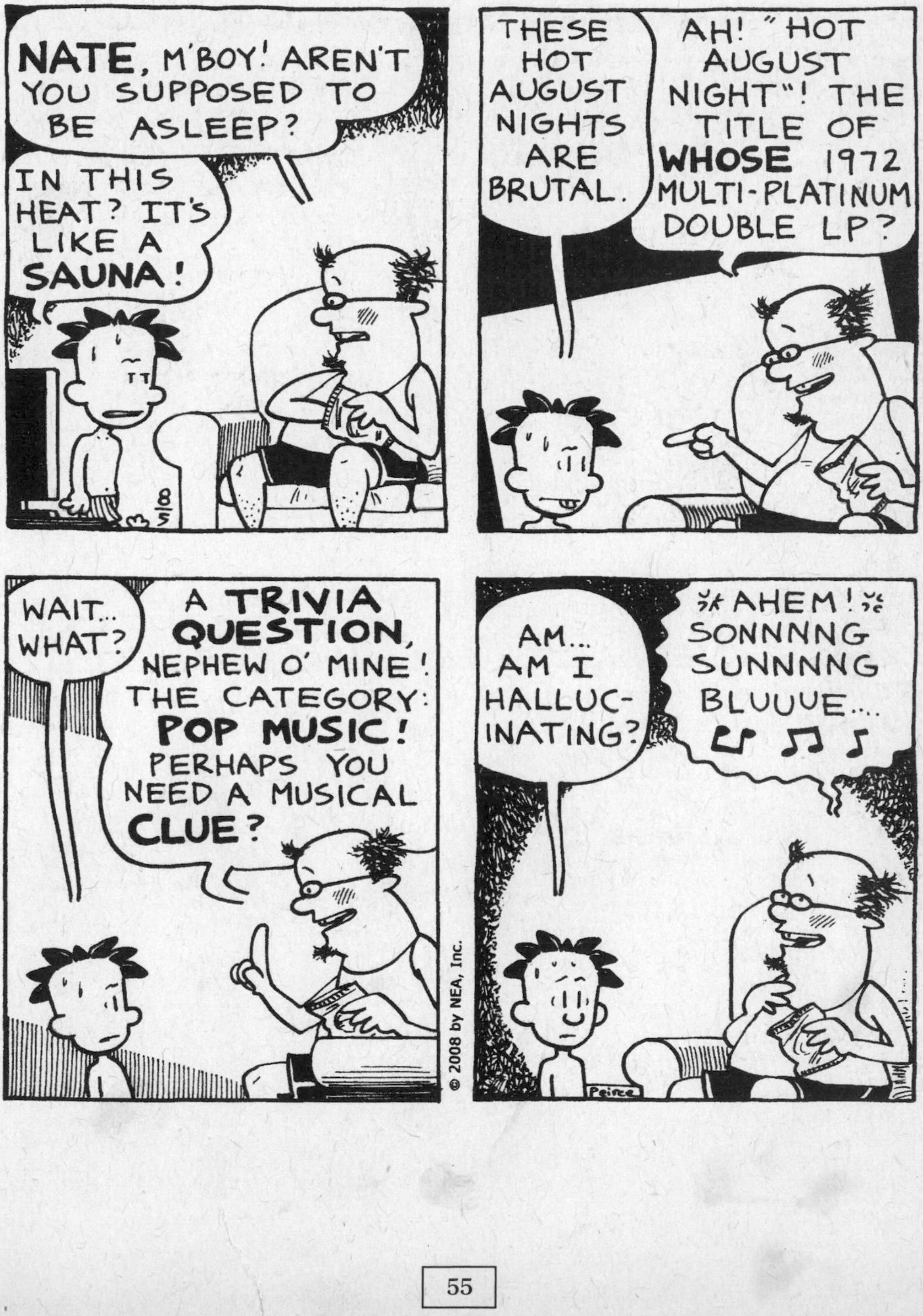
NATE, M'BOY! AREN'T YOU SUPPOSED TO BE ASLEEP?
IN THIS HEAT? IT'S LIKE A SAUNA!
8/5
THESE HOT AUGUST NIGHTS ARE BRUTAL.
AH! "HOT AUGUST NIGHT"! THE TITLE OF WHOSE 1972 MULTI-PLATINUM DOUBLE LP?
WAIT... WHAT?
A TRIVIA QUESTION, NEPHEW O' MINE! THE CATEGORY: POP MUSIC! PERHAPS YOU NEED A MUSICAL CLUE?
© 2008 by NEA, Inc.
AM... AM I HALLUC-INATING?
AHEM! SONNNNG SUNNNNG BLUUUE...
Peirce

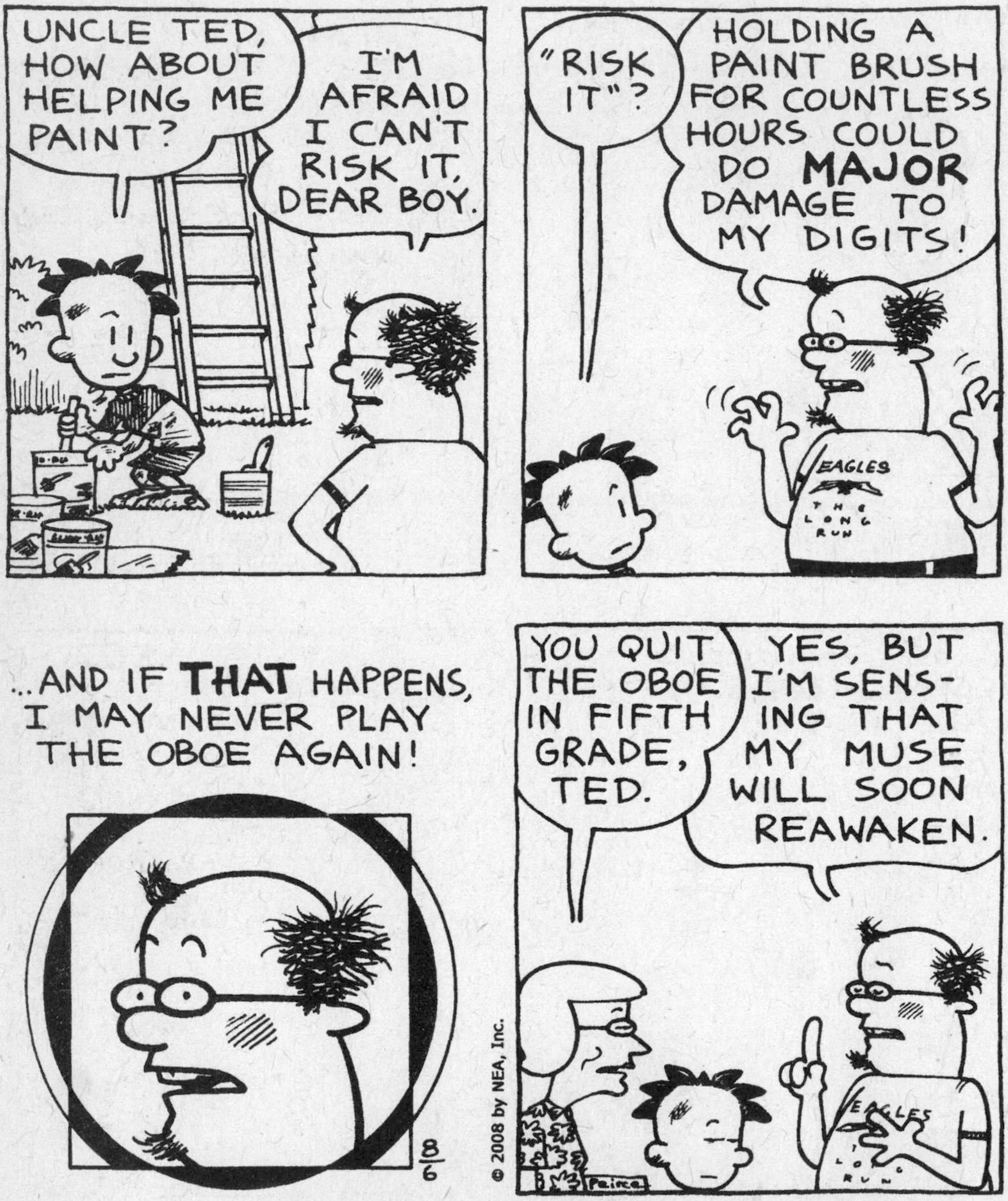

UNCLE TED, HOW ABOUT HELPING ME PAINT?
I'M AFRAID I CAN'T RISK IT, DEAR BOY.
"RISK IT"?
HOLDING A PAINT BRUSH FOR COUNTLESS HOURS COULD DO **MAJOR** DAMAGE TO MY DIGITS!
EAGLES THE LONG RUN
...AND IF **THAT** HAPPENS, I MAY NEVER PLAY THE OBOE AGAIN!
YOU QUIT THE OBOE IN FIFTH GRADE, TED.
YES, BUT I'M SENSING THAT MY MUSE WILL SOON REAWAKEN.
EAGLES
8/6
© 2008 by NEA, Inc.
Peirce

GRAMPS, UNCLE TED ISN'T HELPING WITH THE PAINTING!
I'VE ASKED HIM **NICELY**, I'VE TRIED TO **GUILT** HIM, I'VE TRIED TO **FORCE** HIM TO HELP!
...BUT HE KEEPS COMING UP WITH ALL THESE LAME EXCUSES NOT TO DO ANY WORK!
WELCOME TO MY WORLD, SON.
I NEED TO LIE DOWN. I FEEL A TOUCH OF MALARIA COMING ON.
© 2008 by NEA, Inc.
Peirce

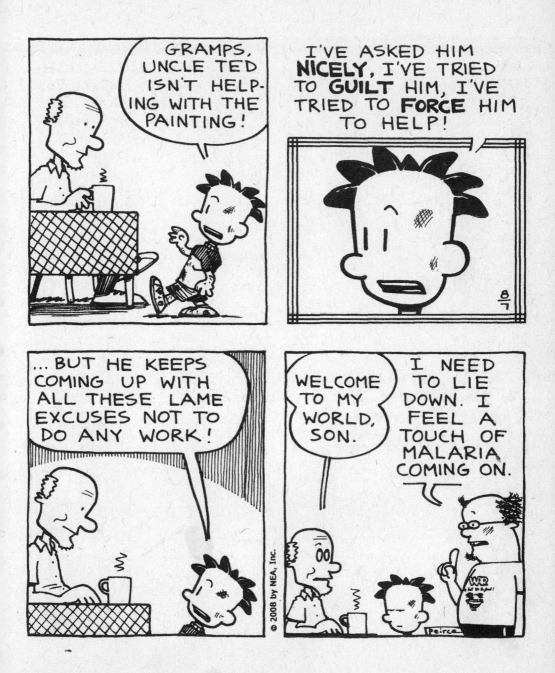

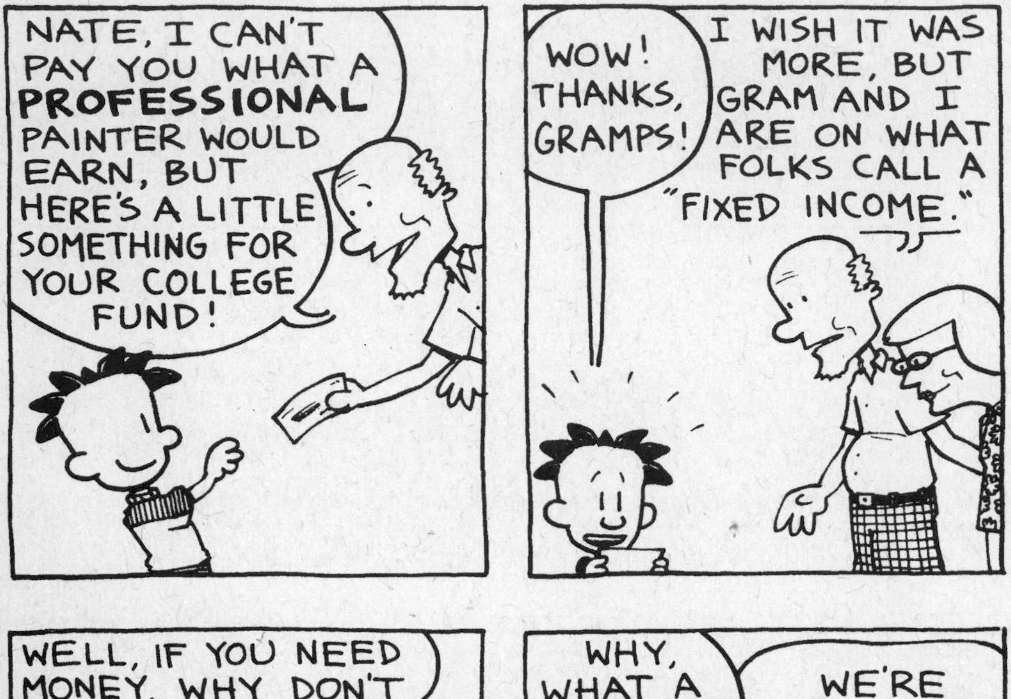
NATE, I CAN'T PAY YOU WHAT A **PROFESSIONAL** PAINTER WOULD EARN, BUT HERE'S A LITTLE SOMETHING FOR YOUR COLLEGE FUND!
WOW! THANKS, GRAMPS!
I WISH IT WAS MORE, BUT GRAM AND I ARE ON WHAT FOLKS CALL A "FIXED INCOME."
WELL, IF YOU NEED MONEY, WHY DON'T YOU START CHARGING UNCLE TED FOR ROOM AND BOARD?
WHY, WHAT A **NOVEL IDEA**!
WE'RE OUT OF "TRISCUITS."

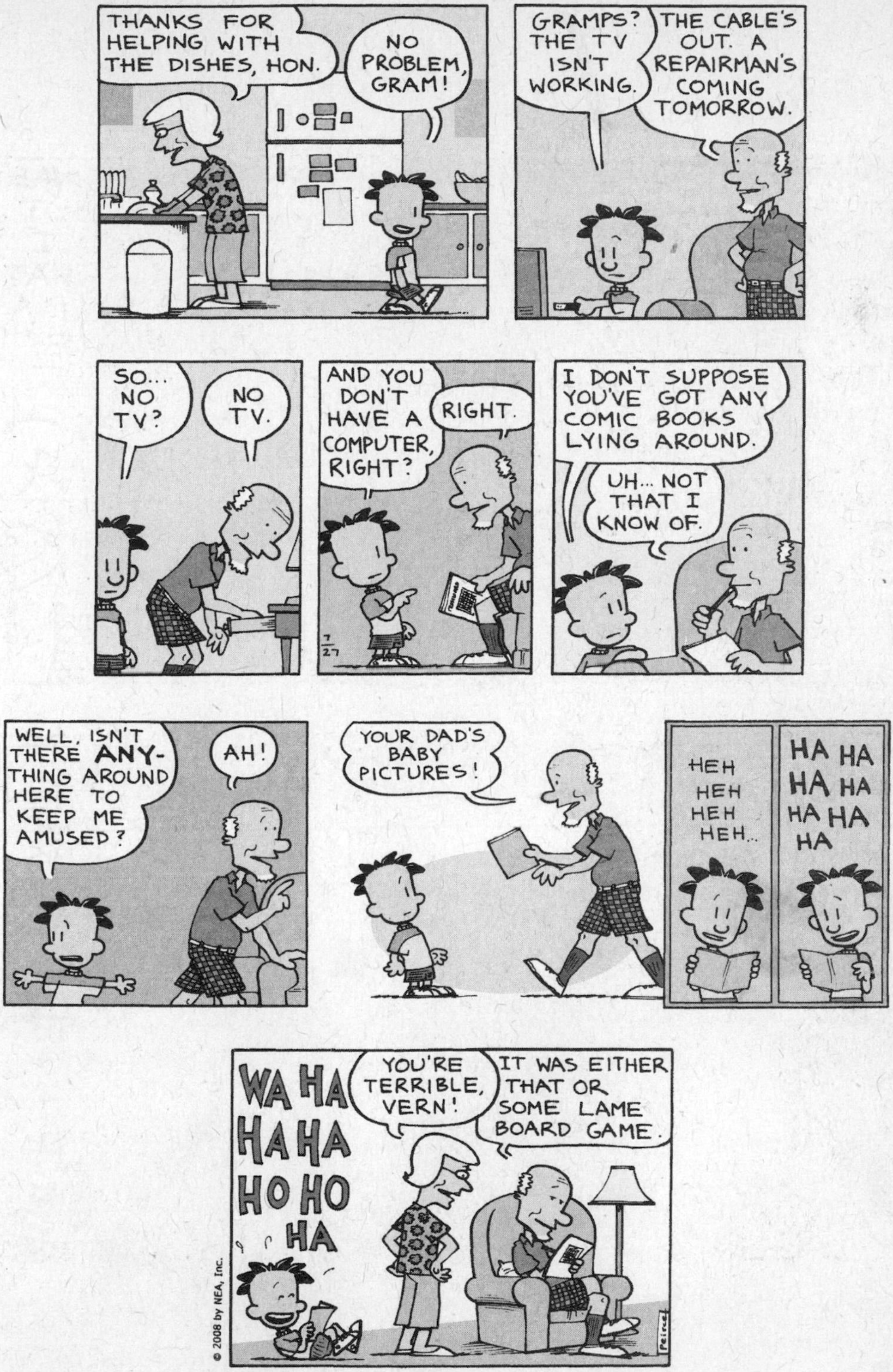
THANKS FOR HELPING WITH THE DISHES, HON.
NO PROBLEM, GRAM!
GRAMPS? THE TV ISN'T WORKING.
THE CABLE'S OUT. A REPAIRMAN'S COMING TOMORROW.
SO... NO TV?
NO TV.
AND YOU DON'T HAVE A COMPUTER, RIGHT?
RIGHT.
I DON'T SUPPOSE YOU'VE GOT ANY COMIC BOOKS LYING AROUND.
UH... NOT THAT I KNOW OF.
WELL, ISN'T THERE ANY-THING AROUND HERE TO KEEP ME AMUSED?
AH!
YOUR DAD'S BABY PICTURES!
HEH HEH HEH HEH...
HA HA HA HA HA HA HA HA
WA HA HA HA HO HO HA
YOU'RE TERRIBLE, VERN!
IT WAS EITHER THAT OR SOME LAME BOARD GAME.
© 2008 by NEA, Inc.

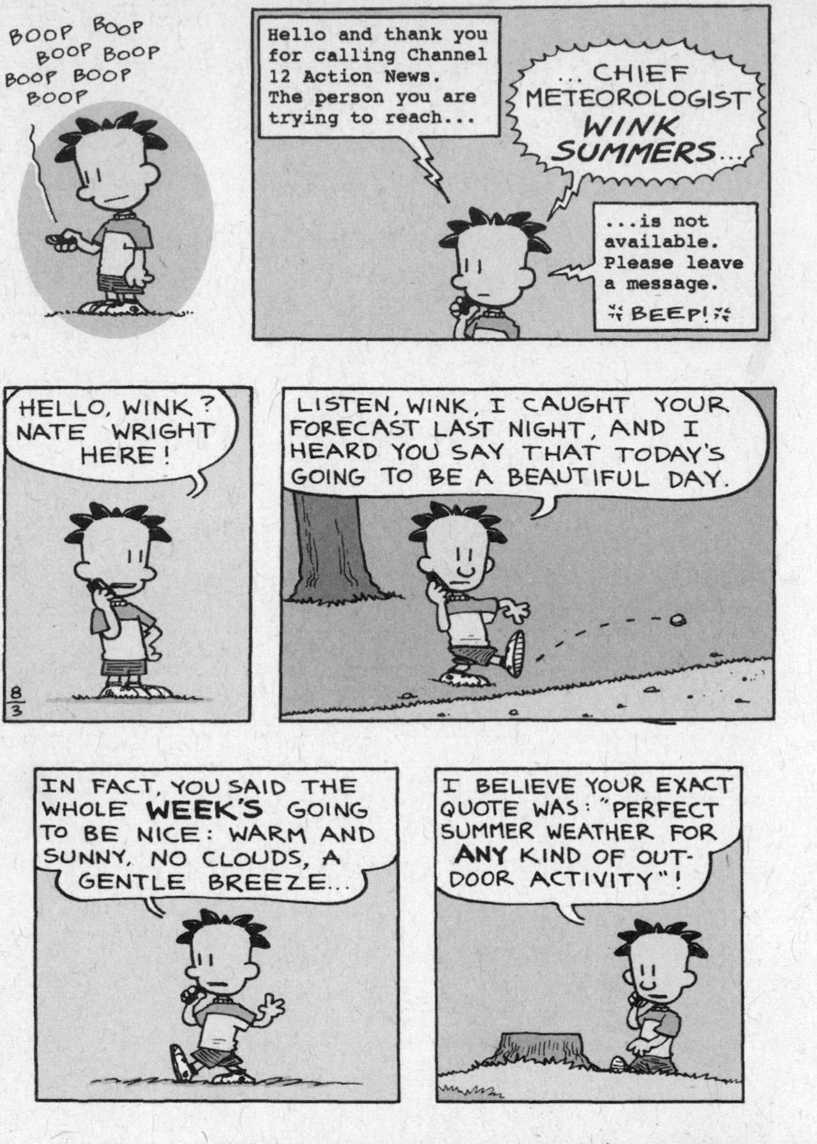

BOOP BOOP BOOP BOOP BOOP BOOP BOOP
Hello and thank you for calling Channel 12 Action News. The person you are trying to reach...
... CHIEF METEOROLOGIST WINK SUMMERS...
...is not available. Please leave a message.
BEEP!
HELLO, WINK? NATE WRIGHT HERE!
8/3
LISTEN, WINK, I CAUGHT YOUR FORECAST LAST NIGHT, AND I HEARD YOU SAY THAT TODAY'S GOING TO BE A BEAUTIFUL DAY.
IN FACT, YOU SAID THE WHOLE WEEK'S GOING TO BE NICE: WARM AND SUNNY, NO CLOUDS, A GENTLE BREEZE...
I BELIEVE YOUR EXACT QUOTE WAS: "PERFECT SUMMER WEATHER FOR ANY KIND OF OUT-DOOR ACTIVITY"!
AND YOU KNOW WHAT? YOU NAILED IT! YOUR FORE-CAST WAS 100% ACCURATE!
© 2008 by NEA, Inc.
YOU'RE KILLING ME, WINK.
LET'S GO, SON! THIS HOUSE WON'T PAINT ITSELF!

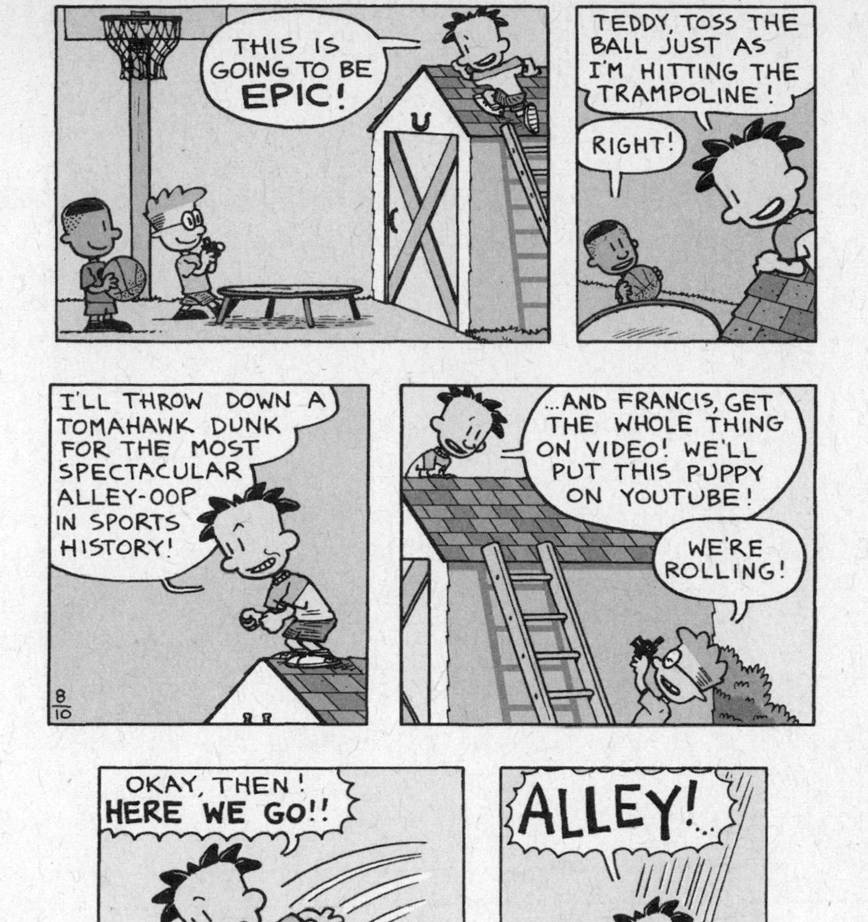
THIS IS GOING TO BE EPIC!
TEDDY, TOSS THE BALL JUST AS I'M HITTING THE TRAMPOLINE!
RIGHT!
I'LL THROW DOWN A TOMAHAWK DUNK FOR THE MOST SPECTACULAR ALLEY-OOP IN SPORTS HISTORY!
8/10
...AND FRANCIS, GET THE WHOLE THING ON VIDEO! WE'LL PUT THIS PUPPY ON YOUTUBE!
WE'RE ROLLING!
OKAY, THEN! HERE WE GO!!
ALLEY!...
CLANNG!
© 2008 by NEA, Inc.
...OOP.
WE CAN STILL PUT THIS ON YOUTUBE, BUT INSTEAD OF "SPORTS," WE'LL POST IT UNDER "COMEDY."
Peirce

WELCOME TO THE REAL WORLD

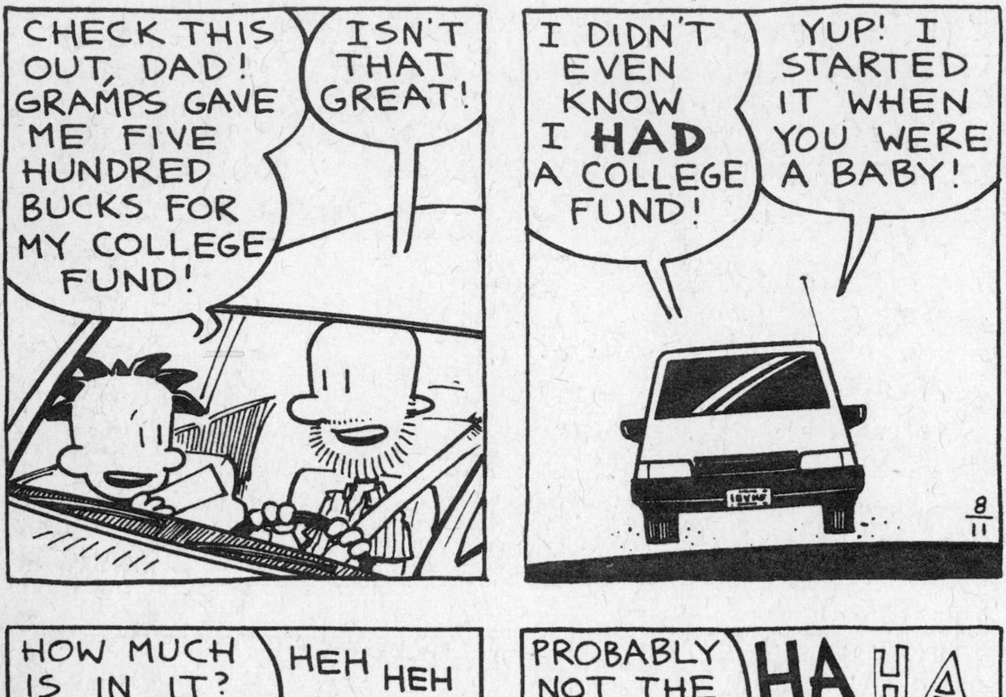
CHECK THIS OUT, DAD! GRAMPS GAVE ME FIVE HUNDRED BUCKS FOR MY COLLEGE FUND!
ISN'T THAT GREAT!
I DIDN'T EVEN KNOW I **HAD** A COLLEGE FUND!
YUP! I STARTED IT WHEN YOU WERE A BABY!
8/11
HOW MUCH IS IN IT? DO WE HAVE ENOUGH TO PAY FOR COLLEGE?
HEH HEH HA HA HA HA HA HA
PROBABLY NOT THE RIGHT QUESTION TO ASK IN A MOVING CAR.
HA HA HA HA HA HA
© 2008 by NEA, Inc.

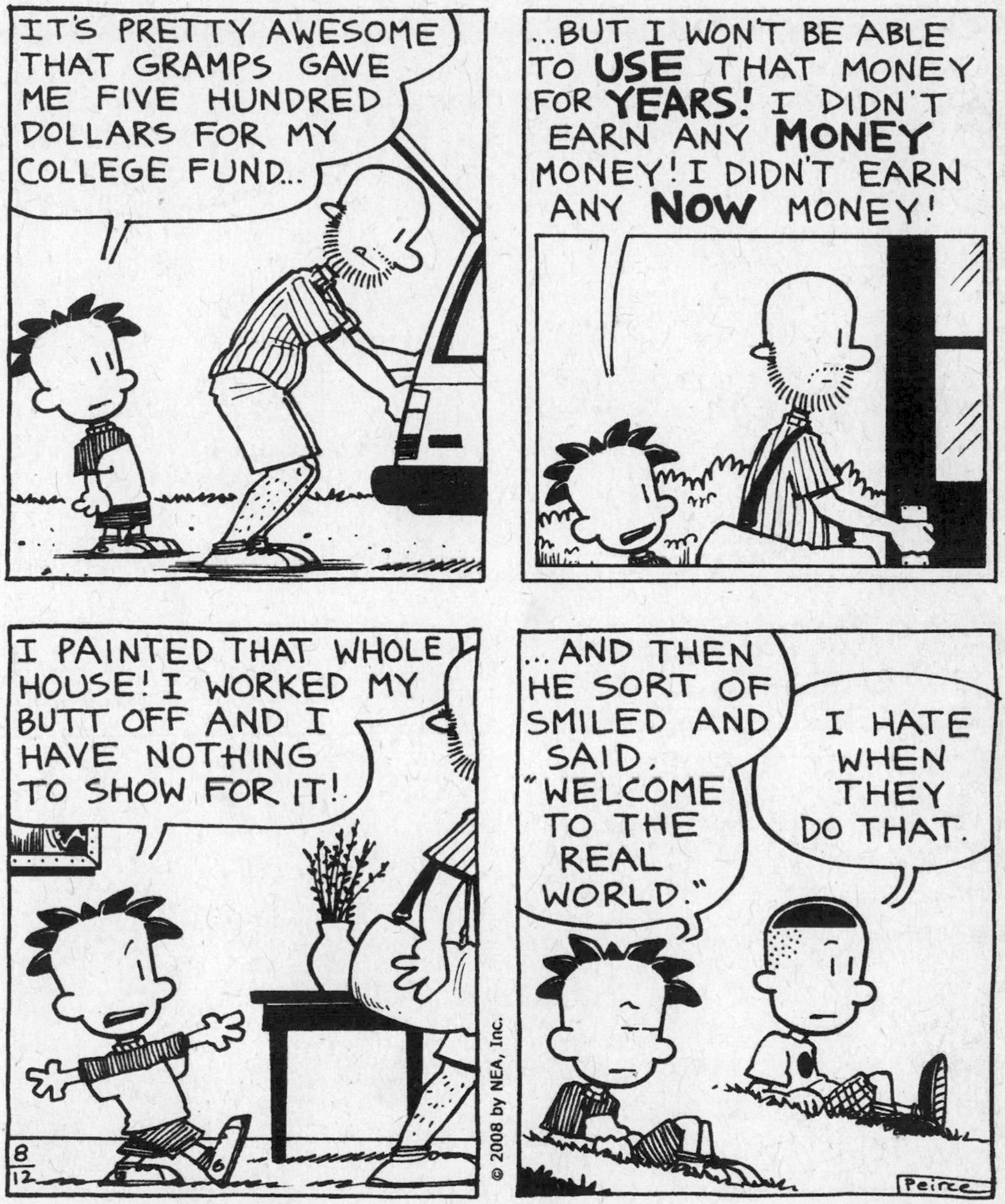
IT'S PRETTY AWESOME THAT GRAMPS GAVE ME FIVE HUNDRED DOLLARS FOR MY COLLEGE FUND...
...BUT I WON'T BE ABLE TO **USE** THAT MONEY FOR **YEARS!** I DIDN'T EARN ANY **MONEY** MONEY! I DIDN'T EARN ANY **NOW** MONEY!
I PAINTED THAT WHOLE HOUSE! I WORKED MY BUTT OFF AND I HAVE NOTHING TO SHOW FOR IT!
8/12
© 2008 by NEA, Inc.
...AND THEN HE SORT OF SMILED AND SAID, "WELCOME TO THE REAL WORLD."
I HATE WHEN THEY DO THAT.
Peirce

NOTHING TO DO

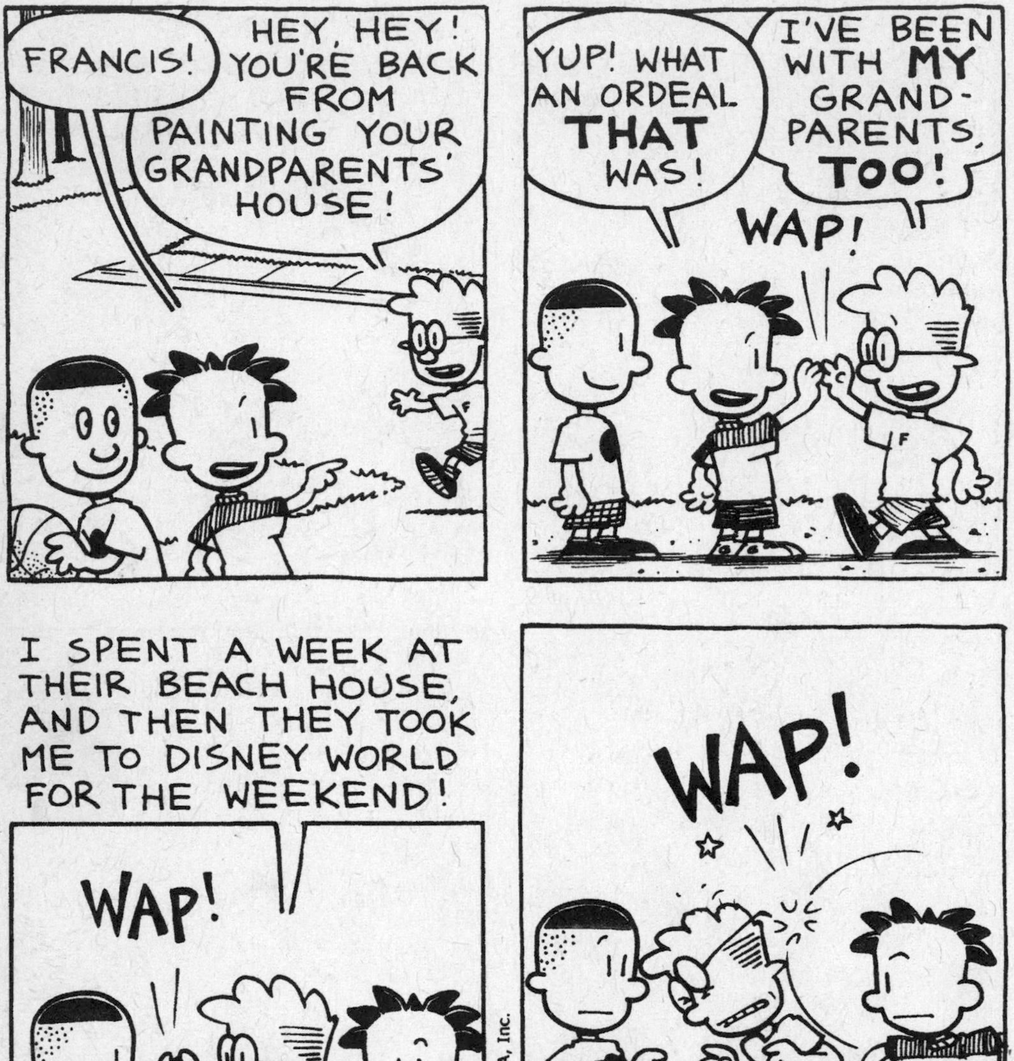
FRANCIS!
HEY, HEY! YOU'RE BACK FROM PAINTING YOUR GRANDPARENTS' HOUSE!
YUP! WHAT AN ORDEAL **THAT** WAS!
I'VE BEEN WITH **MY** GRANDPARENTS, **TOO!**
WAP!
I SPENT A WEEK AT THEIR BEACH HOUSE, AND THEN THEY TOOK ME TO DISNEY WORLD FOR THE WEEKEND!
WAP!
8/13
© 2008 by NEA, Inc.
WAP!
Peirce

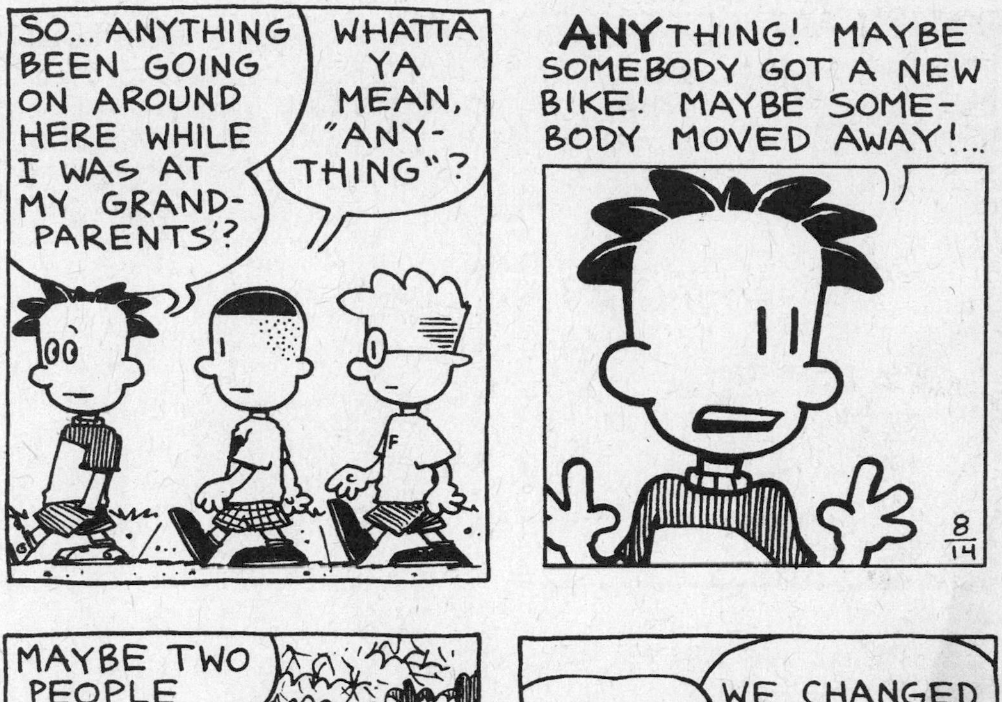
SO... ANYTHING BEEN GOING ON AROUND HERE WHILE I WAS AT MY GRAND-PARENTS'?
WHATTA YA MEAN, "ANY-THING"?
ANYTHING! MAYBE SOMEBODY GOT A NEW BIKE! MAYBE SOME-BODY MOVED AWAY!...
8/14
MAYBE TWO PEOPLE WHO'VE BEEN GOING OUT FOR A WHILE DECIDED TO BR...
JENNY AND ARTUR ARE STILL TOGETHER.
© 2008 by NEA, Inc.
CURSES.
WE CHANGED OUR BRAND OF CAT FOOD!
Peirce

THERE'S NOTHING TO DO.
HEY, I'VE GOT AN IDEA!
WE COULD SHOP FOR BACK-TO-SCHOOL SUPPLIES! WE COULD GET SOME BINDERS, PENCILS, PENS, RULERS...
8/15
OR, WE COULD GIVE FRANCIS A TURBO WEDGIE.
© 2008 by NEA, Inc.
THERE'S NOTHING TO DO.
Peirce

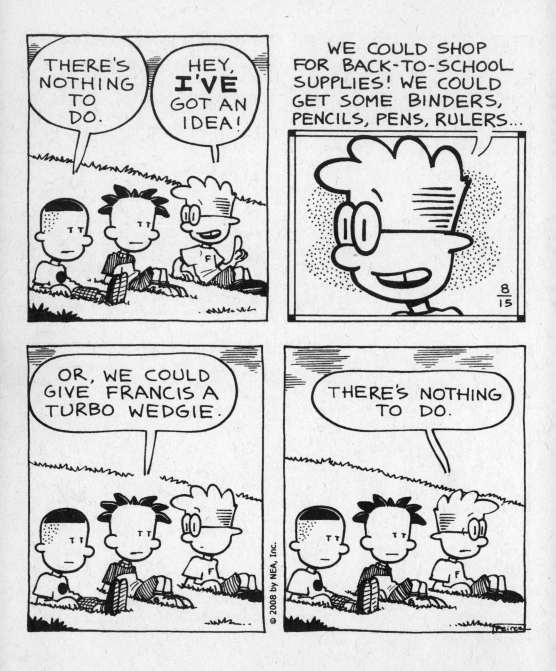

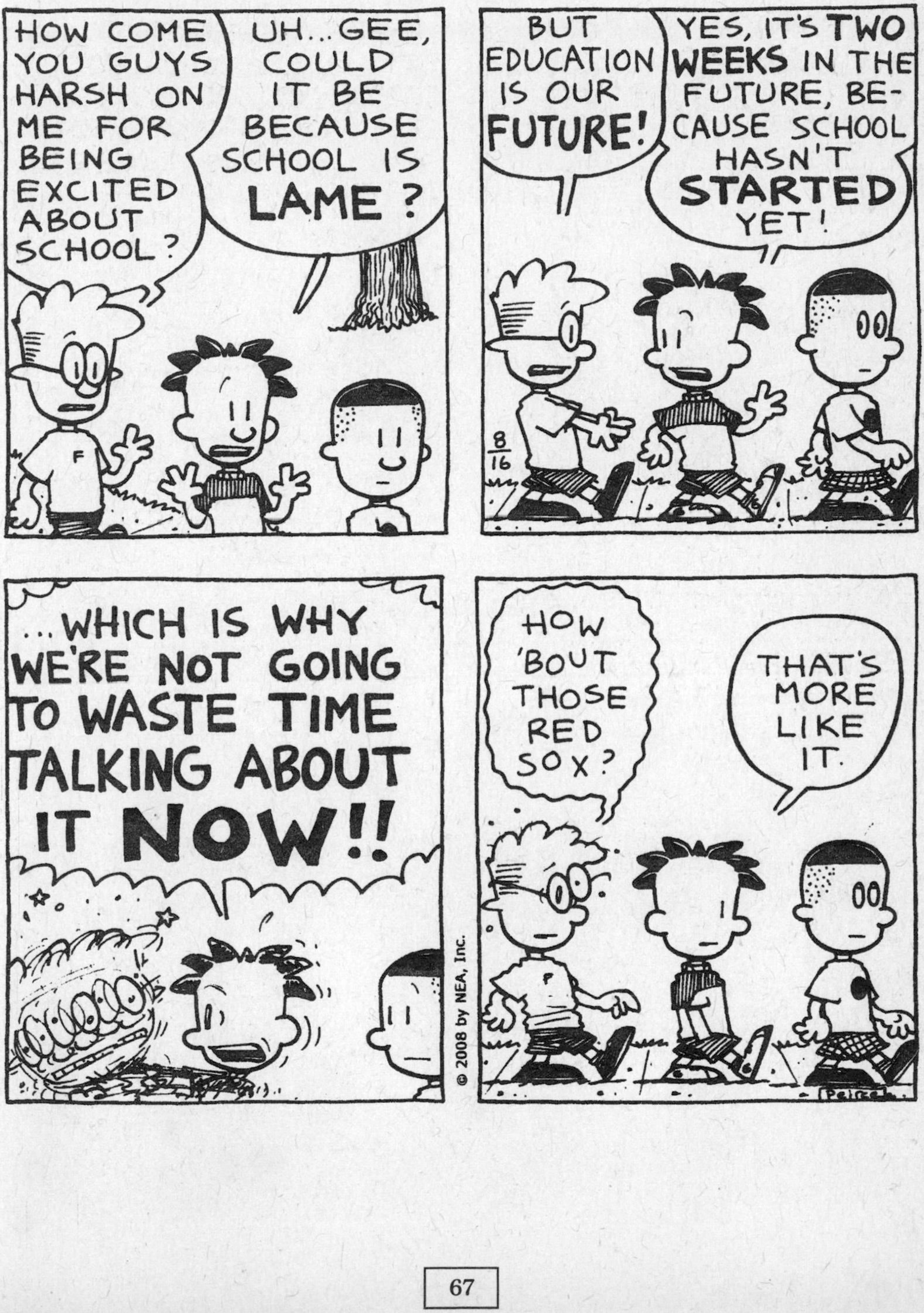
HOW COME YOU GUYS HARSH ON ME FOR BEING EXCITED ABOUT SCHOOL?
UH...GEE, COULD IT BE BECAUSE SCHOOL IS LAME?
BUT EDUCATION IS OUR FUTURE!
YES, IT'S TWO WEEKS IN THE FUTURE, BECAUSE SCHOOL HASN'T STARTED YET!
8/16
...WHICH IS WHY WE'RE NOT GOING TO WASTE TIME TALKING ABOUT IT NOW!!
HOW 'BOUT THOSE RED SOX?
THAT'S MORE LIKE IT.
© 2008 by NEA, Inc.
Peirce

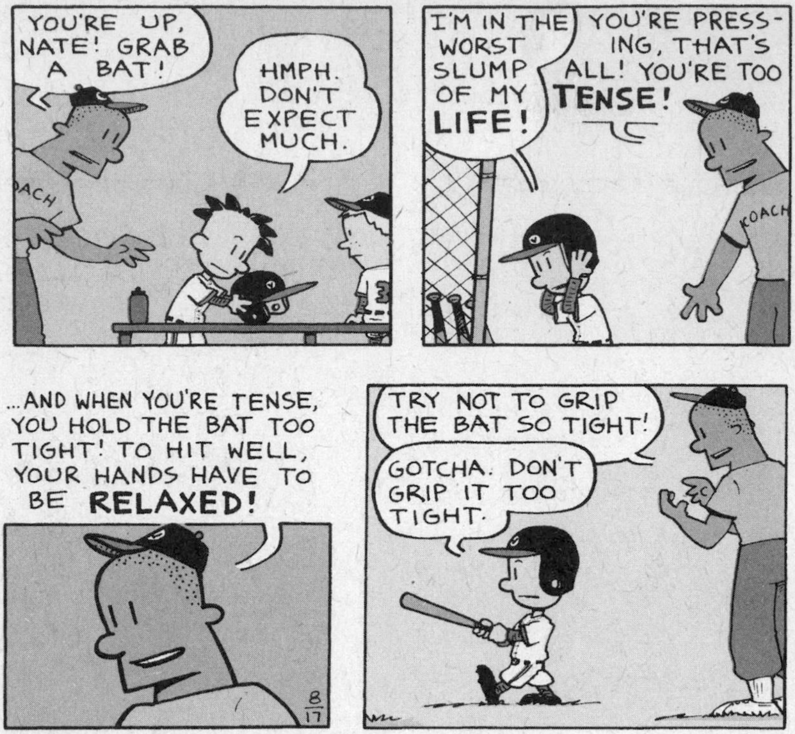
YOU'RE UP, NATE! GRAB A BAT!
HMPH. DON'T EXPECT MUCH.
I'M IN THE WORST SLUMP OF MY LIFE!
YOU'RE PRESSING, THAT'S ALL! YOU'RE TOO TENSE!
...AND WHEN YOU'RE TENSE, YOU HOLD THE BAT TOO TIGHT! TO HIT WELL, YOUR HANDS HAVE TO BE RELAXED!
8/17
TRY NOT TO GRIP THE BAT SO TIGHT!
GOTCHA. DON'T GRIP IT TOO TIGHT.

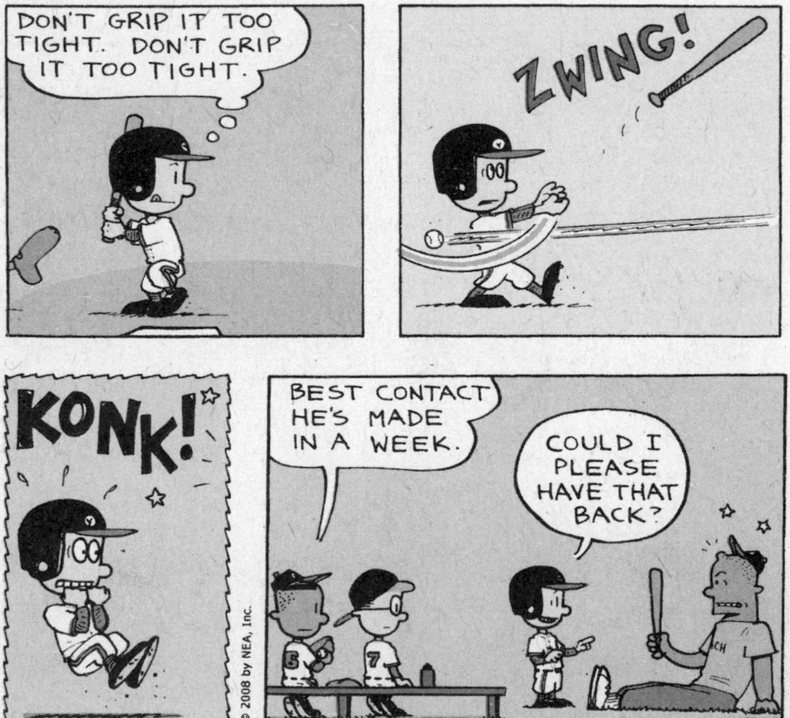
DON'T GRIP IT TOO TIGHT. DON'T GRIP IT TOO TIGHT.
ZWING!
KONK!
© 2008 by NEA, Inc.
BEST CONTACT HE'S MADE IN A WEEK.
COULD I PLEASE HAVE THAT BACK?
Peirce

MASTER OF DISASTER

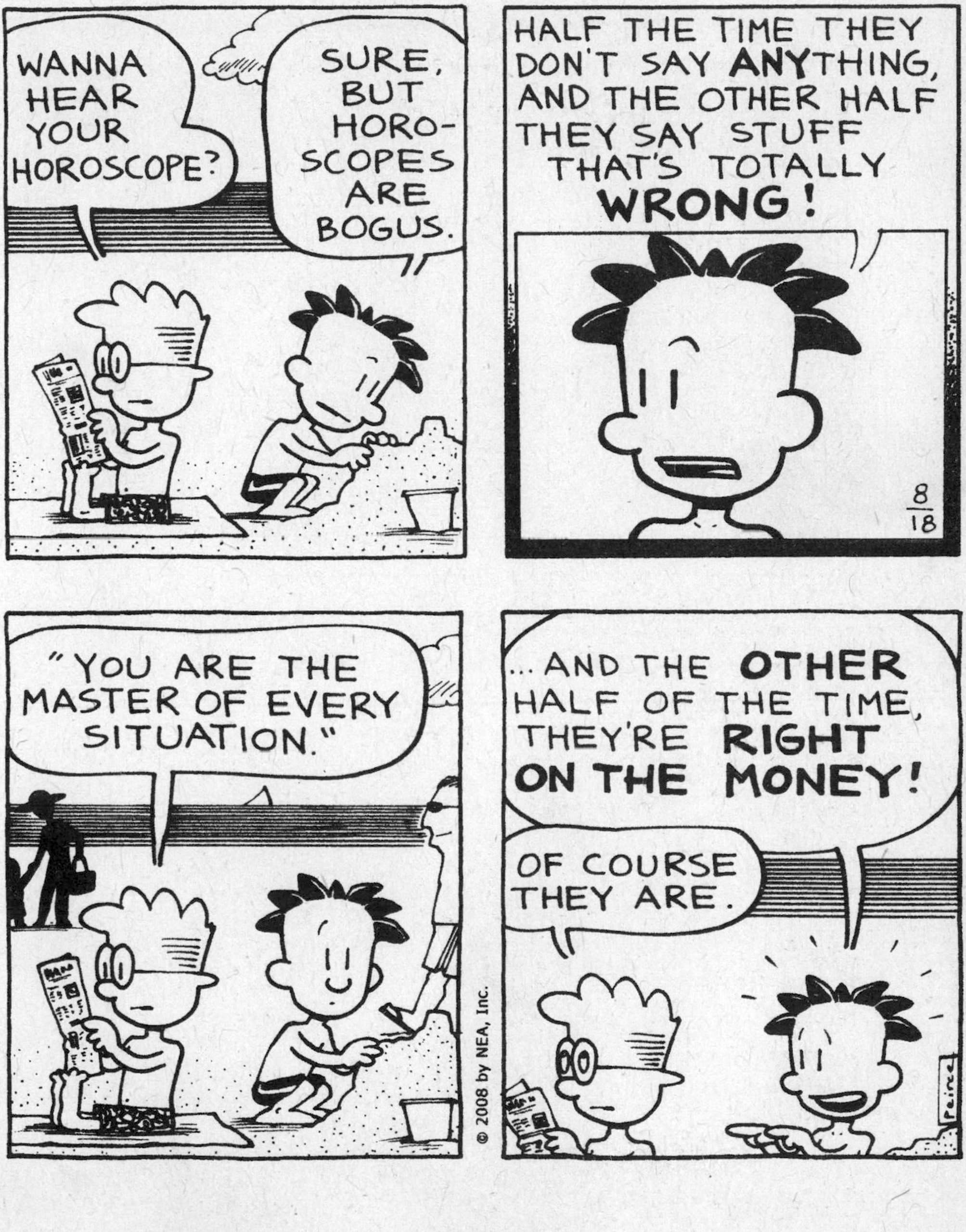
WANNA HEAR YOUR HOROSCOPE?
SURE, BUT HORO-SCOPES ARE BOGUS.
HALF THE TIME THEY DON'T SAY ANYTHING, AND THE OTHER HALF THEY SAY STUFF THAT'S TOTALLY WRONG!
8/18
"YOU ARE THE MASTER OF EVERY SITUATION."
© 2008 by NEA, Inc.
...AND THE OTHER HALF OF THE TIME, THEY'RE RIGHT ON THE MONEY!
OF COURSE THEY ARE.
Peirce

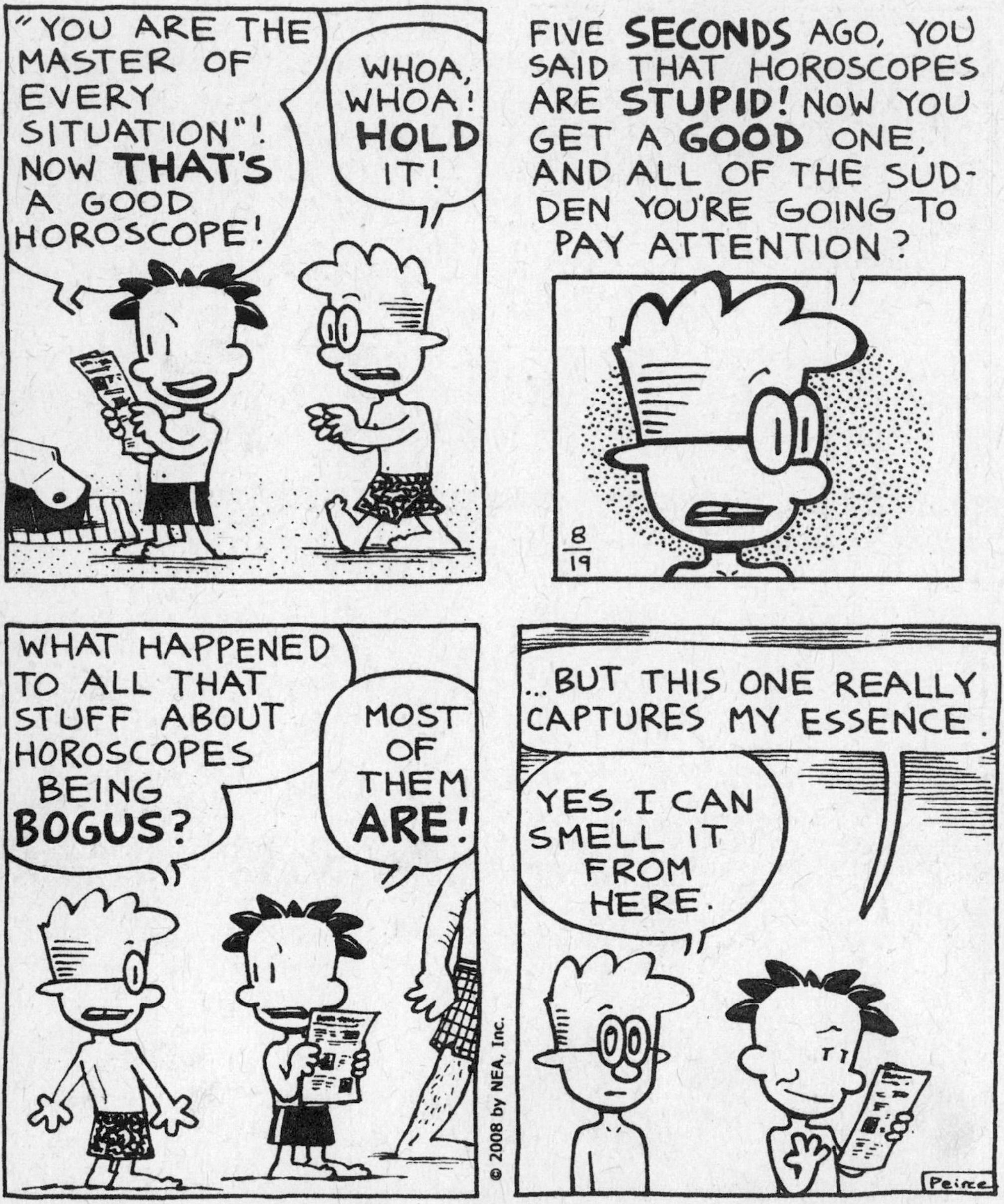
"YOU ARE THE MASTER OF EVERY SITUATION"! NOW THAT'S A GOOD HOROSCOPE!
WHOA, WHOA! HOLD IT!
FIVE SECONDS AGO, YOU SAID THAT HOROSCOPES ARE STUPID! NOW YOU GET A GOOD ONE, AND ALL OF THE SUDDEN YOU'RE GOING TO PAY ATTENTION?
8
19
WHAT HAPPENED TO ALL THAT STUFF ABOUT HOROSCOPES BEING BOGUS?
MOST OF THEM ARE!
© 2008 by NEA, Inc.
...BUT THIS ONE REALLY CAPTURES MY ESSENCE.
YES, I CAN SMELL IT FROM HERE.
Peirce

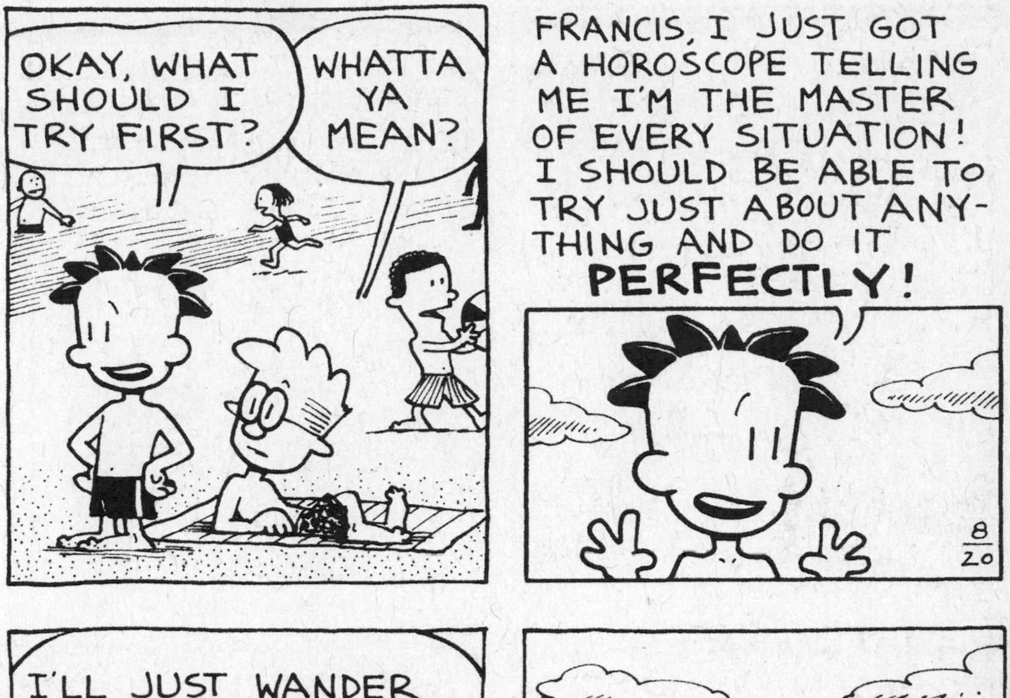
OKAY, WHAT SHOULD I TRY FIRST?
WHATTA YA MEAN?
FRANCIS, I JUST GOT A HOROSCOPE TELLING ME I'M THE MASTER OF EVERY SITUATION! I SHOULD BE ABLE TO TRY JUST ABOUT ANYTHING AND DO IT PERFECTLY!
8/20
I'LL JUST WANDER DOWN THE BEACH AND FIND SOME RANDOM SITUATION TO MASTER!
© 2008 by NEA, Inc.

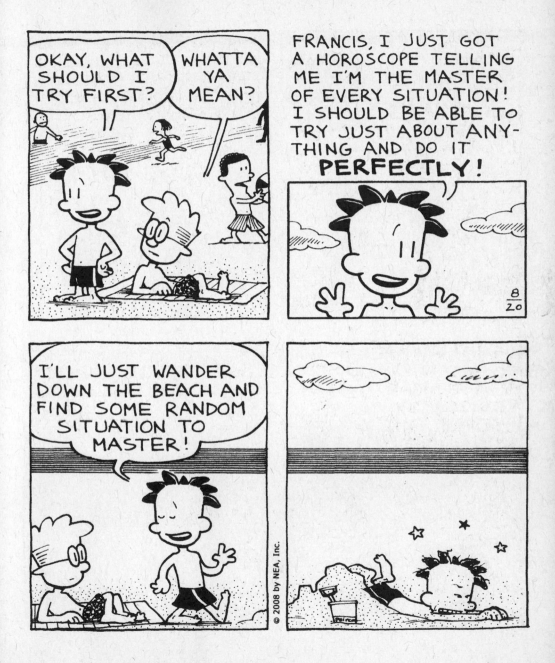

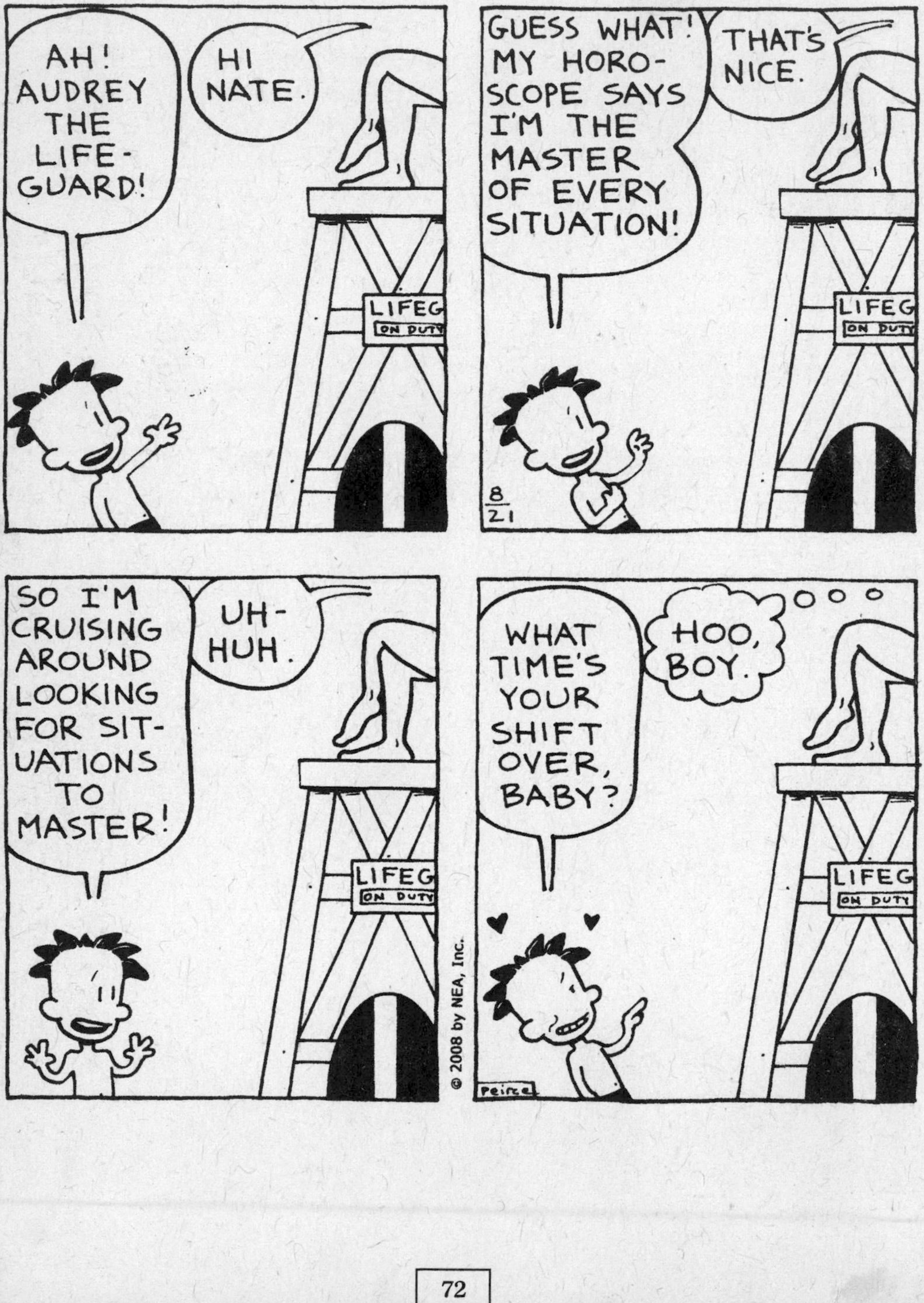
AH! AUDREY THE LIFE-GUARD!
HI NATE.
LIFEG
ON DUTY
GUESS WHAT! MY HORO-SCOPE SAYS I'M THE MASTER OF EVERY SITUATION!
THAT'S NICE.
8/21
SO I'M CRUISING AROUND LOOKING FOR SIT-UATIONS TO MASTER!
UH-HUH.
WHAT TIME'S YOUR SHIFT OVER, BABY?
HOO, BOY.
© 2008 by NEA, Inc.
Peirce

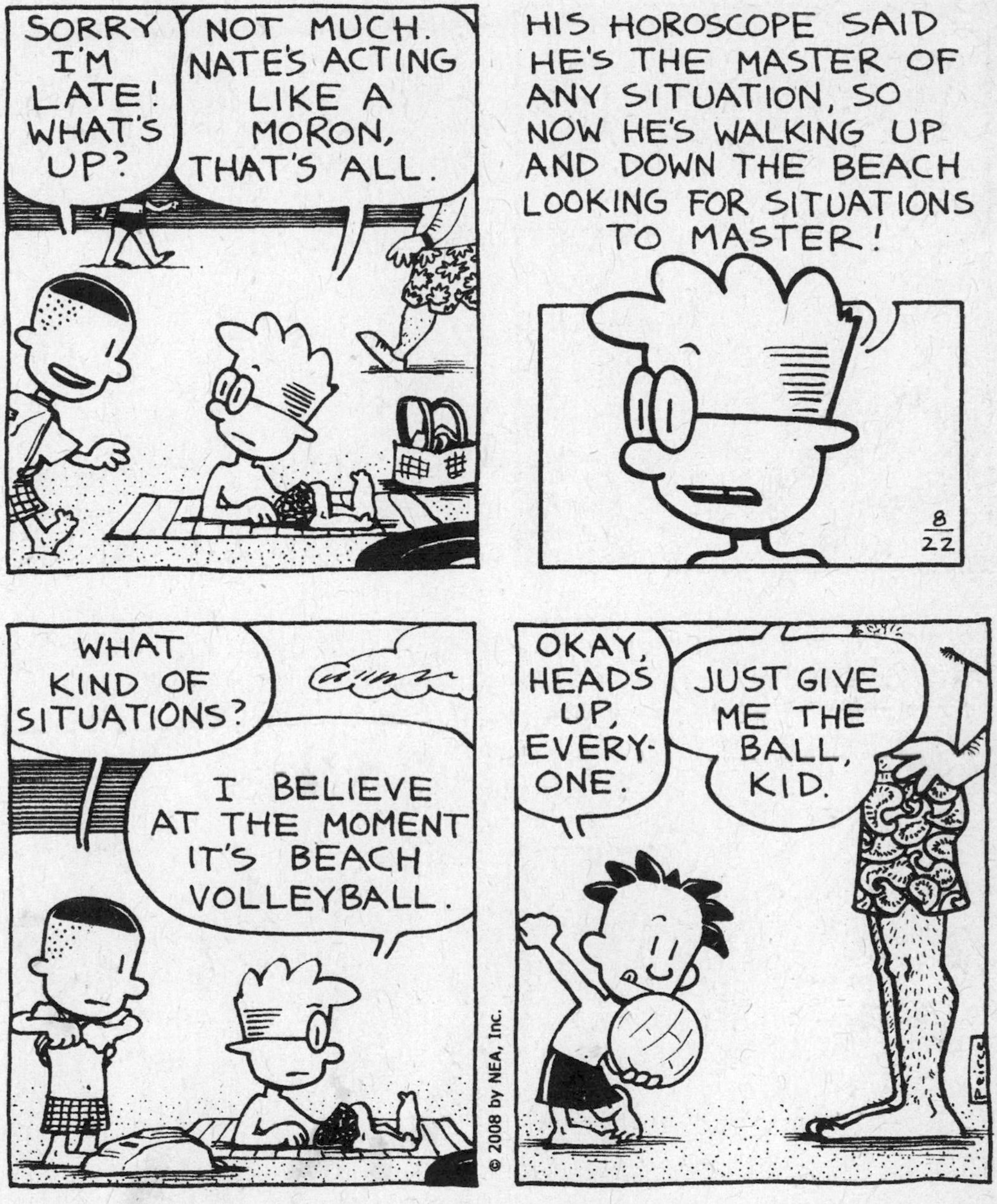
SORRY I'M LATE! WHAT'S UP?
NOT MUCH. NATE'S ACTING LIKE A MORON, THAT'S ALL.
HIS HOROSCOPE SAID HE'S THE MASTER OF ANY SITUATION, SO NOW HE'S WALKING UP AND DOWN THE BEACH LOOKING FOR SITUATIONS TO MASTER!
8/22
WHAT KIND OF SITUATIONS?
I BELIEVE AT THE MOMENT IT'S BEACH VOLLEYBALL.
© 2008 by NEA, Inc.
OKAY, HEADS UP, EVERY-ONE.
JUST GIVE ME THE BALL, KID.
Peirce

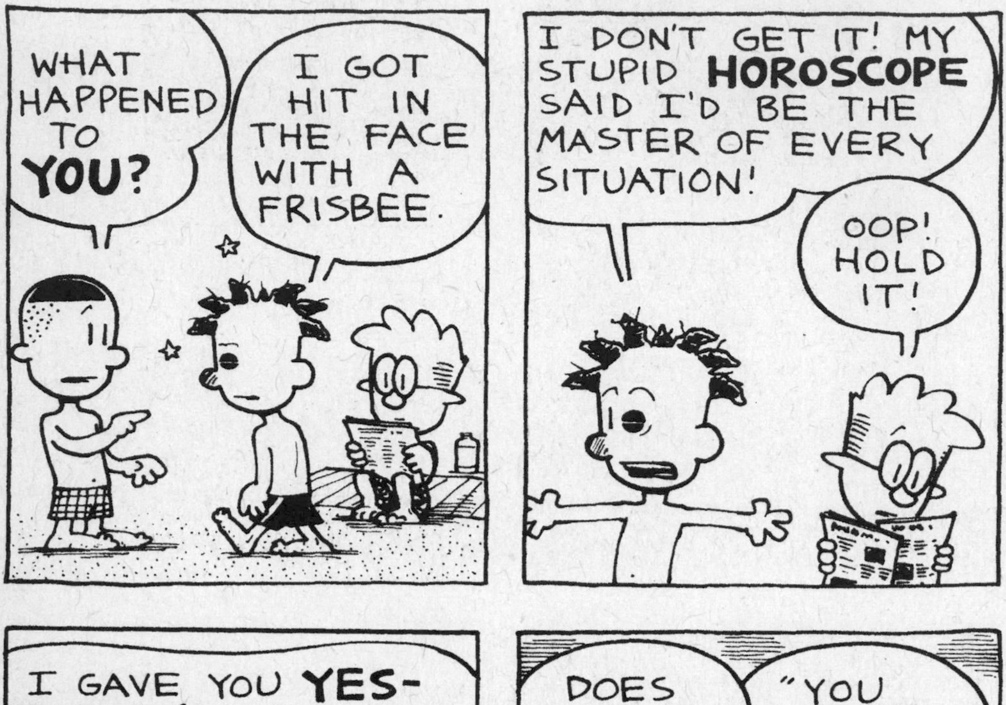
WHAT HAPPENED TO **YOU?**
I GOT HIT IN THE FACE WITH A FRISBEE.
I DON'T GET IT! MY STUPID **HOROSCOPE** SAID I'D BE THE MASTER OF EVERY SITUATION!
OOP! HOLD IT!
I GAVE YOU **YESTERDAY'S** HOROSCOPE BY MISTAKE! **THIS** IS TODAY'S!
8/23
DOES IT MENTION FRISBEES?
"YOU HAVE A SASSY, FUN-LOVING SPIRIT."
Peirce

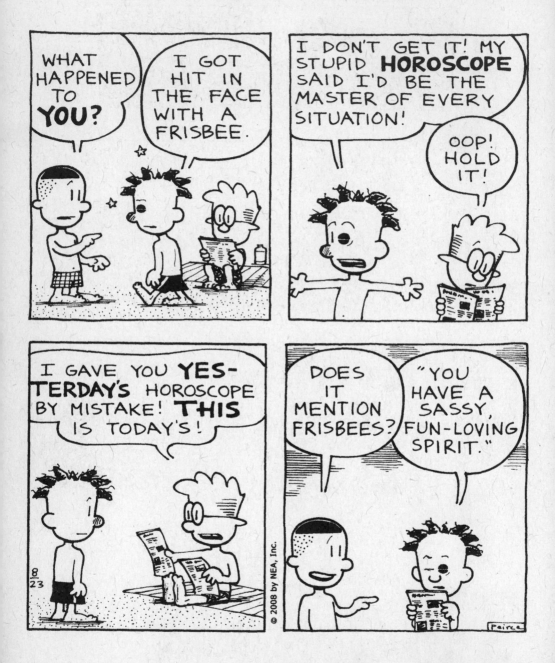

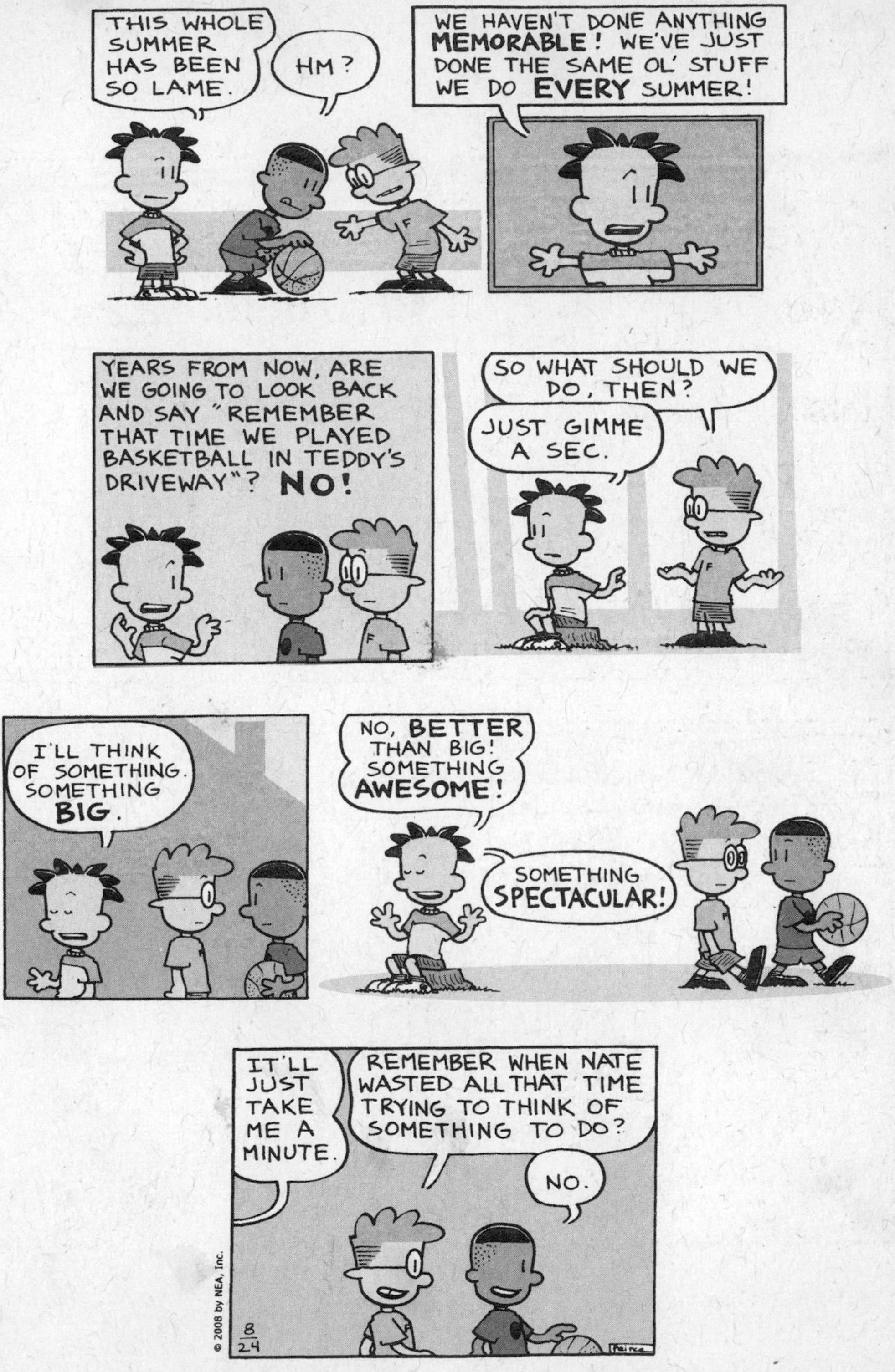
THIS WHOLE SUMMER HAS BEEN SO LAME.
HM?
WE HAVEN'T DONE ANYTHING **MEMORABLE**! WE'VE JUST DONE THE SAME OL' STUFF WE DO **EVERY** SUMMER!
YEARS FROM NOW, ARE WE GOING TO LOOK BACK AND SAY "REMEMBER THAT TIME WE PLAYED BASKETBALL IN TEDDY'S DRIVEWAY"? **NO!**
SO WHAT SHOULD WE DO, THEN?
JUST GIMME A SEC.
I'LL THINK OF SOMETHING. SOMETHING **BIG**.
NO, **BETTER** THAN BIG! SOMETHING **AWESOME**!
SOMETHING **SPECTACULAR**!
IT'LL JUST TAKE ME A MINUTE.
REMEMBER WHEN NATE WASTED ALL THAT TIME TRYING TO THINK OF SOMETHING TO DO?
NO.
8/24
© 2008 by NEA, Inc.

BUY BYE

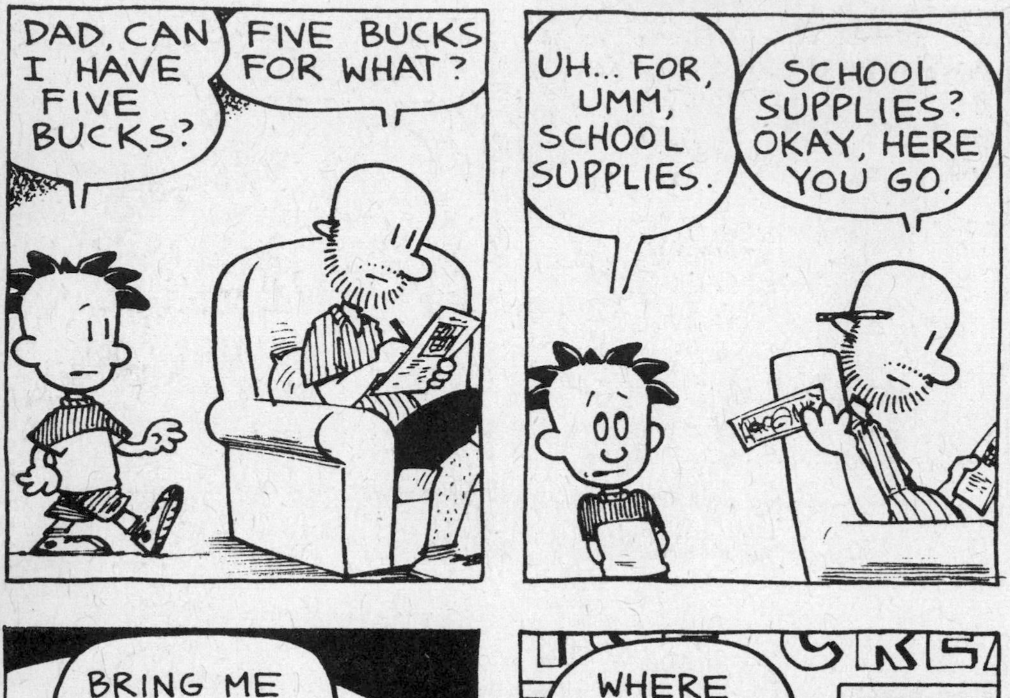
DAD, CAN I HAVE FIVE BUCKS?
FIVE BUCKS FOR WHAT?
UH... FOR, UMM, SCHOOL SUPPLIES.
SCHOOL SUPPLIES? OKAY, HERE YOU GO.
BRING ME BACK THE RECEIPT.
8/25
WHERE IS THE **TRUST**?
Peirce
© 2008 by NEA, Inc.

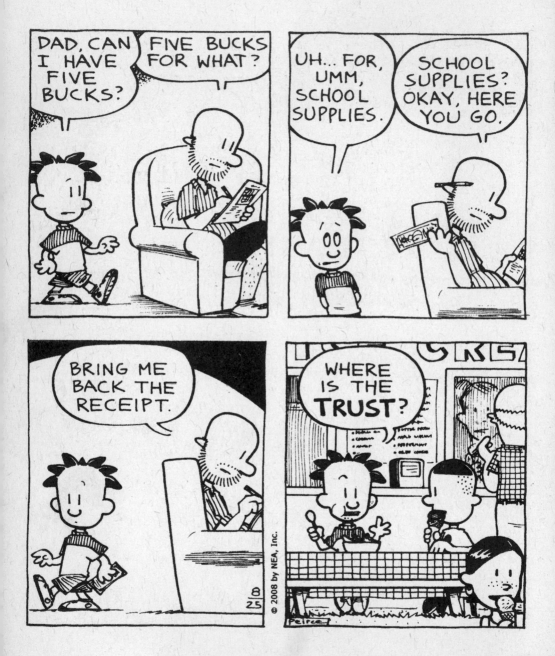

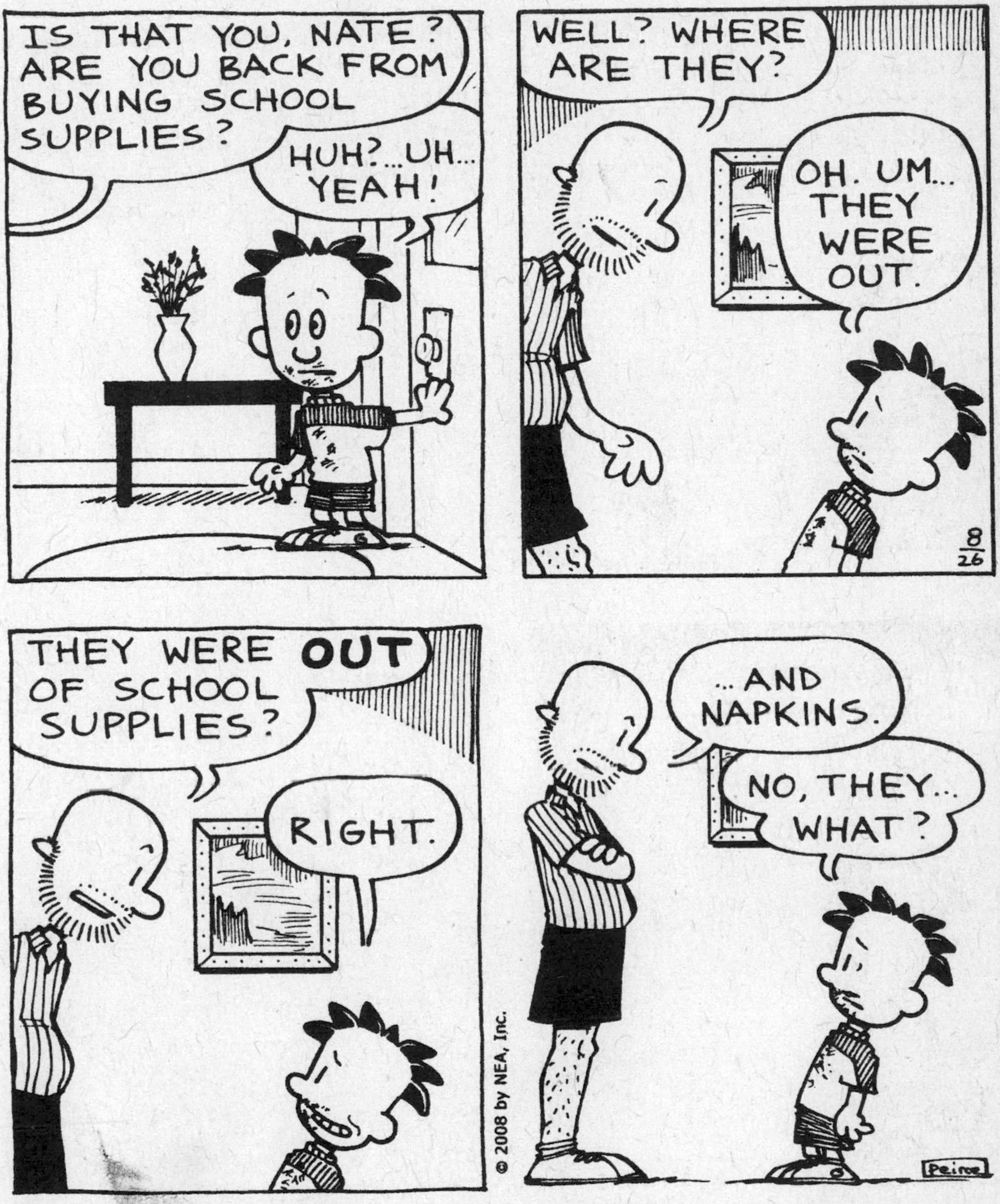
IS THAT YOU, NATE? ARE YOU BACK FROM BUYING SCHOOL SUPPLIES?
HUH?... UH... YEAH!
WELL? WHERE ARE THEY?
OH. UM... THEY WERE OUT.
8/26
THEY WERE **OUT** OF SCHOOL SUPPLIES?
RIGHT.
© 2008 by NEA, Inc.
... AND NAPKINS.
NO, THEY... WHAT?
Peirce

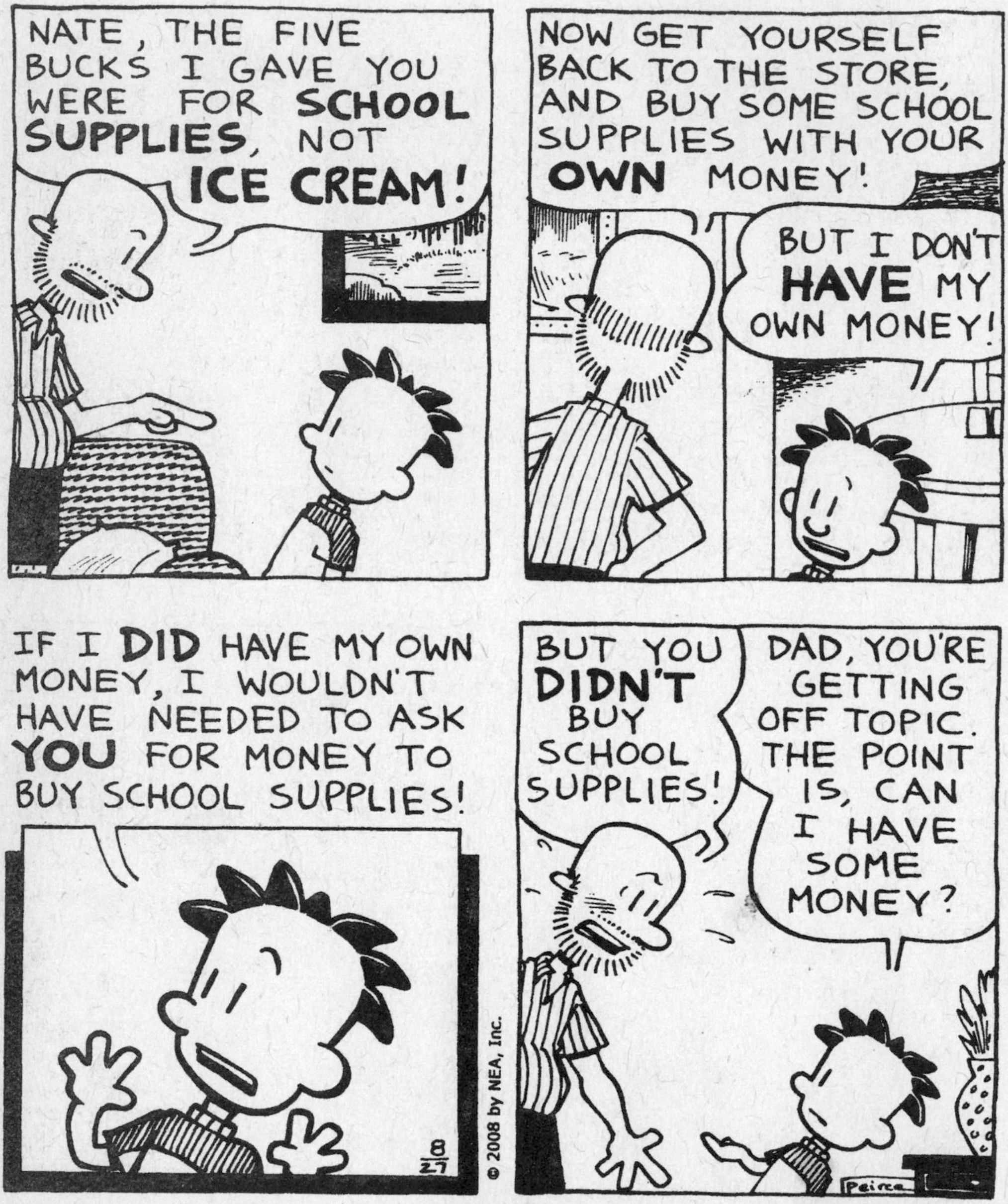
NATE, THE FIVE BUCKS I GAVE YOU WERE FOR **SCHOOL SUPPLIES**, NOT **ICE CREAM!**
NOW GET YOURSELF BACK TO THE STORE, AND BUY SOME SCHOOL SUPPLIES WITH YOUR **OWN** MONEY!
BUT I DON'T **HAVE** MY OWN MONEY!
IF I **DID** HAVE MY OWN MONEY, I WOULDN'T HAVE NEEDED TO ASK **YOU** FOR MONEY TO BUY SCHOOL SUPPLIES!
BUT YOU **DIDN'T** BUY SCHOOL SUPPLIES!
DAD, YOU'RE GETTING OFF TOPIC. THE POINT IS, CAN I HAVE SOME MONEY?
© 2008 by NEA, Inc.

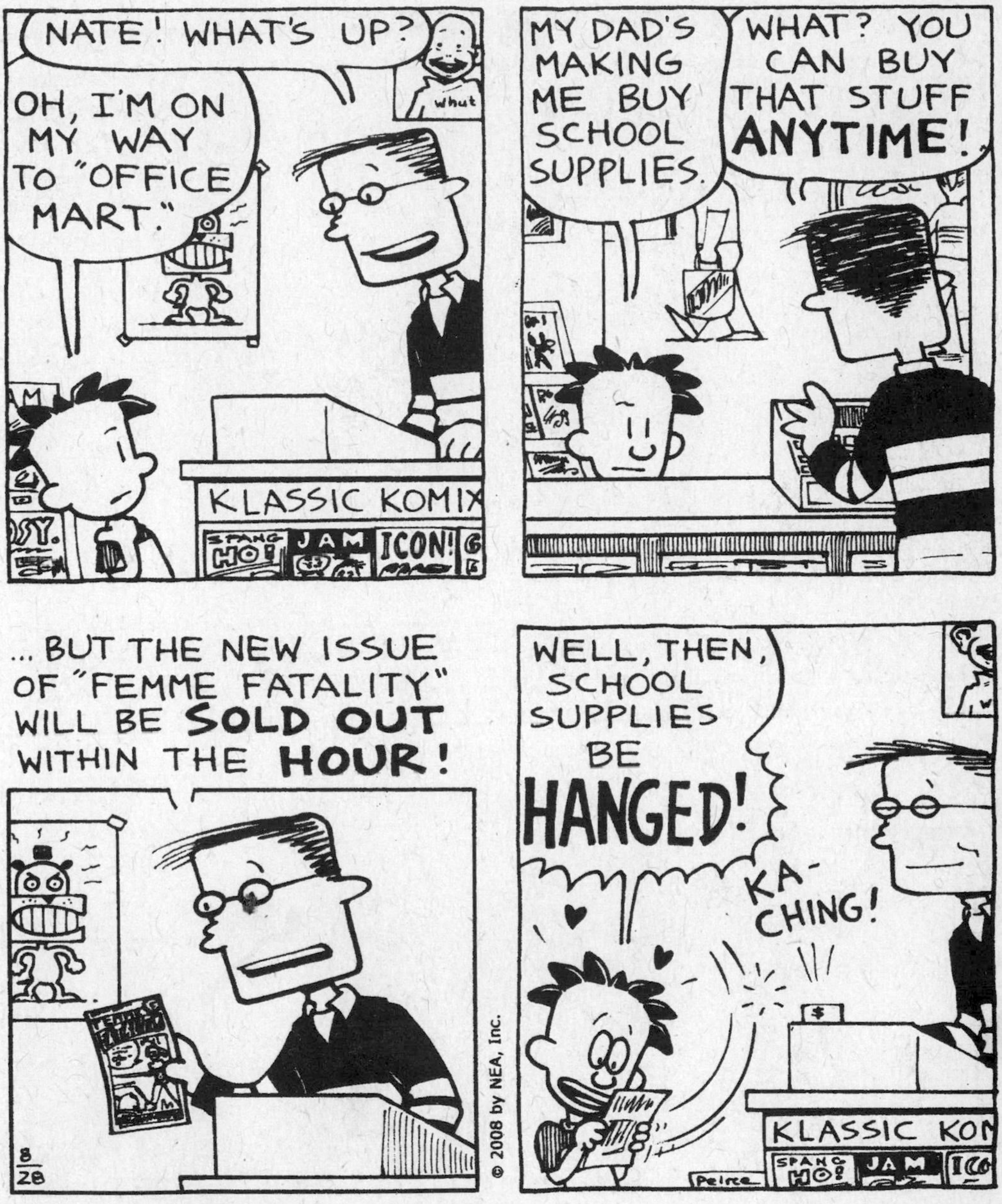
NATE! WHAT'S UP?
OH, I'M ON MY WAY TO "OFFICE MART."
KLASSIC KOMIX
MY DAD'S MAKING ME BUY SCHOOL SUPPLIES.
WHAT? YOU CAN BUY THAT STUFF **ANYTIME**!
... BUT THE NEW ISSUE OF "FEMME FATALITY" WILL BE **SOLD OUT** WITHIN THE **HOUR**!
WELL, THEN, SCHOOL SUPPLIES BE **HANGED**!
KA-CHING!
KLASSIC KOM
Peirce
© 2008 by NEA, Inc.

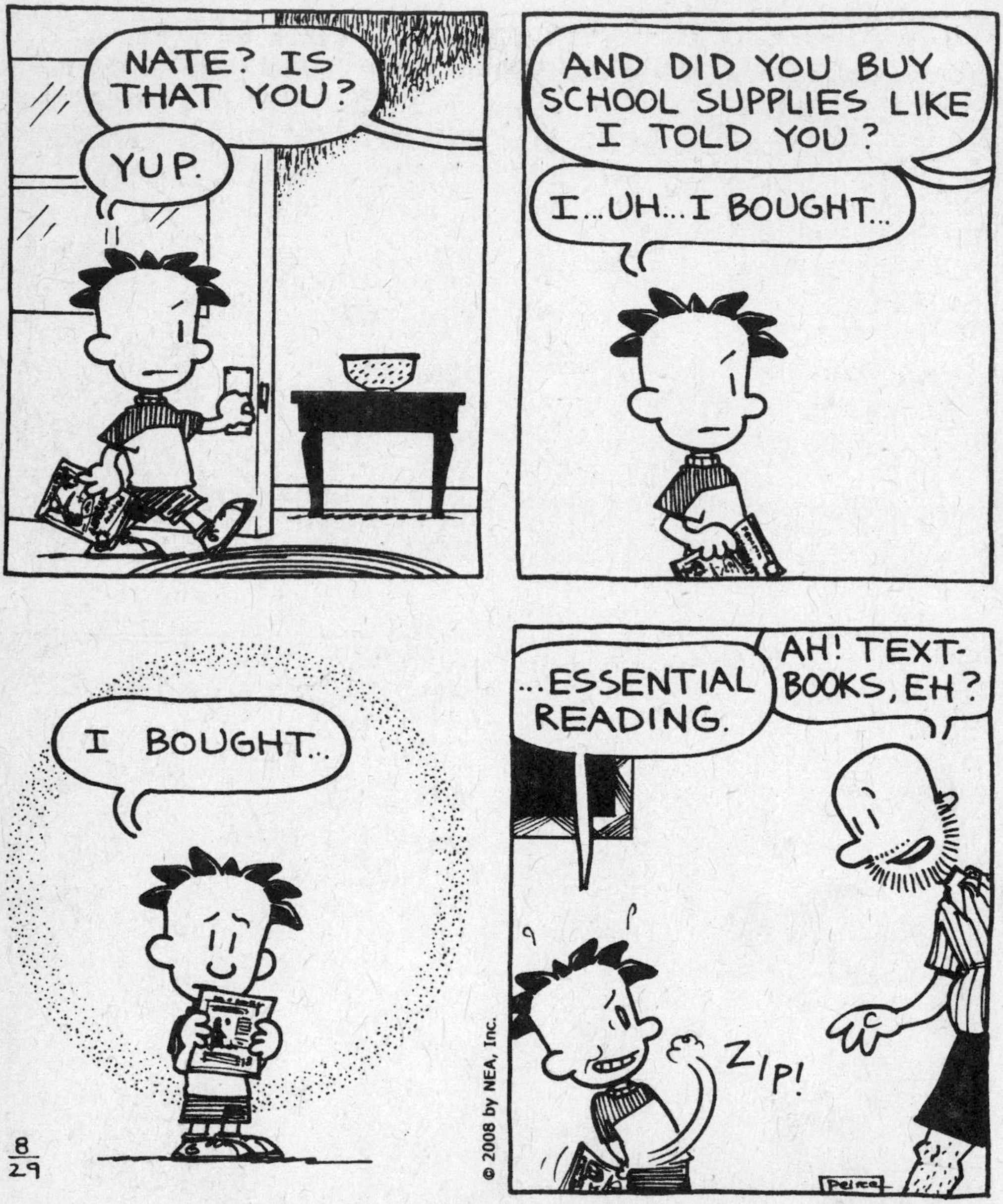
NATE? IS THAT YOU?
YUP.
AND DID YOU BUY SCHOOL SUPPLIES LIKE I TOLD YOU?
I...UH...I BOUGHT...
I BOUGHT...
8/29
...ESSENTIAL READING.
AH! TEXT-BOOKS, EH?
ZIP!
Peirce

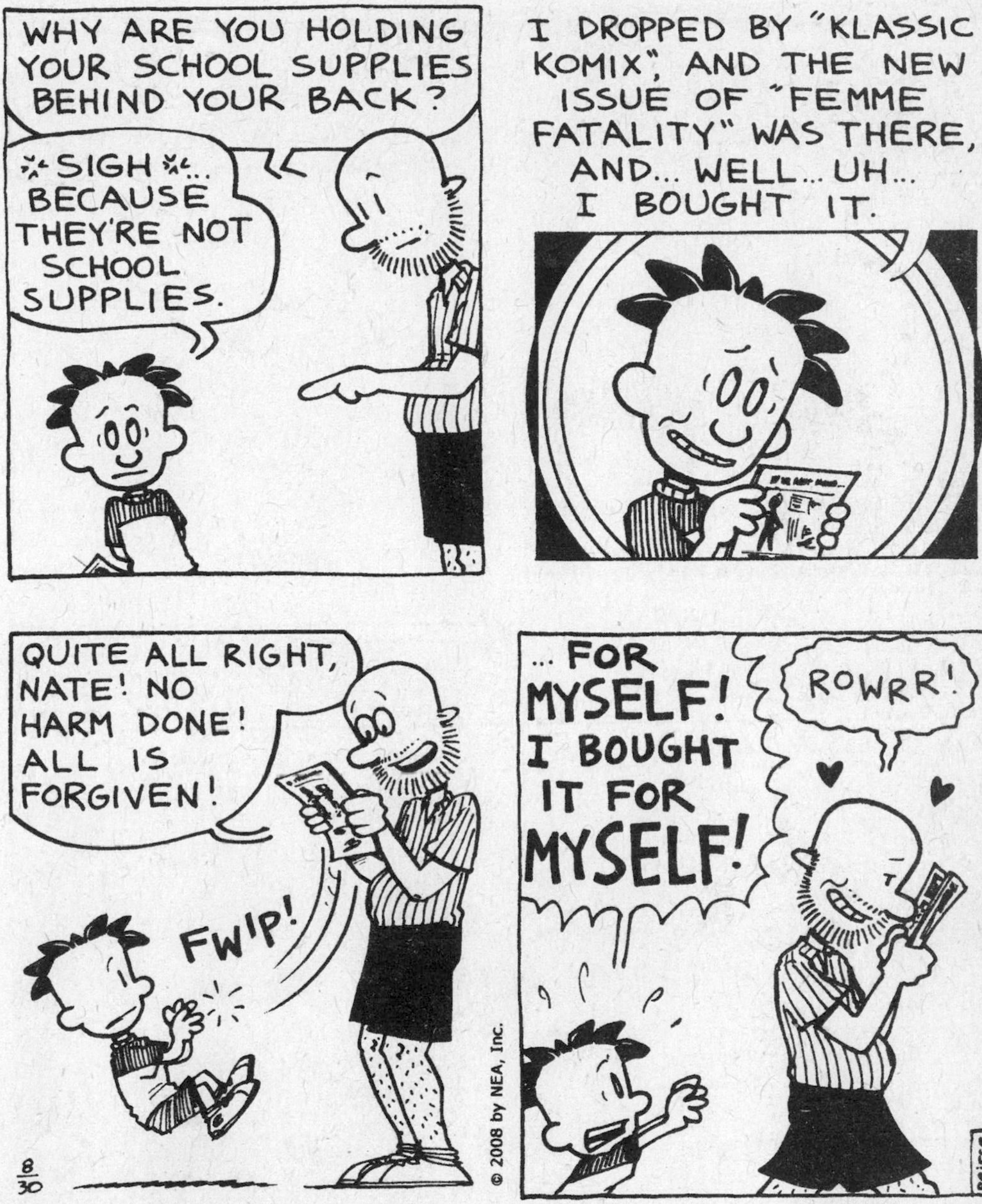
WHY ARE YOU HOLDING YOUR SCHOOL SUPPLIES BEHIND YOUR BACK?
SIGH... BECAUSE THEY'RE NOT SCHOOL SUPPLIES.
I DROPPED BY "KLASSIC KOMIX", AND THE NEW ISSUE OF "FEMME FATALITY" WAS THERE, AND... WELL... UH... I BOUGHT IT.
QUITE ALL RIGHT, NATE! NO HARM DONE! ALL IS FORGIVEN!
FW'IP!
8/30
© 2008 by NEA, Inc.
... FOR MYSELF! I BOUGHT IT FOR MYSELF!
ROWRR!
peirce

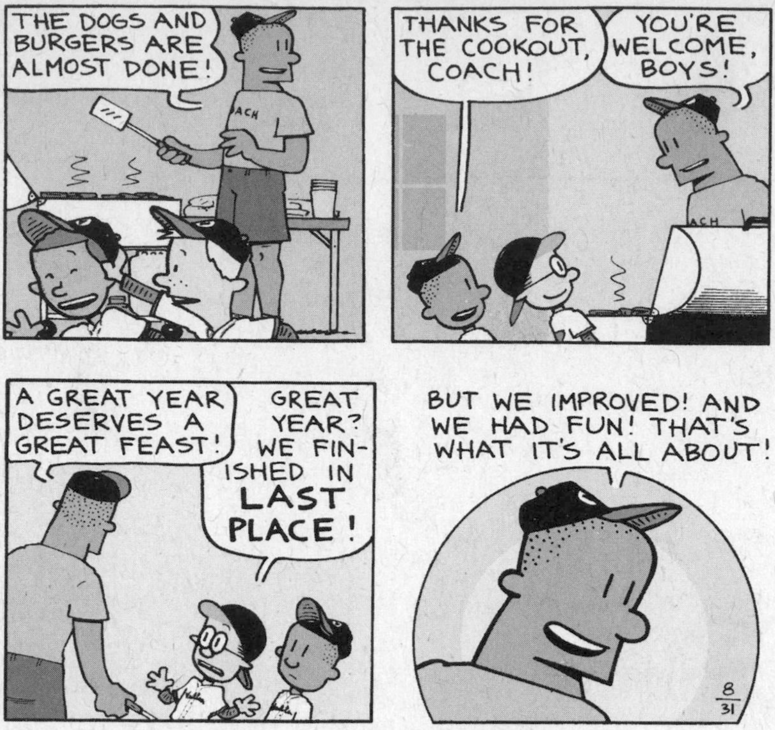
THE DOGS AND BURGERS ARE ALMOST DONE!
THANKS FOR THE COOKOUT, COACH!
YOU'RE WELCOME, BOYS!
A GREAT YEAR DESERVES A GREAT FEAST!
GREAT YEAR? WE FIN-ISHED IN LAST PLACE!
BUT WE IMPROVED! AND WE HAD FUN! THAT'S WHAT IT'S ALL ABOUT!
8/31

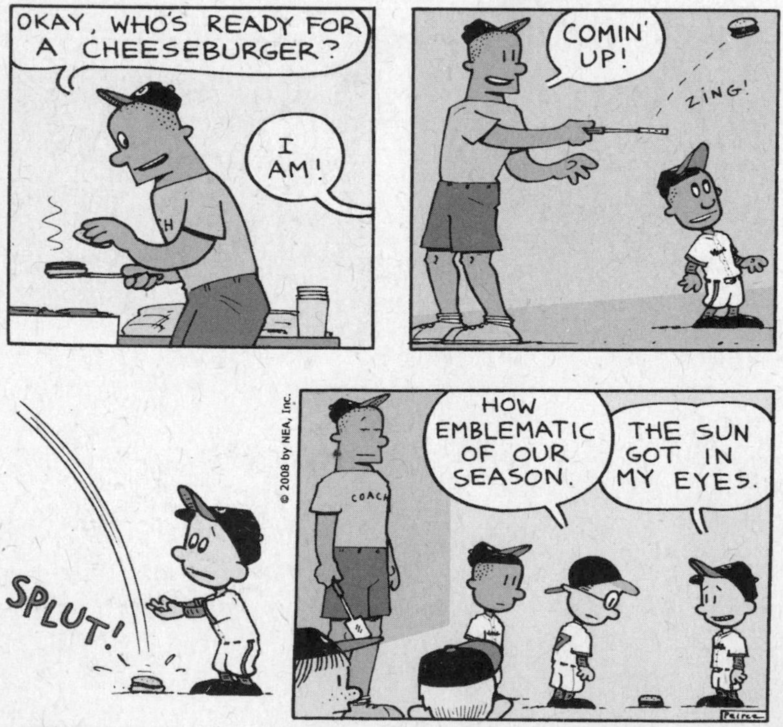
OKAY, WHO'S READY FOR A CHEESEBURGER?
I AM!
COMIN' UP!
ZING!
SPLUT!
HOW EMBLEMATIC OF OUR SEASON.
THE SUN GOT IN MY EYES.

MOLD!

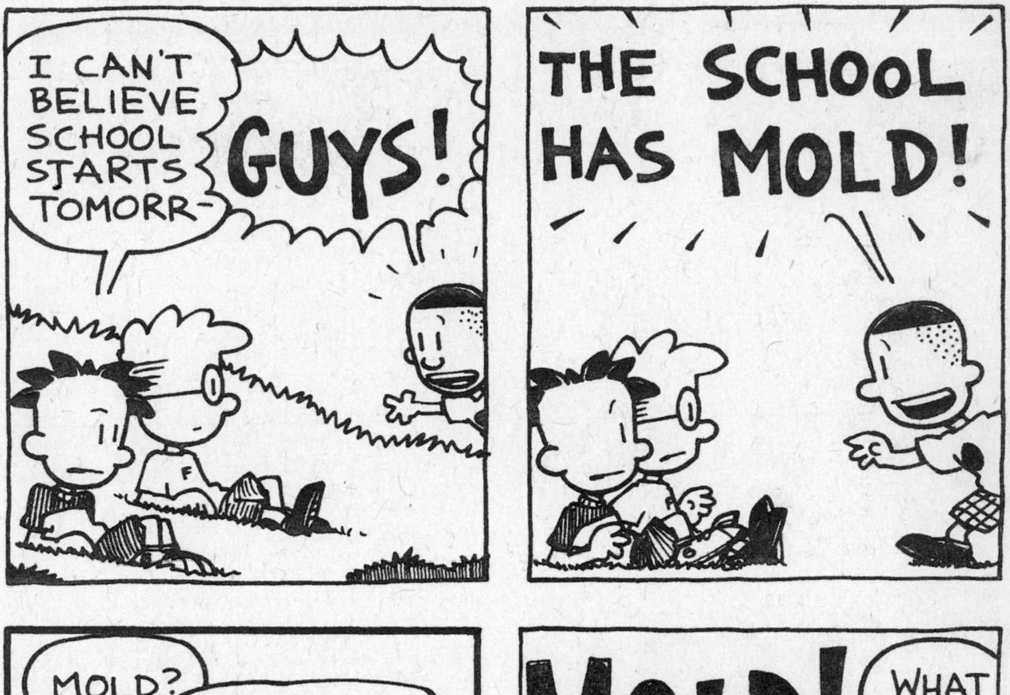

I CAN'T BELIEVE SCHOOL STARTS TOMORR-
GUYS!
THE SCHOOL HAS MOLD!
MOLD?
MOLD!!
MOLD?
MOLD!
!
!
!
MOLD!
WHAT THE...?
© 2008 by NEA, Inc.
9/1
Peirce

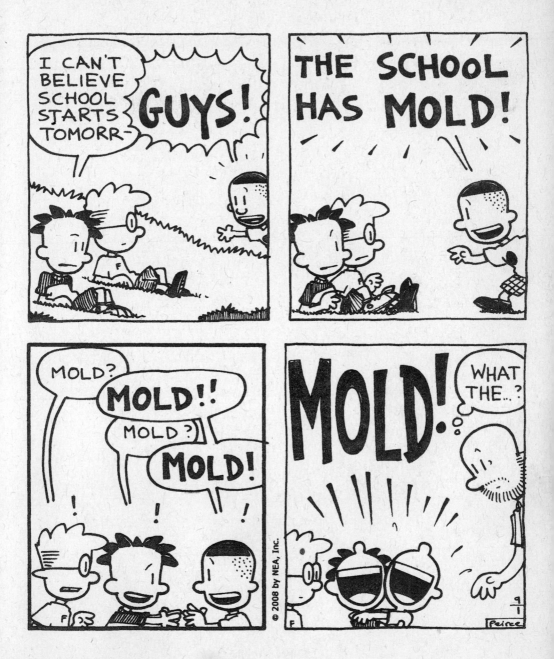

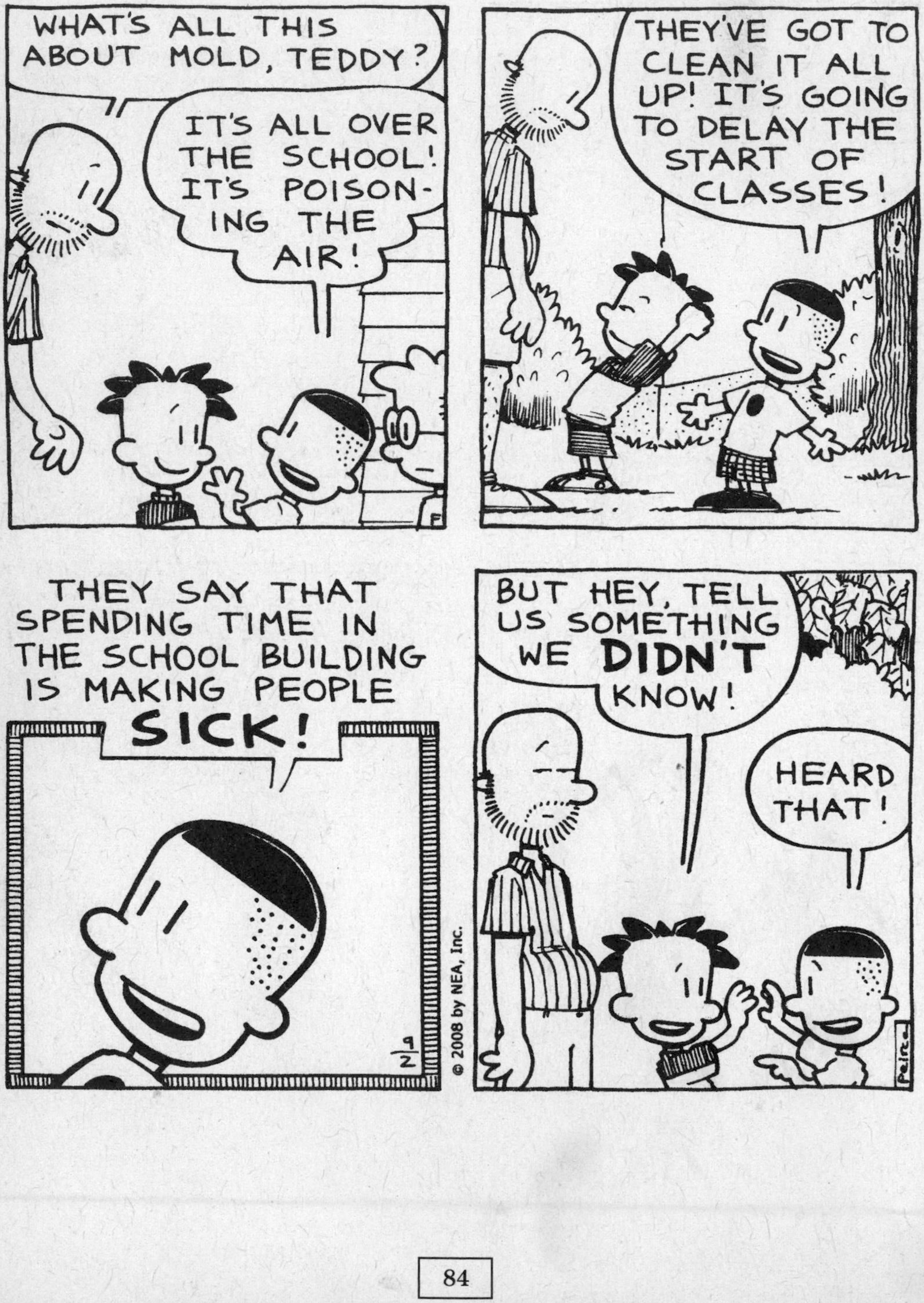
WHAT'S ALL THIS ABOUT MOLD, TEDDY?
IT'S ALL OVER THE SCHOOL! IT'S POISONING THE AIR!
THEY'VE GOT TO CLEAN IT ALL UP! IT'S GOING TO DELAY THE START OF CLASSES!
THEY SAY THAT SPENDING TIME IN THE SCHOOL BUILDING IS MAKING PEOPLE **SICK!**
© 2008 by NEA, Inc.
BUT HEY, TELL US SOMETHING WE **DIDN'T** KNOW!
HEARD THAT!

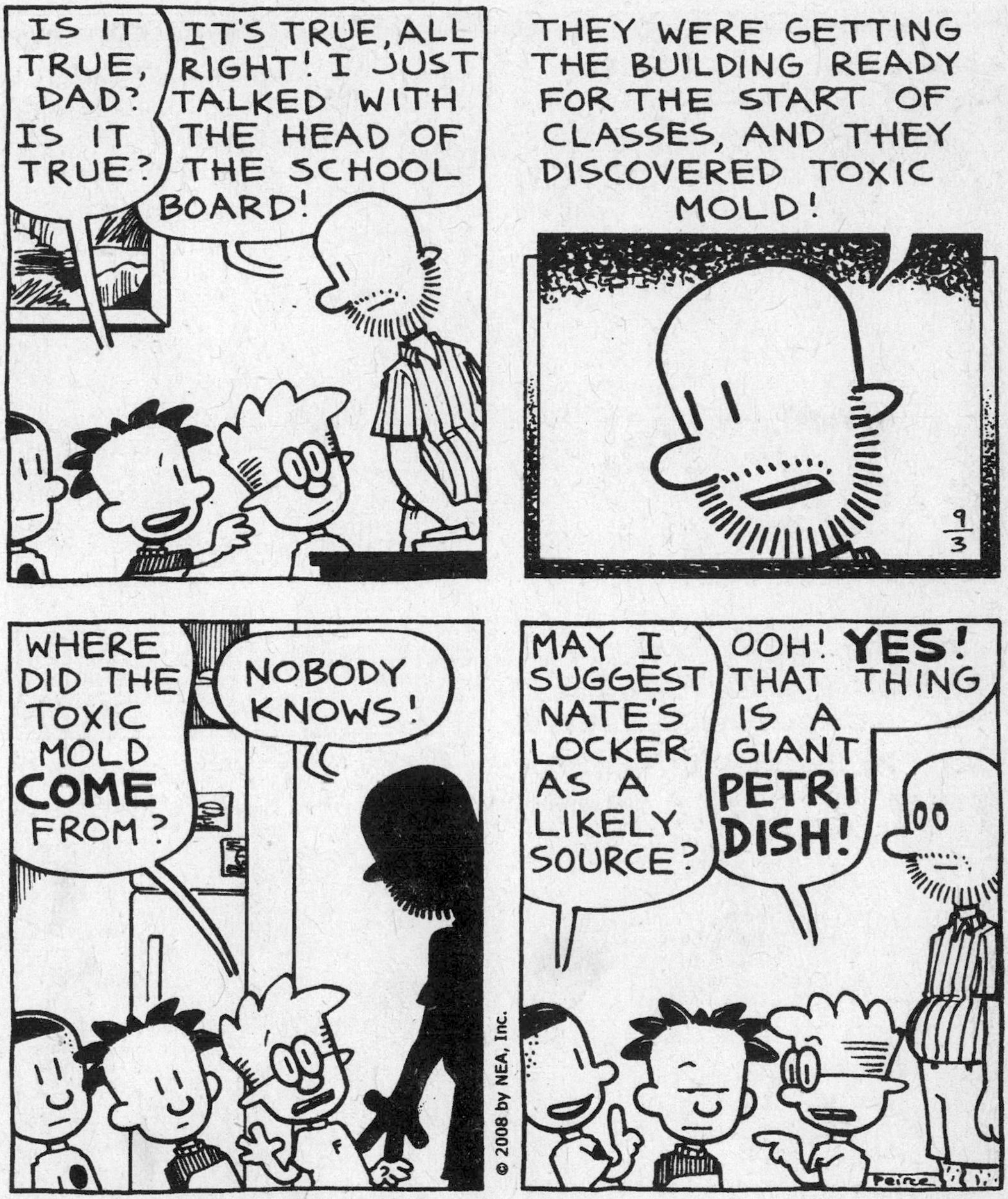
IS IT TRUE, DAD? IS IT TRUE?
IT'S TRUE, ALL RIGHT! I JUST TALKED WITH THE HEAD OF THE SCHOOL BOARD!
THEY WERE GETTING THE BUILDING READY FOR THE START OF CLASSES, AND THEY DISCOVERED TOXIC MOLD!
9/3
WHERE DID THE TOXIC MOLD **COME** FROM?
NOBODY KNOWS!
© 2008 by NEA, Inc.
MAY I SUGGEST NATE'S LOCKER AS A LIKELY SOURCE?
OOH! **YES!** THAT THING IS A GIANT **PETRI DISH!**
PEIRCE

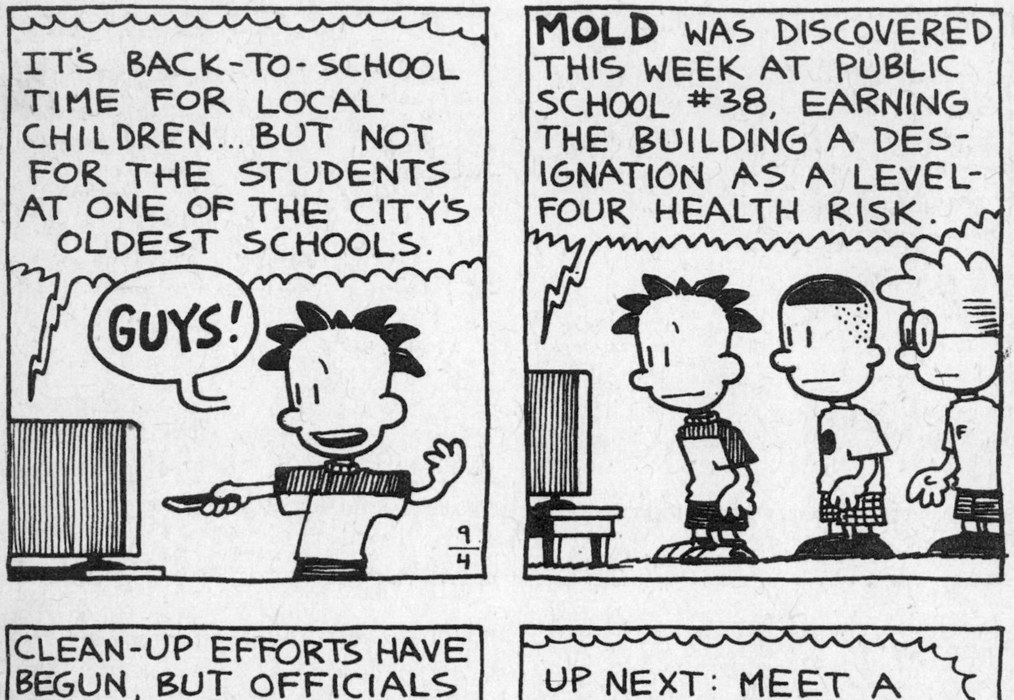
IT'S BACK-TO-SCHOOL TIME FOR LOCAL CHILDREN... BUT NOT FOR THE STUDENTS AT ONE OF THE CITY'S OLDEST SCHOOLS.
GUYS!
9/4
MOLD WAS DISCOVERED THIS WEEK AT PUBLIC SCHOOL #38, EARNING THE BUILDING A DESIGNATION AS A LEVEL-FOUR HEALTH RISK.
CLEAN-UP EFFORTS HAVE BEGUN, BUT OFFICIALS WILL NOT COMMENT ON THE TIMETABLE FOR COMPLETION. FOR NOW, THEY ARE SAYING ONLY THAT THE SCHOOL WILL REMAIN CLOSED "INDEFINITELY."
© 2008 by NEA, Inc.
UP NEXT: MEET A WACKY PARROT WHO SINGS OPERA!
INDEFINITELY!
Peirce

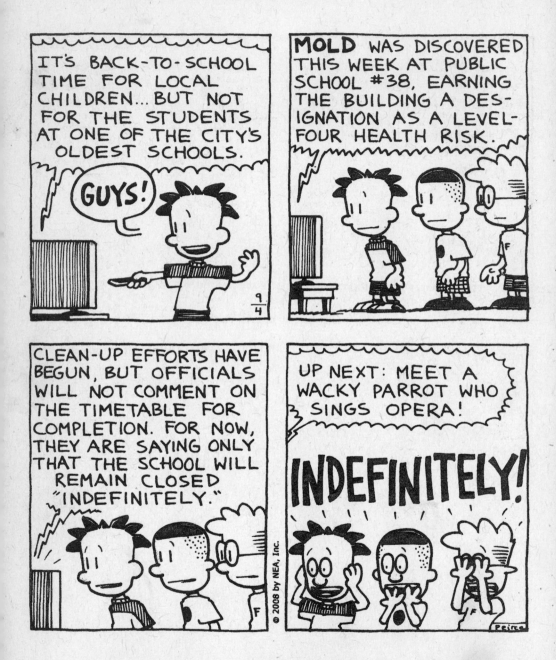

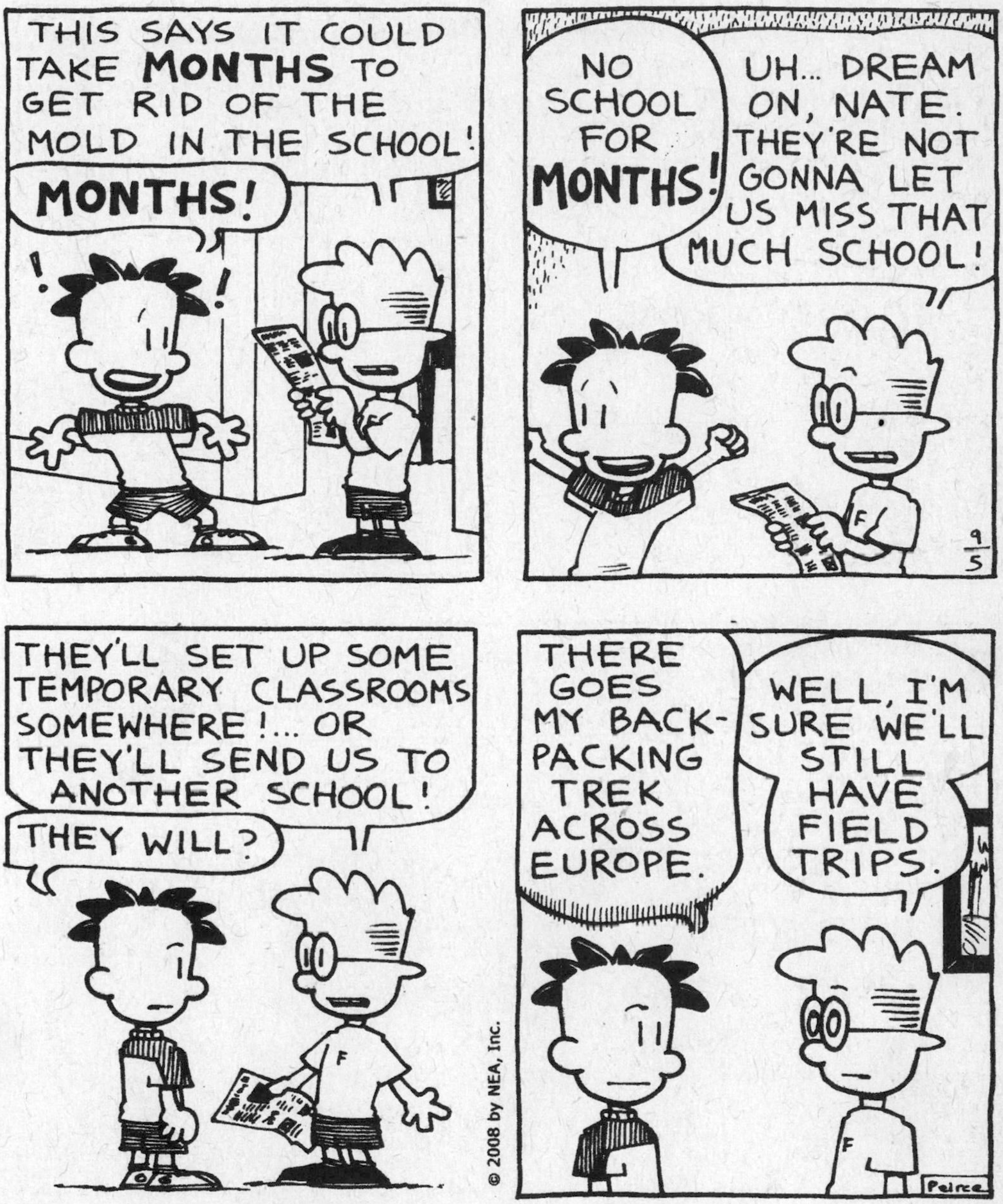
THIS SAYS IT COULD TAKE MONTHS TO GET RID OF THE MOLD IN THE SCHOOL!
MONTHS!
!
!
NO SCHOOL FOR MONTHS!
UH... DREAM ON, NATE. THEY'RE NOT GONNA LET US MISS THAT MUCH SCHOOL!
9/5
THEY'LL SET UP SOME TEMPORARY CLASSROOMS SOMEWHERE!... OR THEY'LL SEND US TO ANOTHER SCHOOL!
THEY WILL?
THERE GOES MY BACK-PACKING TREK ACROSS EUROPE.
WELL, I'M SURE WE'LL STILL HAVE FIELD TRIPS.
Peirce

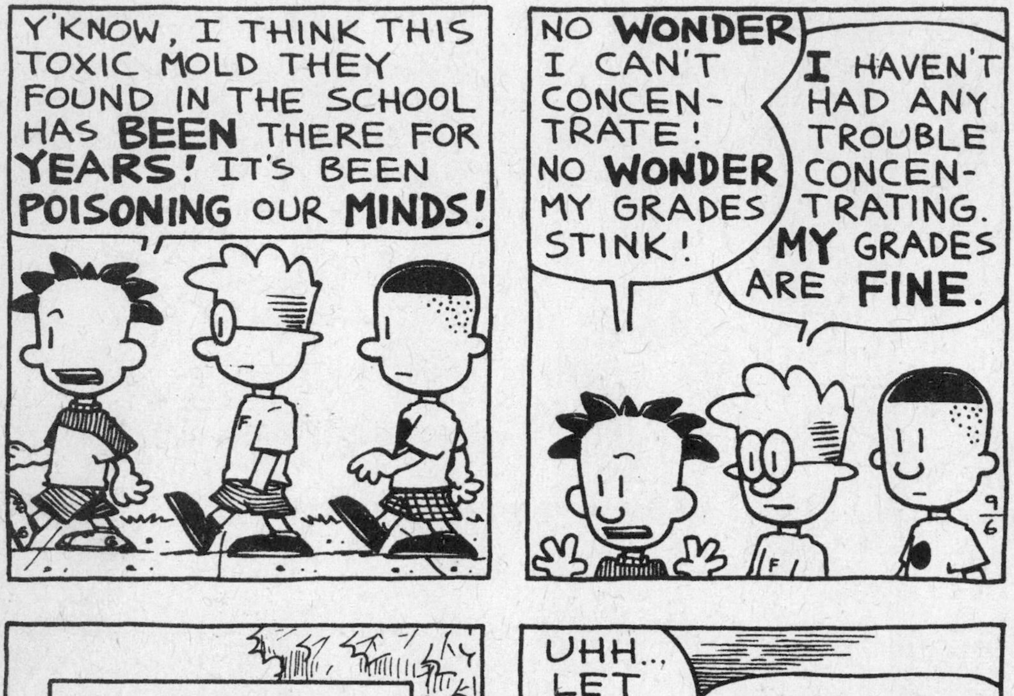
Y'KNOW, I THINK THIS TOXIC MOLD THEY FOUND IN THE SCHOOL HAS BEEN THERE FOR YEARS! IT'S BEEN POISONING OUR MINDS!
NO WONDER I CAN'T CONCENTRATE! NO WONDER MY GRADES STINK!
I HAVEN'T HAD ANY TROUBLE CONCENTRATING. MY GRADES ARE FINE.
9/6
HOW DO YOU EXPLAIN THAT?
© 2008 by NEA, Inc.
UHH... LET ME THINK.
THIS COULD TAKE A WHILE!
HE'S GOT MOLD ON THE BRAIN!
Peirce

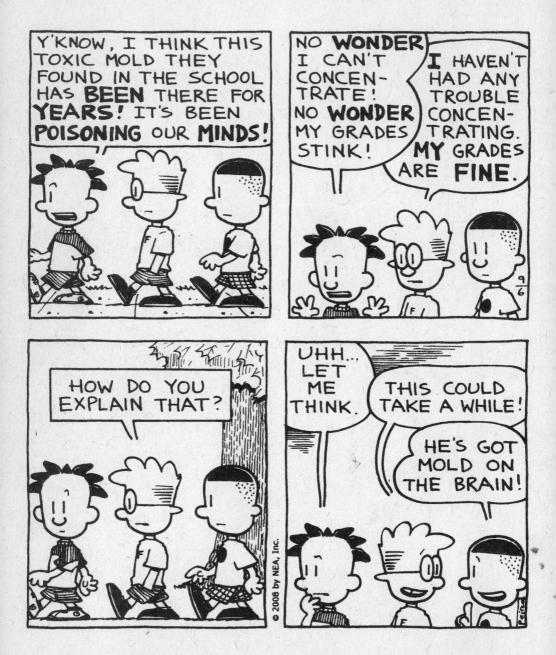

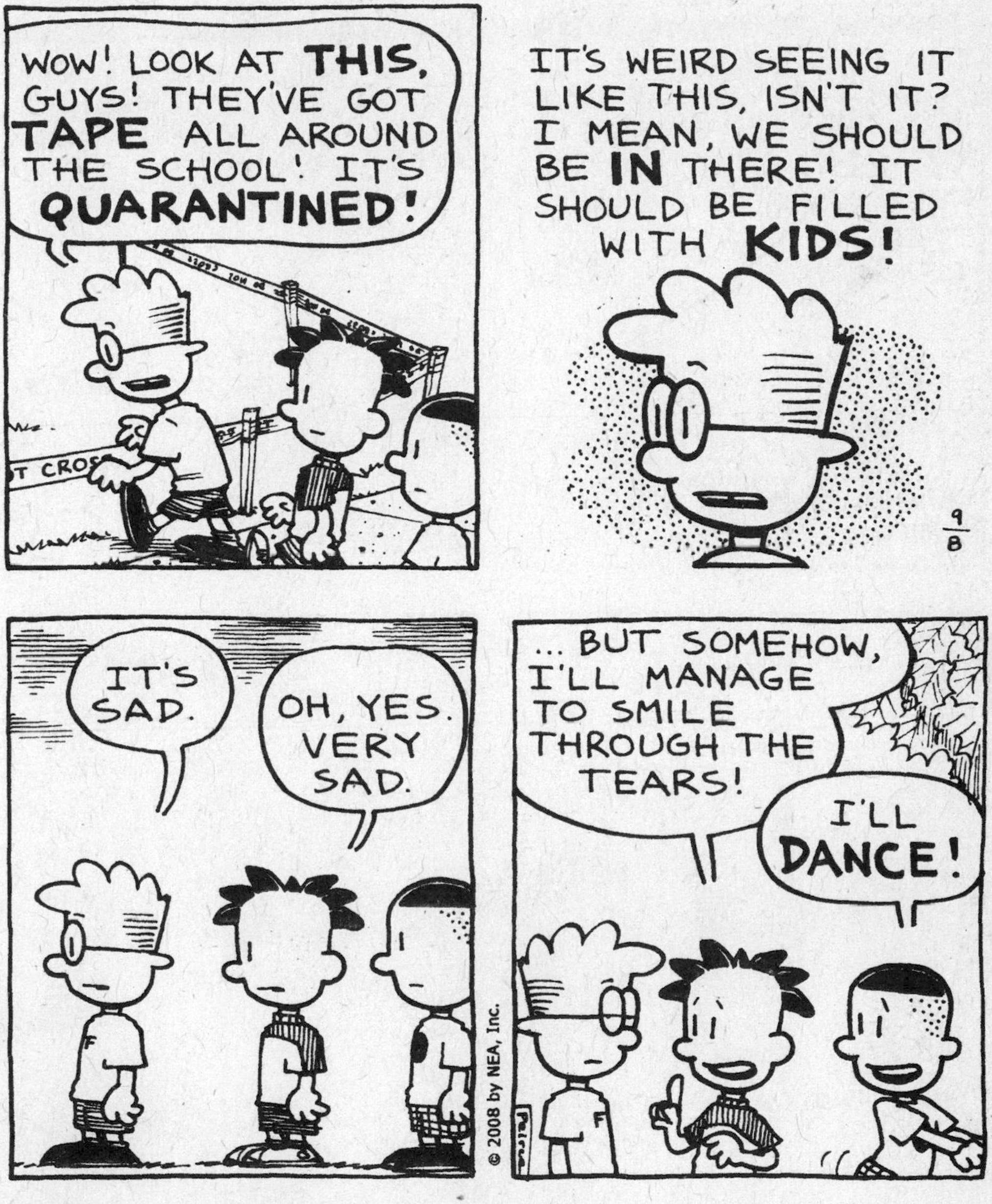
WOW! LOOK AT **THIS**, GUYS! THEY'VE GOT **TAPE** ALL AROUND THE SCHOOL! IT'S **QUARANTINED**!
IT'S WEIRD SEEING IT LIKE THIS, ISN'T IT? I MEAN, WE SHOULD BE **IN** THERE! IT SHOULD BE FILLED WITH **KIDS**!
9/8
IT'S SAD.
OH, YES. VERY SAD.
... BUT SOMEHOW, I'LL MANAGE TO SMILE THROUGH THE TEARS!
I'LL **DANCE**!
© 2008 by NEA, Inc.

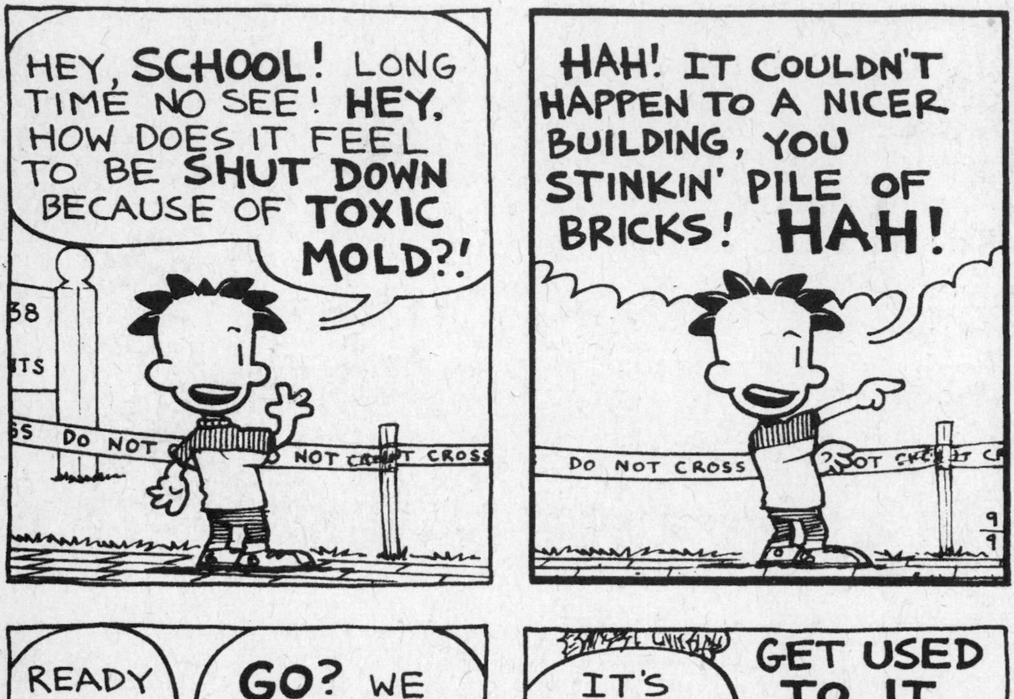
HEY, SCHOOL! LONG TIME NO SEE! HEY, HOW DOES IT FEEL TO BE SHUT DOWN BECAUSE OF TOXIC MOLD?!
DO NOT CROSS
HAH! IT COULDN'T HAPPEN TO A NICER BUILDING, YOU STINKIN' PILE OF BRICKS! HAH!
DO NOT CROSS
READY TO GO?
GO? WE JUST GOT HERE! I'M JUST WARMING UP!
© 2008 by NEA, Inc.
IT'S PAYBACK TIME.
GET USED TO IT, CHUMP! I'M HERE ALL WEEK!

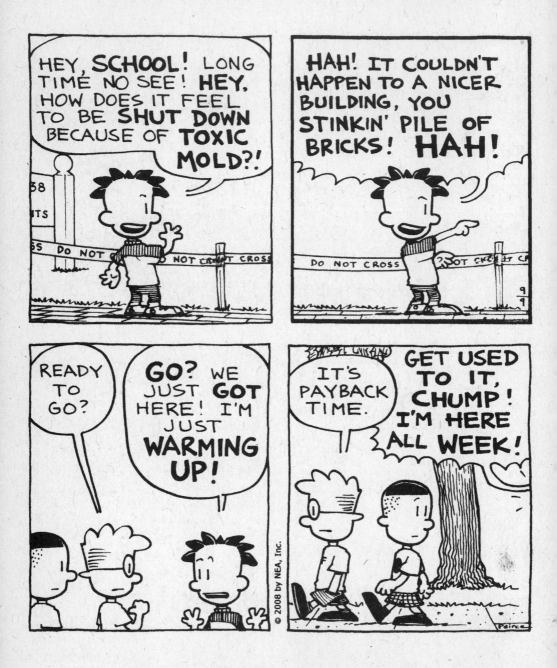

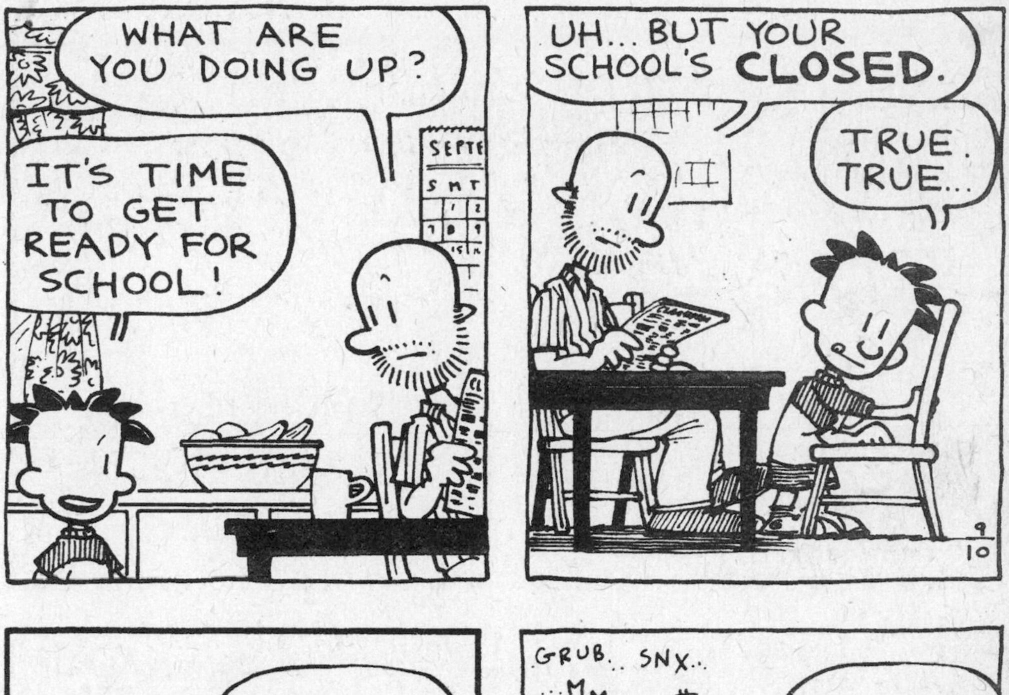
WHAT ARE YOU DOING UP?
IT'S TIME TO GET READY FOR SCHOOL!
UH... BUT YOUR SCHOOL'S **CLOSED**.
TRUE. TRUE...
...BUT **ELLEN'S** ISN'T!
GRUB... SNX... ...MMMPH... ZZZZZZ
COULDN'T MISS **THIS!**
© 2008 by NEA, Inc.

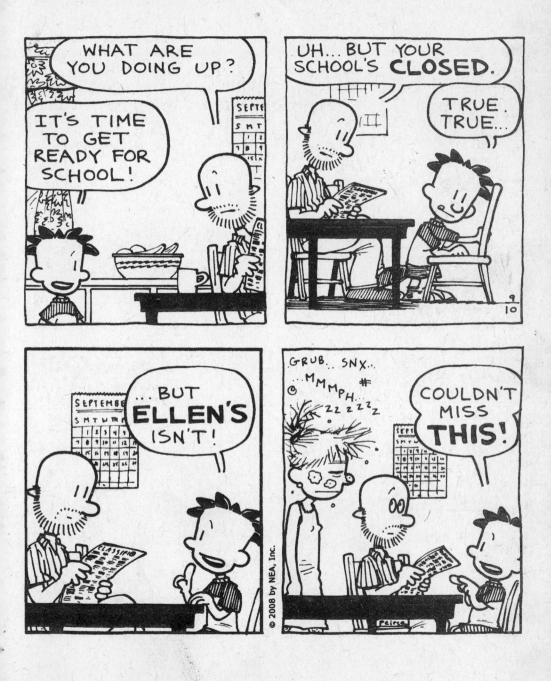

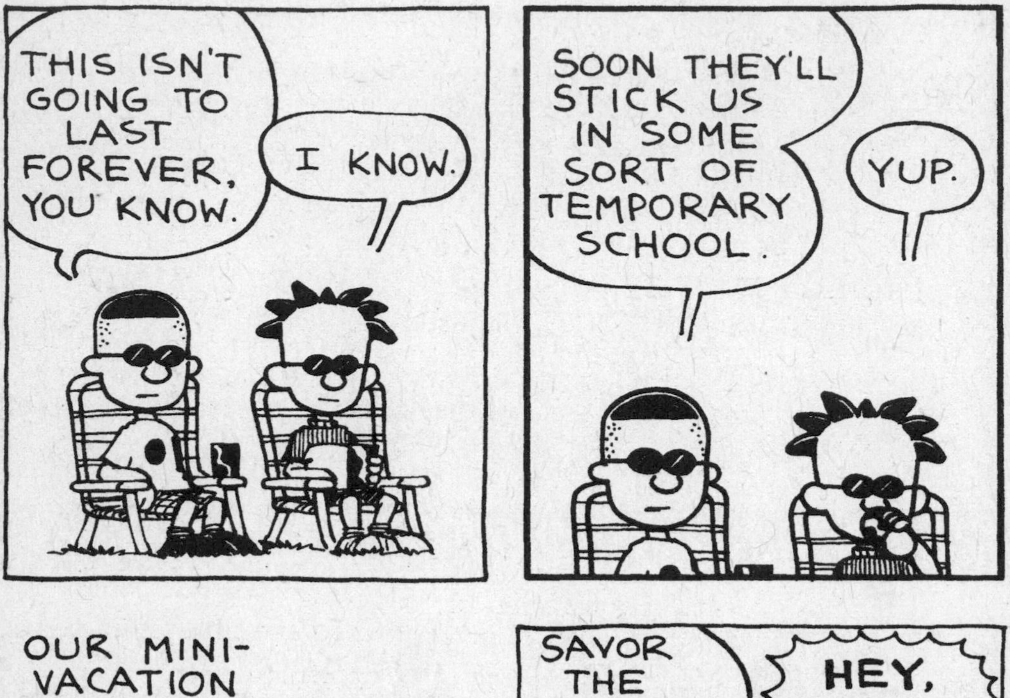
THIS ISN'T GOING TO LAST FOREVER, YOU KNOW.
I KNOW.
SOON THEY'LL STICK US IN SOME SORT OF TEMPORARY SCHOOL.
YUP.
OUR MINI-VACATION BECAUSE OF THE TOXIC MOLD WILL BE OVER.
UH-HUH.
SAVOR THE AWESOMENESS.
KLINK!
HEY, ELLEN! STUDY HARD!
9/11
Peirce

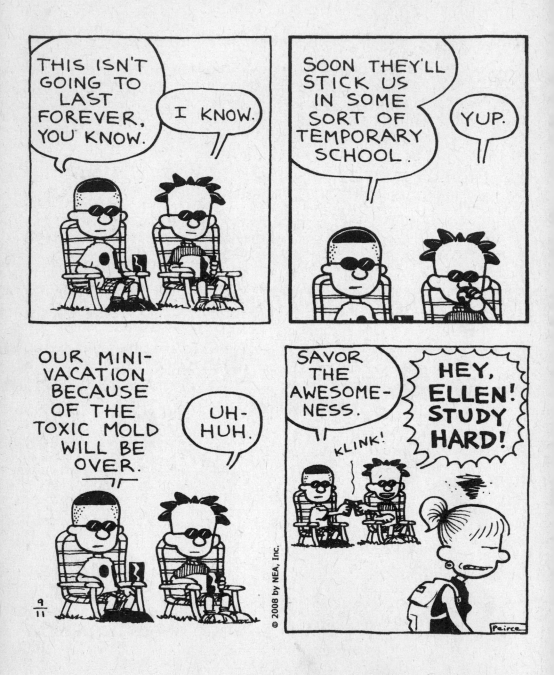

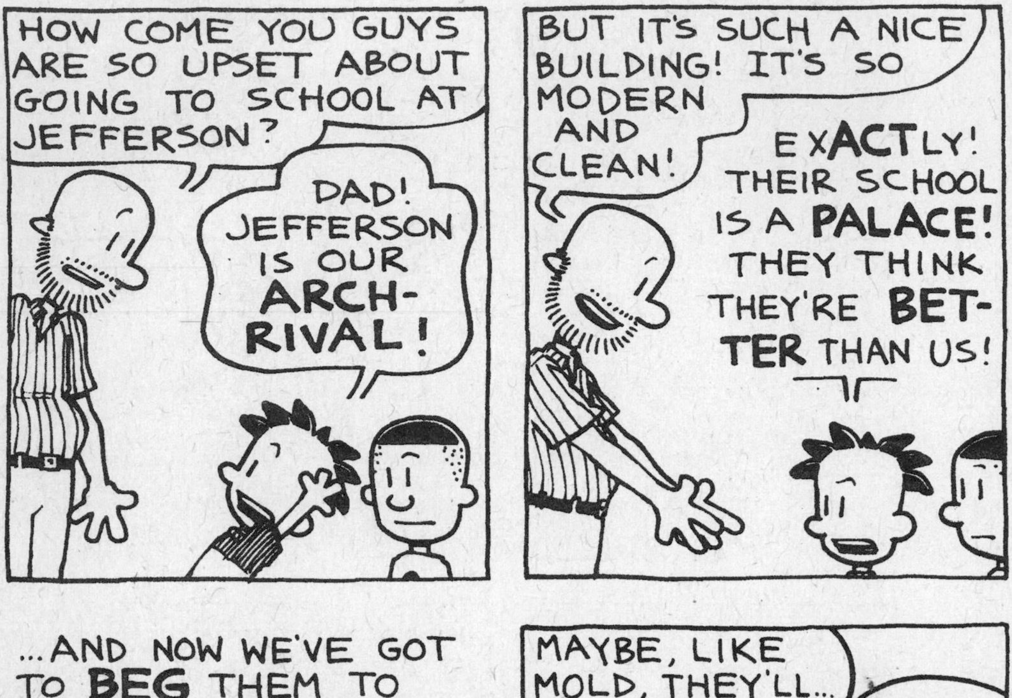
HOW COME YOU GUYS ARE SO UPSET ABOUT GOING TO SCHOOL AT JEFFERSON?
DAD! JEFFERSON IS OUR ARCH-RIVAL!
BUT IT'S SUCH A NICE BUILDING! IT'S SO MODERN AND CLEAN!
EXACTLY! THEIR SCHOOL IS A PALACE! THEY THINK THEY'RE BETTER THAN US!
...AND NOW WE'VE GOT TO BEG THEM TO SPARE US A FEW STINKIN' CLASSROOMS BECAUSE OUR SCHOOL HAS MOLD!
9/13
MAYBE, LIKE MOLD, THEY'LL... HA HA!... GROW ON YOU!
NICE, DAD. WAY TO MAKE LIGHT OF OUR SHAME.
Peirce
© 2008 by NEA, Inc.

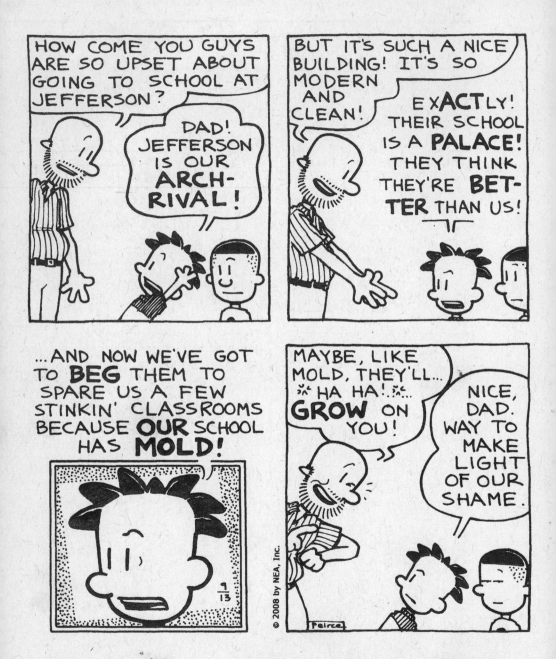

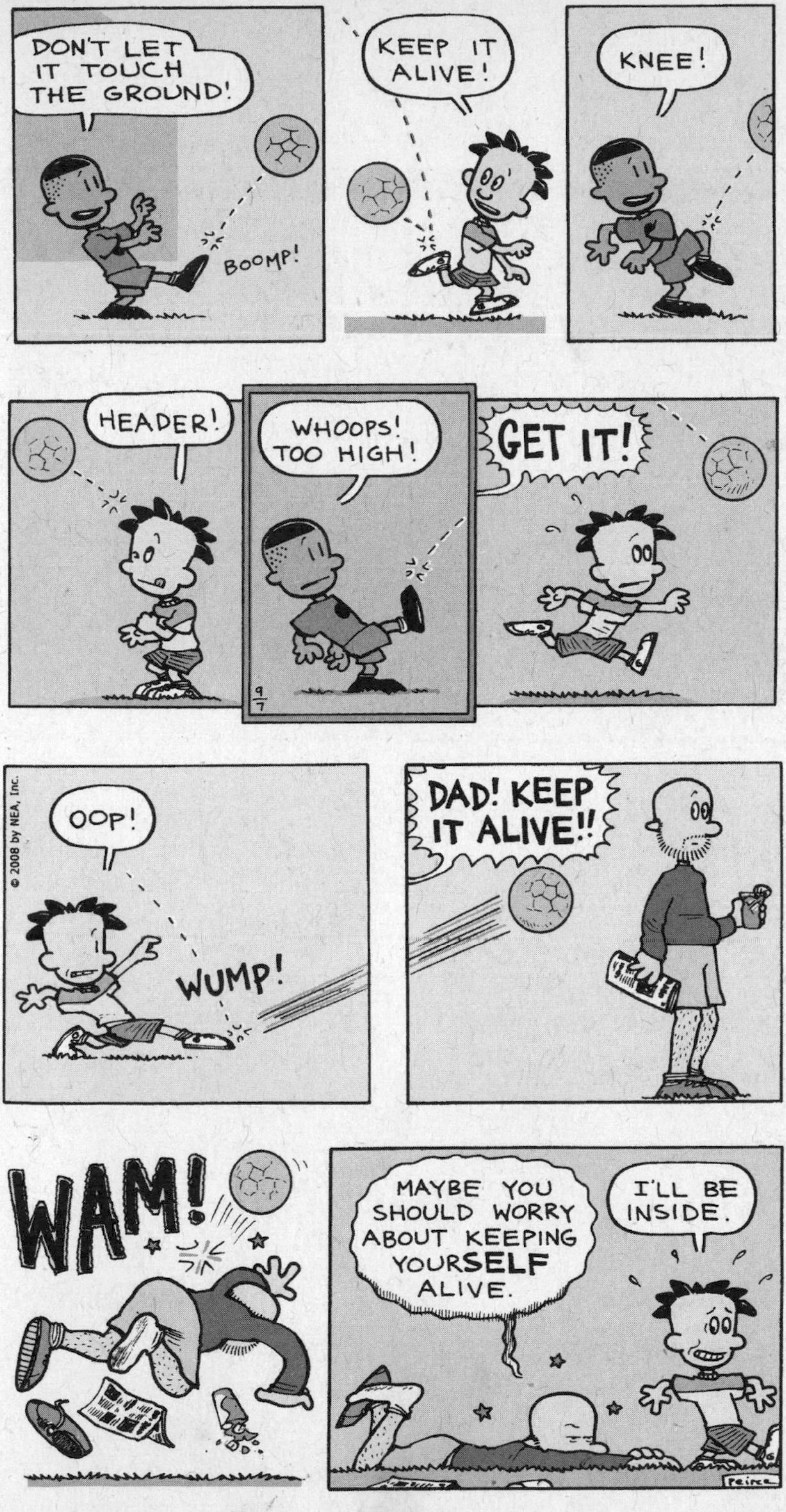
DON'T LET IT TOUCH THE GROUND!
BOOMP!
KEEP IT ALIVE!
KNEE!
HEADER!
WHOOPS! TOO HIGH!
9/7
GET IT!
© 2008 by NEA, Inc.
OOP!
WUMP!
DAD! KEEP IT ALIVE!!
WAM!
MAYBE YOU SHOULD WORRY ABOUT KEEPING YOURSELF ALIVE.
I'LL BE INSIDE.
Peirce

WHAT A DUMP

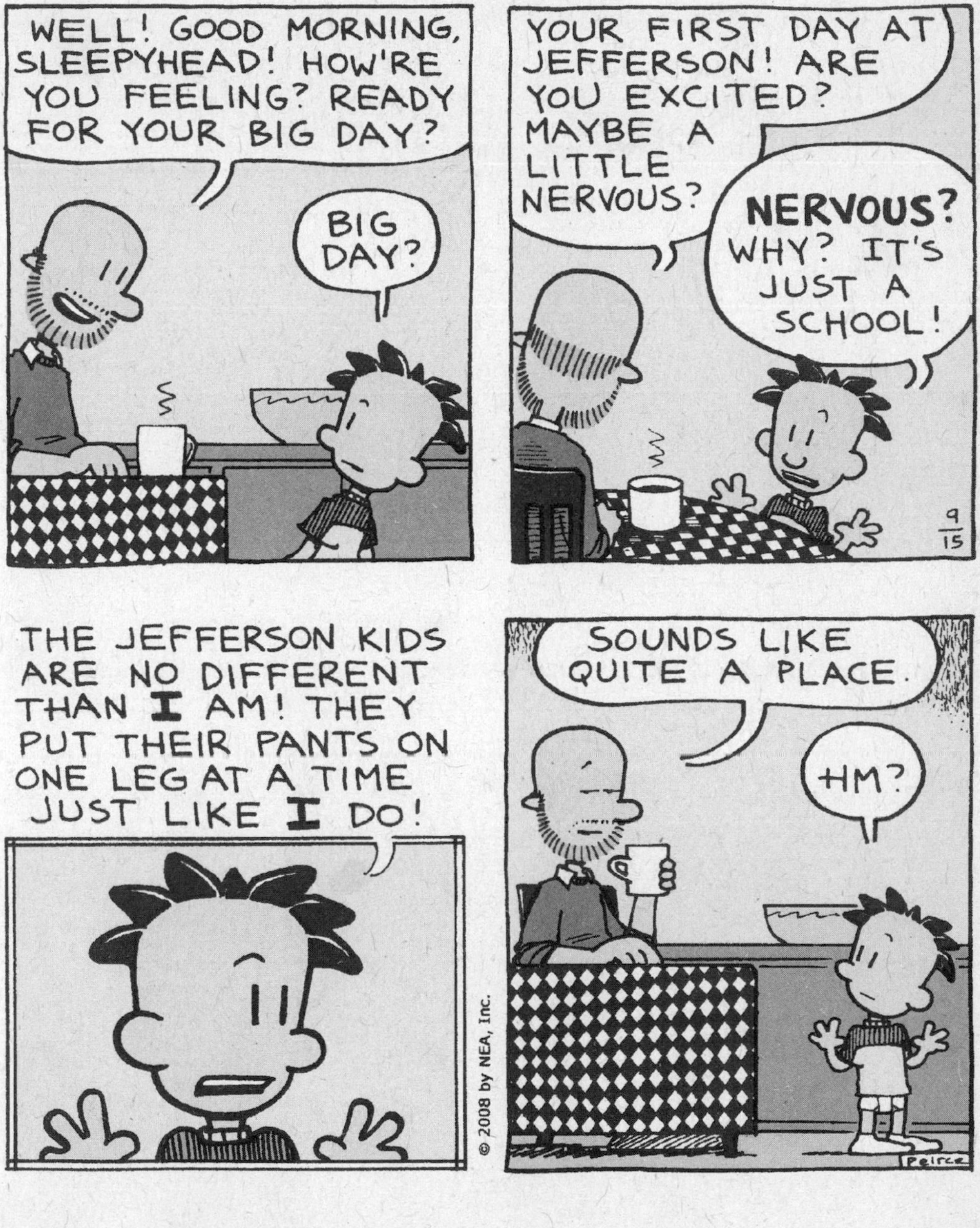
WELL! GOOD MORNING, SLEEPYHEAD! HOW'RE YOU FEELING? READY FOR YOUR BIG DAY?
BIG DAY?
YOUR FIRST DAY AT JEFFERSON! ARE YOU EXCITED? MAYBE A LITTLE NERVOUS?
NERVOUS? WHY? IT'S JUST A SCHOOL!
9/15
THE JEFFERSON KIDS ARE NO DIFFERENT THAN **I** AM! THEY PUT THEIR PANTS ON ONE LEG AT A TIME JUST LIKE **I** DO!
SOUNDS LIKE QUITE A PLACE.
HM?
Peirce

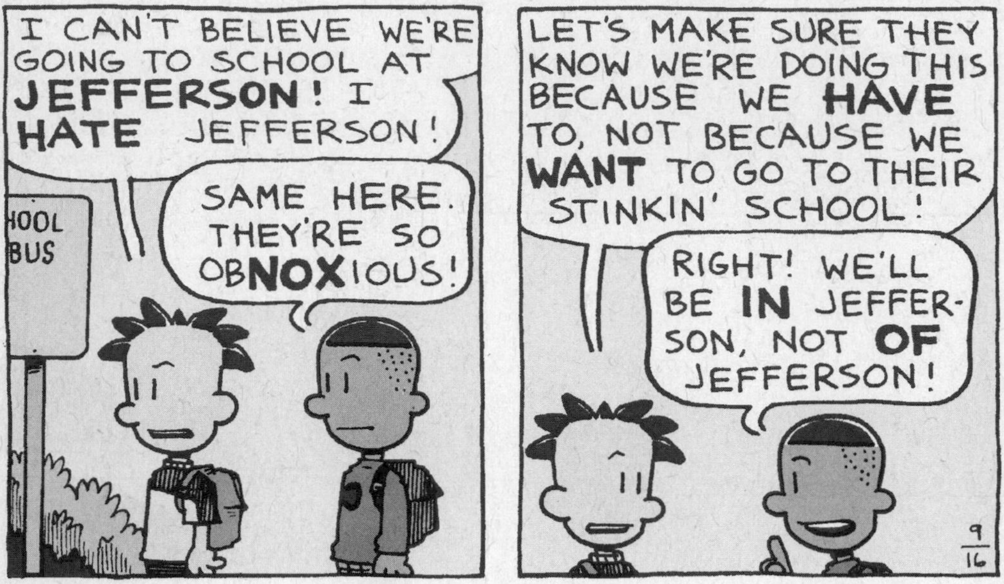
I CAN'T BELIEVE WE'RE GOING TO SCHOOL AT **JEFFERSON**! I **HATE** JEFFERSON!
SAME HERE. THEY'RE SO OB**NOX**IOUS!
LET'S MAKE SURE THEY KNOW WE'RE DOING THIS BECAUSE WE **HAVE** TO, NOT BECAUSE WE **WANT** TO GO TO THEIR STINKIN' SCHOOL!
RIGHT! WE'LL BE **IN** JEFFERSON, NOT **OF** JEFFERSON!
9/16

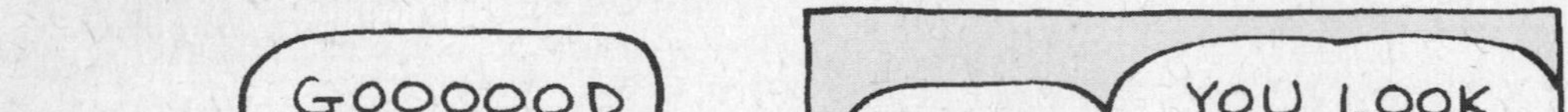
GOOOOOD MORNING, LADS!
SCHOOL SPIRIT!
YOU LOOK LIKE A REJECT FROM AN "ALVIN & THE CHIPMUNKS" AUDITION.

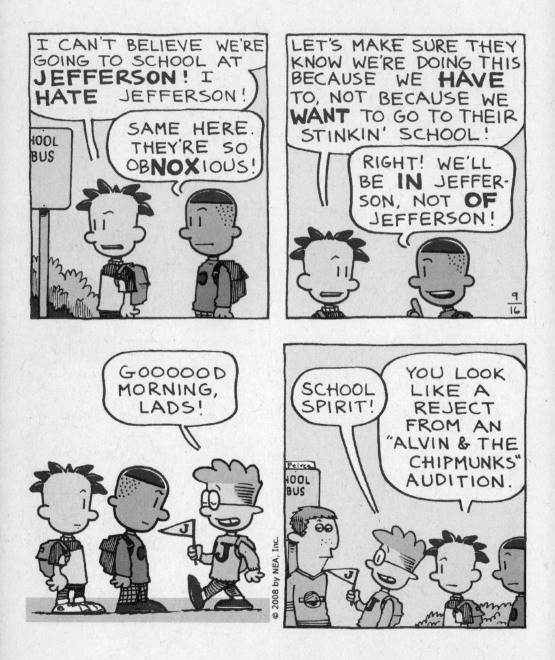

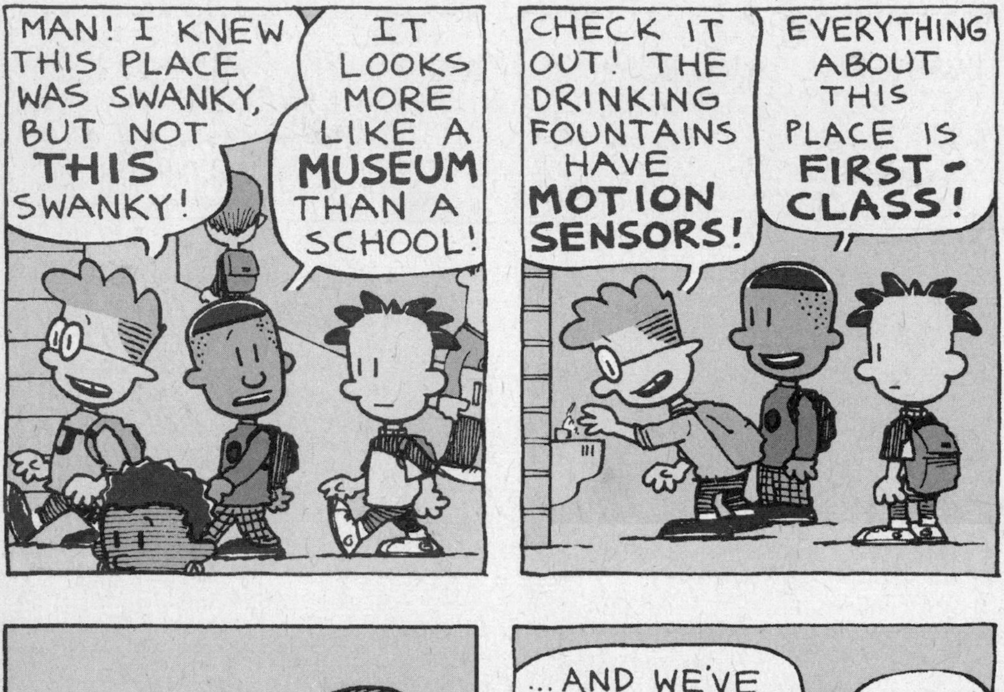
MAN! I KNEW THIS PLACE WAS SWANKY, BUT NOT **THIS** SWANKY!
IT LOOKS MORE LIKE A **MUSEUM** THAN A SCHOOL!
CHECK IT OUT! THE DRINKING FOUNTAINS HAVE **MOTION SENSORS!**
EVERYTHING ABOUT THIS PLACE IS **FIRST-CLASS!**
9/18
© 2008 by NEA, Inc.
...AND WE'VE JUST BEEN DOWNGRADED TO ECONOMY.
WHAT A DUMP.
Peirce

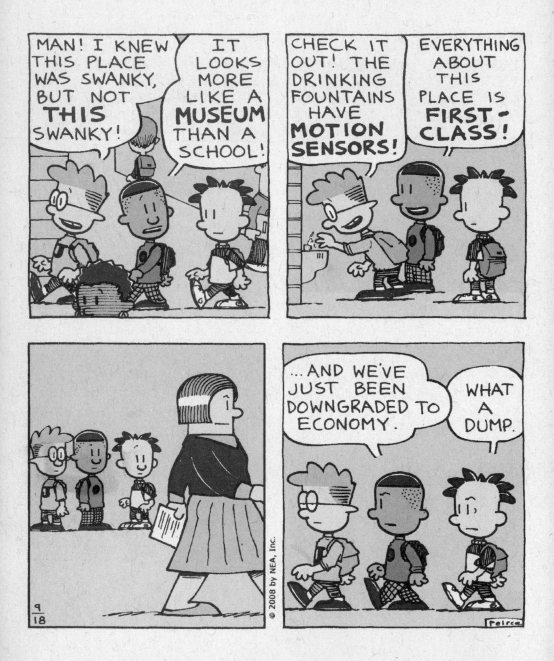

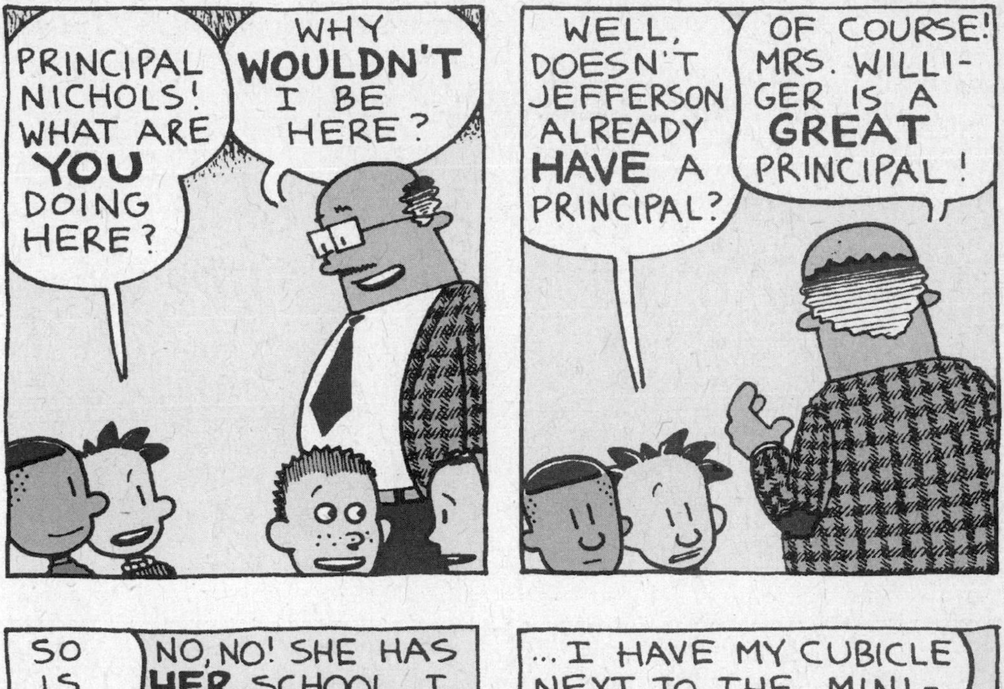
PRINCIPAL NICHOLS! WHAT ARE **YOU** DOING HERE?
WHY **WOULDN'T** I BE HERE?
WELL, DOESN'T JEFFERSON ALREADY **HAVE** A PRINCIPAL?
OF COURSE! MRS. WILLIGER IS A **GREAT** PRINCIPAL!
SO IS SHE YOUR BOSS?
NO, NO! SHE HAS **HER** SCHOOL, I HAVE MINE! SHE HAS **HER** STUDENTS, I HAVE MINE! SHE HAS **HER** OFFICE...
9/19
© 2008 by NEA, Inc.
...I HAVE MY CUBICLE NEXT TO THE MINI-FRIDGE IN THE COPIER ROOM.
SHE'S HIS BOSS.
Peirce

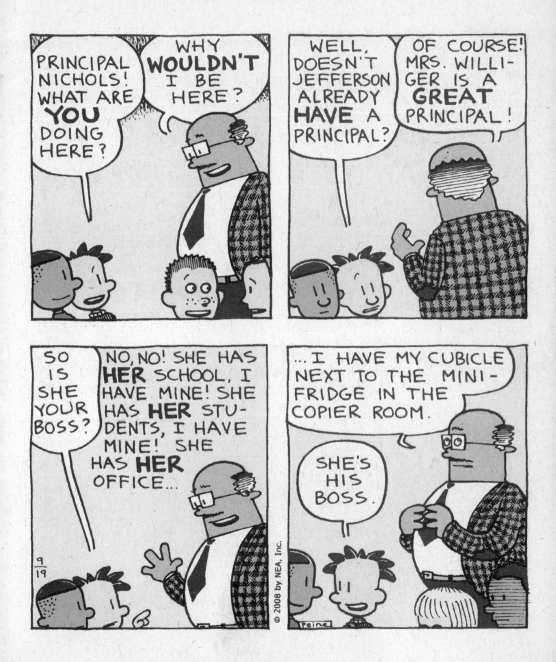

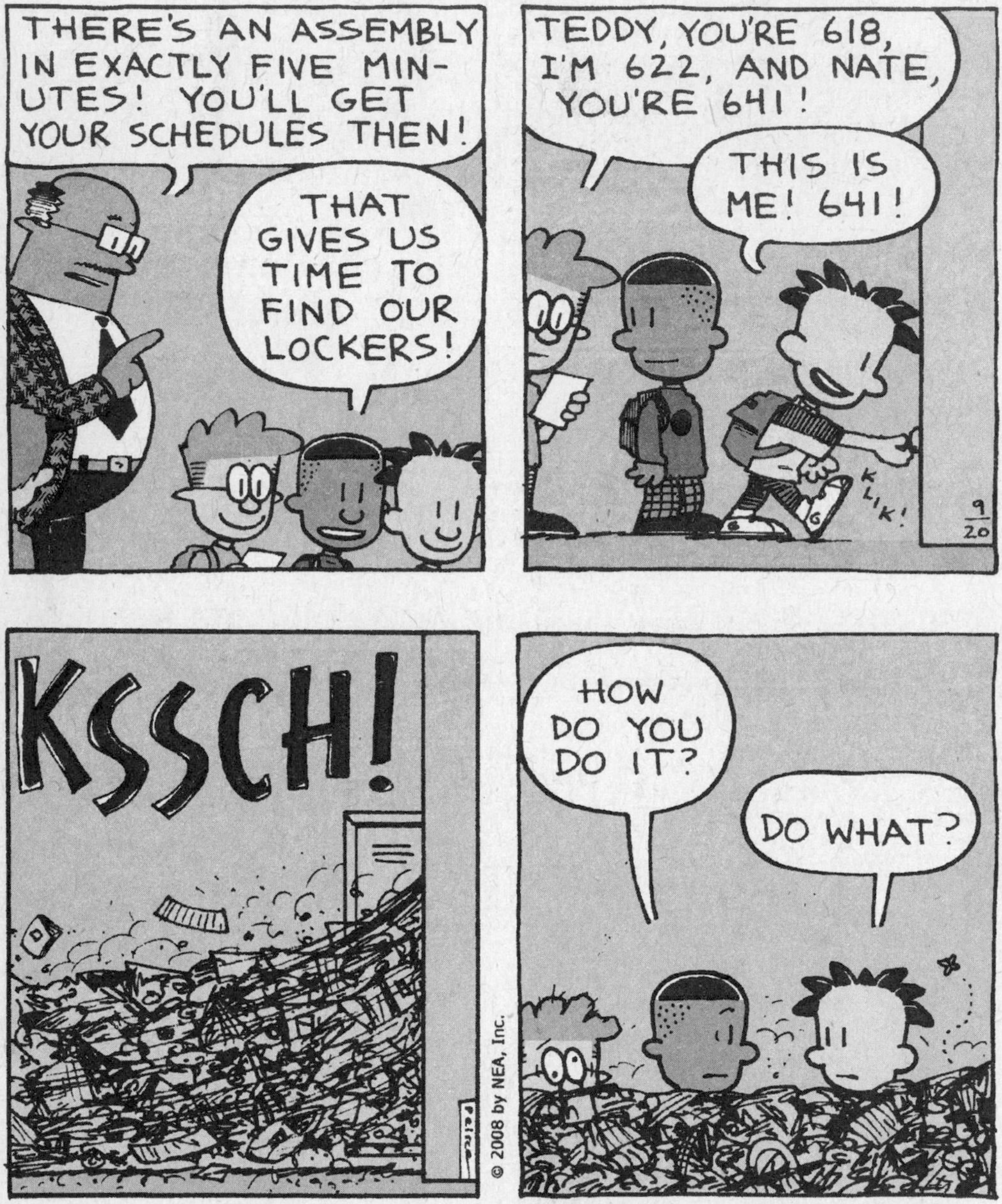
THERE'S AN ASSEMBLY IN EXACTLY FIVE MIN-UTES! YOU'LL GET YOUR SCHEDULES THEN!
THAT GIVES US TIME TO FIND OUR LOCKERS!
TEDDY, YOU'RE 618, I'M 622, AND NATE, YOU'RE 641!
THIS IS ME! 641!
KLIK!
9/20
KSSCH!
© 2008 by NEA, Inc.
HOW DO YOU DO IT?
DO WHAT?

LUCKY, LUCKIER, LUCKIEST

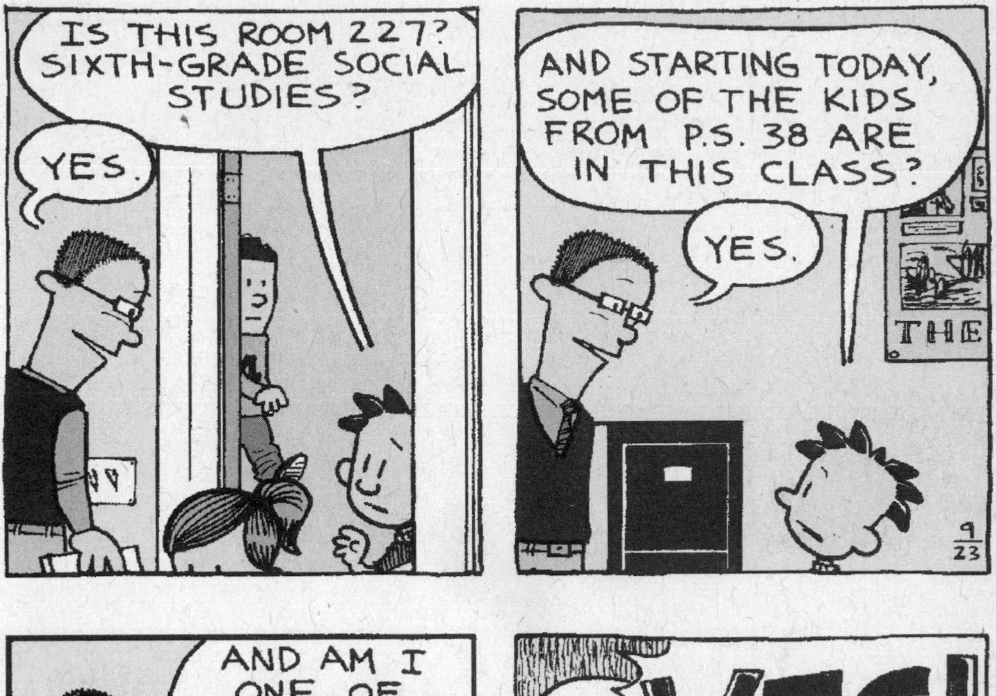
IS THIS ROOM 227? SIXTH-GRADE SOCIAL STUDIES?
YES.
AND STARTING TODAY, SOME OF THE KIDS FROM P.S. 38 ARE IN THIS CLASS?
YES.
THE
9/23
AND AM I ONE OF THOSE KIDS? NATE WRIGHT?
UHHH...
© 2008 by NEA, Inc.
YES
YES!
Peirce

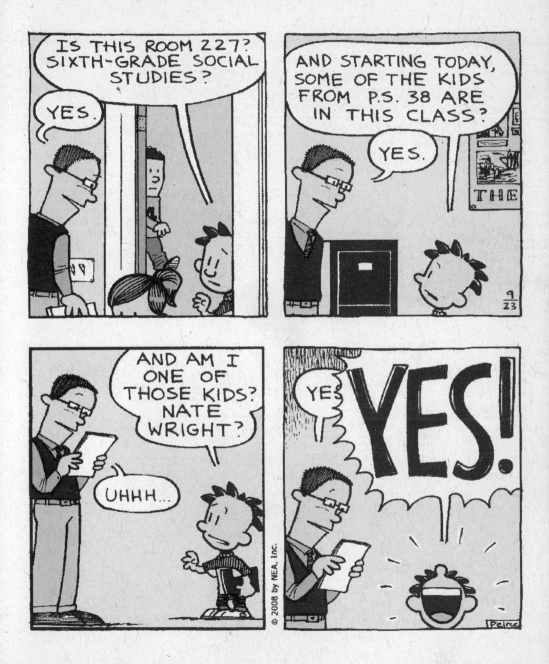

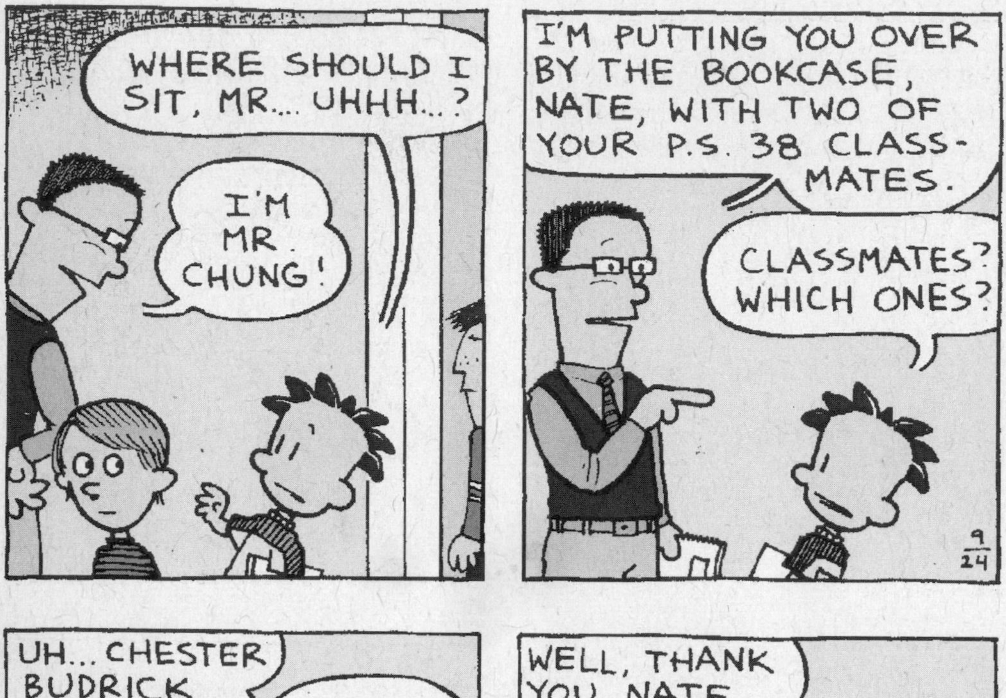
WHERE SHOULD I SIT, MR.... UHHH...?
I'M MR. CHUNG!
I'M PUTTING YOU OVER BY THE BOOKCASE, NATE, WITH TWO OF YOUR P.S. 38 CLASS-MATES.
CLASSMATES? WHICH ONES?
9
24
UH... CHESTER BUDRICK AND GINA HEMPHILL.
OKAY, JUST A WORD TO THE WISE: GINA'S A TOTAL SUCK-UP.
© 2008 by NEA, Inc.
WELL, THANK YOU, NATE, I'LL KEEP THAT IN...
AND CHESTER'S A PSYCHO. TRY NOT TO MAKE EYE CON-TACT.
peirce

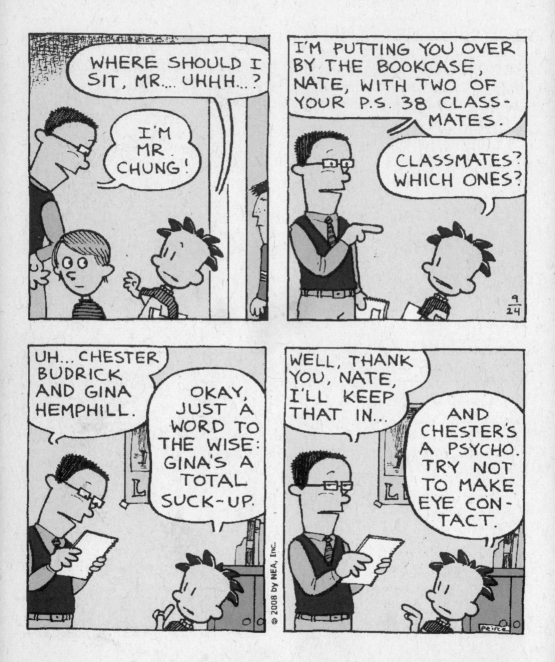

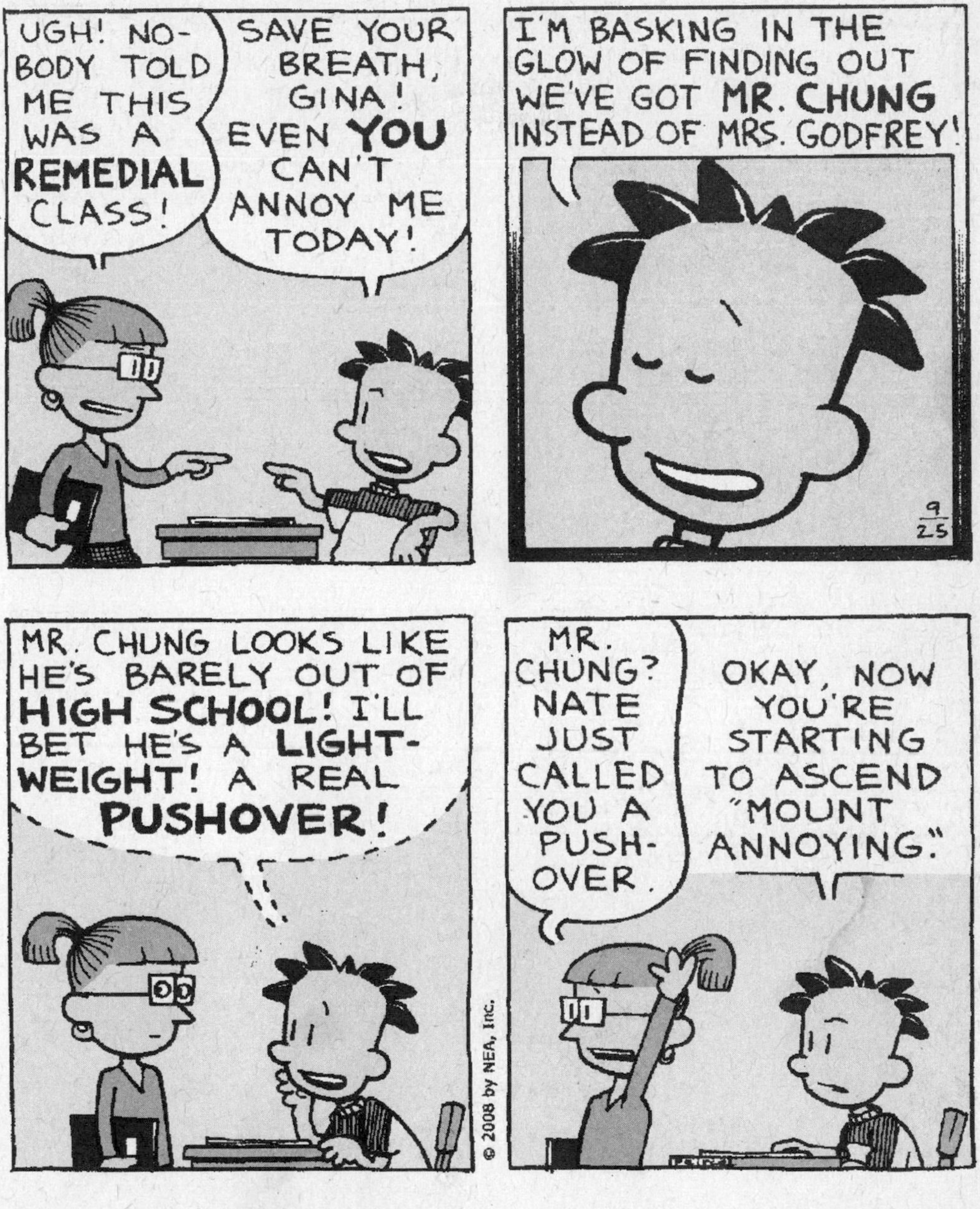
UGH! NOBODY TOLD ME THIS WAS A **REMEDIAL** CLASS!
SAVE YOUR BREATH, GINA! EVEN **YOU** CAN'T ANNOY ME TODAY!
I'M BASKING IN THE GLOW OF FINDING OUT WE'VE GOT **MR. CHUNG** INSTEAD OF MRS. GODFREY!
9/25
MR. CHUNG LOOKS LIKE HE'S BARELY OUT OF **HIGH SCHOOL**! I'LL BET HE'S A **LIGHT-WEIGHT**! A REAL **PUSHOVER**!
© 2008 by NEA, Inc.
MR. CHUNG? NATE JUST CALLED YOU A PUSH-OVER.
OKAY, NOW YOU'RE STARTING TO ASCEND "MOUNT ANNOYING."

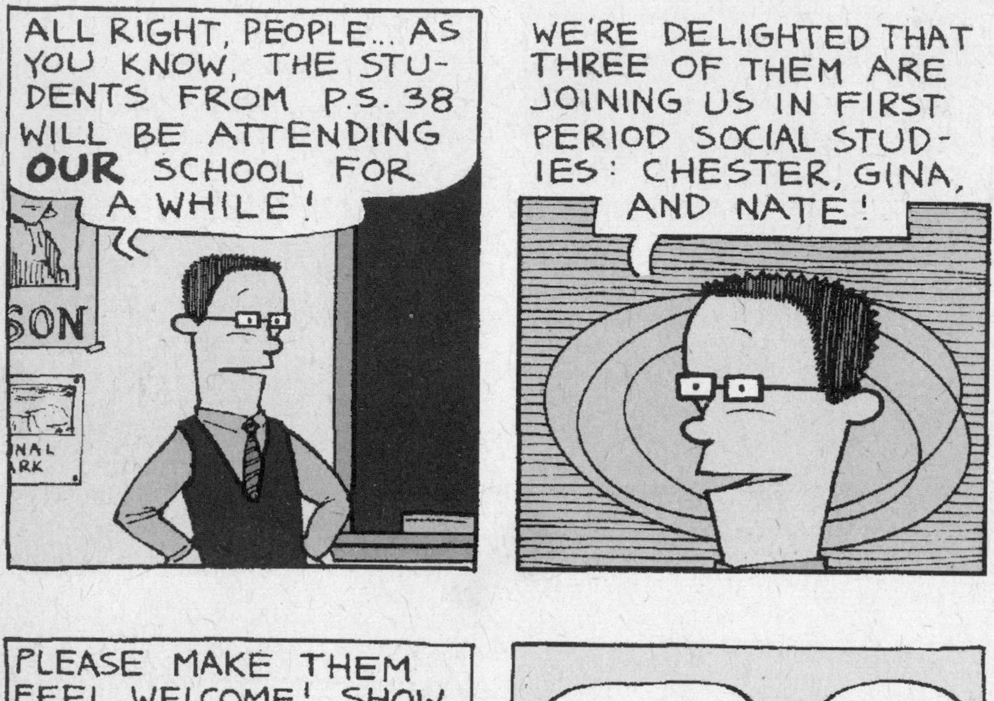
ALL RIGHT, PEOPLE... AS YOU KNOW, THE STUDENTS FROM P.S. 38 WILL BE ATTENDING OUR SCHOOL FOR A WHILE!
SON
WE'RE DELIGHTED THAT THREE OF THEM ARE JOINING US IN FIRST PERIOD SOCIAL STUDIES: CHESTER, GINA, AND NATE!
PLEASE MAKE THEM FEEL WELCOME! SHOW THEM AROUND! BE FRIENDLY!
9/26
Peirce
© 2008 by NEA, Inc.
HELLOOO, FRIEND!
HOO, BOY.

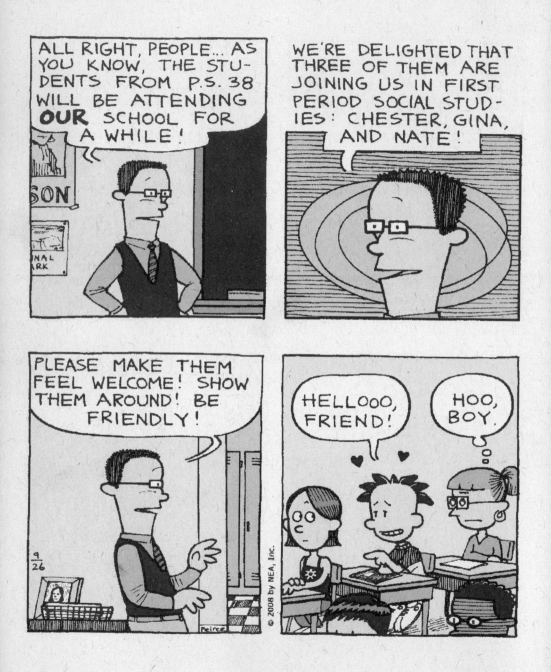

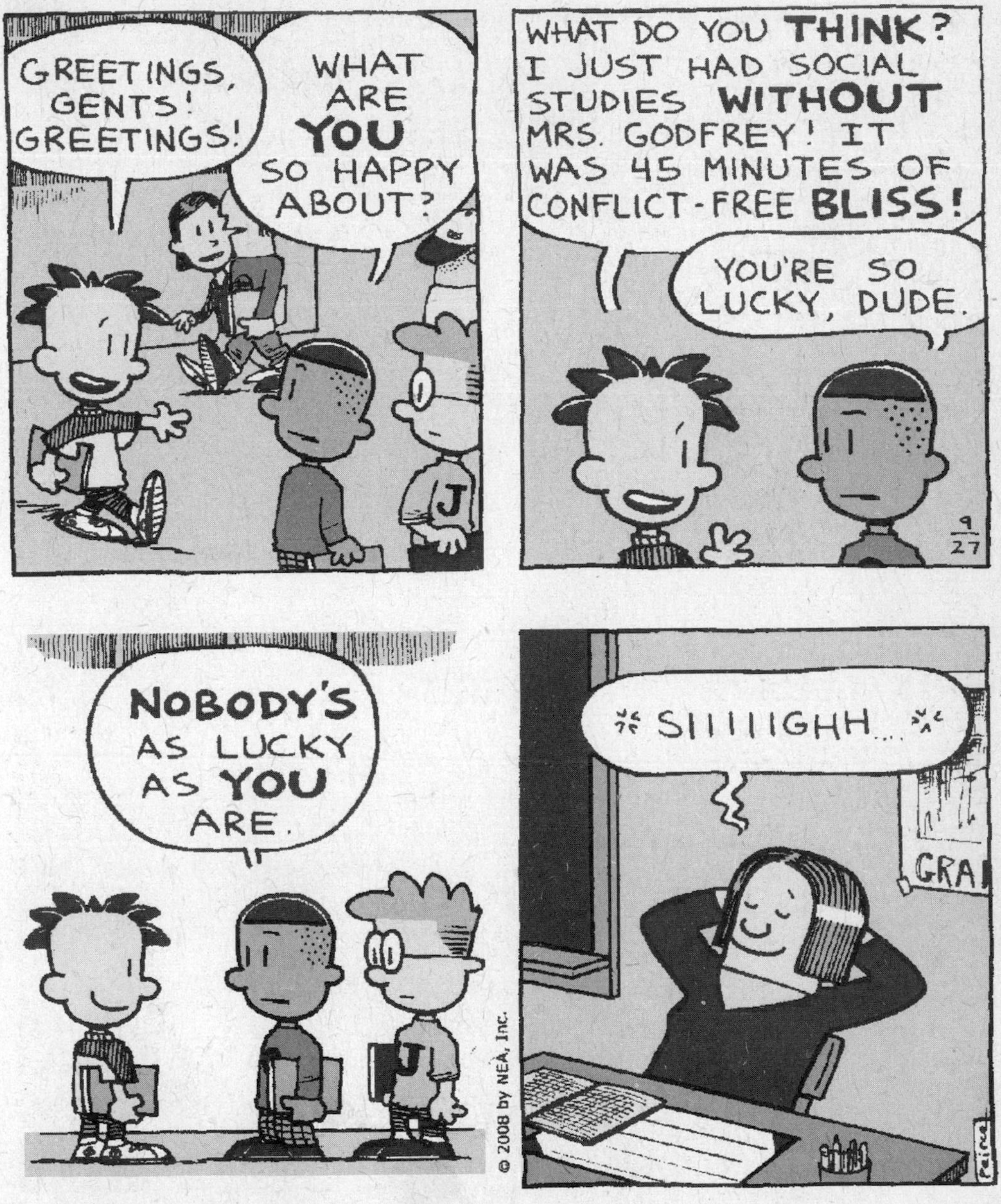
GREETINGS, GENTS! GREETINGS!
WHAT ARE **YOU** SO HAPPY ABOUT?
WHAT DO YOU **THINK**? I JUST HAD SOCIAL STUDIES **WITHOUT** MRS. GODFREY! IT WAS 45 MINUTES OF CONFLICT-FREE **BLISS**!
YOU'RE SO LUCKY, DUDE.
9/27
NOBODY'S AS LUCKY AS **YOU** ARE.
© 2008 by NEA, Inc.
SIIIIIGHH...
GRA
Peirce

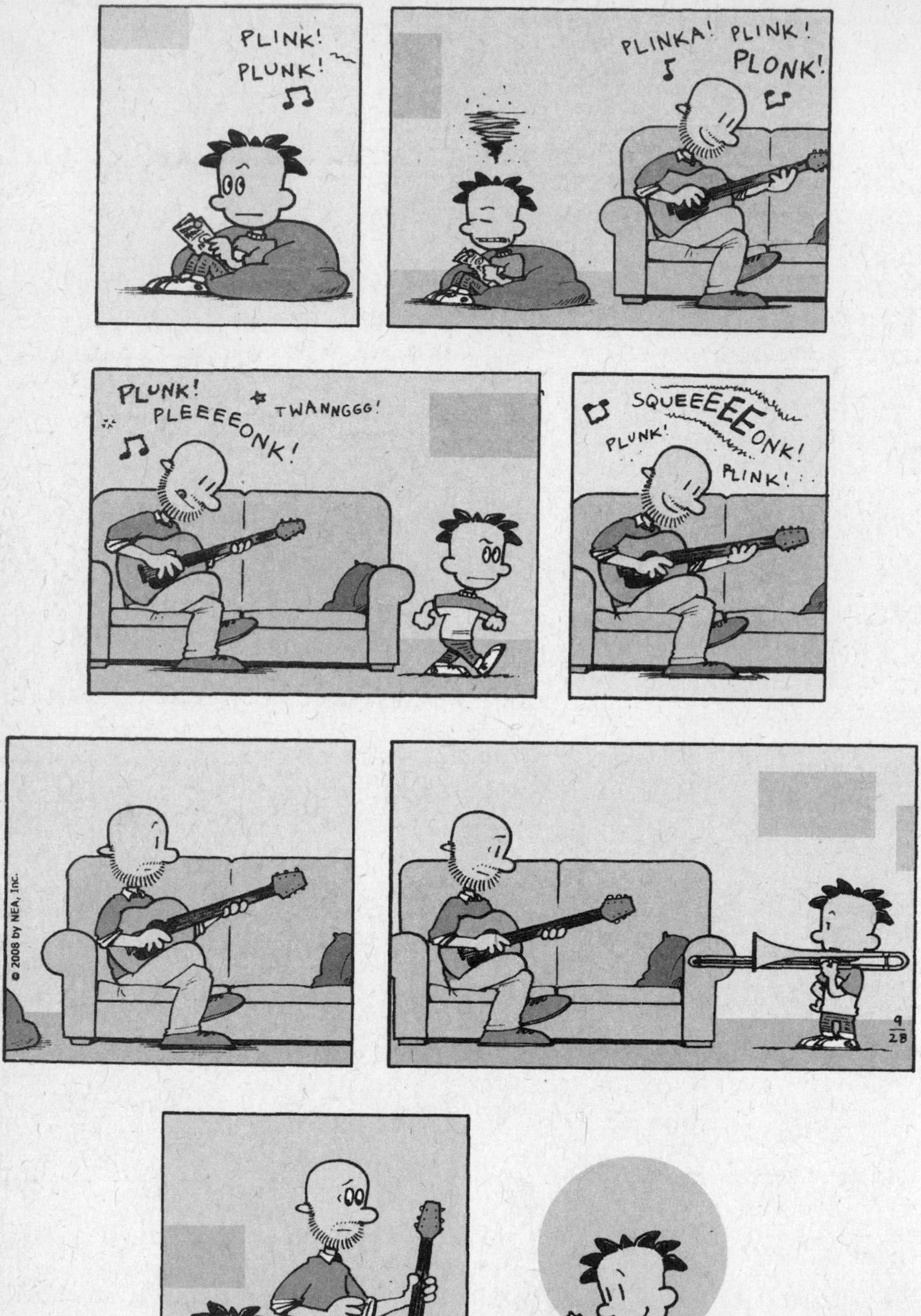
PLINK!
PLUNK!
PLINKA! PLINK!
PLONK!
PLUNK!
PLEEEEEONK!
TWANNGGG!
SQUEEEEEEONK!
PLUNK!
PLINK!
© 2008 by NEA, Inc.
9
28
Peirce

GET REAL

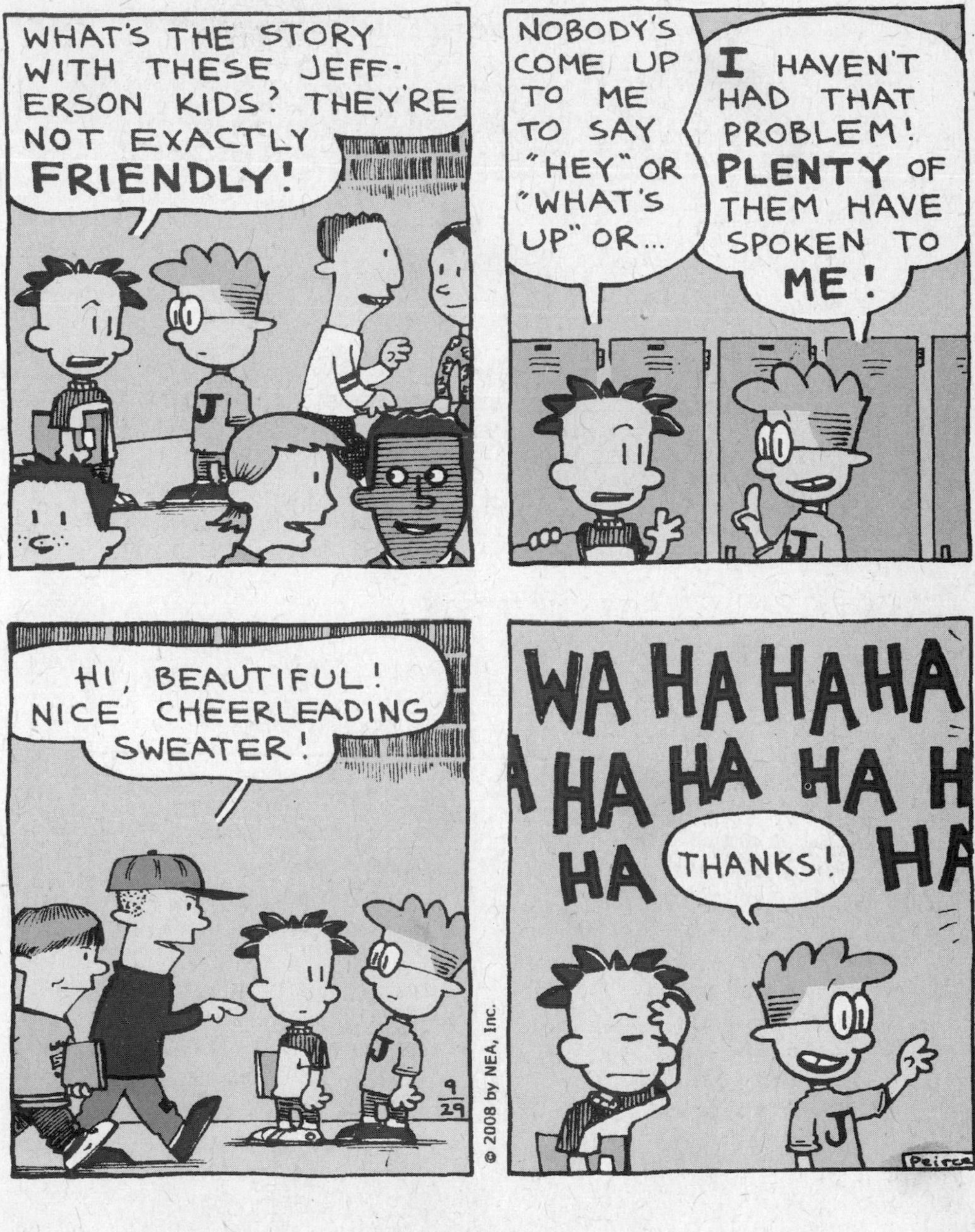
WHAT'S THE STORY WITH THESE JEFF-ERSON KIDS? THEY'RE NOT EXACTLY **FRIENDLY**!
NOBODY'S COME UP TO ME TO SAY "HEY" OR "WHAT'S UP" OR...
I HAVEN'T HAD THAT PROBLEM! **PLENTY** OF THEM HAVE SPOKEN TO **ME**!
HI, BEAUTIFUL! NICE CHEERLEADING SWEATER!
9/29
WA HA HAHA HA HA HA HA H HA HA
THANKS!
Peirce

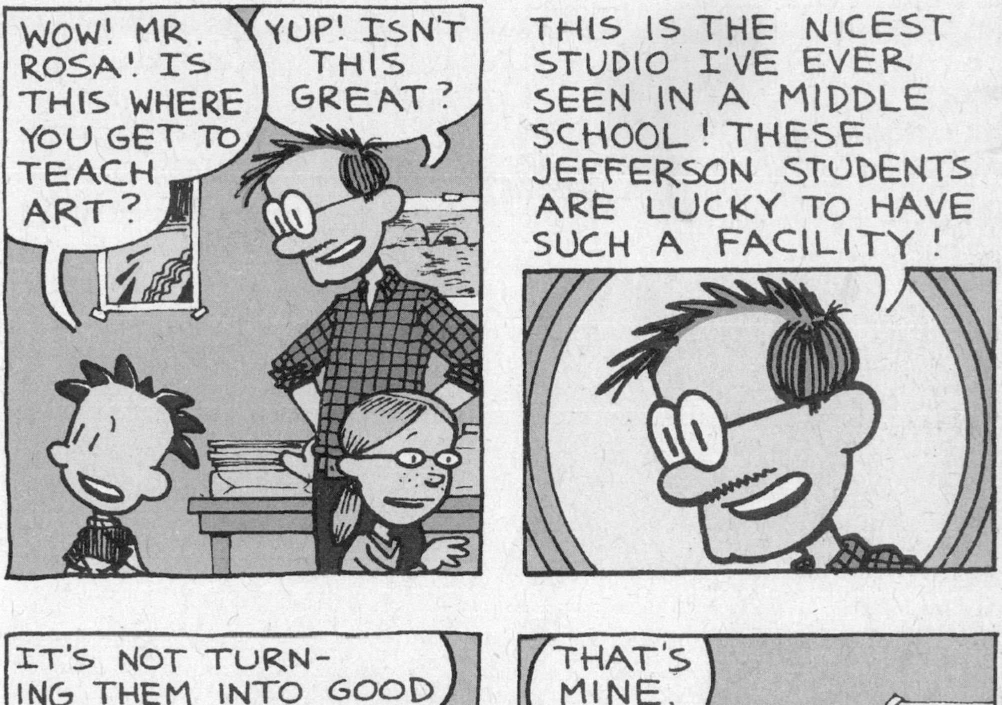
WOW! MR. ROSA! IS THIS WHERE YOU GET TO TEACH ART?
YUP! ISN'T THIS GREAT?
THIS IS THE NICEST STUDIO I'VE EVER SEEN IN A MIDDLE SCHOOL! THESE JEFFERSON STUDENTS ARE LUCKY TO HAVE SUCH A FACILITY!
IT'S NOT TURNING THEM INTO GOOD ARTISTS, THOUGH. I MEAN, THAT PAINTING IS **HIDEOUS!**
THAT'S MINE, SON.
HIDEOUS IN A **GOOD** WAY.
10/1
© 2008 by NEA, Inc.
Peirce

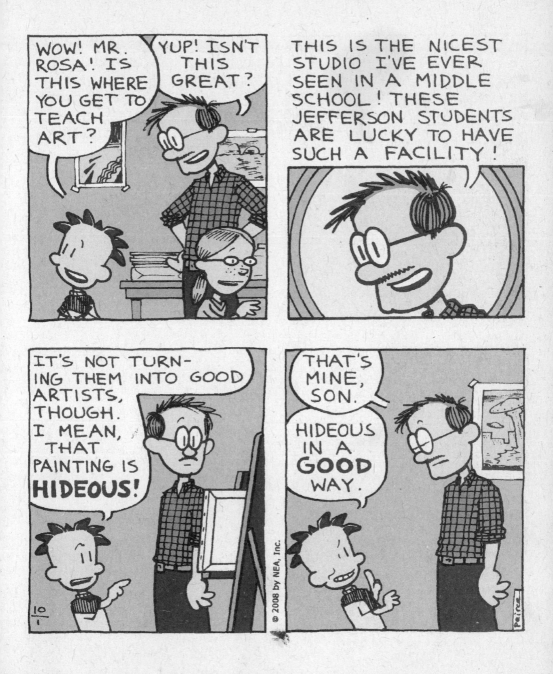

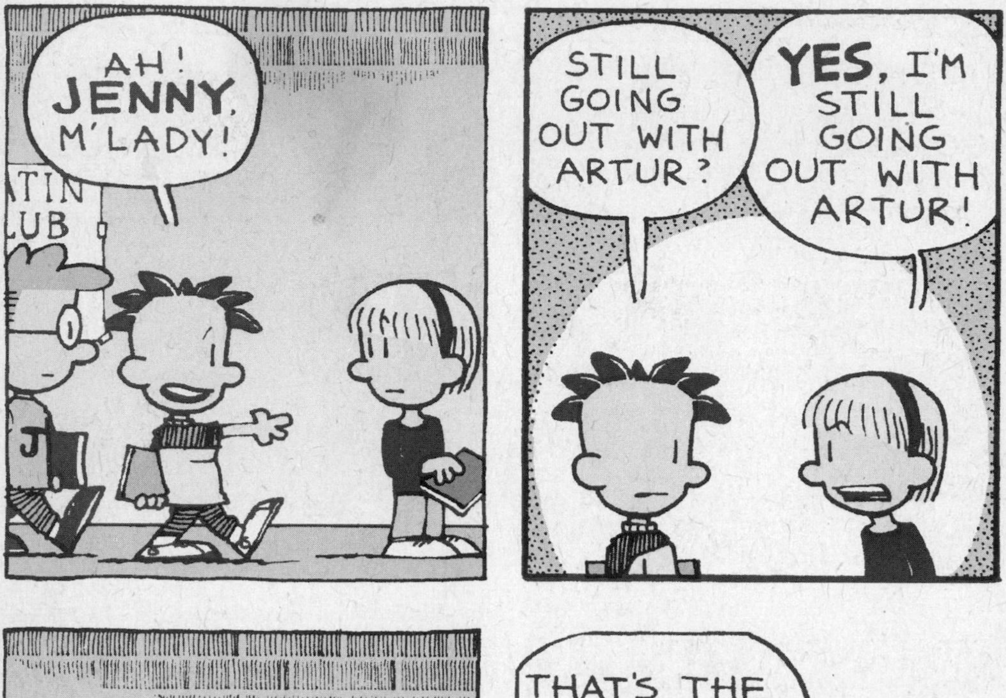
AH! JENNY, M'LADY!
LATIN CLUB
STILL GOING OUT WITH ARTUR?
YES, I'M STILL GOING OUT WITH ARTUR!
LATIN CLUB
THAT'S THE THIRD TIME TODAY YOU'VE ASKED HER THAT.
I LIKE TO STAY CURRENT.
10/2
© 2008 by NEA, Inc.
Peirce

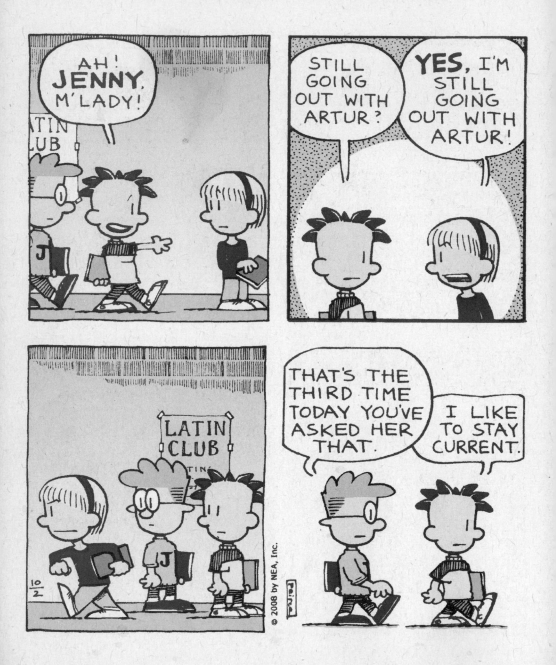

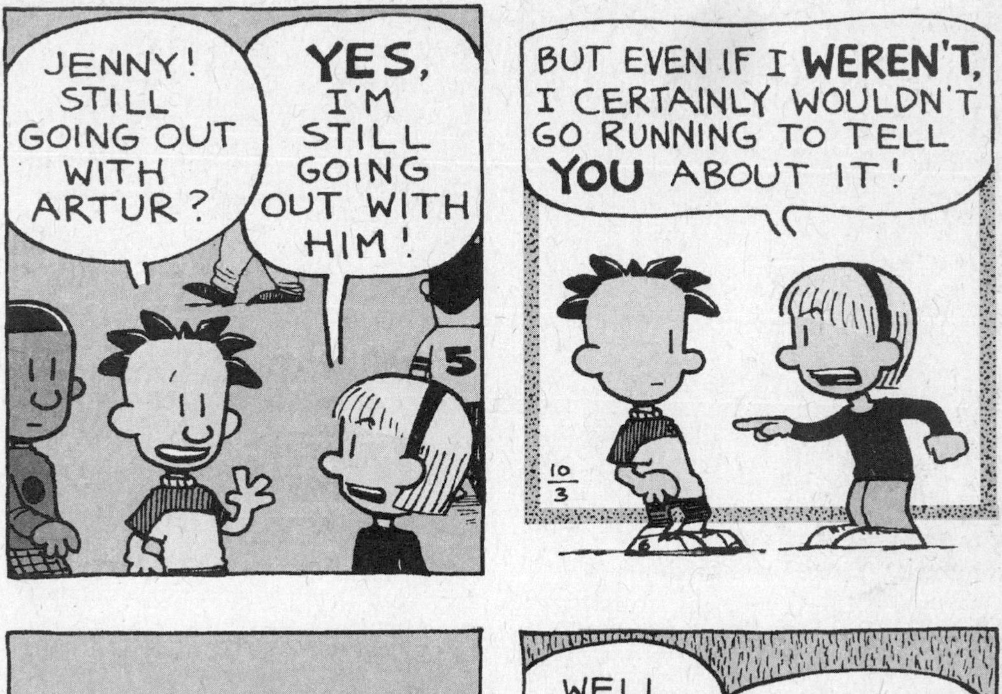
JENNY! STILL GOING OUT WITH ARTUR?
YES, I'M STILL GOING OUT WITH HIM!
BUT EVEN IF I WEREN'T, I CERTAINLY WOULDN'T GO RUNNING TO TELL YOU ABOUT IT!
10/3
WELL, YOU CAN'T MAKE IT MUCH CLEARER THAN...
SO SHE MIGHT NOT BE STILL GOING OUT WITH HIM!
Peirce

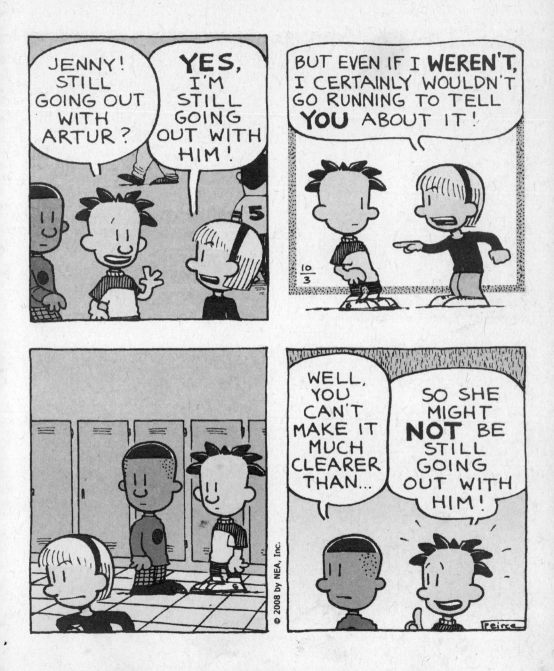

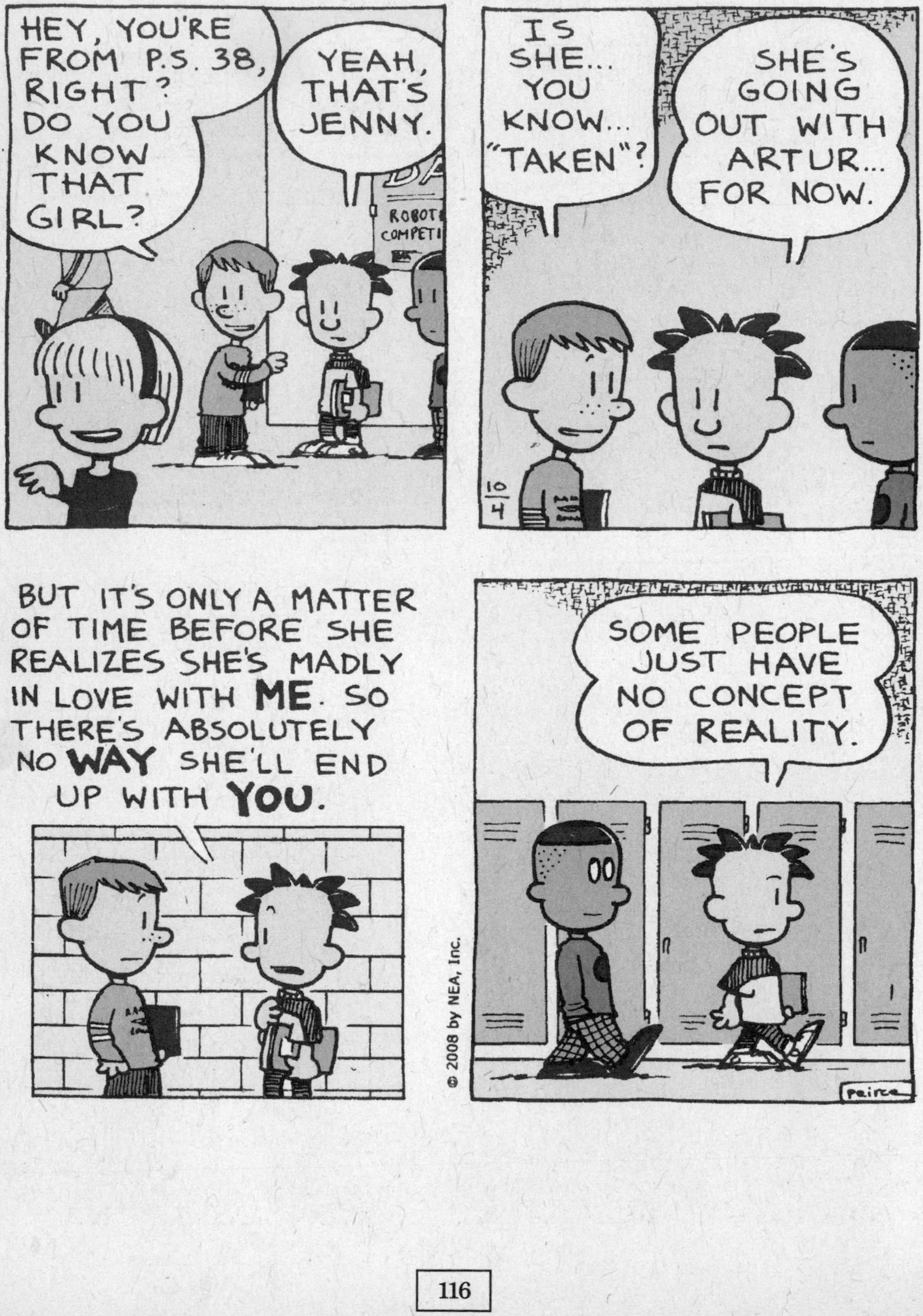
HEY, YOU'RE FROM P.S. 38, RIGHT? DO YOU KNOW THAT GIRL?
YEAH, THAT'S JENNY.
IS SHE... YOU KNOW... "TAKEN"?
SHE'S GOING OUT WITH ARTUR... FOR NOW.
10/4
BUT IT'S ONLY A MATTER OF TIME BEFORE SHE REALIZES SHE'S MADLY IN LOVE WITH **ME**. SO THERE'S ABSOLUTELY NO **WAY** SHE'LL END UP WITH **YOU**.
SOME PEOPLE JUST HAVE NO CONCEPT OF REALITY.
peirce

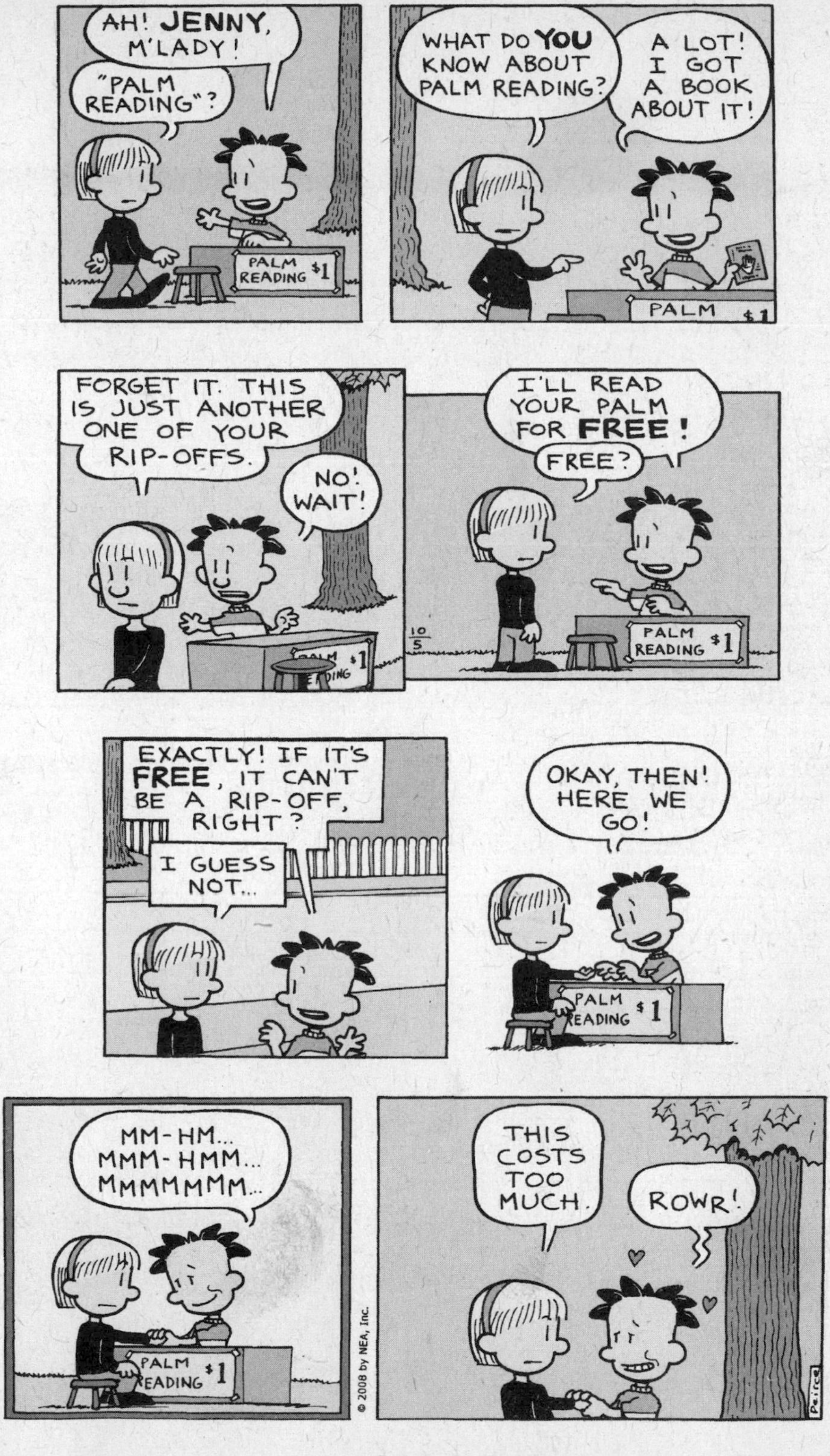
AH! JENNY, M'LADY!
"PALM READING"?
PALM READING $1
WHAT DO YOU KNOW ABOUT PALM READING?
A LOT! I GOT A BOOK ABOUT IT!
PALM $1
FORGET IT. THIS IS JUST ANOTHER ONE OF YOUR RIP-OFFS.
NO! WAIT!
I'LL READ YOUR PALM FOR FREE!
FREE?
10
5
PALM READING $1
EXACTLY! IF IT'S FREE, IT CAN'T BE A RIP-OFF, RIGHT?
I GUESS NOT...
OKAY, THEN! HERE WE GO!
PALM READING $1
MM-HM... MMM-HMM... MMMMMMM...
PALM READING $1
© 2008 by NEA, Inc.
THIS COSTS TOO MUCH.
ROWR!
Peirce

HERE GOES NOTHING

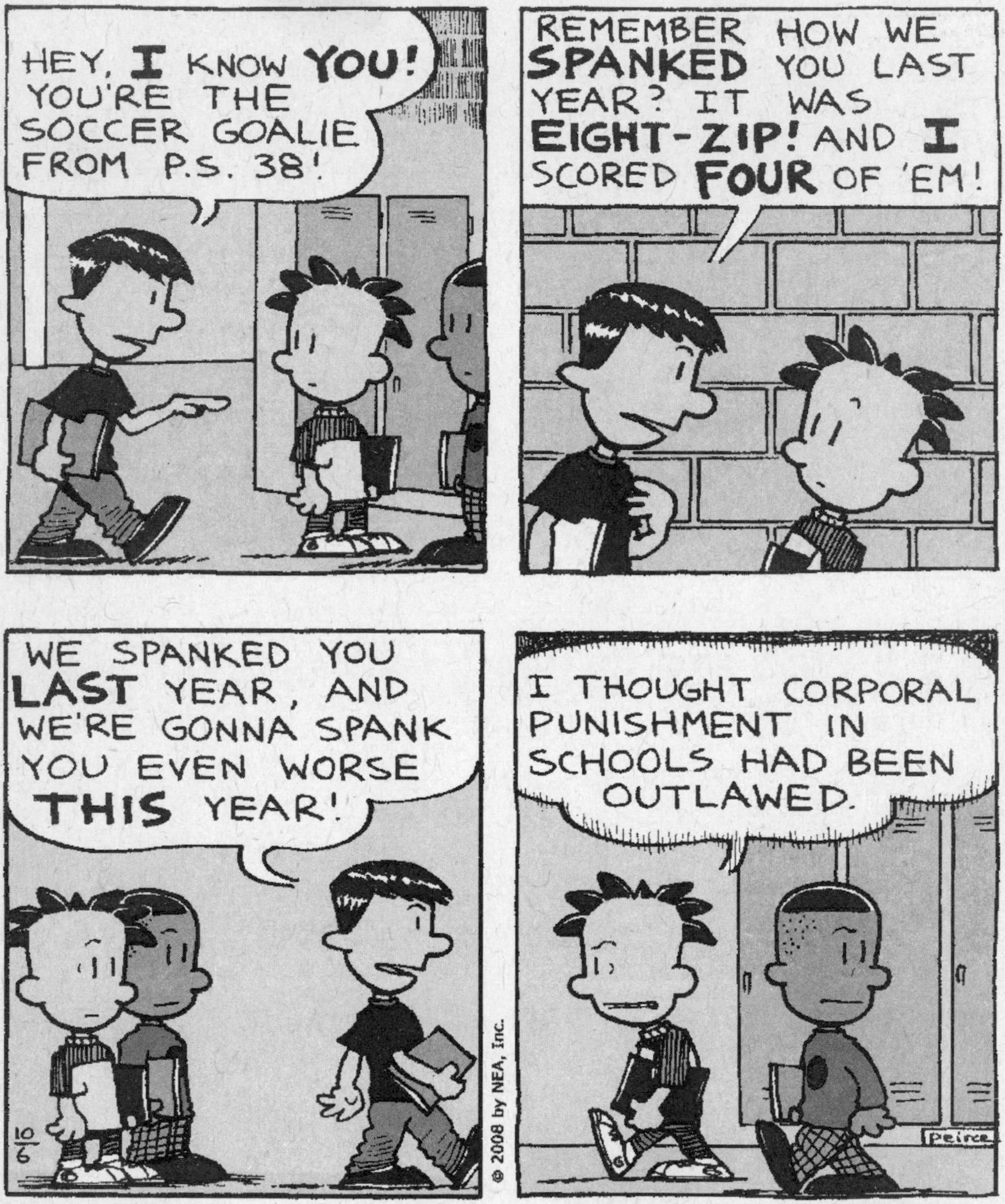

HEY, I KNOW YOU! YOU'RE THE SOCCER GOALIE FROM P.S. 38!
REMEMBER HOW WE SPANKED YOU LAST YEAR? IT WAS EIGHT-ZIP! AND I SCORED FOUR OF 'EM!
WE SPANKED YOU LAST YEAR, AND WE'RE GONNA SPANK YOU EVEN WORSE THIS YEAR!
I THOUGHT CORPORAL PUNISHMENT IN SCHOOLS HAD BEEN OUTLAWED.
10/6
© 2008 by NEA, Inc.
peirce

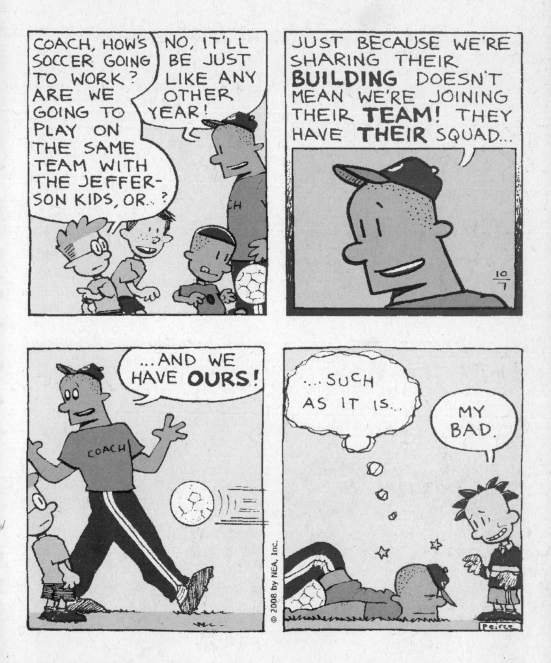

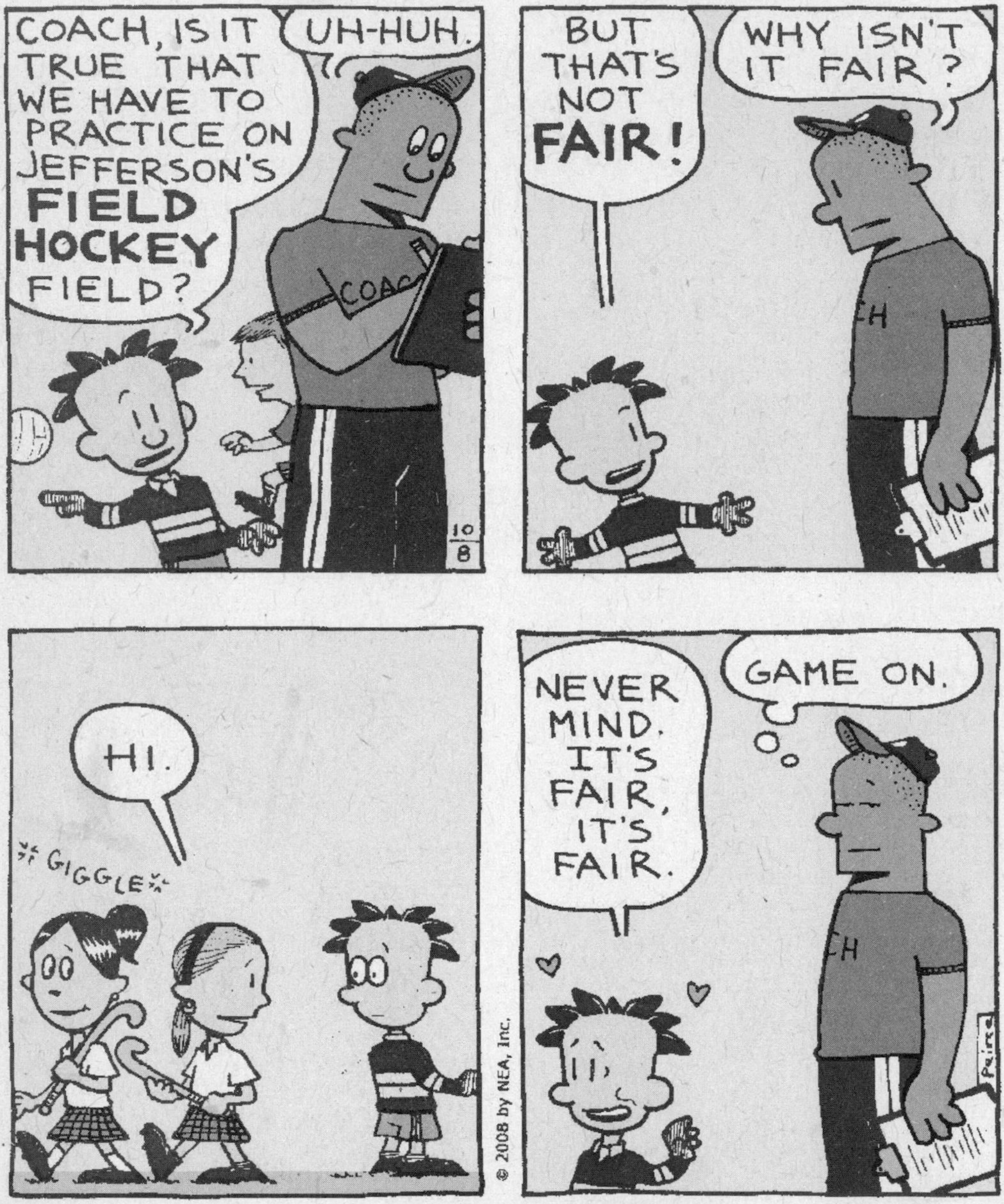
COACH, IS IT TRUE THAT WE HAVE TO PRACTICE ON JEFFERSON'S FIELD HOCKEY FIELD?
UH-HUH.
COACH
10/8
BUT THAT'S NOT FAIR!
WHY ISN'T IT FAIR?
HI.
GIGGLE
NEVER MIND. IT'S FAIR, IT'S FAIR.
GAME ON.
Peirce
© 2008 by NEA, Inc.

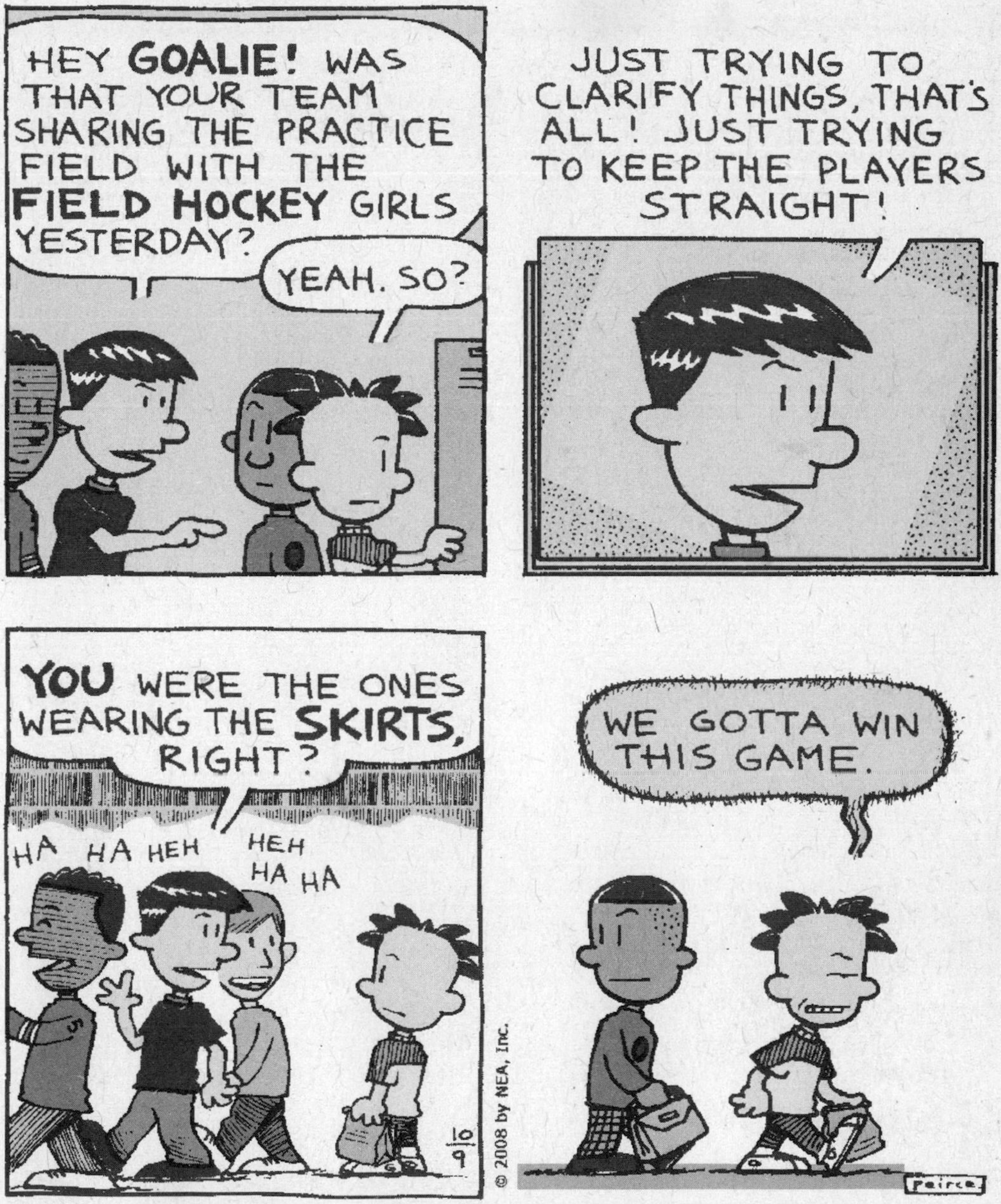
HEY **GOALIE!** WAS THAT YOUR TEAM SHARING THE PRACTICE FIELD WITH THE **FIELD HOCKEY** GIRLS YESTERDAY?
YEAH. SO?
JUST TRYING TO CLARIFY THINGS, THAT'S ALL! JUST TRYING TO KEEP THE PLAYERS STRAIGHT!
YOU WERE THE ONES WEARING THE **SKIRTS**, RIGHT?
HA HA HEH
HEH HA HA
10/9
© 2008 by NEA, Inc.
WE GOTTA WIN THIS GAME.
peirce

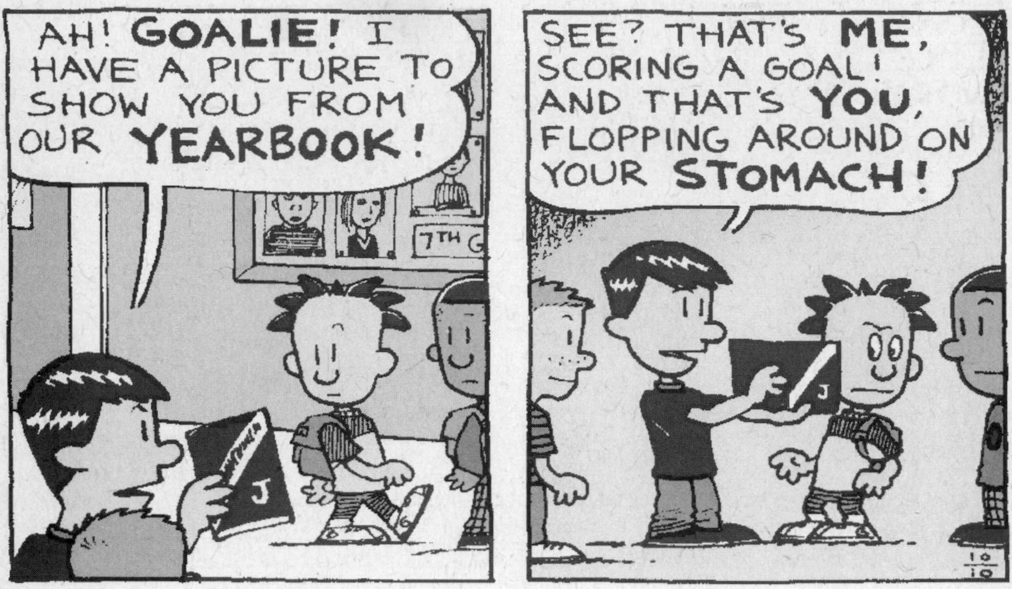
AH! GOALIE! I HAVE A PICTURE TO SHOW YOU FROM OUR YEARBOOK!
7TH G
SEE? THAT'S ME, SCORING A GOAL! AND THAT'S YOU, FLOPPING AROUND ON YOUR STOMACH!
10/10

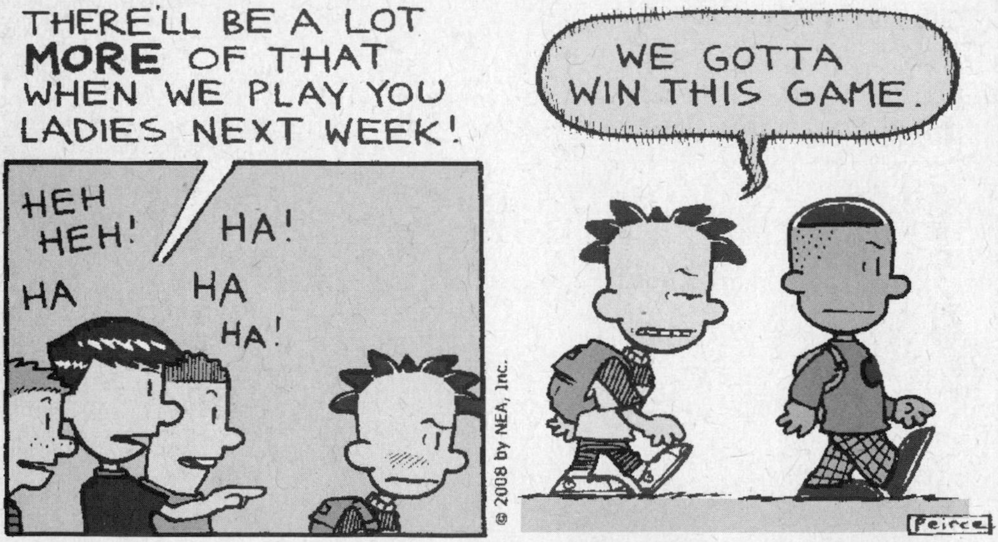
THERE'LL BE A LOT MORE OF THAT WHEN WE PLAY YOU LADIES NEXT WEEK!
HEH HEH!
HA!
HA
HA HA!
WE GOTTA WIN THIS GAME.
Peirce

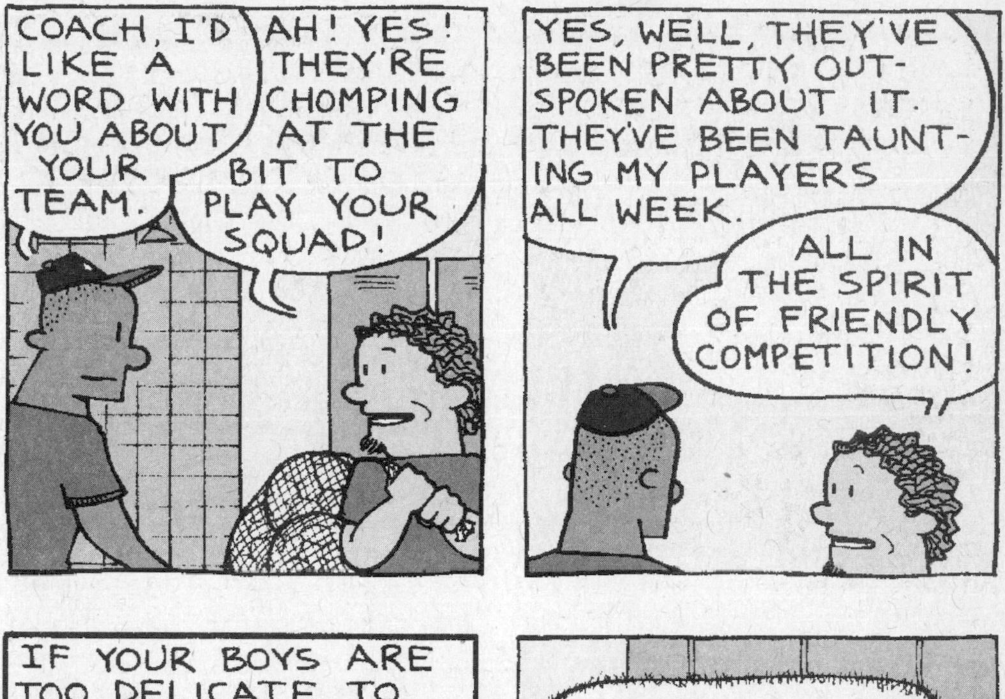
COACH, I'D LIKE A WORD WITH YOU ABOUT YOUR TEAM.
AH! YES! THEY'RE CHOMPING AT THE BIT TO PLAY YOUR SQUAD!
YES, WELL, THEY'VE BEEN PRETTY OUT-SPOKEN ABOUT IT. THEY'VE BEEN TAUNT-ING MY PLAYERS ALL WEEK.
ALL IN THE SPIRIT OF FRIENDLY COMPETITION!
IF YOUR BOYS ARE TOO DELICATE TO **TAKE** IT, MAYBE THEY SHOULD TAKE UP **NEEDLEPOINT**!
HAW!
10/11
© 2008 by NEA, Inc.
WE GOTTA WIN THIS GAME.
Peirce

THE CAPTAIN OF THE JEFFERSON TEAM KEEPS TRASH-TALKING ME! I'M GONNA SERVE HIM UP A STEAMING PLATE OF **SMACK**!

NO, NATE!

WE'RE **GUESTS** HERE AT JEFFERSON! I DON'T WANT ANY OF OUR STUDENTS CONTRIBUTING TO A **CONFLICT**!

DON'T GET DRAGGED DOWN TO HIS LEVEL, NATE! BE THE BIGGER MAN!

COA

10/13

© 2008 by NEA, Inc.

...WHICH ISN'T EASY TO DO WHEN YOU'RE ONLY 4'6"!

YOU'RE NOT HELPING.

PAT PAT!

Peirce

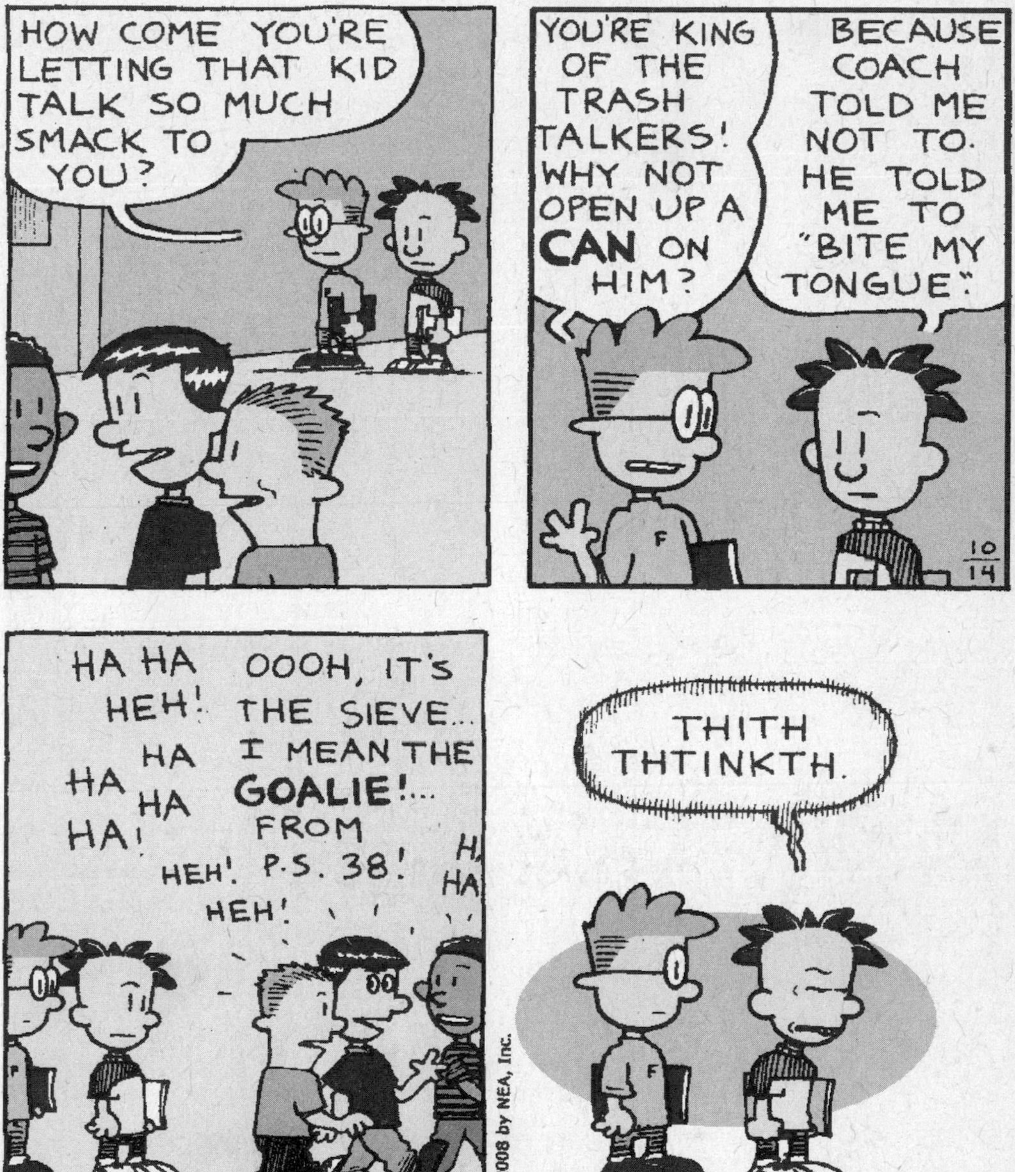
HOW COME YOU'RE LETTING THAT KID TALK SO MUCH SMACK TO YOU?
YOU'RE KING OF THE TRASH TALKERS! WHY NOT OPEN UP A **CAN** ON HIM?
BECAUSE COACH TOLD ME NOT TO. HE TOLD ME TO "BITE MY TONGUE."
10/14
HA HA HEH! HA HA HA HA HA!
OOOH, IT'S THE SIEVE... I MEAN THE **GOALIE**!... FROM P.S. 38!
HEH! HEH!
HA HA
THITH THTINKTH.
Peirce

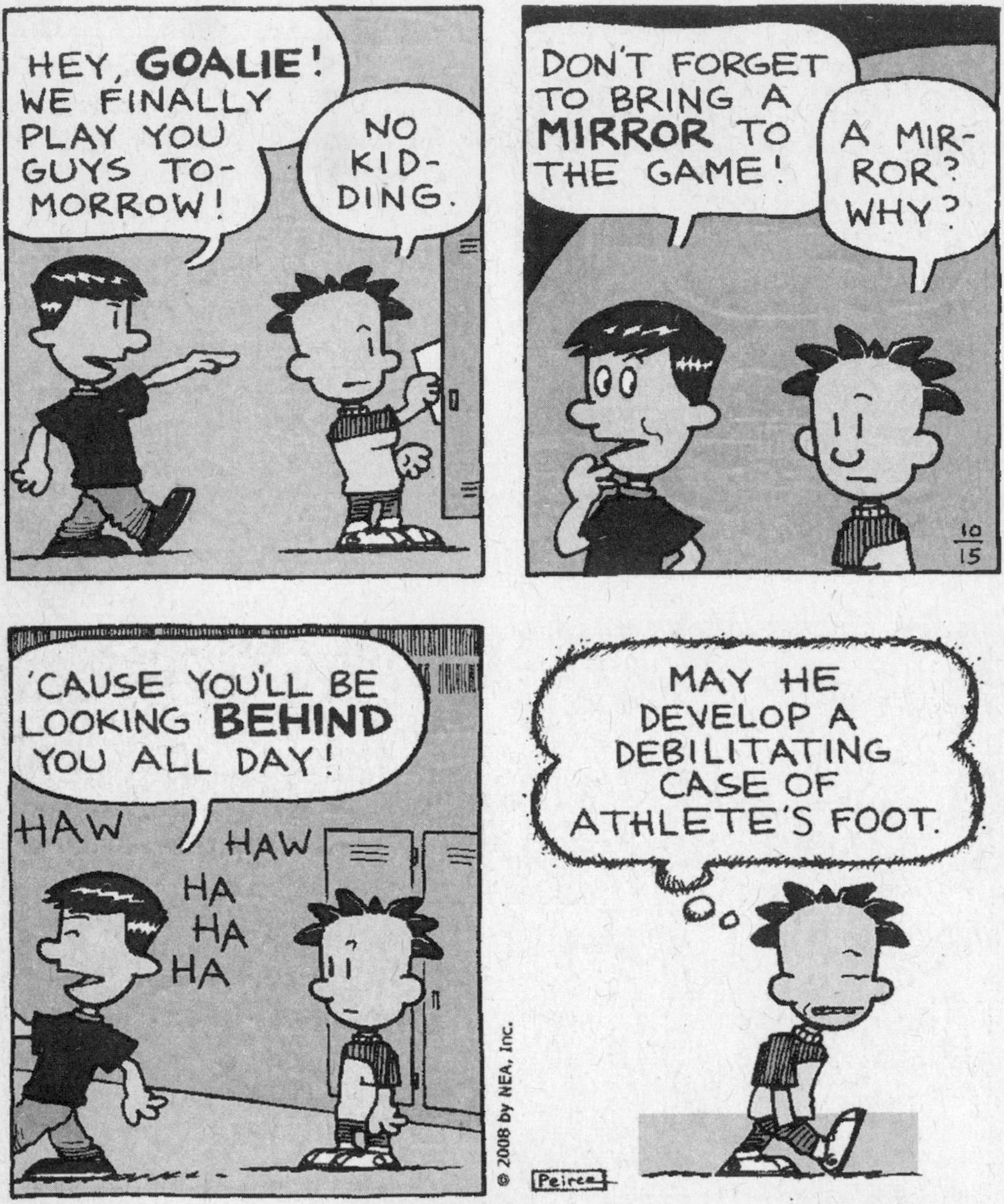
HEY, GOALIE! WE FINALLY PLAY YOU GUYS TO-MORROW!
NO KID-DING.
DON'T FORGET TO BRING A MIRROR TO THE GAME!
A MIR-ROR? WHY?
10/15
'CAUSE YOU'LL BE LOOKING BEHIND YOU ALL DAY!
HAW
HAW
HA HA HA
© 2008 by NEA, Inc.
Peirce
MAY HE DEVELOP A DEBILITATING CASE OF ATHLETE'S FOOT.

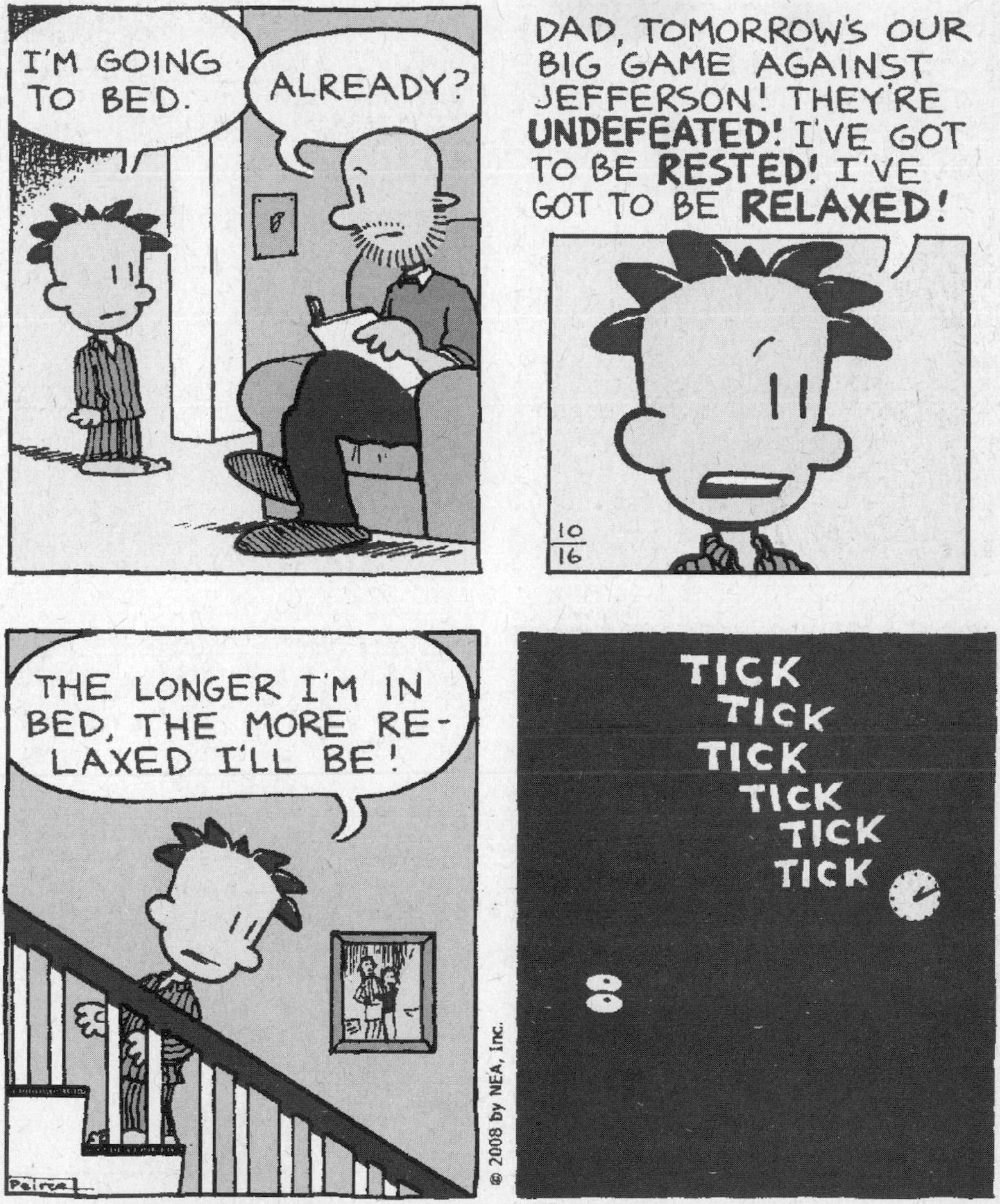
I'M GOING TO BED.
ALREADY?
DAD, TOMORROW'S OUR BIG GAME AGAINST JEFFERSON! THEY'RE **UNDEFEATED!** I'VE GOT TO BE **RESTED!** I'VE GOT TO BE **RELAXED!**
10/16
THE LONGER I'M IN BED, THE MORE RE-LAXED I'LL BE!
TICK
TICK
TICK
TICK
TICK
TICK

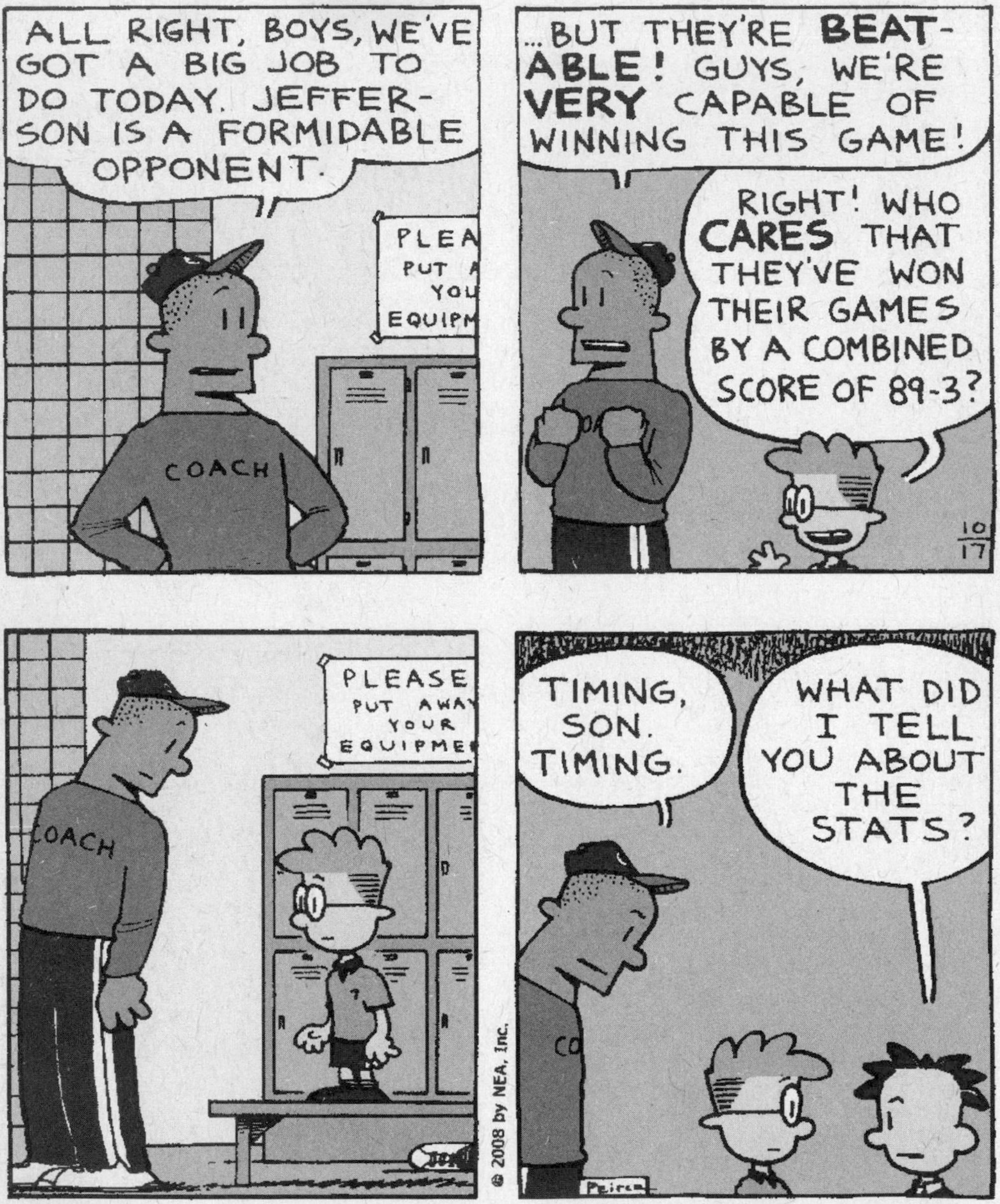
ALL RIGHT, BOYS, WE'VE GOT A BIG JOB TO DO TODAY. JEFFERSON IS A FORMIDABLE OPPONENT.
PLEA PUT A YOU EQUIPM
COACH
...BUT THEY'RE BEATABLE! GUYS, WE'RE VERY CAPABLE OF WINNING THIS GAME!
RIGHT! WHO CARES THAT THEY'VE WON THEIR GAMES BY A COMBINED SCORE OF 89-3?
10/17
PLEASE PUT AWAY YOUR EQUIPME
COACH
© 2008 by NEA, Inc.
TIMING, SON. TIMING.
WHAT DID I TELL YOU ABOUT THE STATS?
Peirce

© 2008 by NEA, Inc.

10/20

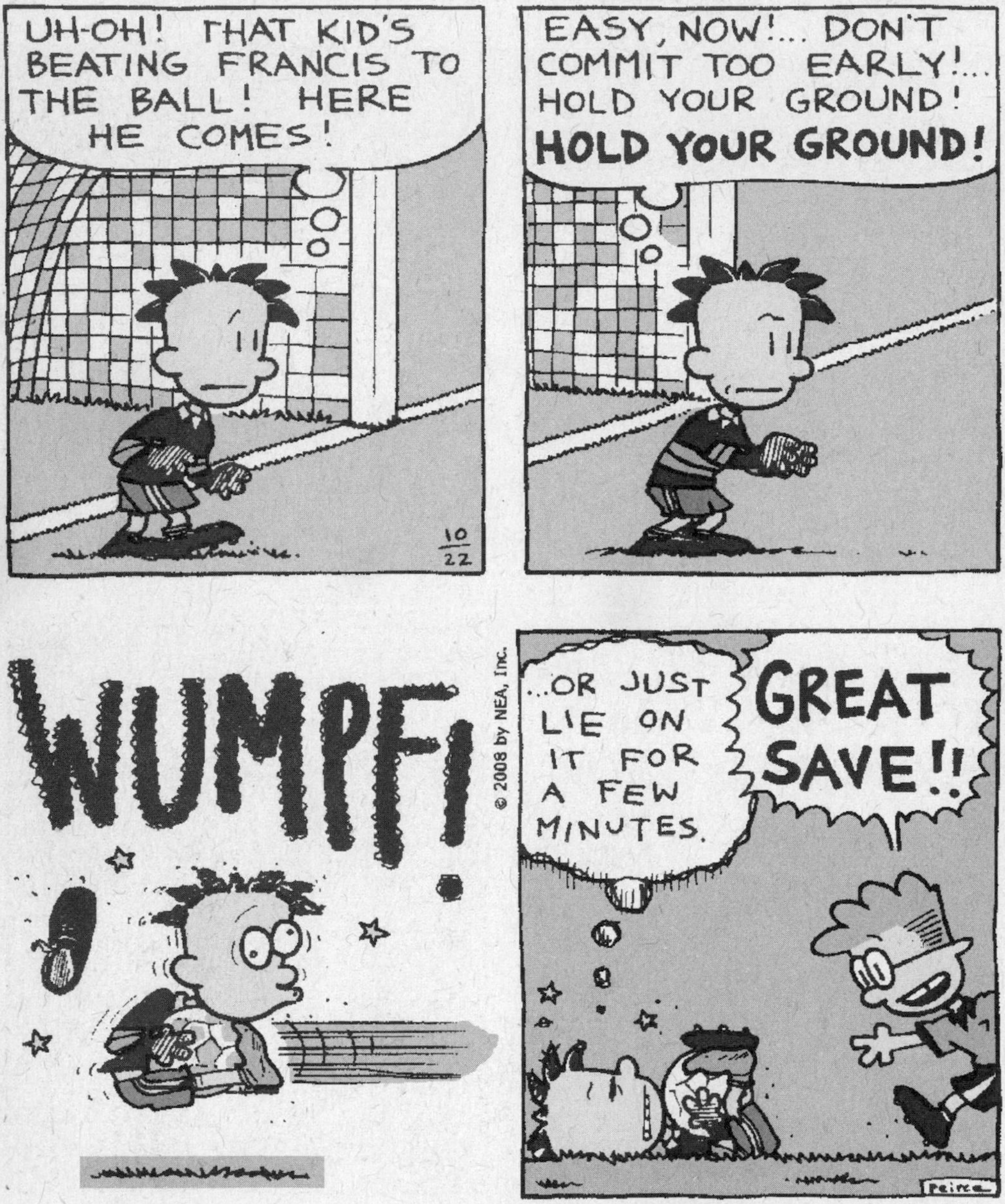
UH-OH! THAT KID'S BEATING FRANCIS TO THE BALL! HERE HE COMES!
10/22
EASY, NOW!... DON'T COMMIT TOO EARLY!... HOLD YOUR GROUND! **HOLD YOUR GROUND!**
WUMPF!
...OR JUST LIE ON IT FOR A FEW MINUTES.
GREAT SAVE!!
Peirce

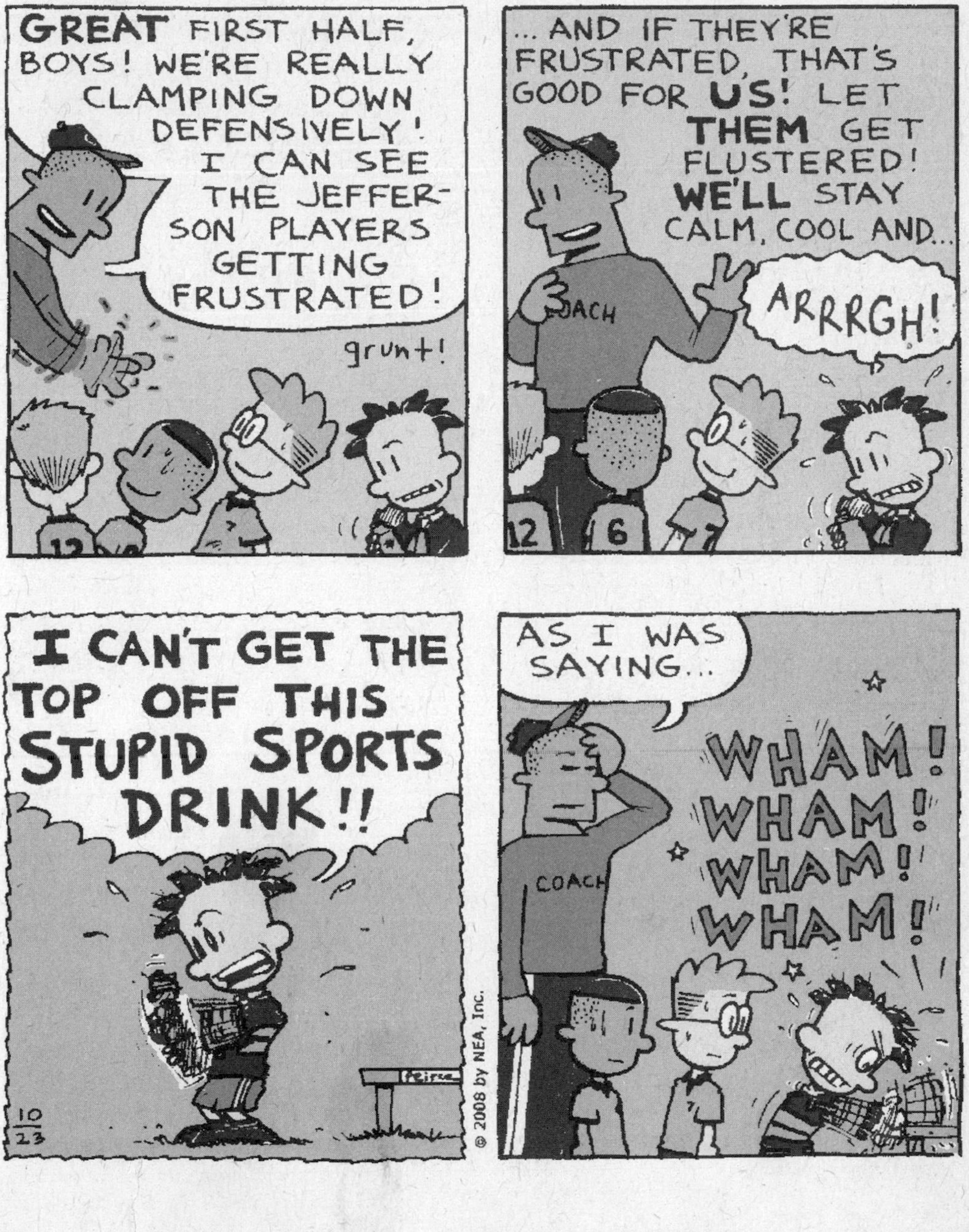
GREAT FIRST HALF, BOYS! WE'RE REALLY CLAMPING DOWN DEFENSIVELY! I CAN SEE THE JEFFERSON PLAYERS GETTING FRUSTRATED!
grunt!
... AND IF THEY'RE FRUSTRATED, THAT'S GOOD FOR US! LET THEM GET FLUSTERED! WE'LL STAY CALM, COOL AND...
ARRRGH!
COACH
I CAN'T GET THE TOP OFF THIS STUPID SPORTS DRINK!!
10/23
© 2008 by NEA, Inc.
AS I WAS SAYING...
WHAM! WHAM! WHAM! WHAM!
COACH

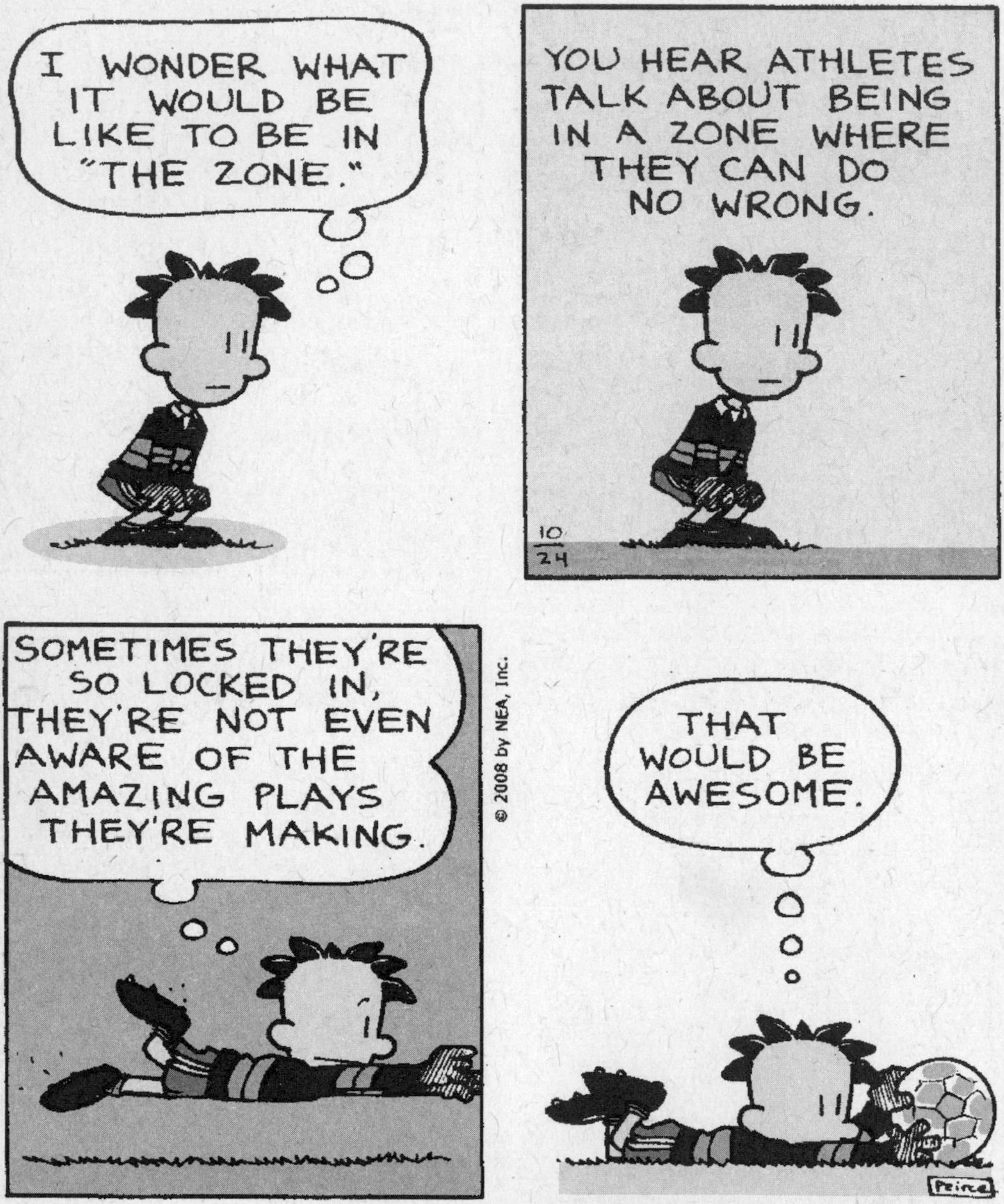
I WONDER WHAT IT WOULD BE LIKE TO BE IN "THE ZONE."
YOU HEAR ATHLETES TALK ABOUT BEING IN A ZONE WHERE THEY CAN DO NO WRONG.
10/24
SOMETIMES THEY'RE SO LOCKED IN, THEY'RE NOT EVEN AWARE OF THE AMAZING PLAYS THEY'RE MAKING.
© 2008 by NEA, Inc.
THAT WOULD BE AWESOME.
Peirce

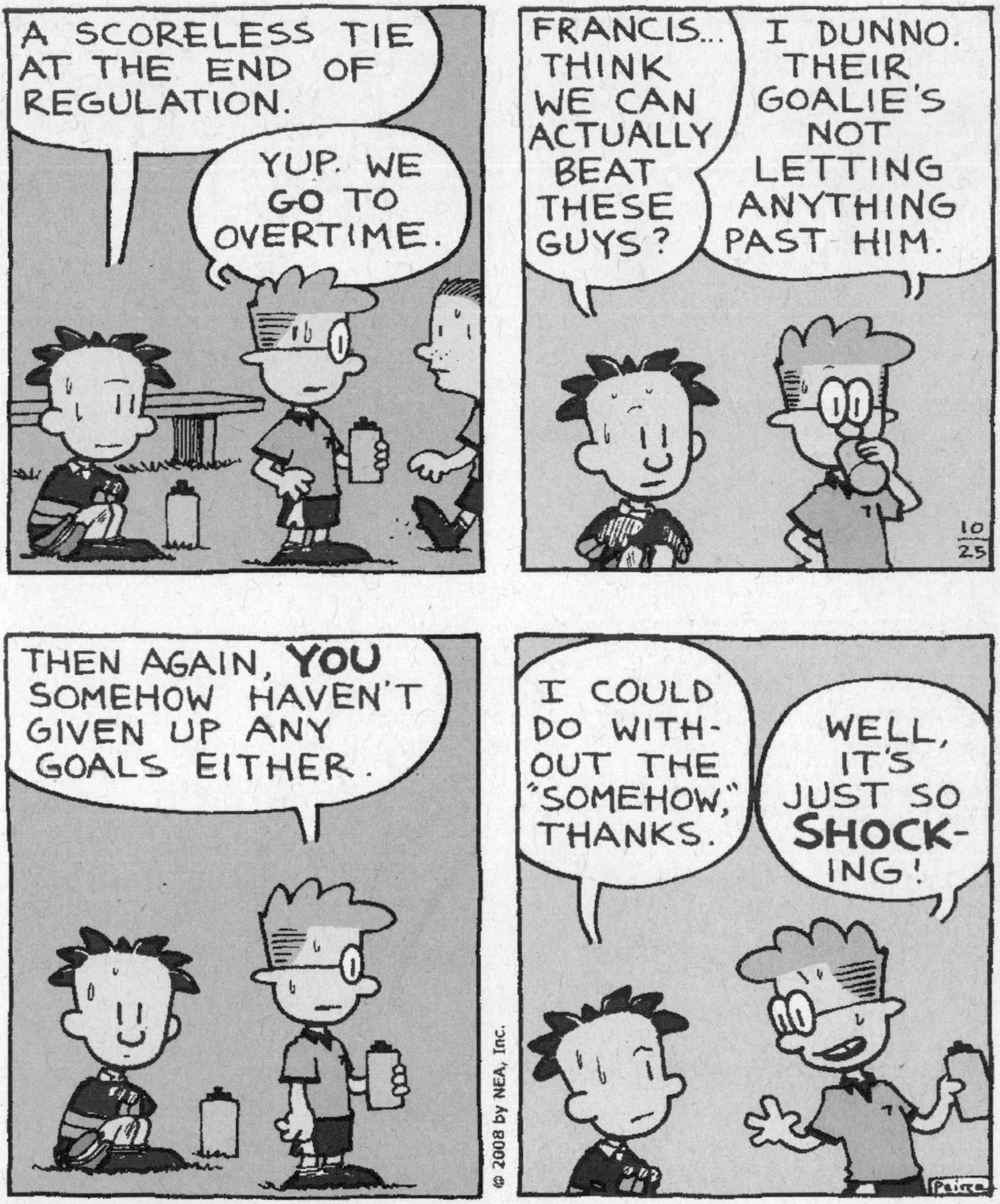
A SCORELESS TIE AT THE END OF REGULATION.
YUP. WE GO TO OVERTIME.
FRANCIS... THINK WE CAN ACTUALLY BEAT THESE GUYS?
I DUNNO. THEIR GOALIE'S NOT LETTING ANYTHING PAST HIM.
10/25
THEN AGAIN, **YOU** SOMEHOW HAVEN'T GIVEN UP ANY GOALS EITHER.
I COULD DO WITHOUT THE "SOMEHOW," THANKS.
WELL, IT'S JUST SO **SHOCKING**!
© 2008 by NEA, Inc.
Peirce

RULE 7.2 If the score is tied at the conclusion of a 70-minute match, a ten-minute overtime period is played.
RULE 7.3 If at the conclusion of the overtime period no winner has been determined, the outcome of the match is decided by a series of penalty kicks.
PHYS. ED
VIS
0
0
FORMAT Five players from each side are selected by their respective coaches to take penalty kicks in alternating order.
The team that successfully converts more penalty kicks than its opponent is declared the winner.
GULP!
© 2008 by NEA, Inc.

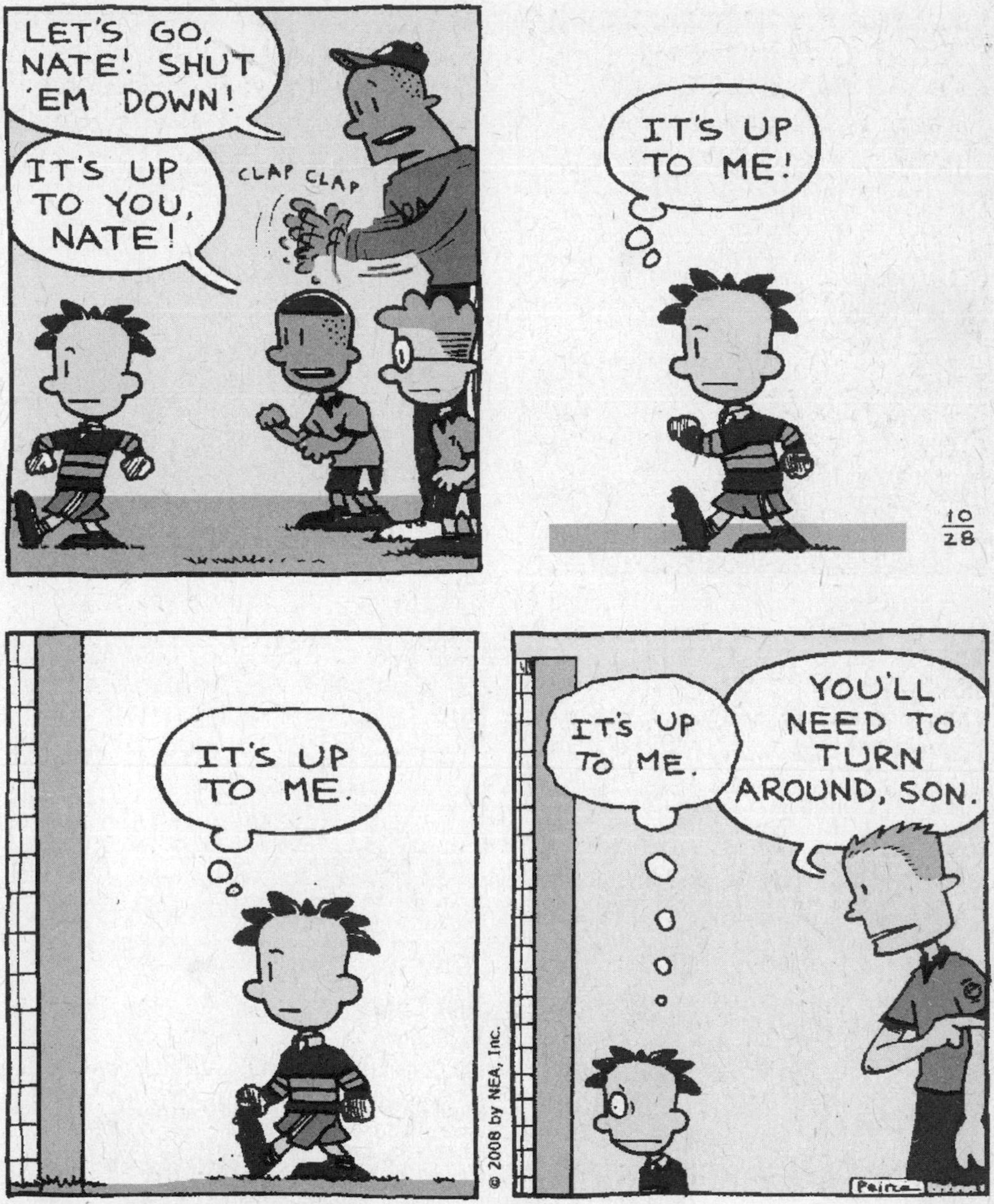
LET'S GO, NATE! SHUT 'EM DOWN!
IT'S UP TO YOU, NATE!
CLAP CLAP
IT'S UP TO ME!
10/28
IT'S UP TO ME.
© 2008 by NEA, Inc.
IT'S UP TO ME.
YOU'LL NEED TO TURN AROUND, SON.
Peirce

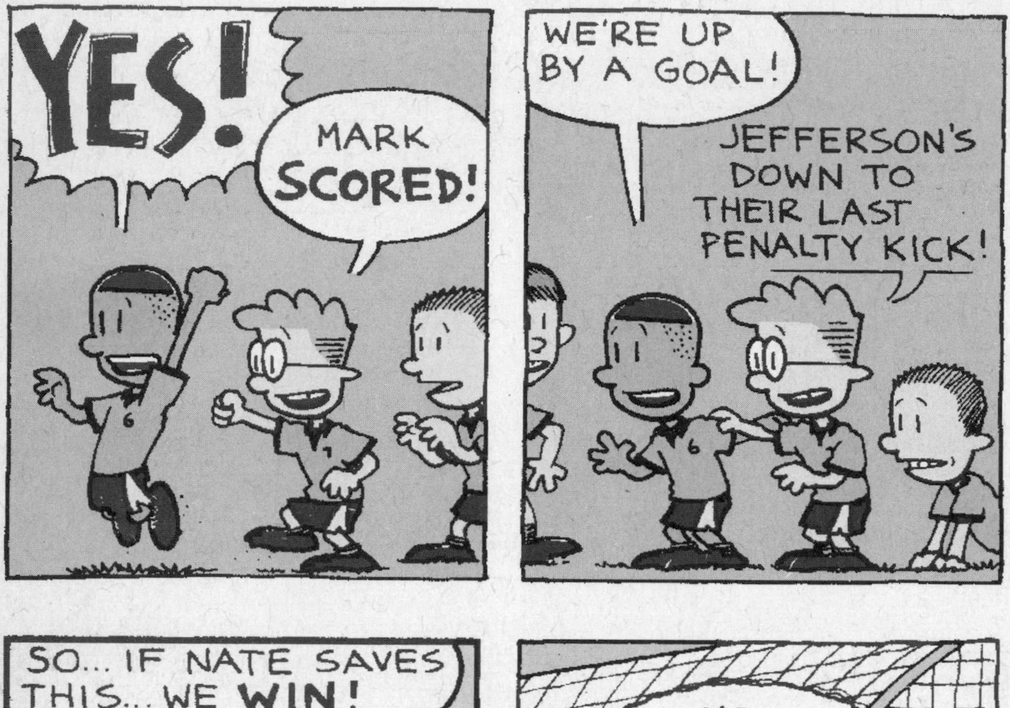
YES!
MARK SCORED!
WE'RE UP BY A GOAL!
JEFFERSON'S DOWN TO THEIR LAST PENALTY KICK!
SO... IF NATE SAVES THIS... WE WIN!
WE'LL BE THE FIRST TEAM TO BEAT JEFFERSON IN FOUR YEARS!
© 2008 by NEA, Inc.
NO PRESSURE, THOUGH.
Peirce

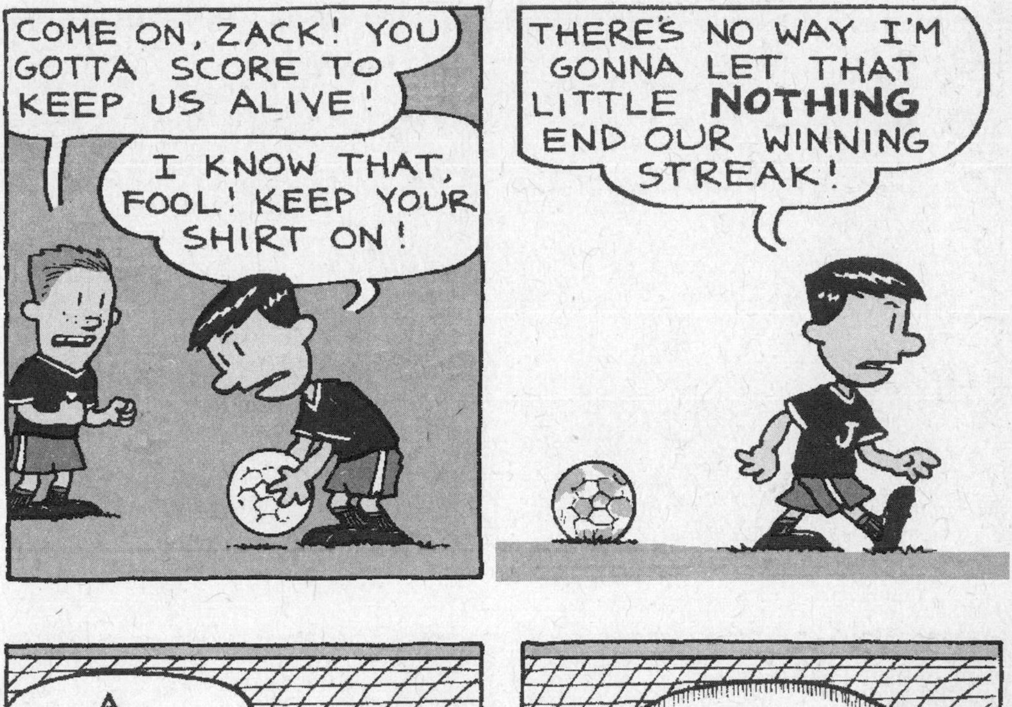
COME ON, ZACK! YOU GOTTA SCORE TO KEEP US ALIVE!
I KNOW THAT, FOOL! KEEP YOUR SHIRT ON!
THERE'S NO WAY I'M GONNA LET THAT LITTLE **NOTHING** END OUR WINNING STREAK!
A NOTHING?
THAT KID CALLED ME A **NOTHING**!
10/30
© 2008 by NEA, Inc.
HERE GOES NOTHING.
peirce

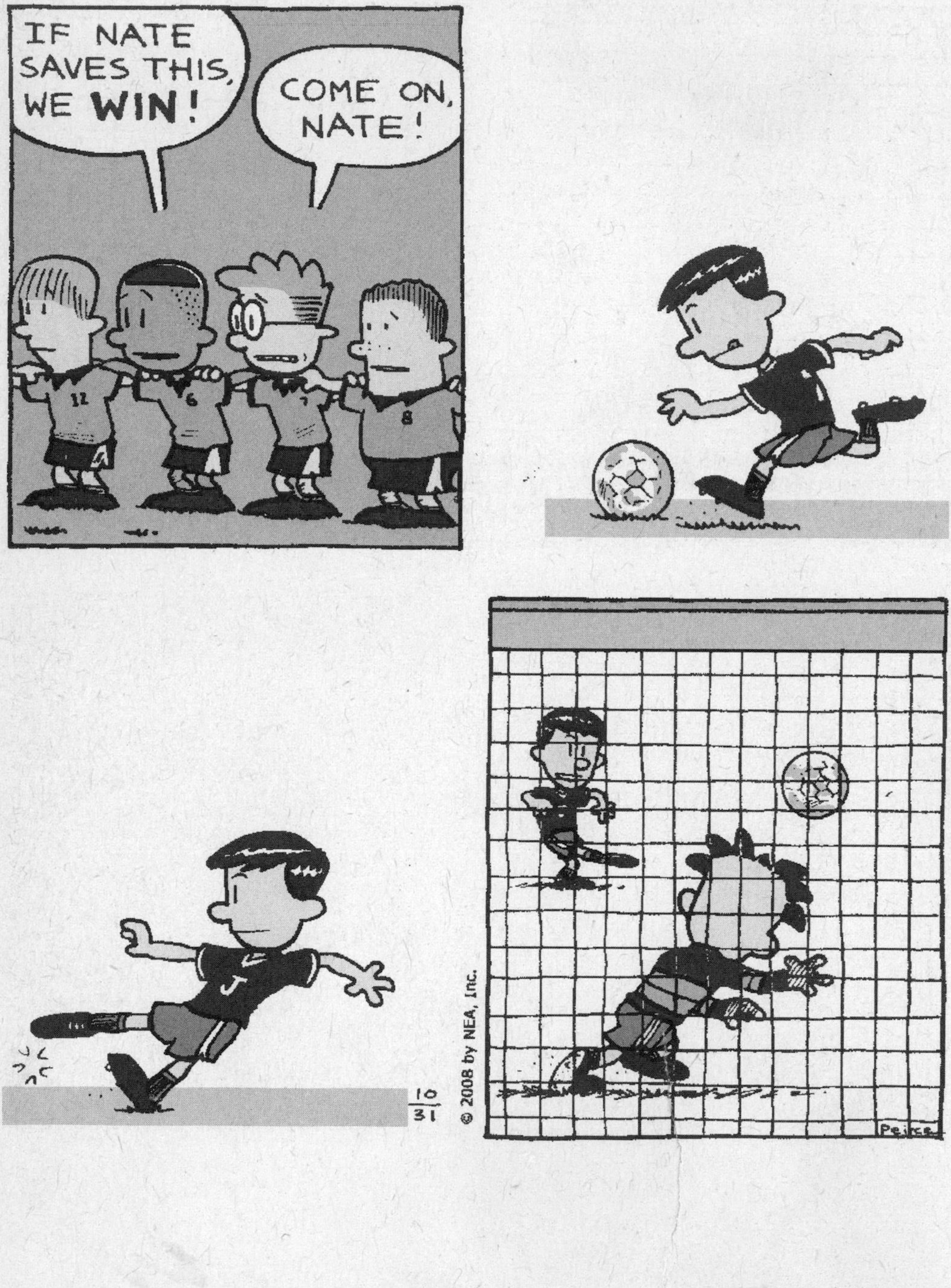
IF NATE SAVES THIS, WE **WIN**!
COME ON, NATE!
10/31
Peirce

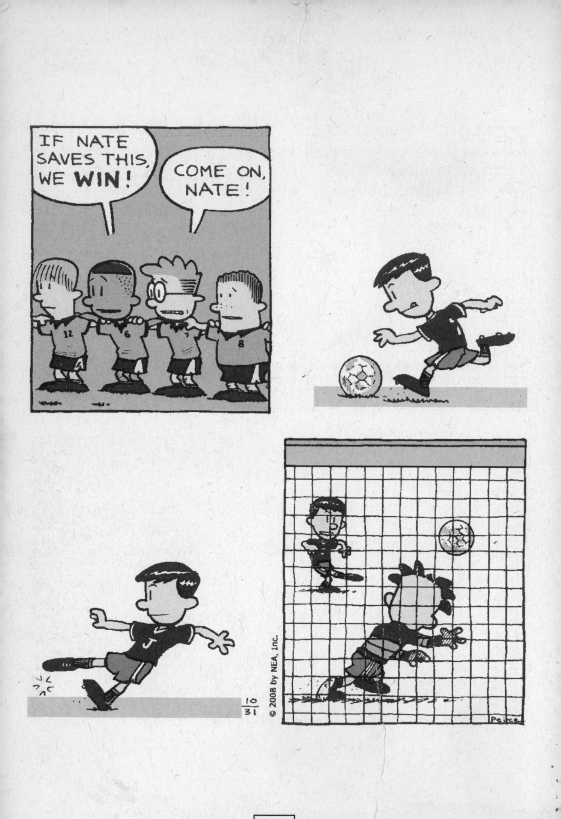

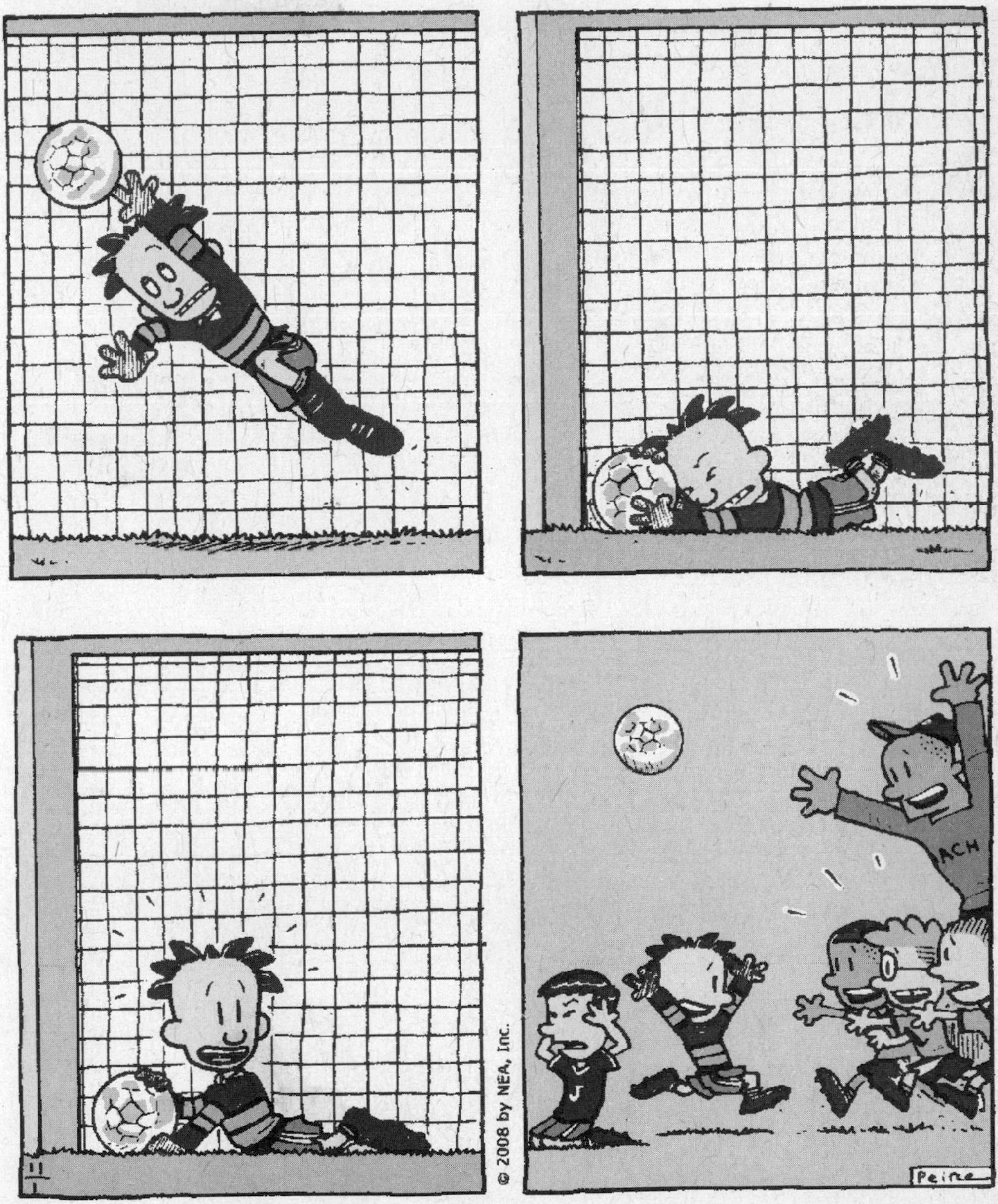
ACH
J
Peirce

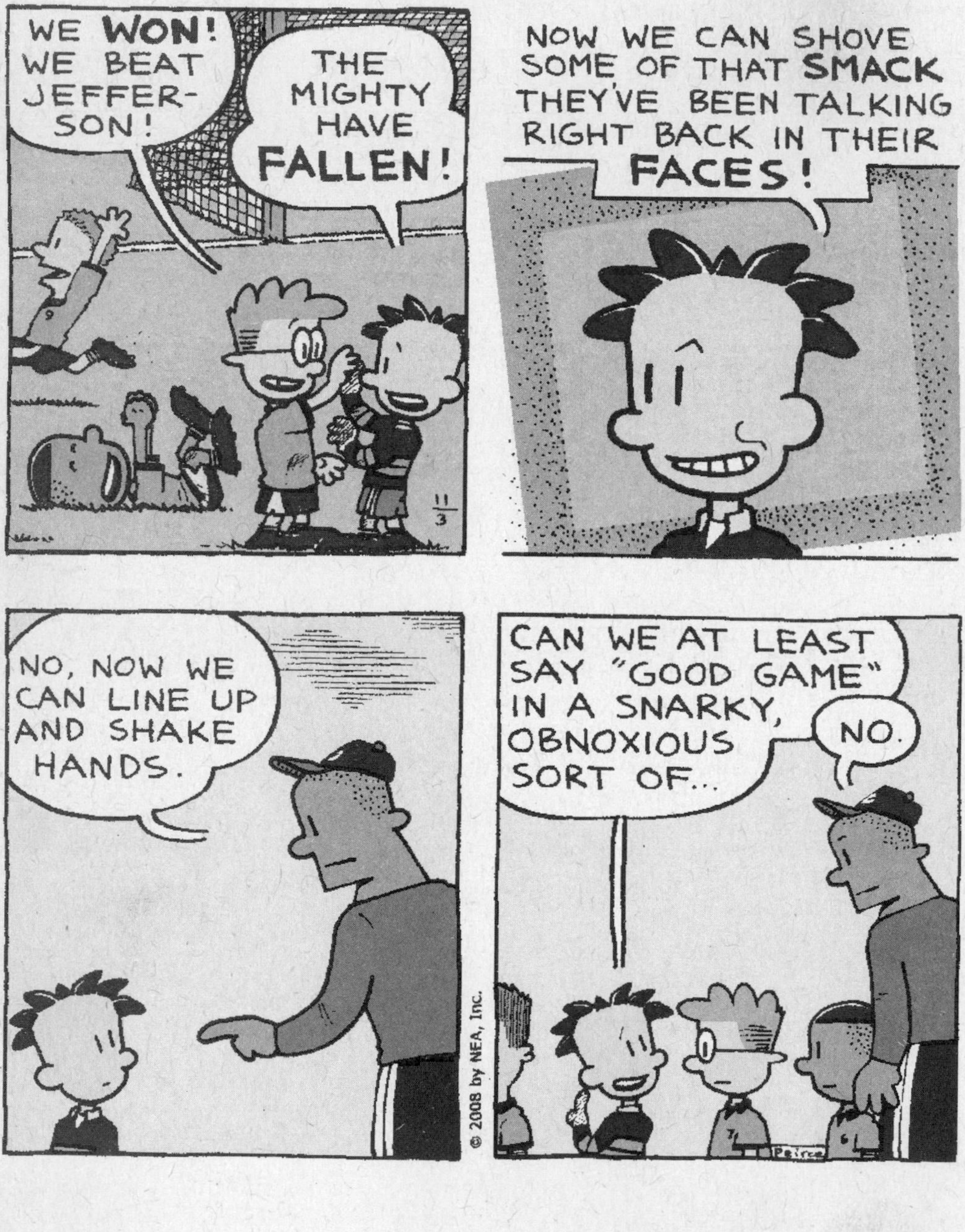
WE WON! WE BEAT JEFFERSON!
THE MIGHTY HAVE FALLEN!
11/3
NOW WE CAN SHOVE SOME OF THAT SMACK THEY'VE BEEN TALKING RIGHT BACK IN THEIR FACES!
NO, NOW WE CAN LINE UP AND SHAKE HANDS.
© 2008 by NEA, Inc.
CAN WE AT LEAST SAY "GOOD GAME" IN A SNARKY, OBNOXIOUS SORT OF...
NO.
Peirce

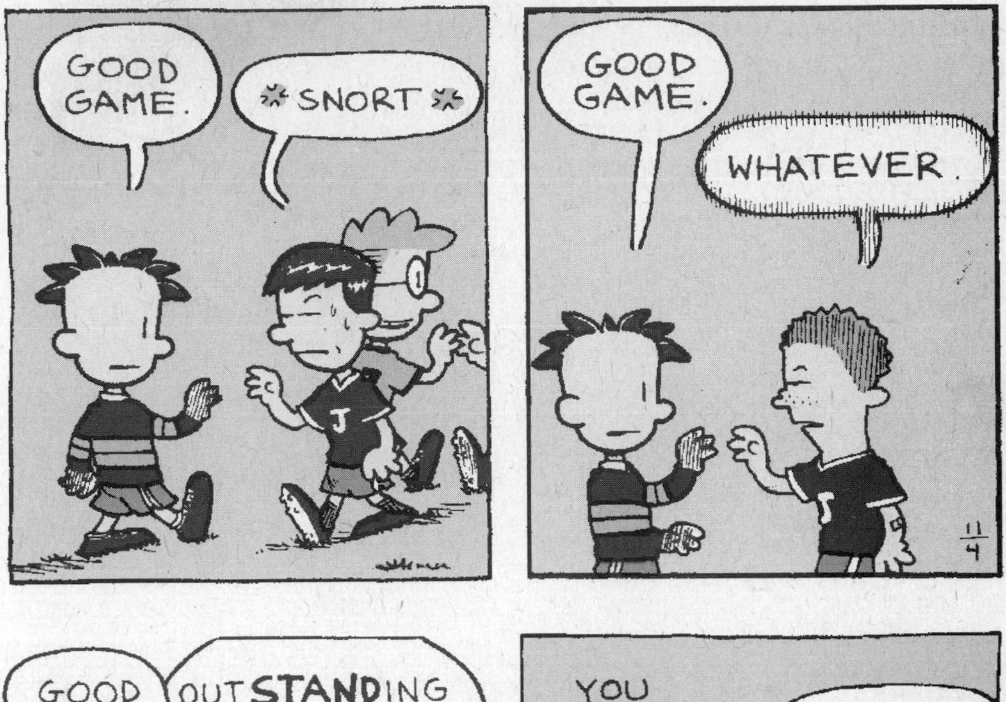

GOOD GAME.
SNORT
GOOD GAME.
WHATEVER.
11/4
GOOD GAME.
OUTSTANDING GAME! YOU GUYS PLAYED GREAT! YOU DESERVED IT!
© 2008 by NEA, Inc.
YOU GOTTA LOVE TEAM MANAGERS!
...WHERE SPORTSMANSHIP LIVES.
Peirce

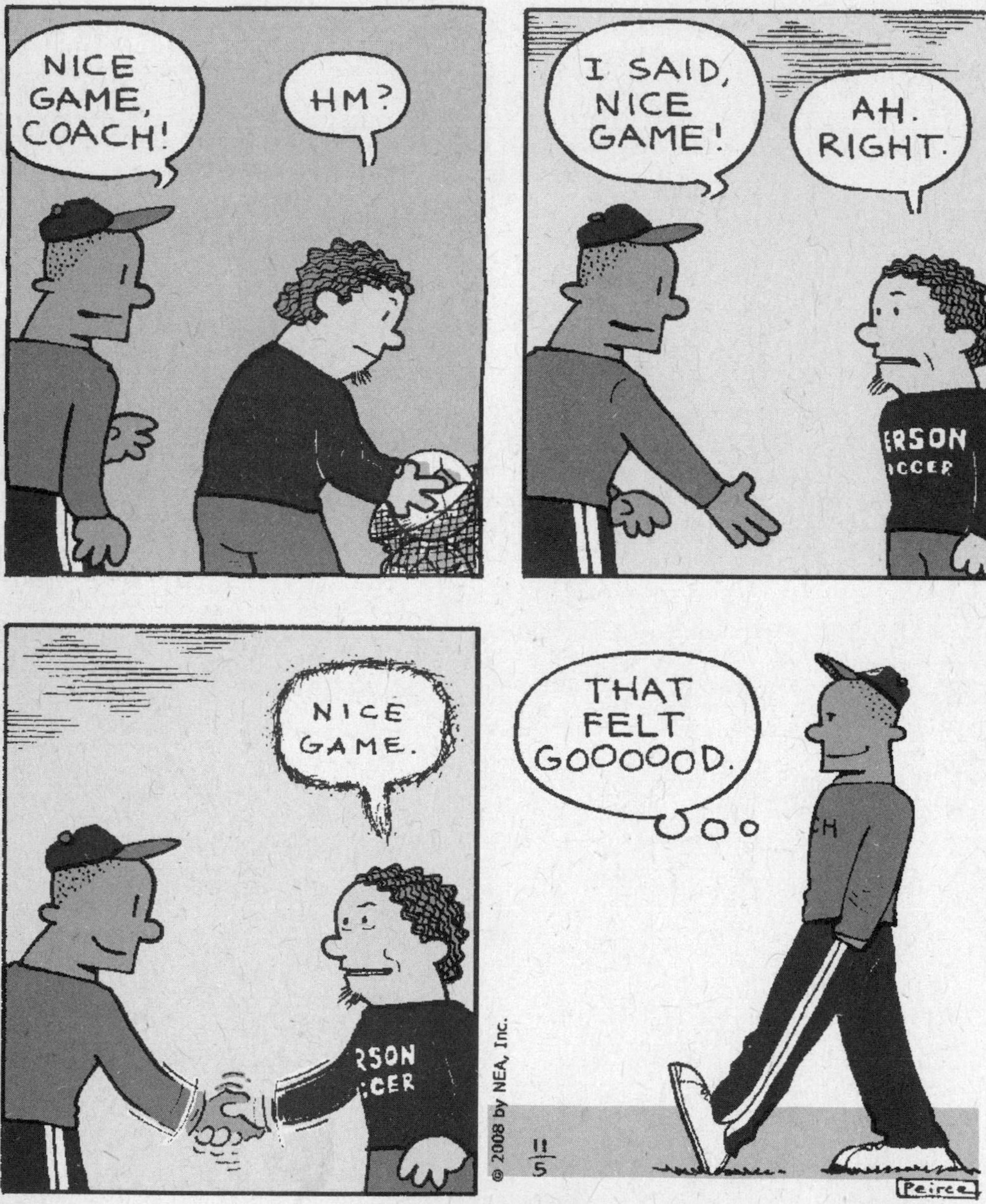

NICE GAME, COACH!
HM?
I SAID, NICE GAME!
AH. RIGHT.
NICE GAME.
THAT FELT GOOOOOD.
© 2008 by NEA, Inc.
11/5
Peirce

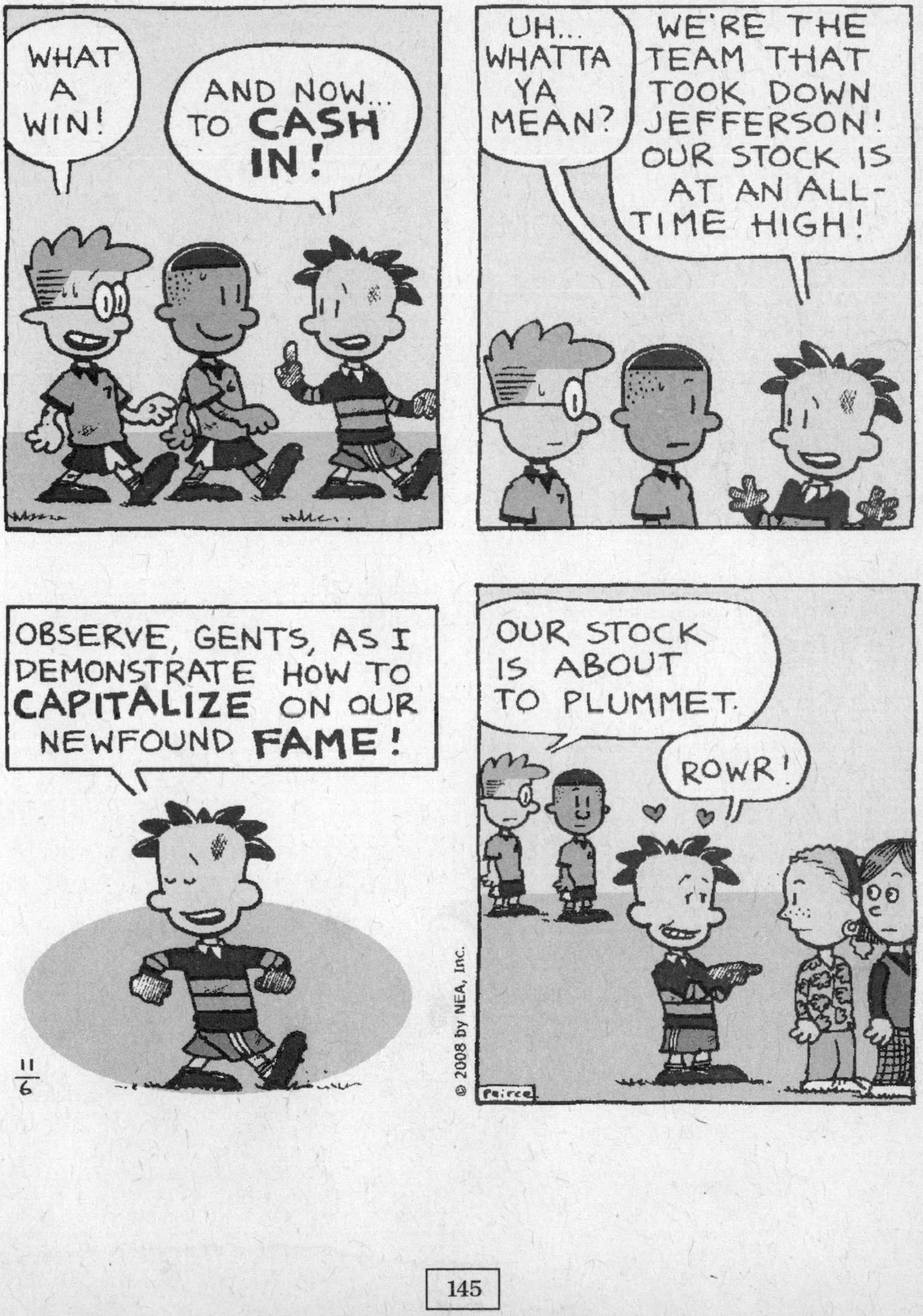
WHAT A WIN!
AND NOW... TO CASH IN!
UH... WHATTA YA MEAN?
WE'RE THE TEAM THAT TOOK DOWN JEFFERSON! OUR STOCK IS AT AN ALL-TIME HIGH!
OBSERVE, GENTS, AS I DEMONSTRATE HOW TO CAPITALIZE ON OUR NEWFOUND FAME!
11/6
© 2008 by NEA, Inc.
OUR STOCK IS ABOUT TO PLUMMET.
ROWR!
Peirce

CHECK IT OUT, NATE! FRONT PAGE OF THE SPORTS SECTION! "P.S. 38 SHOCKS JEFFERSON"!

OOH! READ IT!

"IN A STUNNING UPSET, THE BOYS' SOCCER TEAM FROM P.S. 38 ENDED JEFFERSON MIDDLE SCHOOL'S FOUR-YEAR UNBEATEN STREAK YESTERDAY WITH A THRILLING 1-0 WIN DECIDED BY PENALTY KICKS."

11/8

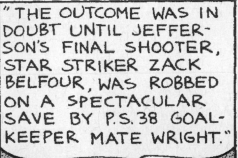

"THE OUTCOME WAS IN DOUBT UNTIL JEFFERSON'S FINAL SHOOTER, STAR STRIKER ZACK BELFOUR, WAS ROBBED ON A SPECTACULAR SAVE BY P.S. 38 GOALKEEPER MATE WRIGHT."

© 2008 by NEA, Inc.

"MATE WRIGHT"?

THAT SOUNDS DIRTY.

Pierce

147

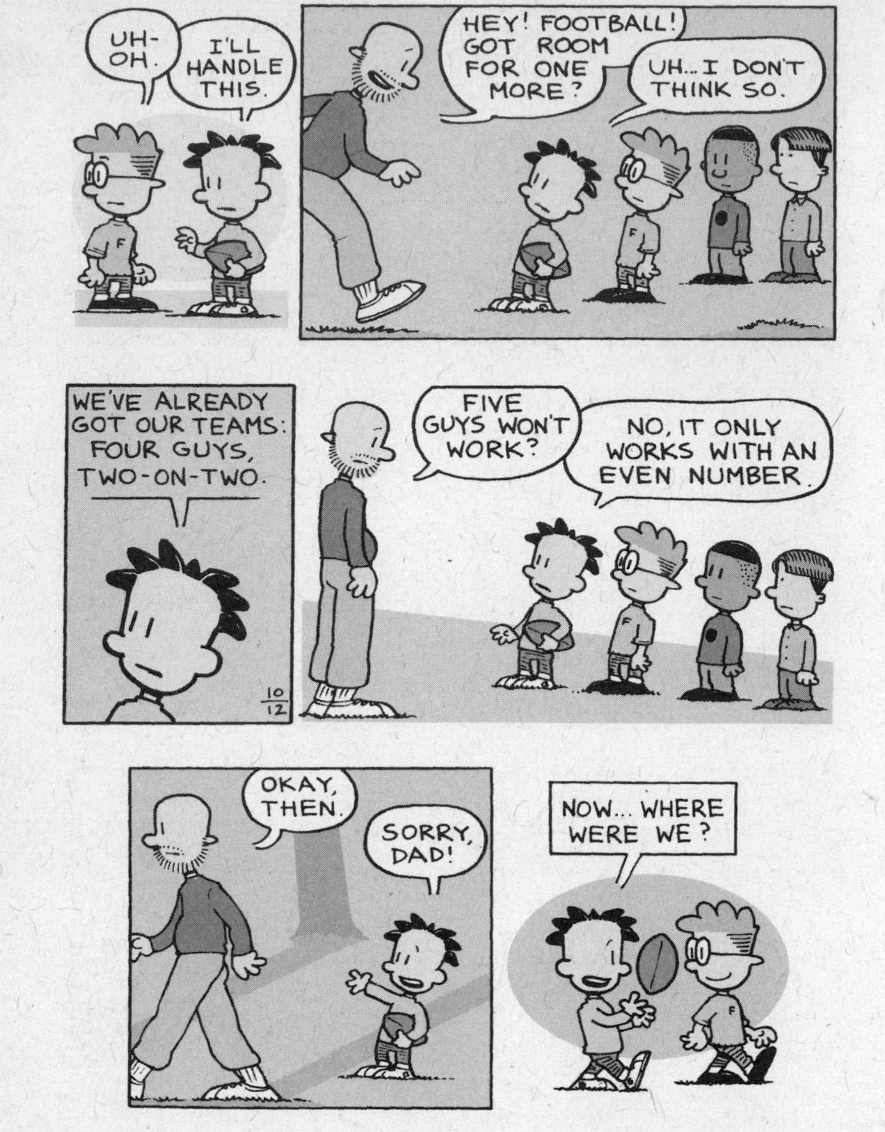
UH-OH.
I'LL HANDLE THIS.
HEY! FOOTBALL! GOT ROOM FOR ONE MORE?
UH... I DON'T THINK SO.
WE'VE ALREADY GOT OUR TEAMS: FOUR GUYS, TWO-ON-TWO.
FIVE GUYS WON'T WORK?
NO, IT ONLY WORKS WITH AN EVEN NUMBER.
10/12
OKAY, THEN.
SORRY, DAD!
NOW... WHERE WERE WE?
MR. EUSTIS WANTS IN! NOW WE'VE GOT AN EVEN NUMBER!
© 2008 by NEA, Inc.
"I'LL HANDLE THIS."
SHUT UP.
CAN I BE QUARTERBACK?
Peirce

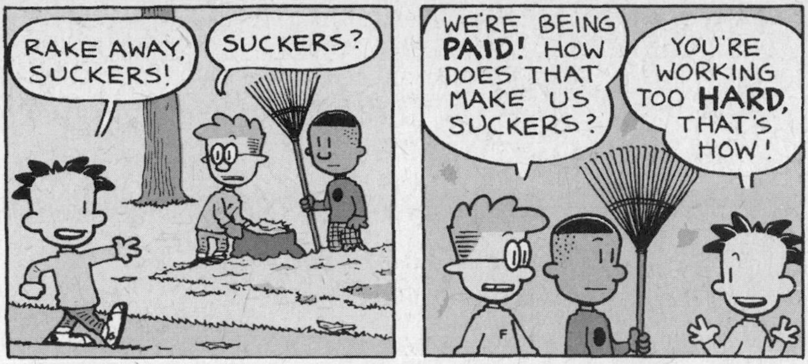
RAKE AWAY, SUCKERS!
SUCKERS?
WE'RE BEING **PAID!** HOW DOES THAT MAKE US SUCKERS?
YOU'RE WORKING TOO **HARD,** THAT'S HOW!

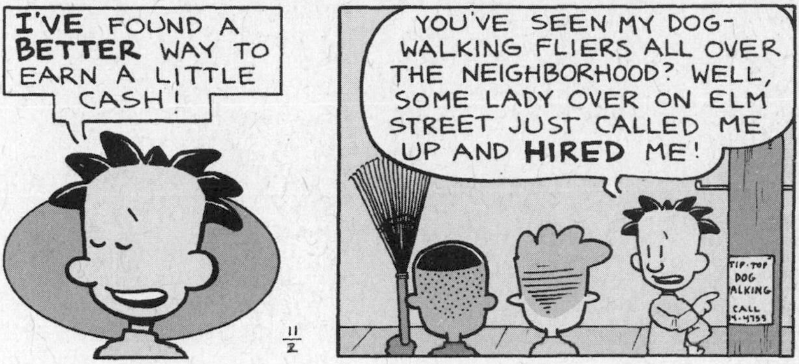
I'VE FOUND A **BETTER** WAY TO EARN A LITTLE CASH!
11/2
YOU'VE SEEN MY DOG-WALKING FLIERS ALL OVER THE NEIGHBORHOOD? WELL, SOME LADY OVER ON ELM STREET JUST CALLED ME UP AND **HIRED** ME!
TIP-TOP DOG WALKING
CALL

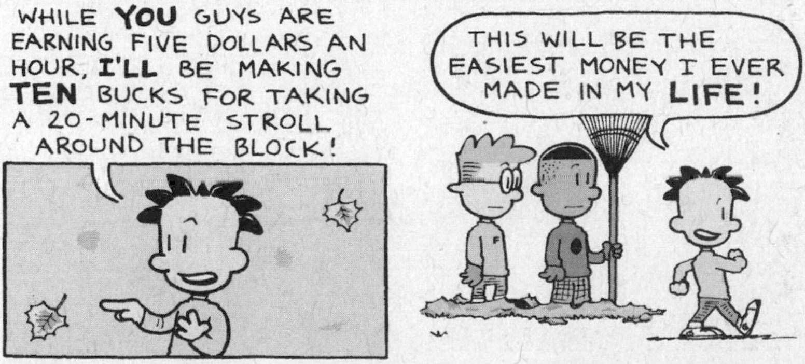
WHILE **YOU** GUYS ARE EARNING FIVE DOLLARS AN HOUR, **I'LL** BE MAKING **TEN** BUCKS FOR TAKING A 20-MINUTE STROLL AROUND THE BLOCK!
THIS WILL BE THE EASIEST MONEY I EVER MADE IN MY **LIFE!**

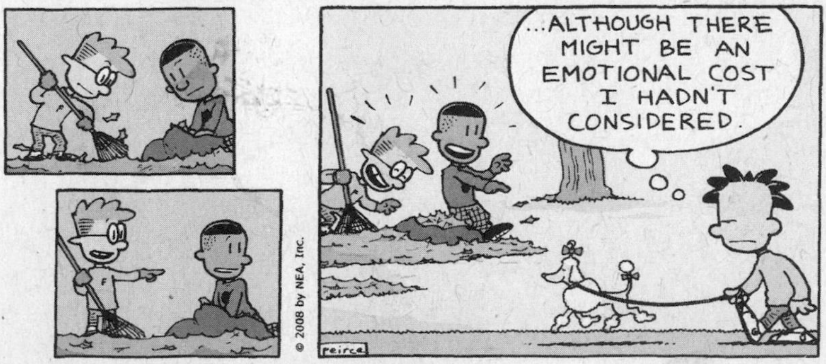
...ALTHOUGH THERE MIGHT BE AN EMOTIONAL COST I HADN'T CONSIDERED.
peirce

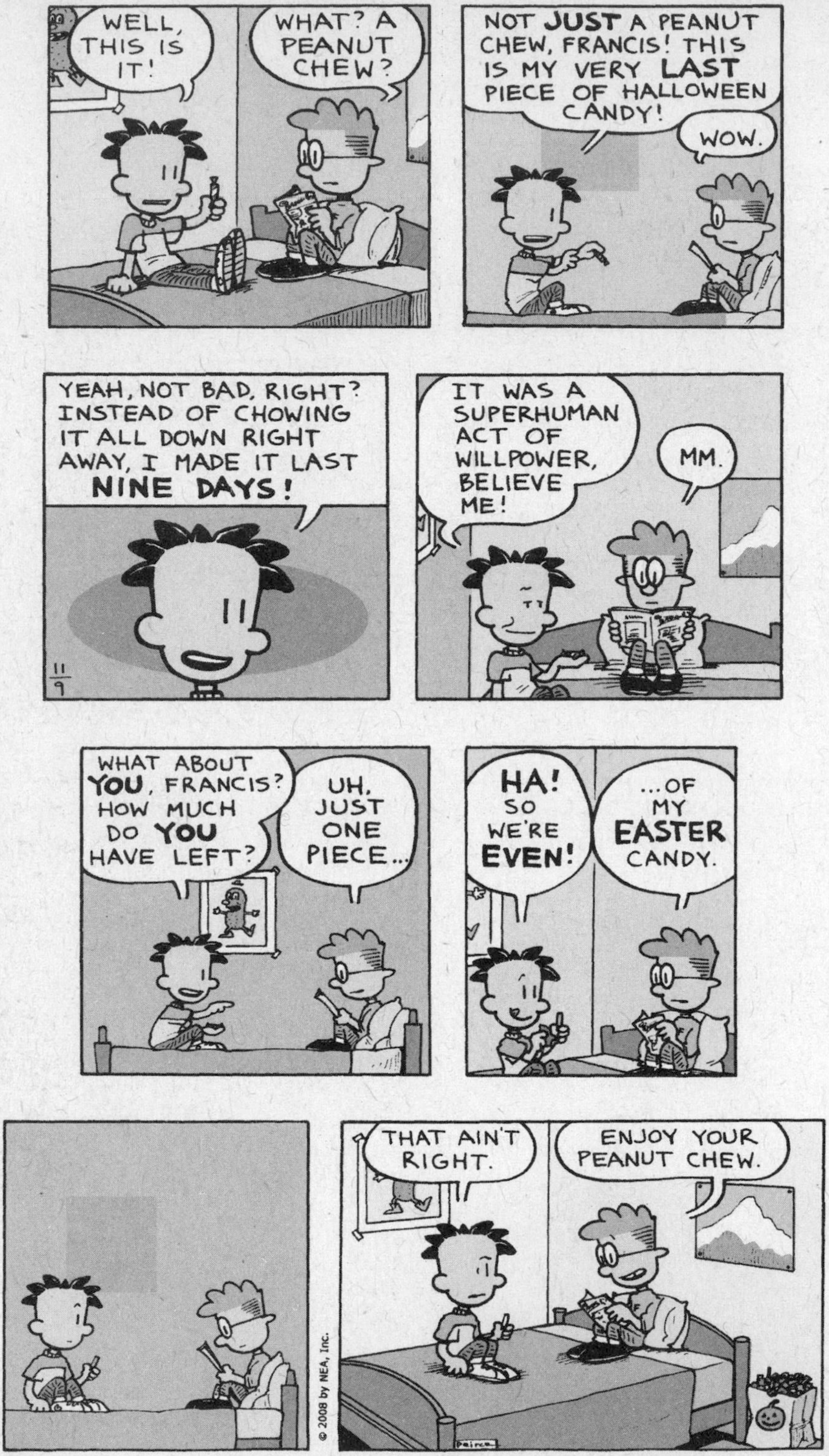
WELL, THIS IS IT!
WHAT? A PEANUT CHEW?
NOT JUST A PEANUT CHEW, FRANCIS! THIS IS MY VERY LAST PIECE OF HALLOWEEN CANDY!
WOW.
YEAH, NOT BAD, RIGHT? INSTEAD OF CHOWING IT ALL DOWN RIGHT AWAY, I MADE IT LAST NINE DAYS!
11/9
IT WAS A SUPERHUMAN ACT OF WILLPOWER, BELIEVE ME!
MM.
WHAT ABOUT YOU, FRANCIS? HOW MUCH DO YOU HAVE LEFT?
UH. JUST ONE PIECE...
HA! SO WE'RE EVEN!
...OF MY EASTER CANDY.
© 2008 by NEA, Inc.
THAT AIN'T RIGHT.
ENJOY YOUR PEANUT CHEW.

CATFIGHT!

...AND THEIR BIG OFF-SEASON MOVE WAS SIGNING RON ARTEST. HE'S DEFINITELY GOING TO IMPROVE THEIR DEFENSE.

PLUS, THEY'VE STILL GOT TRACY McGRADY, WHO CAN SCORE FROM ANYWHERE. THE GUY'S A TOTAL ANIMAL.

11/10

...BUT ULTIMATELY, IT ALL COMES DOWN TO THE BIG FELLA. IF HIS FOOT IS COMPLETELY HEALED, THE ROCKETS CAN DOMINATE THE NBA.

© 2008 by NEA, Inc.

THIS CONCLUDES MY REPORT ON THE MING DYNASTY.

YOW.

MR. CHUNG

Peirce

156

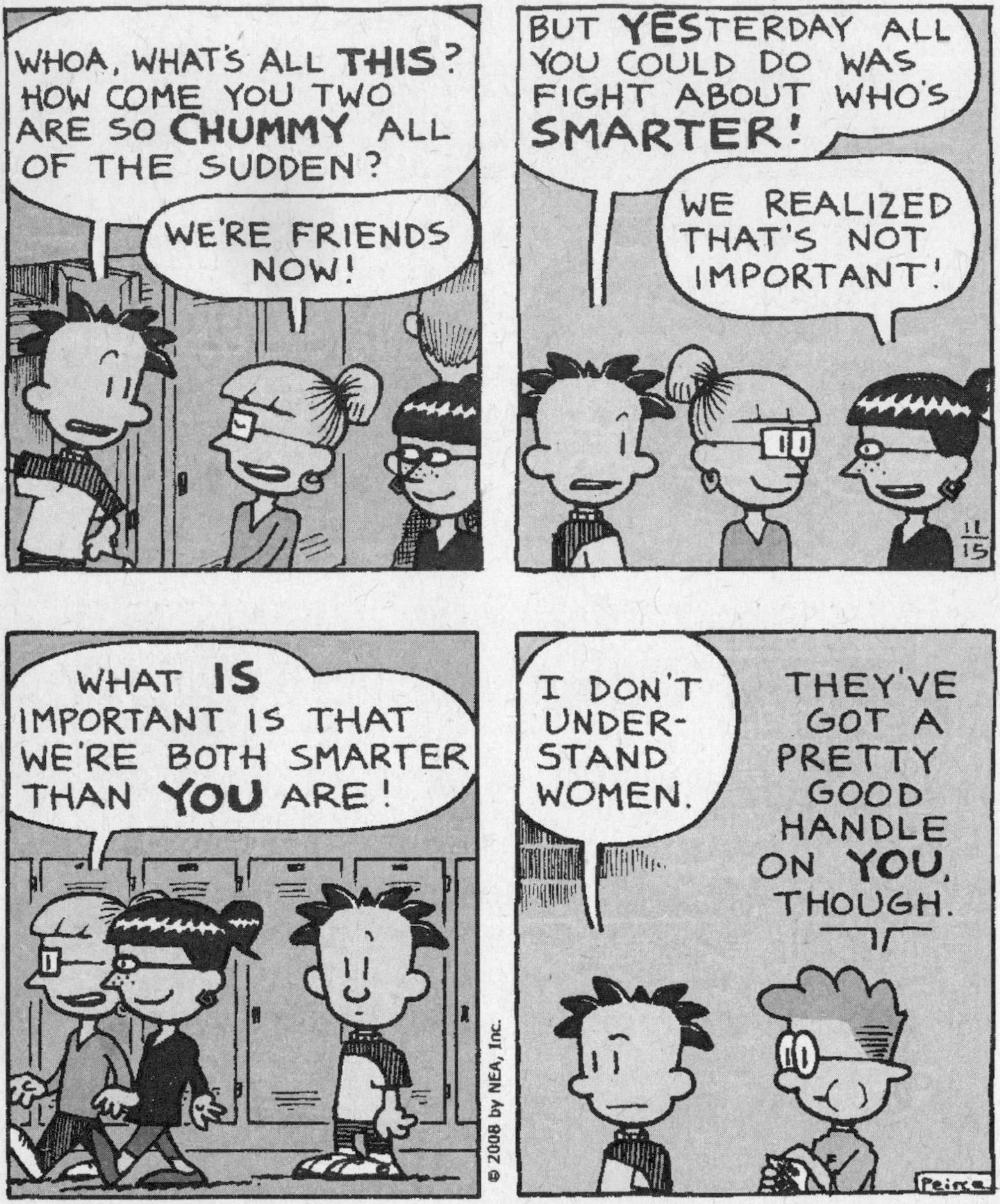
WHOA, WHAT'S ALL THIS? HOW COME YOU TWO ARE SO CHUMMY ALL OF THE SUDDEN?
WE'RE FRIENDS NOW!
BUT YESTERDAY ALL YOU COULD DO WAS FIGHT ABOUT WHO'S SMARTER!
WE REALIZED THAT'S NOT IMPORTANT!
11/15
WHAT IS IMPORTANT IS THAT WE'RE BOTH SMARTER THAN YOU ARE!
© 2008 by NEA, Inc.
I DON'T UNDER-STAND WOMEN.
THEY'VE GOT A PRETTY GOOD HANDLE ON YOU, THOUGH.
Peirce

159

NATE WRIGHT, SUPERBLOGGER

NATE'S "FIRST" THANKSGIVING

Panel 1:
MR. CHUNG, INSTEAD OF **WRITING** MY REPORT ON THE FIRST THANKSGIVING, CAN I DO IT IN COMIC BOOK FORMAT?

HM. I DON'T KNOW, NATE.

Panel 2:
PLEASE? PLEEEEEZ? I'VE DONE **OTHER** REPORTS THAT WAY! MRS. GODFREY LETS ME DO IT **ALL THE TIME!**

Panel 3:
WHOA. HOLD IT. I JUST... ✷KOFF!✷... I JUST USED **MRS. GODFREY** AS AN EXAMPLE OF THE WAY A TEACHER SHOULD DO THINGS!

11/24

© 2008 by NEA, Inc.

Panel 4:
FEELING QUEASY... CALL THE SCHOOL NURSE...

...OR PERHAPS THE DRAMA TEACHER.

Peirce

OH, THE PAIN!

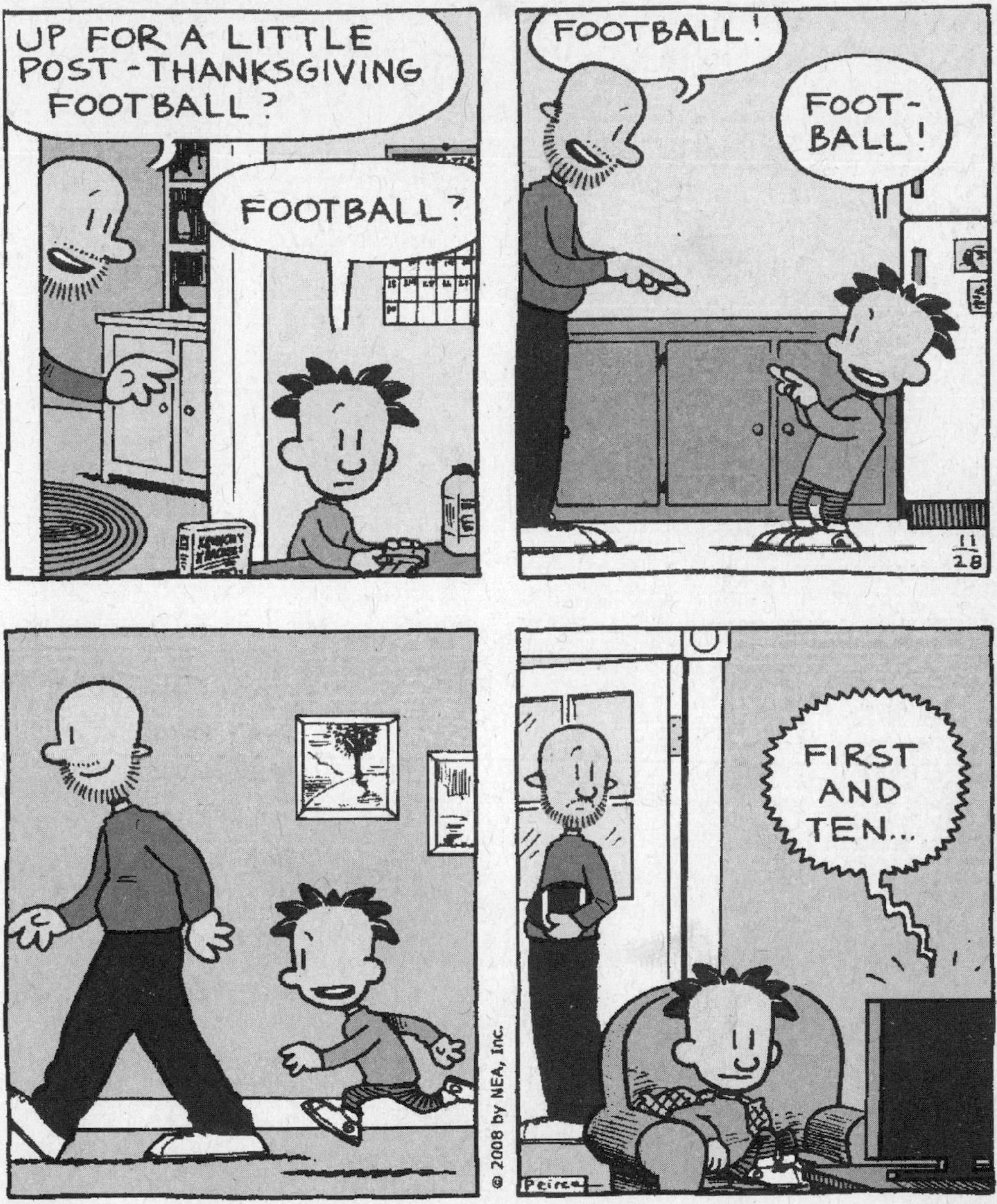
UP FOR A LITTLE POST-THANKSGIVING FOOTBALL?
FOOTBALL?
FOOTBALL!
FOOT-BALL!
11 28
© 2008 by NEA, Inc.
Peirce
FIRST AND TEN...

THE MEANING
OF WOOF

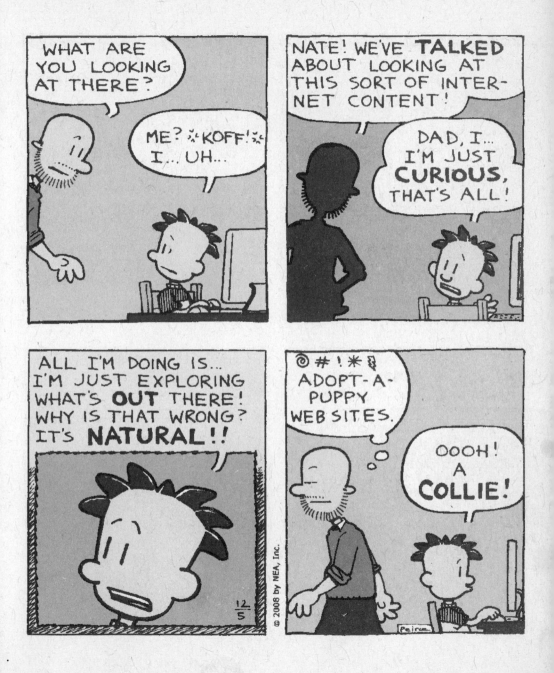

KISS THIS JOINT GOOD-BYE!

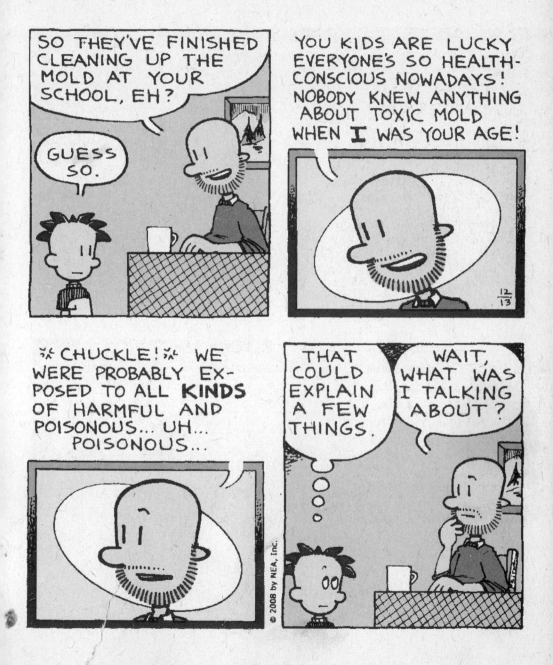

185

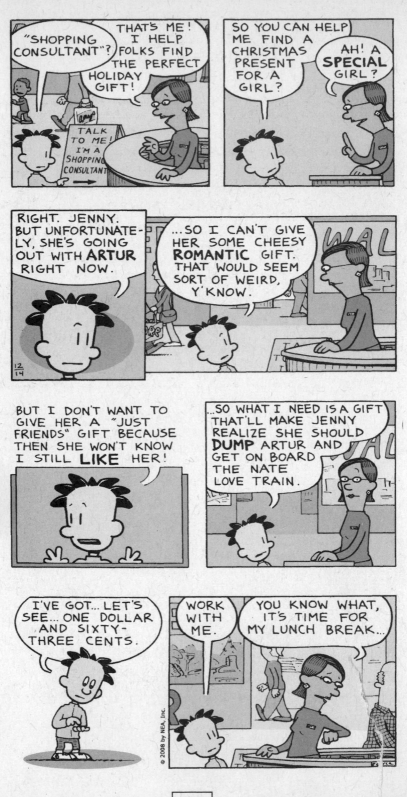

HOW BAD
CAN IT BE?

188

Panel 1:
TIME FOR SOCIAL STUDIES.

212

GREAT.

Panel 2:
AFTER THREE MONTHS OF SOCIAL STUDIES WITH MR. CHUNG, NOW I'VE GOT TO GET USED TO **MRS. GODFREY** AGAIN!

12/20

Panel 3:
LOOK, YOU'VE ONLY GOT TO DEAL WITH HER FOR **ONE DAY!** THEN IT'S **VACATION!**

RIGHT! HOW BAD CAN IT BE?

© 2008 by NEA, Inc.

Panel 4:
POP QUIZ, PEOPLE! TAKE YOUR SEATS!

OH, HOW I HATE HER.

HOUSE
GUEST PEST

198

199

NO MORE MONOPOLY

Panel 1:
UNCLE TED, I'LL TRADE YOU MARVIN GARDENS FOR NEW YORK AVENUE!

MARVIN GARDENS, YOU SAY? I THINK **NOT**!

Panel 2:
THE NAME "MARVIN" CONJURES UP TRAUMATIC MEMORIES OF A **BULLY** NAMED MARVIN WHO USED TO **TORMENT** ME WHEN I WAS YOUNGER!

Panel 3:
THE HORRIBLE DAY WHEN HE SMASHED MY "THUNDERCATS" LUNCHBOX AGAINST A WALL IS INDELIBLY **SEARED** INTO MY **BRAIN**!

Panel 4:
THIS IS THE WEIRDEST GAME OF MONOPOLY OF ALL TIME.

HIGH SCHOOL CAN BE NASTY, LADS. RE-MEMBER THAT.

MAKE IT
OR BREAK IT

209

PET NAMES

WHAT A PRETTY FACE!

Nate's dad has framed some of Nate's self-portraits. Draw yourself doing the same things as Nate!

RHYTHM & RHYME

A picture is worth a thousand words. Fill in these limerick poems and create your own, all inspired by Nate's Sunday strip art!

Nate is a pretty swell guy
But one day a ball flew into his _eye_.
It made him quite sad,
Though he couldn't get _mad_,
He did yell "Why, ball, _____?!"

_____
_____
_____
_____

Francis loves to read most of all
Even on a wave standing _tall_.
I'd be willing to bet
(If the book didn't get _____)
He wouldn't notice a _____!

AWESOME ANNOUNCEMENTS

Have you suffered through those BOOORING announcements at school? What would you say if you had the microphone? Change it up and shout out something FUN!

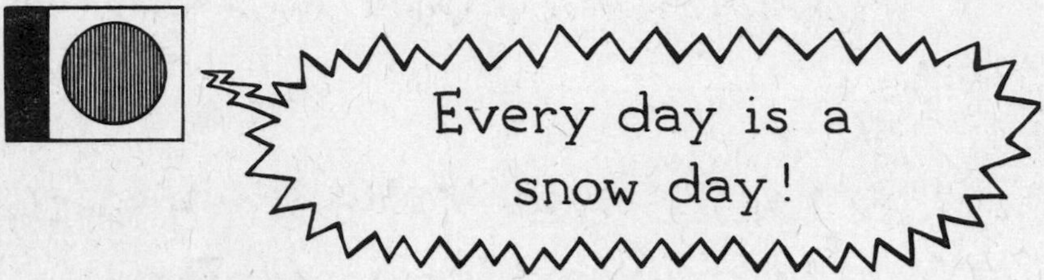
Every day is a snow day!

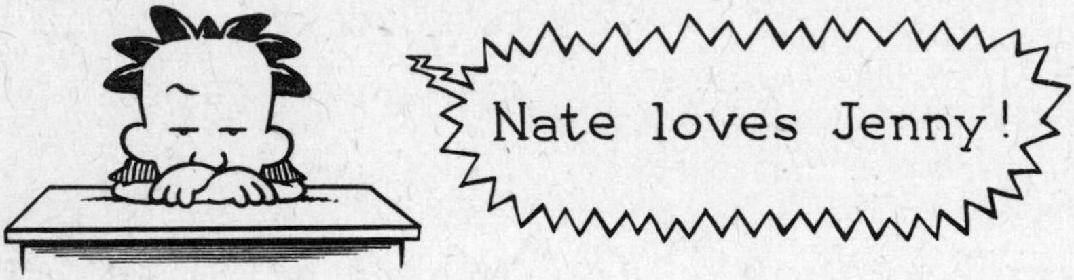
Nate loves Jenny!

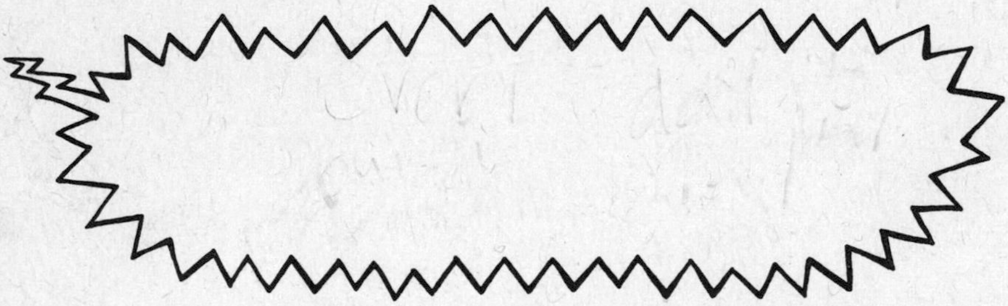

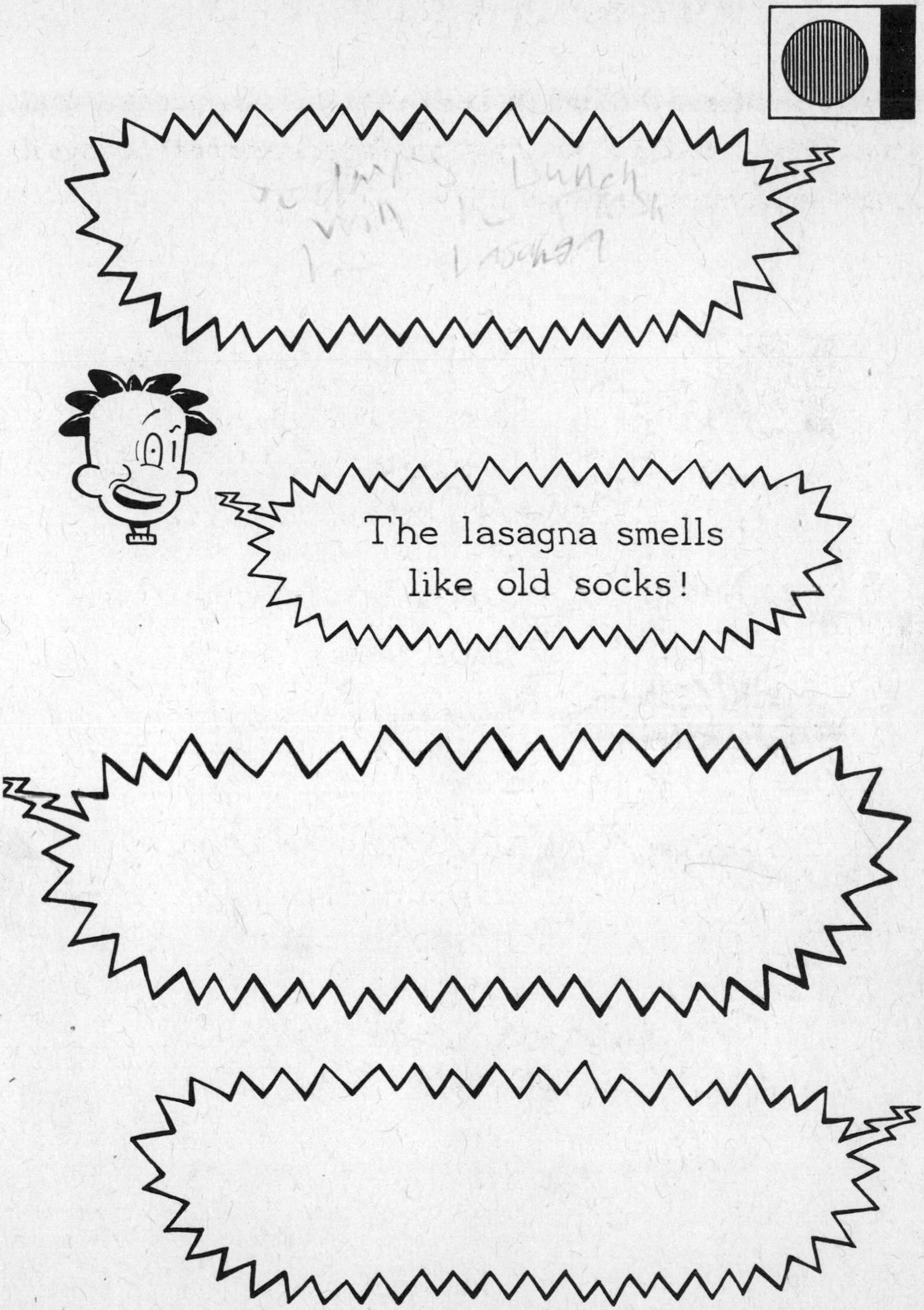
The lasagna smells like old socks!

NATE ≠ NEAT

Have you ever scrambled the letters in your name to see if they spell anything else? Well, **I** have. And guess what: **MY** letters spell **N·E·A·T!**

KSSSCH!

Pretty ironic, right? Hey, I realize I'm not exactly Joe Tidy. **EVERYBODY** knows it. But that doesn't stop Francis, who color-codes his underwear, from pointing it out about a jillion times a day.

Your desk is **DISGUSTING**. You have paint on your shirt. Oh, and you have Cheez Doodle stains all over your face. What a SLOB you are!

Francis has been telling me to clean up my act since I poured applesauce down his pants back in kindergarten. Of course, I've always ignored him. But then last week my sloppiness got Francis in trouble ... and he **NEVER** gets in trouble!

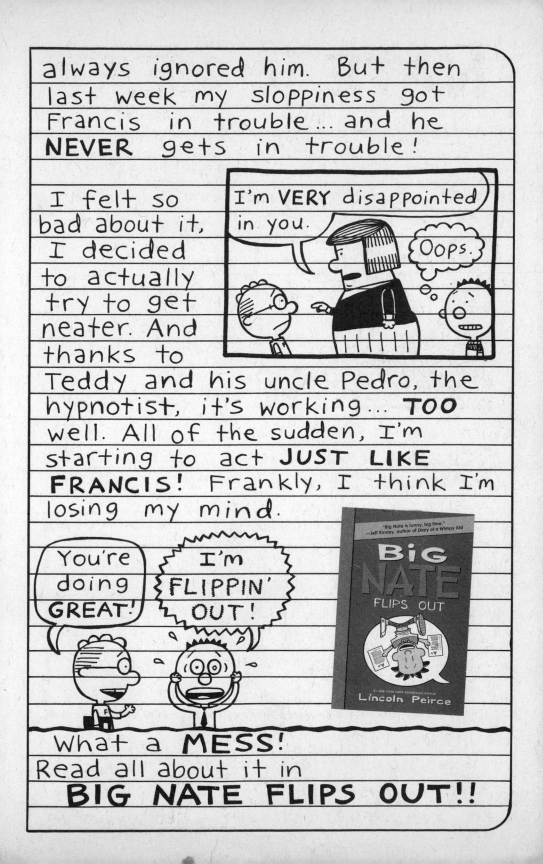

I'm **VERY** disappointed in you.
Oops.

I felt so bad about it, I decided to actually try to get neater. And thanks to Teddy and his uncle Pedro, the hypnotist, it's working ... **TOO** well. All of the sudden, I'm starting to act **JUST LIKE FRANCIS!** Frankly, I think I'm losing my mind.

You're doing **GREAT!**
I'm **FLIPPIN' OUT!**

"Big Nate is funny, big time."
—Jeff Kinney, author of Diary of a Wimpy Kid
BIG NATE
FLIPS OUT
Lincoln Peirce

What a **MESS!**
Read all about it in
BIG NATE FLIPS OUT!!

Lincoln Peirce

(pronounced "purse") is a cartoonist/writer and *New York Times* bestselling author of the hilarious Big Nate book series (www.bignatebooks.com), now published in twenty-five countries worldwide. He is also the creator of the comic strip *Big Nate*, which appears in over two hundred and fifty U.S. newspapers and online daily at www.bignate.com. Lincoln's boyhood idol was Charles Schulz of *Peanuts* fame, but his main inspiration for Big Nate has always been his own experience as a sixth grader. Just like Nate, Lincoln loves comics, ice hockey, and Cheez Doodles (and dislikes cats, figure skating, and egg salad). His Big Nate books have been featured on *Good Morning America* and in *USA Today*, the *Washington Post*, and the *Boston Globe*. He has also written for Cartoon Network and Nickelodeon. Lincoln lives with his wife and two children in Portland, Maine.

For exclusive information on your favorite authors and artists, visit www.authortracker.com.

GINA RATES ALL THE BIG NATE BOOKS!

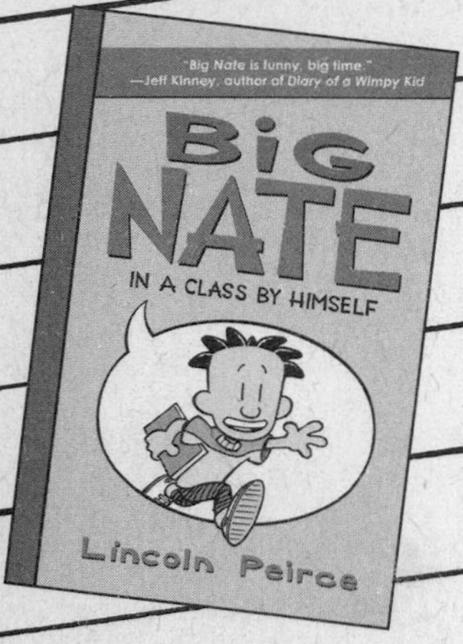
"Big Nate is funny, big time."
—Jeff Kinney, author of Diary of a Wimpy Kid
BIG NATE
IN A CLASS BY HIMSELF
Lincoln Peirce

Grade: A+

Comments: Nate Wright gets detention all day? I approve!

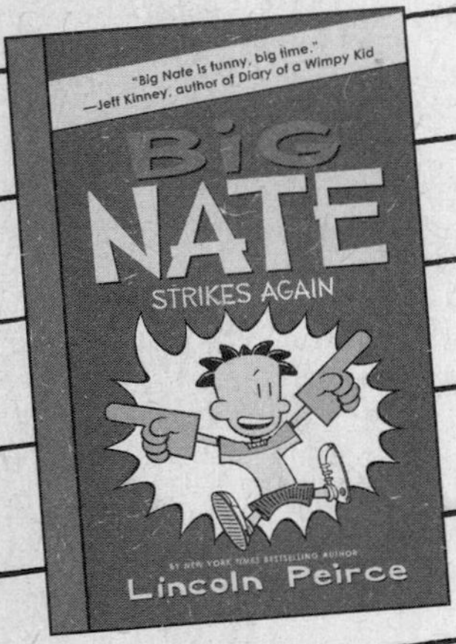
"Big Nate is funny, big time."
—Jeff Kinney, author of Diary of a Wimpy Kid
BIG NATE
STRIKES AGAIN
Lincoln Peirce

Grade: A++

Comments: As far as I'm concerned, I'm the hero here.

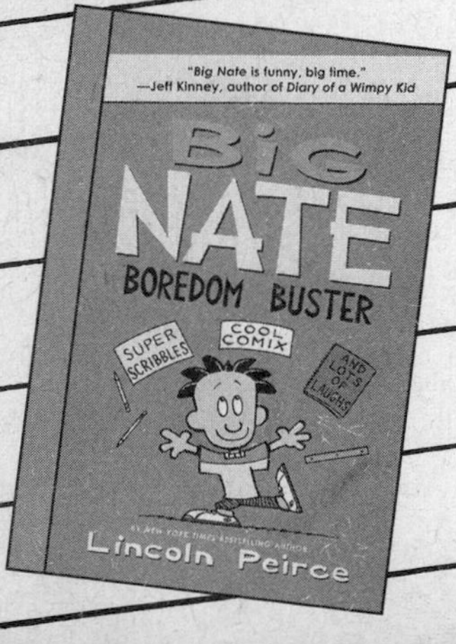
"Big Nate is funny, big time."
—Jeff Kinney, author of Diary of a Wimpy Kid
BIG NATE
BOREDOM BUSTER
SUPER SCRIBBLES
COOL COMIX
AND LOTS OF LAUGHS
Lincoln Peirce

Grade: A+

Comments: Like doing extra-credit assignments . . . my dream come true!